AF271300

TORONTO
PUBLIC
LIBRARY
Sale of this book
supports literacy programs

Also by Caroline Bishop:

The Other Daughter

The Lost Chapter

Caroline Bishop

PUBLISHED BY SIMON & SCHUSTER
New York   London   Toronto   Sydney   New Delhi

SIMON &
SCHUSTER
CANADA

Simon & Schuster Canada
A Division of Simon & Schuster, Inc.
166 King Street East, Suite 300
Toronto, Ontario M5A 1J3

This book is a work of fiction. Any references to historical events, real people, or real places are used fictitiously. Other names, characters, places, and events are products of the author's imagination, and any resemblance to actual events or places or persons, living or dead, is entirely coincidental.

Copyright © 2022 by Caroline Bishop

All rights reserved, including the right to reproduce this book or portions thereof in any form whatsoever. For information, address Simon & Schuster Canada Subsidiary Rights Department, 166 King Street East, Suite 300, Toronto, Ontario, M5A 1J3.

This Simon & Schuster Canada edition May 2022

SIMON & SCHUSTER CANADA and colophon are trademarks of Simon & Schuster, Inc.

For information about special discounts for bulk purchases, please contact Simon & Schuster Special Sales at 1-800-268-3216 or CustomerService@simonandschuster.ca.

Manufactured in the United States of America

10   9   8   7   6   5   4   3   2   1

Library and Archives Canada Cataloguing in Publication
Title: The lost chapter / Caroline Bishop.
Names: Bishop, Caroline H. (Helen), author.
Description: Simon & Schuster Canada edition.
Identifiers: Canadiana (print) 20210313803 | Canadiana (ebook) 20210313811 |
    ISBN 9781982196912 (softcover) | ISBN 9781982196929 (ebook)
Classification: LCC PR6102.I84 L67 2022 | DDC 823/.92—dc23

ISBN 978-1-9821-9691-2
ISBN 978-1-9821-9692-9 (ebook)

For my friends, near and far

The Lost
Chapter

Prologue

The question I suppose you might ask me, when you get to the end of this story, is whether I would have changed anything had I known how it was going to turn out, and the answer is absolutely not. Of course, there are myriad ways in which my life could have turned out differently, many dependent on the actions of other people, but regarding my own actions – the only ones I, Eleanor 'Lenny' Cranshaw, could control, after all – I can tell you right now that I wouldn't have changed a damned thing.

But back then, on that chilly spring night in April 1958, loitering on a street corner in the dark, looking at my watch every ten seconds as I waited for Fran, I felt less confident than my actions in the previous months had hitherto implied. What the hell had I done? How had my year at school in France, which had started with such giddy excitement, ended in this remarkably abrupt and unexpected manner? I looked down at my shoes – black leather Oxfords, a little dirty – and hysteria bubbled up in my chest to think of our esteemed headmistress Madame Bouchard catching

1

me standing on the street in the dark like a lady of the evening, all her judgements about me confirmed.

You've demeaned yourself, Eleanor, wasted all that potential.

I tried to breathe evenly to quell the laughter; white wisps appeared and then dissolved on the cold night air. But it wasn't funny, the situation I found myself in. In fact, though I hadn't ever said it aloud, it was actually a little daunting.

That certainly wasn't a word I'd used with Fran when the two of us had discussed our plan late at night, talking in whispers in our bedroom at the school. Daunting? Hardly. *It's going to be wonderful, honey*, I'd said. *I'm going to make it wonderful, I promise.* I was the confident one, the persuader, cajoling her with my boundless enthusiasm. I had to be, since she wasn't. I had to tell her that we'd conquer this new life we were embarking on, Fran and I. Fleeing the school would be liberating, and possibly quite thrilling. We could do this because we'd have each other; together, we'd make it work.

I'd convinced myself in the end, I really had (all these years later, I am still good at convincing myself to do things I possibly shouldn't), and I thought I'd convinced her, too.

I looked at my watch again. It was nearly ten past eleven. *Come on, Fran.* There was only so long I could hang around before the lights would come on in the chateau, the alarm would be raised and Bouchard would send out a search party in an attempt to drag me back. And that simply could not happen. I was finished with that place, with its rules and conventions and double standards and constraints. And it was finished with me, too, though not in the way it had intended, and I still derive considerable satisfaction from that.

I understood, in that moment, that I was going to do this regardless. Yes, I needed Fran. Without her, how would I possibly manage? And more importantly, I *wanted* Fran, because I'd miss her so desperately if she wasn't with me. However, she'd been right about something: I *was* brave (or perhaps foolhardy, as Ma would have said) and I was going to deal with the consequences of my actions in my own way, whatever happened.

I looked up at the clouds drifting across the moon. When the lunar glow shone down on me again, I'd go. I'd walk to the bus stop and head into Lyon city centre. I'd follow through with the plan – *our* plan – because I had to, because the alternative was unacceptable to me, and if she failed to show up, I'd leave her behind. That was her choice to make, just as this was mine. I nodded to myself – decision made, that's that – and swallowed down a lump in my throat.

A few moments later the clouds parted and the road lit up, the moonlight so bright I could see my shadow on the pavement, the shadow of an 18-year-old woman, wearing a woollen dress, coat and hat, a small suitcase at her feet. It's a silhouette I remember still – it's seared into my head – because it was the end of the first phase of my life and the start of a new one, one that would mould me into the person I am now. And I like that person. I'm proud of her.

I glanced up at the school building, this strange mock-castle that had been my home and my prison for the previous seven months, picked up my case and turned up the road. Something shattered inside me, but I didn't look back.

Bye bye, Fran.

PART ONE

1

It's only when the mug hits the floor that Flo notices it's fallen from her grasp. In the millisecond before it shatters, everything freezes – her hand halfway to her mouth, her eyes on the newspaper, her mind fixated on the image; everything freezes except the cup freefalling through the air. And then the dog is barking and milky tea is puddling on the kitchen floor and her slippers are splattered like a Jackson Pollock. She is too old for shocks, damnit.

'Shoo, Ernie, shoo!' She sticks out a leg and pushes the dog away before he can put his fat pink tongue in the scalding liquid or snaffle up any shards. The cat flap slams; Eric has sensibly fled, ears back, ginger tail high. Flo sighs. She should clear up the mess straight away, but she doesn't. Instead she smooths the newspaper on the kitchen table and looks at it again, this thing that made her drop her tea, this thing that near stopped her heart.

Later, she thinks: *this was put here for me.* Of course, it's always put here for her – she has the paper delivered to her door every day. But she doesn't always get around to reading the whole thing. Usually, she catches half a book review or theatre preview upside-down or sideways, partly obscured by smears of ink or shavings of linoleum, and wishes she'd taken the time to read the arts section properly before it ended up as fodder for her studio.

But today, the day this particular item is published, she did take the time. She came in from the studio – it's a shed really, but Flo feels a place she spends so much time in, a place that is responsible for nurturing her creativity over so many years, deserves a grander name than that – to have one of the many cuppas that punctuate her working day. She could have a kettle in the studio – there is electricity and a sink – but keeping it here in the kitchen means she will actually get up and walk down the garden path to the house if she wants some tea, and she considers that small but regular act of movement to be essential. She becomes so easily immersed in the meditative rhythm of carving and printing that she could happily spend all day immobile in her chair in the studio if it weren't for tea and the toilet – so she is thankful that, at her age, she regularly needs both.

Now, she leans forward over the newspaper and pushes her reading glasses further up her nose. *EXCLUSIVE: READ THE PROLOGUE OF THE NEW NOVELLA BY BESTSELLING AMERICAN WRITER L. P. HENRI.* It wasn't the author's name that shocked her, since she doesn't recognize it – a pseudonym or a married name, perhaps – neither was it the excerpted prologue itself, although as she read it, the scenario seemed vaguely familiar, the image of a girl loitering outside a school provoking an eerie déjà vu that unnerved her. No, it was the picture of the author, of this *L. P. Henri*, that sent her tea flying to the floor. She knew, the instant she laid eyes on it and the mug slipped from her hand, that it was Lilli, but now she scrutinizes it more carefully. Could it really be her? She looks at the woman's hair, a short crop of vivid white. She looks at the lines framing her cheeks, and the plumpness of her body, which used to be so slim. And she knows that despite these differences, it is her old school friend, captured within a physical shell that is not how it used to be, more than half a century after she last saw her, but still, unmistakeably, Lilli.

When the front doorbell rings, Flo jumps again, her heart racing at the abrupt interruption. She curses under her breath as she pushes herself up from the table, steps around the puddle of tea, and walks down the hall, Ernie trotting after her. Is she expecting someone? She can't think, but when she opens the door and sees the girl on the front step – ah yes, of course.

'Alice? My goodness, I'd clean forgotten you were coming.' She smiles but the girl's own mouth barely flickers. She holds her hands in front of her, fidgeting with a nail, head down but eyes up, as though hedging her bets, dithering between the two.

'Sorry if . . .' the girl says, clearly taking Flo's greeting as a rejection. 'I mean, Mum said you wanted me to come round, but if this isn't a good time . . . oh!' She bends down as Ernie pushes his way around Flo's legs and barks once in friendly greeting at the newcomer. 'He's so beautiful.'

The girl smiles then – properly this time – and Flo sees the uncertainty dissolve, transforming her face as though a silent shift has taken place within her and is shining through to the outside. She is fairly tall, with that same litheness of youth Flo supposes she and Lilli had at eighteen, but her posture is awkward, as though she wishes she were shorter than she is, and her long light brown hair is messy – two things Flo's old school never would have tolerated. She thinks of her and Lilli pin-curling each other's hair in their bedroom in the chateau so long ago, while gossiping about the other students and dreaming of escaping. Yes, escaping together. Flo puts her hand on the door to steady herself as the scene blooms in her head.

'It's the perfect time – do come in,' she says, but she has to force herself to say it, to close the door and usher Alice down the hall, because all the while her head is replaying the prologue she's just read, the sense of déjà vu it provoked, and then it hits her.

Lilli's book is about them.

Alice knows this is a bad idea. She was surprised her mum even suggested it, given how little she likes Alice doing much of anything, ever. At first she objected, nearly outright refused; after all, Mrs Carter is known at school as the mad old cat lady, the spinster who isn't far off dying and being eaten by her pets. Alice doesn't know why some of the kids call her that, apart from the fact she is old and has a cat and lives on her own. It probably started after Jake Pearson in the year below saw her in the supermarket wearing slippers, which is a bit weird, to be fair. So as she walked to the house, Alice ran through scenarios in her head, just to be prepared for all eventualities: she might be knocked over the head with a walking stick and left lying in a pool of blood, locked in a dark cupboard to starve to death, or maybe poisoned with some weird cat-lady potion and kept prisoner as the old woman plays out some strange fantasy of the child she never had.

It doesn't entirely surprise her, then, to arrive at the house and find Mrs Carter, in said slippers and a grubby shirt, looking flustered and a little lost, with a puddle of tea and shards of broken mug all over the kitchen floor. After Alice follows her down the corridor from the front door into the kitchen, the old woman sits down at the table with a little *oof* of effort and doesn't even attempt to clean up the mess. Mad as a box of frogs, clearly.

'Do you want me to . . .' Alice gestures to the floor. She feels rude drawing attention to it, but she's worried about the dog, the beautiful black Lab. She doesn't want him to hurt his paws on the shards. The dog is the only reason she's here.

'Oh, would you?' Mrs Carter says. 'My knees object to me crouching down, I'm sorry to say.' She tears a page out of the newspaper on the table and gives the rest to Alice. 'There's a mop in the cupboard over there. Thank you, dear.' She folds up the piece of paper she ripped out and puts it in her pocket, then takes off her glasses, rubs her eyes. She seems distracted, not all there, and Alice wonders what's going on in her head. Maybe she's got Alzheimer's or something. That would account for the slippers in the supermarket.

Alice wraps the shards in the newspaper, making sure to sweep up every last little bit that might otherwise become lodged in the dog's paw or swallowed, leading to internal bleeding and a slow, painful death. She hopes he didn't already get too close, or it might be too late. She pushes the wad of paper right down to the bottom of the bin. She wouldn't want the bin men to cut themselves and end up with sepsis and die.

'Shame.' Mrs Carter nods to the broken mug. 'A ceramicist friend gave me that – well, traded for one of my prints.' Alice must look blank because she adds, 'I'm a printmaker. Didn't your mum say? I'll show you my studio later, if you're interested. As long as you promise not to call it a shed.' She laughs.

Alice doesn't know what she's talking about. All her mum said about Florence Carter was that she was a lovely woman with all her marbles, maybe just a bit lonely, and Alice shouldn't listen to the kids at school, particularly since she was willing to pay Alice to walk her dog, which was probably the easiest and best summer job there is. And even though Alice wasn't at all sure, even though, on her way over here, she convinced herself she was unlikely to leave this house alive, she was drawn here almost against her will by the thought of spending time every day with a dog. She loves dogs. All animals, in fact. They are far easier than humans.

'Right then,' Mrs Carter says when Alice has finished with the bin. 'About the job. Much as I love my walks with Ernie, he's much younger than me and far more agile, and with my knees I just can't give him the sort of long, boisterous outings he wants, so your task will be to simply come round once a day and take him off for a good old romp.'

Alice nods. She's already decided where she'll take him. Not to the reservoir – it might be dangerous if he went in for a swim – and not into town, in case he ran into the road. They'll go along the footpath to the meadow, that big open space where there aren't any trees for weirdos to hide behind and no main roads to put Ernie in danger.

'Fifteen quid a walk, plus the gratitude of a woman past her prime and a handsome fellow still very much in his,' Mrs Carter says, patting Ernie's head. As she does, a ginger tom emerges through the cat flap and jumps up on the table, nuzzling his owner's arm. *Mad old cat lady.* Jake's words float into Alice's head. She remembers walking past this house the day after last Halloween, when Liam and some other dickheads from her year chucked eggs at the front door. His Snapchat post showed the yellow slime running down the door, peppered with bits of shell, drying to a hard, slick varnish over the red paint. It probably wouldn't have been easy to clean it off, especially with dodgy knees.

'Okay,' Alice says, as Mrs Carter rubs the cat under his chin and mutters, *You don't need walking do you, Eric.* 'Thank you for the job.'

'Well it's not going to make you a millionaire, but every bit helps. You're going to university this autumn, yes?'

Alice nods. She pictures the offer letter that came in the spring, her dad's congratulations over the phone, her mum's tearful delight that she wouldn't be moving away, and her hand goes to her right arm, rubs at the raised, puckered skin of her scar.

'This should give you some G&T money at least.' Mrs

Carter grins. 'Speaking of which, why don't you take Ernie out now for an hour or so, and by the time you get back it'll be gin o'clock.'

Alice nods, smiles. Perhaps she's not so crazy, after all.

But she'll sniff the gin before she drinks it, just to make sure.

When Alice has gone, Flo opens the back door and walks down to the end of the garden. Eric watches from his usual place on the doormat, tail curled around his white socks. Inside her studio she sits on the chair in front of her workbench. Pegged to strings strewn across half the room are her latest efforts, finally finished after many days and multiple layers of ink. It's one of her most complicated reduction prints to date – a landscape of the local reservoir, boats on the water, a lone jogger on the path and more than half the picture a mass of swirling cloud and sky – and she thinks it'll sell well in Harriet's shop. She should start something new; she can barely keep up with demand as it is. She picks up a gouge and feels the smooth wooden handle in her palm. It's been fifteen years since she first tried lino printing, a new hobby to fill her days after James died and she retired and moved here from London, and now she doesn't know what she'd do without it. But she doesn't think she can plan anything new today. She doesn't have the focus.

She takes the folded sheet of newspaper out of her pocket and looks once more at the face of L. P. Henri. Lilli. There was a time when she thought that face would always be in her life. But as it happened, their lives only converged for less than one short year – the year they both turned eighteen – then parted to follow what Flo imagines were such different directions. But she doesn't actually know what direction Lilli took, or how different it was from hers, because sixty-two years have passed. Sixty-two years! She can never quite believe she's that old. She doesn't feel much different to twenty, thirty years ago, apart from her creaky knees and tissue-paper skin. But sixty-two years? Then, way back then, she was different. The same, but different.

She looks at her watch. There's time to nip into town before Alice comes back. She returns to the house, remembering, for once, to exchange her tatty old boot slippers for pumps, but not bothering to change out of the ink-stained old shirt she wears when printmaking, and gets in her Mini. In the bookshop the sales assistant greets her by name, though Flo can't for the life of her remember what she's called, so she just mumbles *hello dear*, as the girl likely expects the 80-year-old cat lady to say, and heads for the fiction aisle. H for Henri. Her palms feel slightly damp as she searches. What if it's not in stock? She knows she must have it, this *semi-autobiographical novella set in southern France in the late 1950s*, as the paper described it. Only *semi*-autobiographical. Not entirely real. She holds on to that thought as she scours the shelves, runs her fingers across the spines of the H row, knowing that Lilli couldn't possibly have written the absolute truth of what happened back then because she doesn't know it, does she? Not all of it.

Her hand pauses. There it is, just one copy. A slim volume with a cover depicting two young women, their backs to each other, against a city backdrop, the title in elaborate script: *The Way We Were.*

She turns it over and reads the blurb on the back.

When she leaves New York for a finishing school in Lyon in 1957, the indomitable Lenny Cranshaw may only be seventeen, but she's ready to set the world on fire – whether the world is ready for her or not. But she's soon to learn that going your own way in buttoned-up 1950s society comes with certain consequences. Through the eyes of a young woman fighting for emancipation, *The Way We Were* paints a portrait of a conservative society pitted against those who set out to challenge it.

Flo's heart speeds up and sweat prickles her neck. She is hot, too hot, and she puts a hand out to steady herself against the bookshelf, and then the sales assistant is there – Jenna, she remembers now – asking if she's okay, if she wants some water or some fresh air. She shakes her head, unable to speak for a moment, and hands the book to Jenna. 'Just this, I'll just take this,' she says eventually.

She pays and leaves the shop. Across the road is a small park with a couple of benches, where she sits, the book in her hands, waiting to feel calm enough to drive home. She watches people passing by, heading to the pub after work or hurrying to the supermarket to get something for dinner. Over by the post office she sees Doug, the nice man who fixes her car when it breaks down, and there's Alice's mother, Carla, going into Boots. It's not a big place, this town, and Flo has lived here long enough to know a bit about most people.

She runs her hand over the book, feeling the spot laminate title. She never knew, after the day they parted so long ago, whether Lilli had ever given her a second thought. She never knew if the path she took back then was as momentous for Lilli as it was for her. For years she's wondered where life would have taken her if she'd been stronger, braver, if she hadn't cast herself into purgatory for a reason that was long ago banished to the back of her mind, shadowed by sixty-two years of trying her hardest to forget. A reason that Lilli couldn't possibly have written about.

Could she?

She opens the cover and turns the page and her heart skips when she sees the dedication.

For F.

⟋⟍

Calm descends over Alice when she gets to the meadow and lets Ernie off the lead. She was tense all the way here, worried he might be too strong for her and the leash would slip from her hand, or they might encounter another dog and Ernie would go berserk. So now they're here, she's relieved they made it.

She loves the meadow – so many long summer afternoons spent here with Ella. She stands still for a minute as the dog runs about, the sun prickling her bare shoulders. The sky is a rich shade of blue, that gorgeous summer hue she so loves, criss-crossed by fading vapour trails. She tries to let herself enjoy it for a minute, tries to hold on to this calm, this sense of freedom. But it soon slips away. What if Ernie runs off and she can't find him again? Then Mrs Carter will be mad at her and very sad because she's a lonely old woman without any family or probably many friends and so the dog is her best buddy and she might be devastated by his loss and die of a broken heart and it would be all Alice's fault.

She blinks away the image, takes a breath, tries again. Isn't it nice, she tells herself, that she's finally finished her A Level exams and school is over? Doesn't she feel free? But it doesn't work. The other side of her brain grinds the thought into the ground – it's only a few months until she's supposed to start at Birmingham University and she might hate it, she might not make any friends, she might get mugged or raped or murdered on the journey home. All for a degree she isn't sure she wants to do in a place that makes her feel trapped.

She sighs, looks down, scuffs her shoes on the ground. It's exhausting, being her.

She hears Ella's voice then, her laugh. *C'mon, Alice, live a little!*

Sure, she fires back in her head, *but look what happened to you!*

If Ella were here they'd be lying on their backs looking up at the sky, trying to find patterns and shapes in the clouds and vapour trails. Ella would always make her laugh. *Doesn't that one look like Mrs Jackson's enormous bottom?* Or, *Look, it's Harry Styles in his man-bun phase.*

At least, she *used* to make her laugh, when they were kids, before Vicky and Nick and Liam came on the scene, back when Ella was hers, before she changed and Alice didn't.

A breeze blows warm over her skin and her scar prickles.

She touches it, running a finger down the pinkish trail of damaged skin on her right forearm. She is almost glad she has it, this constant reminder of how she failed Ella, though she knows she could never forget, in any case.

She hears a bark and looks up to see Ernie running towards her, a stick in his mouth. He reaches her and bends down, a literal downward dog, supplicant before her, eyes big and hopeful. She wrestles the stick from him and throws it as far as she can and Ernie bounds after it, so happy, so joyful, so carefree.

Lucky him.

Mrs Carter's already got the gin out by the time they get back to the house. In fact, Alice thinks she's probably sunk a few in her absence. The old woman puts down the book she's reading – a slim volume with the title *The Way We Were* – and fetches a second glass. She adds ice cubes from the freezer, sloshes in a generous amount of gin, a splash of tonic and a squeeze of lime, and hands it to her.

'Cheers,' she says and they clink glasses. 'How did it go? Did my boy behave himself?'

Alice nods. 'He's great, Mrs Carter.' She bends down to pat Ernie's head and can't help but smile. She already loves this dog.

'Flo, please,' Mrs Carter says. 'Or Florence if you must, but no one's called me that since school – and you can imagine how long ago that was!'

Flo. It's a jaunty name, a name with a sense of mischief, a name for a regular gin drinker. Not a name for someone like herself. *Come on, Alice, don't be so dull, Alice.* She sniffs her drink – gin, definitely gin – and takes a sip. It's so strong it makes her cough. She rarely drinks much, just the occasional glass of wine at home with her mum. She's heard the gossip from her classmates' eighteenth birthday parties down the local rugby club, listened to their tales of hangovers and drunken snogs and sexual exploits. But most weekends – and weekdays come to think of it – Alice stays at home with her mother, binge-watching Netflix or reading a book, breaking from time to time to scroll through social media like a silent stalker of other people's lives. She doesn't want to go out – especially not after what happened – but staying in with her mum on a Saturday night only makes her feel even more of a freak than she has long known she is. But at least it puts a smile on her mother's face.

'Much as I'm glad you're here,' Flo continues, 'I'm imagining summer jobs are a little thin on the ground if this is all you can get, a bright girl like you?'

'I have a Saturday job,' Alice says. 'In a café in town. I was hoping there'd be more shifts over the summer but it's not doing too well so Merryn can't afford it. I don't think it'll last long.'

'What, that little café by the town hall? Oh, what a shame, I often go there for a morning coffee in the week.'

Alice nods. She knows. She told Merryn, the café's manager, that she might be doing some dog walking for Mrs Carter – Flo – and she only raised her eyebrows in that sardonic way she has, as if to say *poor you*. Alice wasn't sure if it was because Merryn doesn't like dogs or doesn't like Florence Carter. But then Merryn, a 22-year-old former carnival queen who's worked at the café since she left school at sixteen, doesn't seem to like anyone. Alice thinks that's the real reason the café won't last too much longer, but she wouldn't dare tell Merryn that.

'Well, I shall have to find a new coffee spot.' Flo smiles. 'I don't suppose they'd let me in that other place – Gigi's, is it? They'd probably think an old duffer like me would put off the trendy young things.'

Alice smiles. She finds, despite herself, that she likes this old duffer; she feels more relaxed here than she ever has with the trendy young things in Gigi's or the Cross Keys. Alice isn't like them. She doesn't really know what she *is* like, but she knows she's not like them.

'Their loss then,' she says. 'You make a better G&T anyway.'

The Way We Were

Let's rewind a little.

Seven months before fleeing the place, I arrived at Château Mont d'Or in the autumn of fifty-seven thinking I was going on a fabulous adventure. What you must understand about me is that I was all about the fabulous adventures (still am, as it happens), but until then, my teenage escapades had been confined to New York, or even to my home neighbourhood of Brooklyn. I'd spend whole days at Coney Island beach with my best friend Jennifer, impose myself on my brother Bobby's baseball game in Prospect Park until I'd hit a home run (*She's bossy, your sister*, his friends would observe, eliciting a weary *Don't I know it*, from my darling brother), and occasionally venture into Manhattan, where Jen and I would ride the Staten Island ferry, buy ice-cream from our favourite vendor in Central Park, and put far too much on Ma's account at Macy's. But *this* adventure was in a different league altogether. Pop had promised me it would be the greatest of my little life

22

(ha! If only he knew), and Ma had been almost as excited for me as I was for myself (excited to have me out of her hair, I suspected). Even Bobby, about to start his third year at college right there in New York, had raised what I considered to be an envious eyebrow at the prospect of my journey across the Atlantic. Because what was special about this particular adventure was that it was in France!

I'd boarded the plane at Idlewild Airport having never been abroad in my life, and after hopping along the refuelling stops from New York to Gander to Shannon to Paris, my excitement rising incrementally with each leg until I was just about fit to burst, I'd been met at Orly Airport by a petite, neat Frenchwoman and chaperoned on the train ride down to Lyon, most of which I spent watching cornfields and vineyards and towns rush by under a vast blue sky, my nose near-glued to the window. *Isn't it just wonderful?* I'd gushed, but my chaperone had only shrugged and returned to her book, so I'd returned to the window, to the freedom I glimpsed on the other side of the glass – the freedom and the opportunity.

And now there I was, in a city of rivers and fine food and chic Frenchwomen and ... *je ne sais quoi*. Actually, I really didn't know what, but I sure was looking forward to finding out. It wasn't Paris – oh, how I wished it had been Paris! – because despite Pop's entreaties to his new highfalutin so-called friends, no quiet word had been enough to get me, a daughter of new money, into one of the French capital's elite finishing schools, which only took girls whose family wealth and status went back centuries (the kind who pooped pearls, as Jen's electrician father used to say). But I was, apparently, good enough for Château Mont d'Or in Lyon – that, or they really needed Pop's cash.

So the upshot was, I was pretty darn excited when I stepped into the reception room at the school for the welcome event.

I was also, as it turned out, a hopeless optimist (or denialist) about what, exactly, I would do whilst there.

'Do you know when we'll get to go and explore the city?' I asked a brunette in a belted wool dress, a silk scarf tied around her neck. She turned to me, eyes bright, cheeks flushed, epitomizing the nervous anticipation that simmered in the room, where sixteen girls mingled on a polished parquet floor under a sparkling chandelier. The atmosphere was infectious; excitement fizzed in my chest.

'Oh, I really couldn't say,' she replied and I tried to place her accent – Canadian, I guessed. 'Maybe there'll be a chaperone for trips outside the school?'

I pictured the disinterested woman on the train, who had communicated mostly through pursed lips and severely pencilled eyebrows. 'I sure hope not,' I said, my smile fading. Ma was usually too busy with her Tupperware parties and luncheons and PTA meetings and housework to chaperone me and Jennifer to the movie theatre or the shops, so we'd been trusted to go by ourselves, which suited us just fine. Lately it hadn't seemed to suit Pop so well, though. *She's running wild, Bel*, I'd overheard him say to Ma one day. *Gotta nip that in the bud or she'll never get hitched – at least not to the right sorta guy.*

The Canadian opened her mouth to say something else, but I turned away to grab another glass of non-alcoholic sparkling wine (though I wished it was a tumbler of Pop's best bourbon instead – another thing Jen and I did when we weren't being supervised). I moved through a gap in the small crowd, headed to the side of the room and lent against the wall, watching my new classmates – all pin-curled hair and trim waists – introducing themselves with varying degrees of confidence. I'd write about all this to Jen as soon as I could. *Tell me everything*, she'd said the day we hugged each other goodbye, tears spilling down our cheeks, *I want to know every little detail.*

'Girls.' The single word, accompanied by a sharp clap of the hands, brought the chatter to an end. 'Welcome to Château Mont d'Or. I am Madame Bouchard, headmistress of this school, and I am delighted to have you here.'

Sixteen pairs of eyes turned to face the speaker, who was standing at the back of the room behind a wooden lectern. It was the first time I'd laid eyes on the headmistress and I observed her with curiosity, imagining how I'd describe her to Jen: short grey hair set in smooth waves; a slim, almost gaunt, figure neatly packaged in a dusky pink jacket and matching calf-length pencil skirt; a double string of pearls lying across the crêpe-paper skin of her collarbone. She spoke with a British accent (the surname Bouchard, I was later informed, came from her late husband, a Frenchman) and there was an assuredness in her voice which I suppose was apt for a teacher of many years' experience but which also told me she was no fool, no pushover – more's the pity.

'We have welcomed young women here every year for thirty years, bar a break during the war, so you should feel honoured to be part of this long and prestigious tradition,' she said. 'The education you will receive from myself and my staff has been granted to the daughters of royalty, politicians, world leaders and society's longest-standing families, and it has served them well throughout their lives. In attending Château Mont d'Or, you will not only learn skills that will be essential in your roles as wives, mothers, homemakers and high society's leading lights, you will receive a training for life itself.' She paused, surveying the room as though to seek eye contact with each and every girl, and when her eyes found mine, I stared right back. I don't know what she saw in my face but I noticed that her smile fell, just a little.

'Whatever path your life may take, this education will be your guiding light, your cornerstone, your trusty handbook. At the end of this year, you will emerge highly skilled in cooking, sewing, nursing a sick child, keeping a house and managing staff. You will know how to present yourself in social situations, host a cocktail party and a formal luncheon, debate the issues of the day over the dinner table and support your husband in his work and hobbies, all the while ensuring that you look and feel your absolute best at all times.'

I looked around the room and took in the delight on the faces of some of the other girls as queasiness rose in my chest, dampening my previous excitement to a mere smoulder. No wonder Pop had been vague about the curriculum when he'd flogged the place to me like the true salesman he was. *You're gonna turn out as fine as any of those European gals, honey,* he'd said, and though that argument didn't really wash with me, since I thought I was pretty fine already, the appeal of travelling to France had been so great that I hadn't thought to consider precisely what I would have to study to make me even finer than I already was.

'What's more, we are blessed with a superb location in one of France's finest cities,' Madame Bouchard continued, 'which allows us to deliver a cultural programme of theatre, opera, music and art alongside your studies in this building. While the feminine mind may not be made for science and mathematics, I believe culture is an important part of any young woman's upbringing.' She smiled. 'I hope you understand that this is a rich opportunity which isn't afforded to many. In return for our hard work in providing you with this excellent education, I ask that you commit to its principles and work to the very best of your ability. I have no doubt that at the end of the academic year you will be transformed from naïve girls into exceptional young women, ready to enter society and make a good marriage.'

A ripple of applause spread through the room as Madame Bouchard finished her speech and stepped forward to mingle among us, but my hands stayed by my side, her words ricocheting in my head. *While the feminine mind may not be made for science . . .* I'd always quite liked science (all those dead bugs in jars and cells morphing under the microscope held a slightly macabre fascination for me) and I'd once had the fanciful idea of going to college to study biology. *Don't waste your time,* my high school teacher had said when I broached my tentative plan. *By all means go to college, but* domestic *science would be a more appropriate course of study for you.* I don't know why I'd thought Europe might be different, but in that moment I realized I had. I really had.

Still, I told myself, it would be all right. Music, Bouchard had said, and art – I liked those things, too. Sewing and nursing sick children not so much, but it would be fine. It really would. I was in *France*, so how could it be anything but?

'And you must be Eleanor Cranshaw.' The headmistress was suddenly in front of me.

I drained my glass, beamed and stuck out my hand. 'How'd you guess? But it's Lenny if you don't mind. Only my old man calls me Eleanor.'

'I'm delighted to meet you, Eleanor.' The woman shook my hand and smiled back. 'However, your father is quite correct. Eleanor is your name, and that's what we will call you here, or Miss Cranshaw, as the situation requires. And please refrain from using slang, it has no place in polite society.' She smiled again and leaned forward, almost conspiratorially. 'Don't worry, we'll have you shipshape in no time at all.'

She clearly thought she was being welcoming, and I suppose she was, in her own way, but as she spoke I instinctively recoiled from her words – just a little, but enough that she noticed. Her smile faded and she stepped back, her eyes locked on to mine. *She's a bright girl, but something of a challenge,* my teachers back home would write in my school reports. *She would do well to talk less and listen more.*

I had the feeling Madame Bouchard quite enjoyed a challenge.

As the headmistress turned to greet the next student I rolled my eyes, not for anyone but myself; however, as I did, I saw another girl looking over at me, a small smile tugging at her mouth. I smiled back, then stuck my tongue out the side of my mouth and crossed my eyes as if to say *I'm done for already*, and the girl laughed, before another student touched her on the arm and drew her into conversation.

At least my bed was comfy. I kicked off my shoes and flopped down on the mattress nearest the window, from where I could stare out at the sky. The lights of Lyon in the far distance were as tantalizing as a bowl of chocolate pudding in an empty kitchen. If I squinted, I felt sure I could make out the spire of Fourvière basilica standing proud on the hill. What a view it must have! First chance I got, I was going right there.

'Hello.'

I turned my head to see a figure standing in the bedroom doorway – the girl who had laughed at my silly face.

'Come on in.' I swung my feet off my bed. 'I guess you're landed with me.'

She put her small case down at the foot of the other single bed. 'Frances. Nice to meet you.'

'Lenny.'

The girl smiled. 'Not Eleanor.'

'You got it.' I grinned.

It's funny to think back to that moment, knowing what good friends we would later become, because on first sight we weren't an obvious pairing. With her clipped English accent, porcelain complexion and hourglass figure – accentuated on that day by a tweed circle skirt and pale pink blouse – Frances was just how I had pictured upper-class English girls to look. Why she needed to be at a finishing school, I couldn't imagine; surely she was already *finished* – and if she wasn't, then I had a hell of a long way to go to catch up.

'Say, new roomie, do you want to go there with me some-time?' I nodded at the window.

'Lyon?' Frances sat on her bed. 'Well I'd love to, but I don't know how much free time we'll get, or whether we'll be permitted to take trips into the city.'

'I'm not talking about getting *permission*.' I beamed at her. Ma always said my smile would get me in trouble one day and I sure hoped it would. 'Oh, I just want to see everything! I've never been to France before, or anywhere abroad. Have you?'

'Well, yes, a few times to Paris, and I've skied in the Alps.'

She delivered what was to me a frankly extraordinary sentence in a completely prosaic manner, with no hint of boastfulness, as though such experiences were so common-place they didn't even merit remark, and I laughed at the contrast with my own experience. My passport was newly issued – though foreign holidays were, in the years since Cranshaw Construction had boomed, within financial reach for our family, let's just say my father's outlook hadn't expanded as fast as his business. Despite his time overseas in the war – or because of it, perhaps – he was scared of *foreign*, I think. Funny foreign food. Funny foreign words. I wasn't, though. Anything but. Foreign meant exotic. Foreign was delicious. Thank goodness Pop's desire to keep up with the Joneses trumped any qualms he might have had about sending me abroad.

'In that case you'll be a fabulous guide,' I said. 'We can go into town and try out our fancy new table manners at a big hotel or go shopping in the luxury boutiques or even go to a nightclub or . . . whatever else it is the French do that's *très* fun.'

Frances smiled. 'You're American.' It was a statement, as though everything I'd said had marked me out as one, accent apart. Perhaps it had. Perhaps I seemed as much of my country as Frances did of hers. But she didn't know that sometimes I felt as alien back there as I did here. She couldn't realize that Pop's transformation from humble construction worker to president of one of the biggest real-estate developers in New York State had propelled me into an environment of unfathomable social codes and unspoken rules that I tripped over every time I was forced to play the obedient daughter at an occasion Pop had been invited to. She couldn't know how much I hated it, how I'd seized upon this year in Europe as a chance to escape. *Out of the frying pan, into the fire* – the phrase popped into my head then as I remembered Bouchard's speech, but I brushed it away, refocused on Frances, who was still smiling at me, head cocked to one side, assessing her own reaction to my Americanness, or so it seemed.

'Yes,' I said to her. 'American, but open to options.' I laughed at my own silly words and she smiled back. And I saw then that if *I* wasn't exactly as I appeared, perhaps Frances wasn't either. Perhaps there was more to this well-spoken English rose than first appeared.

'I should like to do those things, Lenny,' she said finally. 'I'd like this year to be *très* fun.'

2

Flo picks up a small V gouge and makes her first marks on the linoleum, feeling the sharp blade cut cleanly through the industrial grey surface. She traces the outline of the shape and then chooses a larger U gouge to clear away the centre. She works methodically, rhythmically, waiting for that beautiful moment when she will disappear into her work.

Usually, whatever is going on in the world, in this studio she can find calm, peace. Sometimes hours pass without her noticing. As she carves a design with her tools, she lets her mind wander off on whatever path it chooses. Sometimes it silently works through problems, sometimes it thinks of nothing at all and she finds herself in an almost meditative state.

Art has always been her therapy. It has always been there for her, even when she hasn't been bold enough to speak her troubles out loud – especially then, in fact. At first, drawing, from as far back as she can remember, and then oil painting, after she and Peter divorced and she needed something bold and bright to express the melting pot of feelings that poured out of her – relief, guilt, joy, shame. And now, in her old age, lino printing, a graphic, bold form of expression that fills her with delight. Art has been the only constant in her life, through all these years, as people and events have ebbed and flowed around her.

Now, as she feels the gouge slip through the lino, she thinks of Lilli, and her heart aches. Using the name *Lenny* may give her a certain artistic freedom in her writing, but so far the character is just as Flo remembers Lilli in real-life – bold, forthright, vivacious. They'd been such good friends, it seems a tragedy to her now that they didn't maintain that friendship, that Lilli has been absent in the six decades of her life that have passed since Flo stepped into that bedroom and met her for the first time.

Why?

She puts down the gouge, her hand shaking. The reason she abandoned her friend has been lodged like a sliver of shrapnel in her brain for more than sixty years. But she's spent so long trying to forget what happened – what she did – that the memory is no longer a whole, distinct picture; instead, it is a collection of abstract shapes and lines, much like the first layer of a reduction lino print, when the final image is far from clear. And she would prefer it to remain that way. She doesn't want the memory to crystallize, doesn't want to look right at it, because if she did, she knows it would scorch her eyes as badly as if she'd stared at the sun.

Perhaps she shouldn't read this book. Maybe she should give it away, leave it in a book drop or give it to the secondary school library. What will reading it solve, anyway? She can't change anything now. But she knows she won't do that. This is Lilli's account of what happened back then, and maybe if she reads it, if she hears Lilli's side of things, it will finally allow her to make peace with her own.

She looks at the lino and sighs. She can't do this now. She isn't going to disappear into her work. That beautiful meditative state eludes her today. She pushes herself up from her chair and walks slowly back to the house, Eric nearly tripping her up as he demands a snack. She rattles a few biscuits into his bowl, puts the kettle on, walks down the hallway and stoops to collect the post. She must get a cage put in so she doesn't have to bend so far. She thinks this every day, and never does it. Still, at least her knees remain functional. Maybe that little exercise is all that's stopping them from seizing up altogether.

She flicks through the mail. There's a postcard from her great-niece on holiday in Majorca, which makes her smile (nobody sends postcards anymore, Emily always says, and then sends her one anyway, knowing how much her silly old great-aunt will appreciate it), plus two bills and a brochure from a holiday company she used once about ten years ago, remaining on their mailing list ever since. The front cover is an amalgamation of photos from around France: the vineyards of Bordeaux; a Bateau Mouche on the Seine, the Eiffel Tower in the background; and, in the bottom corner, a cityscape at night, showing bridges illuminated over a river, a white basilica high on a hill in the background, and it is this picture that stops her still. Lyon. Today – now – after starting to read that book, she would receive this. Of course, it's not really a coincidence. Holiday brochures flogging tours to France are two-a-penny; she's probably had dozens of them over the years and put them in the recycling without giving them a second glance. But today she looks. She looks and she remembers. The white beacon of Fourvière on the hill, the wide boulevard of Rue de la République, the art galleries and the cathedral, the hotels lining the Rhône, the insalubrious alleyways and secret passageways of Vieux Lyon, the city's Old Town.

Back in the kitchen, she puts the brochure on the table and opens her laptop. Her fingers hover over the keyboard. The school isn't there anymore – she heard it shut down years ago – and Lilli wouldn't be anywhere near it anyway, but the newspaper article said she was still in France. Has she been there all this time? Did she never leave the country she fell in love with back then? She types in the name. L. P. Henri. An author would have a website, surely. She squints at the results and taps on the first link and there she is. Lilli. It's the same photo from the newspaper, so she scrolls down, hoping to find more. But there's only some text about the book and a photo of the cover and some quotes from reviewers. She clicks on 'About' and there's another photo. A smiling Lilli standing in a field of lavender, squinting slightly in the sun. She looks happy. Flo scrolls down again.

Born and raised in New York, L. P. Henri travelled to France at the age of 17 to attend a finishing school near Lyon. On leaving the school in 1958, she settled near Avignon, Provence. After a modest acting career, including a supporting role in the acclaimed independent film *Frédérique*, she spent twenty years as a high-school teacher before setting up a florist's shop in central Avignon with her daughter. *The Way We Were* is her third novel.

A daughter. Acting. Provence. A florist's shop, for goodness sake! Flo stares at the screen, floored by the details of a life she's known nothing about for more than sixty years. Such a long time in which so much can happen. Marriages and lovers and jobs and holidays and illnesses and deaths and disappointments and successes and countless new starts. That's what Flo knows of life; she is sure Lilli knows the same, in her own way. But Flo is suddenly breathless with how quickly it's all gone, and how vividly she remembers sitting in that bedroom in Lyon, meeting the energetic, impulsive lifeforce that was Lilli, this American, and knowing right then and there that this girl could change her life – if she let her.

For so long after they parted, she didn't know how to find Lilli – a get-out clause, she can admit in retrospect, since seeing her would have meant having to face up to that hideous act – but now, staring at her old friend's face on the computer screen, she knows she would love to see her again.

She would love to be able to say sorry.

⁓

It is Sunday and Alice is sitting on the patio at the back of the house scrolling through her phone. There are Instagram stories from last night, posted by Vicky and Nick and Liam and some of the others from her year. Photos of the Lido club, of their outfits and make-up, of tequila shots and beers. #endofexamsparty reads one hashtag. #girlsgowild,

#largingitinLido, #fuckitwerefree. It's what you're meant to do when you're eighteen, as so many people have told her. But it looks intimidating to Alice, who has never actually stepped inside a club, who has never taken the night bus home from the city in the small hours, the party no doubt continuing on the top deck of the N15 as it rattles through sleepy villages, past dark, empty flood plains each side of the main road. If she had gone, she wouldn't have found it easy, like her classmates have made it look. She would have spent the whole time feeling out of her depth, feeling silly if she danced or awkward if she didn't, worrying about losing everyone, about what would happen if they missed the last bus, about the terrors that might await them in the dark streets. For the millionth time she wonders what's wrong with her, why she doesn't feel comfortable getting drunk and dirty dancing with boys and wearing low-cut tops and lashings of make-up. Why it all went wrong when she tried to.

'Here, fresh out of the oven.' Her mother comes onto the patio and hands her a cookie. 'Careful, it's hot.'

Alice takes it and forces a smile but doesn't make eye contact. 'Thanks.'

Her mother cocks her head. 'What's up?'

'Nothing.'

She stands there a moment, concern emanating from her, like a forcefield drawing Alice in. 'Do you fancy going to the cinema tonight? There's that one with Timothée Chalamet in it that you wanted to see.'

Alice shrugs. 'S'pose. After I've walked Ernie.'

Her mum kisses her head. 'Great!' she says. 'We can get

dinner in town beforehand if you like. Steak and chips at that French place?'

Alice recognizes her mother's brightness for the mask it is. She wears it a lot, these days. She makes out that life has moved on and everything's normal (even though it never can be, ever again), but Alice knows her mum better than that – because they are the same, really. She knows that beneath this false brightness, this mask, is a quagmire of worry that has thickened and spread in the past two years. Alice rarely gives her anything to worry *about*, and yet still, she manages it. *Be careful sweetie*, she says, on the rare occasion Alice takes the bus into Birmingham city centre to do some shopping. *There are nasty people in the city. I don't want anything to happen to you.*

Her mother's worry is quicksand and Alice shouldn't try to fight it, shouldn't try to extricate herself, because it's stronger than her – stronger than both of them – and if she struggles, she'll only sink deeper. She doesn't have the conviction to push against it, anyway, because a big part of her thinks she's right.

She leaves the house, her mum's eyes on her back, and walks to Flo's. The route takes her through town and out the other side, past the Cross Keys, the supermarket and the town hall. There's the main square, where everyone at school gathers on New Year's Eve after getting trolleyed in the pub – or so she hears, since she's never been. There's the jewellery shop where Ella worked as an assistant on Saturdays after she turned sixteen, using her considerable charm to sell eternity rings and watches and diamond earrings. *A delightful young girl, such a terrible loss.* And the ice-cream shop run by

Mr Moretti, the first port of call after school most days in the summer term. Alice has lived here all her life, all eighteen years, and it's as familiar to her as the colour of her hair and the worry line between her mother's eyes.

She knocks on the door when she arrives and, getting no answer, uses the key Flo gave her to let herself in. *I'm often in the studio and I won't hear you knocking.* She makes her way down the hall and is warmly greeted by Ernie, whose claws skitter on the wooden floor as he rushes to meet her. She should go straight to the studio to tell Flo she's here, but instead she lingers in the house, held there by the quiet and the emptiness, which invite her to look around without being looked at herself.

It's not the sort of house she thought someone like Flo would live in. She thought an old woman's house would be dark and grubby, with a slight air of neglect, stuffed full of things that have likely been there so long she's forgotten she has them. But Flo's house is bright, clean, homely. It is, however, definitely full of things. Books are packed into the antique mahogany bookcase in the sitting room – travel guides and novels and encyclopaedias and leather-bound volumes of who knows what. There are pieces of art on the walls – colourful oil paintings and pencil sketches and graphic prints – and photos lining the mantelpiece and windowsills. She stops to look at them. There's Flo somewhere abroad in the still-fierce sun of a summer's evening, standing on a hill overlooking orchards and, beyond, the sea. Her arm is linked through a middle-aged man's and they are both laughing as Flo's hair – shoulder-length and light brown, rather than the short grey bob it is now – blows across her face. There she is again, much younger and surprisingly glamorous in a patterned maxi dress, among a row of people who look vaguely familiar, all of them holding cocktail glasses and cigarettes. There's a handwritten inscription below. *To Flo, my right-hand woman, with my love, Guinevere. June 1979.* A more recent photo shows Flo standing next to two women, her arm around both – one who must be in her fifties and another much younger woman with obviously dyed red hair and a nose ring, who leans into Flo with affection. All three are smiling – a similar smile that tells Alice they are related. Above a side table in one corner of the room is another picture hanging on the wall. She peers closely at the figures – it's Flo, in a helmet and goggles, strapped to an instructor, doing a tandem skydive.

Florence Carter. The mad old cat lady. The sad and lonely spinster.

⚓

Flo has forced herself back to the studio, forced herself to carry on with her latest work, meditative state or not. She has left the book on the kitchen table, unwilling to read any more right now. Part of her wants to race through it, to find out what Lilli knows, if she's written about what Flo did, but another part of her can't bear to. Reading the book plunges her right back there, and it feels too intense, too upsetting, to stay in the past for long.

She is in the middle of printing when Alice knocks on the door of the studio.

40

'Ernie's walked, so I'm going now,' she says.

Flo looks up. Alice doesn't smile often, and it strikes her as sad that this young girl with her whole life ahead of her shouldn't find much to smile about.

'Don't feel you have to rush off,' she says. 'Want to have a go?'

Alice comes further into the studio, Eric weaving around her ankles.

'At this?' She nods to the lino, the paper, the freshly printed design in Flo's hands. 'Oh, I couldn't. I'd only mess it up.'

Flo smiles. 'Well yes, probably. Everyone does, the first time. But you have to start somewhere, don't you?'

She pegs the paper she's holding onto the washing line and takes another piece. She doesn't do it for the money – doesn't need it, luckily, with her pension, her inheritance and an ongoing trickle from the shares and bonds in her old trust fund – but for the sheer pleasure of it, the pleasure of making and the pleasure of seeing her artworks bought, seeing others enjoy what she's created.

'Come on, just give it a go.' She gets up from the chair, knees clicking, and beckons Alice over. She can see that, in fact, the girl does want to, but she's shy, or unsure, or appre-hensive – perhaps all three.

Alice hesitates, then takes Flo's place on the chair. Flo hands her a roller.

'Now, you're going to ink up the lino. Roll it in the ink on the tray first until it's smooth and not too sticky, then over the lino, and you'll see the design come to life.'

She watches as Alice tentatively does as she's told, a frown of concentration on her face.

'That's it, now lay the piece of paper over the top,' Flo says. 'Then you use this,' she picks up a wooden baren and holds it out to Alice, 'to press on the back of the paper. Use a circular motion and quite a lot of pressure.'

Alice does as directed and then Flo shows her how to slowly peel back the paper.

'Wow.' Alice looks up, her eyes big with surprise when she sees the design appear in rich blue, and Flo smiles. Ah yes, she remembers the joy of discovering this for the first time, the realization that it was possible to create something from nothing, with just her hands and a few tools.

'Looking good,' she says. 'But don't peel it off entirely just yet. It needs a bit more pressure to transfer the ink a little more.'

Alice presses on the baren again.

'Good, now let's see.'

She peels the paper back once more and lets out a deflated *Oh* at the now-smudged ink, the blurred lines. 'I told you I'd mess it up.'

Flo puts her hand on her shoulder. 'It happens, especially when you've never done it before. You just need practice. And that's the beauty of printmaking – you can just print again and again until you get the result you want.'

'No, I'm useless. I can't do it.' Alice gets up from the chair. 'I'm sorry for wasting the paper. I have to go now.' Her hand rubs at something on her right forearm – a long puckered scar, Flo sees.

'It's not wasted, it's an experience,' Flo says, but Alice is already walking out the studio door. Eric is forced to move from his place on the doormat as she leaves, a perturbed expression on his whiskered face. Flo bends down to stroke his head. 'What are we going to do with her, eh?' she says, watching Alice walk up the garden path, head bent, as though she's carrying a heavy weight on her shoulders. And suddenly Flo recognizes it, this weight of fear, of sadness, of uncertainty, of worry. She recognizes it so clearly because she once carried it herself.

'Alice?' Flo calls up the path. 'Wait a second. You've time for a drink, haven't you?' She tries to keep her tone casual, offhand, belying the rush of desperation she feels for Alice to come back. She can't let her leave like that, feeling like a failure.

The girl turns, hesitates; her face softens and her hand drops from her arm.

'Okay.' She nods.

Flo's chest relaxes. 'Just let me clear up in here, won't you?'

Alice comes back to the studio and together they put the inks away and wash the rollers and inking trays. They move around each other in silence, Flo careful not to make a big deal out of what just happened. But it feels important to her, Alice coming back in here, a tentative first step in a game of trust she's only just realized they are playing.

'How long did it take you to learn?' Alice speaks finally, her voice almost a mumble.

'Oh, I'm still learning. I don't think you ever stop.' Flo dries her hands on her shirt and looks at her. 'But I suppose it took around a year before I thought what I was doing was good enough to sell. The first few pieces I did were atrocious.

I had to learn how to visualize my ideas in a graphic way, how to transfer that into a design, and then get my head around the reduction print process, which can be ever so complicated. This isn't a craft for the impatient. You must be prepared to fail and start all over again.' She laughs. 'Which, when I think about it, is a metaphor for my life.'

Flo sees the question on Alice's face before she says it. 'What have you failed at in life?'

'Well, dear, how long have you got? When you get to my age, it's a mighty big list I can tell you.' She laughs again, rich and croaky, a laugh that's had many outings over the years, she is pleased to be able to say. 'Now, how about that drink?'

They walk back to the house, where Ernie greets them enthusiastically from his usual napping spot by the back door. Flo pours the gin, hands a glass to Alice and beckons her to follow. 'Come with me.' She walks through the kitchen door into the living room, stopping by a photo, one of her favourites, from a trip to Italy sometime in the nineties. 'This is my darling James. He died a long time ago now, but he brought me such joy during the years we were together.'

'You were married?' Alice asks, surprise in her voice.

Sad old spinster. Flo knows her reputation among the youngsters of this town, but it doesn't hurt her, it simply makes her laugh. *Old* is the only part of that phrase that is undeniably true. And don't they know that *spinster* originally meant a woman who spun wool to earn a living? Nothing derogatory in that. *Sad* is the sole word she finds objectionable, because although she has felt desperately sad plenty of times in her life, those times have been more than balanced out by joyous ones.

'Yes,' she says, 'but not to James. I was married to Peter for ten years. But that's my point. I failed at marriage. Well, actually it was very much a mutual failure. But the point is, I was able to be with James – the love of my life – only because I failed at marriage. I never would have met him if I'd still been married to Peter.' She points to a black and white photograph of a group of people, herself and Guinevere standing next to Mick Jagger and Jerry Hall. 'And this here is a picture from my wonderful, wonderful job that I loved so much. But I only ended up doing that because I failed to be a mother and Peter left me for someone who could be. Instead, I became assistant to Guinevere De Souza, one of the most influential British fashion designers of the sixties and seventies, and believe you me, that's never a sentence I thought I'd utter before it happened.'

Alice doesn't say anything and Flo feels a childish sense of triumph to have clearly refuted the girl's assumptions about her. Though to be fair to her, grubby slippers and an ink-splattered old shirt don't really scream cutting-edge fashion.

'And this?' Alice points to the photo of Flo skydiving.

'Oh, that was simply to mark the occasion of still being alive at seventy.' Flo laughs. 'My niece put me up to it.'

'Weren't you scared?'

'Shitting bricks!' Flo says, and Alice snorts. 'But you can't let fear hold you back,' she adds, looking Alice in the eyes, but the girl drops her gaze and stares at her shoes, which are flecked with dust from her walk through the dry meadow, parched after several weeks of no rain.

'I really have to go now,' she mumbles at the floor. 'Mum's expecting me.'

⚬

'You're back! How was it?' Carla says when her daughter comes through the back gate into the garden, where she is sitting.

Alice shrugs and doesn't look at her. 'Fine.'

'Nice walk with the dog?'

'Yeah.'

'And have you seen Flo's prints yet? She's talented, isn't she?'

A nod. 'Yeah.'

Carla sighs. It's like pulling teeth, conversing with her daughter. 'We'll leave for the restaurant in about half an hour then, okay?' she says as Alice disappears into the house. She leans back in her chair and closes her book. She can't read anymore, now.

Carla has spent the two hours since Alice left the house reading in the garden and eating the cookies she made earlier. They are delicious – crunchy on the outside, slightly soft in the middle, the chocolate chips still warm – and she's eaten too many of them (these days it feels like every tiny treat she allows herself is punished tenfold, as if one little biscuit inexplicably adds an extra kilo to her body) but they have failed in their ultimate aim, which was to put a genuine smile on her daughter's face.

The cinema trip won't do it either, or the meal out beforehand. She hopes walking Florence Carter's dog *will* do it, eventually, but so far she's seen no evidence of it, though it's early days. That's why she suggested the idea, after she bumped into Flo in town one day and they got talking about Flo's struggle to give her dog the twice-daily walks he needs. She doesn't like to think of Alice going off who knows where to walk – she's told her to avoid the main roads, and anywhere too remote – but she assumes the dog will protect her from harm, and on balance it seemed like it was worth a shot. Alice loves animals, and pets are a comfort in traumatic times, aren't they? Perhaps they should have got a dog or cat themselves, right after the accident (it wasn't an accident, it was a crime, but that's what she calls it), but at the time Carla couldn't even contemplate that anything, anything at all, could possibly go any way to easing the pain her daughter felt. It would have been a drop in the ocean. But after two years of unsuccessfully trying to coax Alice back to herself, pet therapy is surely worth a go. *Have fun, Alice,* she said as her daughter left the house that afternoon. *Have fun and be careful!* Alice only rolled her eyes and slammed the door behind her, and Carla felt the familiar jolt of dismissal.

How did it get to this? *Two peas in a pod,* that's what Rich used to call them, and they became even closer after the divorce, after Rich abandoned them for Sweden's big pharma and a six-figure salary that will no doubt keep him in meat-balls for life (Carla has refused to shop in IKEA ever since). But recently it's like a glass wall has come down between them and she's left gesticulating wildly one side of it, while Alice remains blank and unresponsive on the other. *I'm fine,* she always says when Carla tries to get her to open up, to tell her what's going on in her head. *I'm fine.*

Carla can think of many words to describe her daughter but *fine* certainly isn't one of them.

At the restaurant – a French chain, one of the only decent places to eat in this small town – they sit in silence looking at menus, though they will undoubtedly order what they always do: steak, skinny fries and a side salad. It pleases her, this small act of consensus between her and her daughter, a reminder that this chasm has not always existed between them.

'The steak frites for two, please, *à point*,' Carla says to the waiter, pleased she remembers the French expression for medium rare.

Alice rolls her eyes. *Mum*, she used to say with a smile, *don't be so embarrassing.* But now Alice is beyond words, beyond smiling; Carla understands that she is an embarrassment to her daughter. Or more than that – something shameful. Or frankly, who knows, because she has no idea what Alice thinks about anything anymore.

'No,' Alice says to the waiter, her objection loud in the quiet restaurant. 'I don't want the steak. The chicken, please.'

Carla brings her glass to her mouth and takes a sip of beer, blinking hard. *Stupid, stupid.* She will not get upset because her daughter doesn't want to eat steak.

'So, how's the dog? Ernie, is it?' Carla asks when the waiter has gone. *So* this, *so* that . . . She starts a lot of sentences with *so* when talking to her daughter, a device to kickstart a new conversation when the last one has failed.

Alice doesn't look at her directly but she nods and Carla sees a flicker of a smile on her face. *Good.*

'He's really cute,' she says.

'Where did you go today?'

'To the meadow again.'

Carla nods. The meadow is safe enough during the day and Alice knows it well. She used to go there with Ella all the time. Carla remembers how they'd come back for dinner, giggling over something silly that they wouldn't share with her, and she almost envied their closeness, their naturalness with each other, something that could only come from being friends from such a young age – from the very first day of primary school, in fact. Ella's allocated coat hook in reception class had a picture of a bright yellow duckling on it, its beak open in an expression of happiness, while Alice's was an owl, neat and serious, and those images have stuck with her through the years because they were so apt, so indicative of the people they would grow into. Such different people, yet they complemented each other. *Sisters from another mister,* they'd always say, and Carla would laugh because she felt like Ella's mother at times, so often was the girl round at theirs.

What damage has it done to Alice to have that taken away?

Her brain flips back to that night, as it is wont to do, presents her with Alice's pale face, streaked with tears, her right arm heavily bandaged, her bright pink fingernails poking out; she relives the jackhammer of her heart as she ran down the hospital corridor, her legs near buckling when she saw her daughter in the bed. *You're okay, you're hurt, you're okay, you never wear nail polish that colour.* And she recalls the way she castigated herself, a feeling that has never left her since: she didn't protect her daughter from this man; she let her get hurt. *You had one job . . .*

49

'You're careful along the roads, though, aren't you,' she says now. 'I don't want Ernie pulling you into the traffic.'

Alice looks down, the tentative smile gone. 'Yes,' she says quietly.

She doesn't say much after that. They eat in near silence and then head for the cinema, relief settling over Carla as the ads come on, releasing her from the pressure of having to try to extract words from her daughter's mouth. The cinema is the only activity they both still seem comfortable doing together.

As the adverts play, she reaches for her phone to put it on silent and glances at the notifications.

'It's Sunday, Susan,' she mutters when she sees an email from her boss, but she opens it anyway. *Lisa starts tomorrow, please could you set aside some time to go through the release schedule with her?* Carla closes the email without replying; there's no rule she has to respond to emails on the weekend, and she has ignored plenty from Susan before. But she's always had the sense that it is *noted* that she doesn't reply out of hours, that she is doing herself a disservice by not playing the game. But the truth is, after so many years at Pulham Press and with no ladder to climb, she simply doesn't care enough. Quality time with her daughter is far more important.

There's also a WhatsApp from her mother in Spain. *Good weekend darling? Roasting here x.* A variation on the same message Carla has received most weekends since her parents emigrated five years ago, just after Rich left her, just when she needed them most. *We're at the end of the telephone whenever you need us*, her mother said at the time. *Every day?* Carla felt like saying. They came back when Alice was in hospital, though;

they were there for her then. And so was Rich, briefly, though he left again as soon as Alice was discharged, fleeing back to Stockholm to his new wife and toddler son. She didn't mind; she wanted to care for Alice by herself anyway, to facilitate her recovery with soup and cake and fresh bedding.

Lastly, there's a Facebook post from an old friend, Kerry, asking for sponsorship money for a charity bungee jump. At their age? God, no. She did one once, though, a long time ago, on an epic post-university trip to Australia, during which she also tried whitewater rafting, scuba diving, windsurfing, snorkelling. She even swam in a lake with a crocodile (*freshies don't bite*, their guide said cheerily, and she chose to believe him). Couldn't now, though. Just couldn't. Not now she knows how easily things can go wrong, how precarious life can be.

Sometimes – like right now, sitting here next to Alice in the semi-dark cinema – her daughter absently touches the scar on her arm and that little gesture fills Carla with something she can't put into words. It is as though everything else has melted away – the aloneness of single motherhood, the forced civility between her and Rich, the night sweats and middle-aged spread and itchy skin that have started to torment her since she slipped past forty-five – and there is only Alice. Alice is all and all is Alice.

But Alice doesn't even talk to her anymore.

The Way We Were

LYON, FRANCE, SEPTEMBER 1957

'Fresh blooms are happiest in spotless vases. A little bleach, scrub them well, rinse in hot water and you'll be ready to display your flowers at their very best.'

I looked around the room. All the other girls, including Frances, seemed rapt. One or two were even writing notes. My notebook remained in the pocket of my skirt.

'Think carefully about where your floral arrangement is to be displayed,' Madame Bouchard continued, but I drifted off then, only vaguely following her instructions on pleasing proportions and table centrepieces and something strange involving rhubarb. Outside, the sky was a vivid autumn blue and if I stretched my neck a little, I could just make out Mont Blanc, hazy in the distance.

'Eleanor, please pay attention.'

'*Oui, Madame,*' I muttered.

'As I was saying,' she threw me a pointed look, 'fruit and vegetable foliage such as rhubarb leaves, artichoke heads, asparagus spears and broccoli leaves can be very complementary within a floral display.' She clapped her hands as I absorbed this extraordinary statement. Back home, Ma would have made a soup from all of that. 'Now, in pairs, I would like you to choose from the selection provided and create a display in an appropriate receptacle.'

I looked towards Fran, but my roommate was already paired up with Barbara, the Canadian I'd met at the welcome reception, a timid, harmless type I knew I'd have little in common with ('I want to study nursing', she'd told me, 'so I can meet a doctor to marry'). The others also quickly fell into pairs: Alia, the daughter of a minor Jordanian royal, with Gina, the child of an Italian actress and a French movie director; Catherine, a British mining heiress who grew up in Zambia before attending boarding school in England, paired with Aurélia, a Swiss girl whose father made his money in powdered milk. I'd chatted briefly to most of my fellow students by now and though I found their varied, exotic backgrounds fascinating, they seemed less enamoured by mine. As I stood alone, unpaired, I wished my friend Jen was there. *Did you know they put* broccoli leaves *in flower arrangements?* I would write later.

'I guess it's you and me, Sandra,' I said to the only other girl left, whom I'd barely had the chance to speak with yet, though word had already reached me that she was the daughter of an earl and a regional schools' champion lacrosse player back home in England. 'Or should I call you Sandy?'

She turned to me and I saw her disappointment. 'I suppose it is.' Her voice was frosty. 'And no.'

'Gotcha.' I beamed and gave a little salute in jest, which was met with a single arched eyebrow, an expression that confirmed to me why she, too, had been left unpartnered. 'Well then,' I picked up a flower, 'these pink chrysanthemums, a bunch of grapes and a few of these rhubarb leaves should do it, don't you think?'

Sandra looked me up and down. 'Weren't you listening? We need to think carefully about this, not just throw any old thing together. Constance Spry would not approve.'

'Constance who?' I twirled the chrysanthemum stem in my hand.

Both of Sandra's eyebrows flew up this time. 'Spry. Only the best floral designer in London. You haven't heard of her? No, I suppose you wouldn't have, being *American*.'

I laughed – partly in shock, I think – at the undisguised disdain in her tone, which was ably supported by the expression on her face. Perhaps my Fodor's *Woman's Guide to Europe* (a parting gift from Jen) was correct in stating that Europeans resented Americans for helping them during the war, though I found that completely ridiculous. What had the war to do with me anyway? I was a toddler in diapers back then.

'I'm glad there are such fabulous floral designers in England, Sandra, but if that's the case then what's the point of learning how to do it yourself? I could have bought the finest bouquet in New York every day for the rest of my life and it would still be cheaper than my tuition here.'

Sandra regarded me with a mix of pity and condescension. 'When I have a home to run and a household budget to manage,' she said slowly, as though speaking to a child,

'I'm sure my husband will be extremely glad I can do such things myself.'

I thought about Pop and Bobby, mostly oblivious to Ma's efforts to beautify our home, and was about to reply *I don't think he'll give a damn about flowers* when Madame Bouchard came up behind us. 'Have you made your choices yet, girls?'

'We're still considering the design, Madame,' Sandra said.

'Very good. It's worth taking your time.' Her eyes flicked to the chrysanthemum in my hand. 'Eleanor, please see your way to handling the flowers with care. Should you bruise the petals, you will ruin the display.'

'Of course.' And then I just couldn't help myself. 'Should I be wearing kid gloves?'

I caught a brief frostiness in Bouchard's expression before canned sunshine returned to her face. 'That won't be necessary,' she said. 'Simply give the task in hand your full attention and utmost care, just as a young woman should approach everything in life.'

When she left us, I picked up the scissors, surveyed the chrysanthemum briefly, and cut the stem with a confident snip.

Flower arranging was just the start. Over my first week at the school, I was taught how to plan a cocktail party for fifty guests, complete with shopping list and staff requirements. I sat through classes in French and needlework, history of art and home economics. Bouchard taught us deportment, manners and conversation skills; a petite woman in her late fifties called Madame Grisaille (whose spinster status quickly led to rumours she was *one of those women*) provided lessons on dinner-party menu-planning and cooking, while after lunch on Tuesdays the bespectacled, white-haired Monsieur Joussot (whose bachelor status sparked no such gossip) taught us musical appreciation. Wednesday afternoons were reserved for tennis on the school's own courts – a game I'd never played but soon loved, since it allowed me to let off steam after all that time cocooned in the school – while each evening after dinner we were coached in singing or piano, neither of which I had the slightest aptitude for.

I did *try* to pay attention, as I was frequently reminded to do, but I couldn't prevent my mind from embarking on adventures, daydreaming about what I might encounter if I ever got the chance to escape into Lyon, imagining the clothes in the shops and the men in the bars and the mystique of the hidden alleyways called *traboules* that I'd read about in my guidebook.

I only had to get out there.

'Does anyone know when we might have one of those promised cultural trips into town?' I asked the others over dinner one night. We had all dressed for the occasion, as per the rules, and under said rules we were meant to be speaking French; however, given none of us anglophones could yet say more than a few words, we resorted to whispering in English as long as a member of staff wasn't in earshot.

'Je ne sais pas,' Sandra said loudly, before lowering her voice. 'But I heard Madame Bouchard discussing an opera production with Monsieur Joussot, so hopefully it won't be long.' She nudged her knife and fork together on the right

side of her plate so they lay in the exact arrangement specified by Bouchard to indicate *one has finished one's meal* — the knife blade facing in, the fork to its left, tines up, so as not to fall as the plate is removed — and sat with Bouchard-approved posture in her high-backed chair, hands in her lap. 'However, I hear Lyon's opera house isn't a patch on Palais Garnier in Paris,' she whispered, eyebrows raised. 'Did I tell you Father took us there to see *Le nozze di Figaro*?' She stressed the words in an exaggerated accent that would have made Jen, an Italian-American, roar with laughter.

'You did,' I said. 'Twice.'

A titter rippled down the table but stopped abruptly when Sandra glared at my classmates. In less than a week she had emerged as the de facto Head Girl, the one praised by Bouchard as an example for the rest of us to follow, the one we all knew you crossed at your peril. I'd met girls like that before and I didn't very much care for them.

'There's no need to be snippy, Eleanor. I don't suppose you can appreciate what a treat it is to go to the opera, having never been yourself. I assume your family doesn't have much history of opera-going, being *new money*. What is it your father does again?'

'His company builds houses for young families in suburban New York State. They're quite the homes to have right now,' I found myself saying with an unfamiliar rush of pride for Pop. It wasn't that I didn't admire how far he'd come since starting his construction company on his return from the war, I just didn't understand why that meant we now had to be chummy with such snobs as Sandra and her ilk.

'Oh yes, those identical rabbit hutches for the aspiring middle classes.' Sandra laughed. 'Well, I suppose not everyone can have a manor house.'

'I think they look rather nice, from the pictures I've seen in the papers. Darling little gardens.' Frances had been silent for much of the meal but her voice, when it came, was a rose among thorns. I threw her a look of gratitude, though I doubted she meant what she said; having grown up in an enormous house herself, she was unlikely to find Pop's suburban split-levels appealing. (Even Ma didn't want to live in one, preferring to stay close to her friends in the Irish community of Brooklyn, though Pop was keen on renovating a grand old house near his golf buddies in Scarsdale.)

Taking Fran's lead, several of the other girls murmured their agreement. I'd noticed that, unlike Sandra, Fran's quiet yet warm presence commanded a certain respect among the other students. She wasn't giggly and silly like some of them, neither was she snooty and condescending like Sandra. She wore her upper-class background lightly.

Sandra pursed her lips. 'Each to their own, I suppose. But I doubt I shall be seeing such people at the opera any time soon.'

I smiled. 'I look forward to you showing me the ropes, Sandra.'

Back in our room that evening, I managed to make Fran laugh with my impression of Sandra's entitled manner.

'Oh Fran, I was so excited about coming to Lyon, but is this how it's going to be?' I flopped down on my bed and looked at my roommate. 'Trapped in an endless cycle of flower arranging and dinner-party planning? We could be in Wisconsin or . . . Peru, for all we've seen of what's out there.'

Fran only shrugged. 'It's not so terrible. And what choice do you have?' She returned to the drawing she was doing, a pencil sketch of the large oak tree outside our window. She was a good artist, I'd quickly discovered in the time I'd known her. Over the course of that first week, we'd settled into a comfortable existence together, spending our late evenings talking, reading and in Fran's case, sketching. She was talented, I could see. She worked quickly, freely, capturing a face, a landscape, a room with what seemed like minimal effort. I could just imagine what inspiration she would find if we could only go into the city.

'Where'd you learn to do that?' I asked.

Fran's eyes remained on the paper. 'I've always sketched.'

'You're terrifically good. You could make a career out of it, I'm sure.' I got up from the bed and stood in front of the mirror, twirling one of Fran's chiffon scarves around my neck. She had some beautiful scarves – beautiful clothes, in fact: cashmere twin sets and silk blouses and tailored dresses and skirts in fabric of a quality that even I, for all my lack of knowledge about these things, could sense. She'd told me her mother ordered fabrics from Harrods in London and had clothes tailored for her by a seamstress in Stow-on-the-Wold, the funny name of the nearest town to their country pile. I couldn't imagine what that was like, how it must feel to have grown up in a world where a family seamstress made you dresses with fabrics from the most exclusive store in England.

For all my family's adopted airs and graces in public, our new money could never buy us the entrenched sense of wealth and standing that Fran had clearly grown up with. My father was essentially a two-bit construction worker who'd made it big by being in the right place at the right time and getting a loan on the GI Bill. My mother still hoarded paper grocery bags and Pop's old shirts, a habit from more frugal times in the thirties when paper bags were used as writing paper and shirts cut up and sewn into clothes for my then-toddling brother Bobby.

'A career?' Fran said. 'Hardly – I'd have to go to art school for that.'

'And why not? You could train to be an illustrator for one of the big women's magazines. That would be so exciting, don't you think?'

Fran smiled. 'I'd only have to give it up when I married, and anyway, Father would never let me. He doesn't approve of my sketching; says I've got my head in the clouds.'

'So?'

'He's always considered it off-putting to potential husbands.'

I pulled one of Fran's hats down on my head and twirled around to face my roommate with a grin. 'I'd better take up drawing quick smart then.'

Frances put her pencil down, surprise on her face. 'You don't want a husband, children?'

I shrugged. 'Sure, I do,' I said, though I wasn't, in fact, at all sure I did, something I'd never confessed to anyone, even Jen. The thought of spending my days doing housework and running after children, as Ma had done, had never been an enticing prospect to me, but I felt quite alone in considering an alternative destiny. I thought of the barely disguised pity and derision Sandra and some of the other girls had for unmarried, childless Madame Grisaille – a failure, a freak. Was there really nothing in between these two female fates – no third way? 'But there's so much I want to do first,' I told Fran, 'like travel the world and get a job and . . . well, I don't really know what else, but I'd like to find out, wouldn't you?'

'I suppose so,' Fran said. 'But I'm already engaged to a man from home. My mother is planning the wedding for when I return from France. We shall be married by the summer.'

Her tone was matter-of-fact, devoid of any excitement. I looked at her. 'And do you love him, this man?'

She seemed taken aback that I should have asked, so I sat down on the bed next to her and took her hand. 'Sorry, honey, but I do find small talk so terribly dull. You don't mind, do you?'

Fran hesitated, then smiled. 'I've known him since I was a small child,' she said. 'Our parents always envisioned us together.'

'Well, that's not what I asked.'

She sighed. 'He's quite nice.'

Something in that response seemed unfathomably sad to me and I didn't really know how to reply. I looked at myself in the mirror, decked out in Fran's pink chiffon scarf, felt hat and pearls, and suddenly all I saw reflected back was someone twice our age. *This is how Fran's mother dresses*, it came to me. *This isn't Fran, it's her mom.*

'Just because you're meant to do something, doesn't mean you have to,' I said. 'In fact, I think it's much more interesting to want to do what you're not meant to, wouldn't you say?'

Fran gave a small smile. 'I couldn't disappoint them, I just couldn't. They've been disappointed enough.'

'In *you*?' I was incredulous. I couldn't imagine Fran had ever broken a rule in her life. Never taken a nip of her pop's bourbon or snuck into the back of a movie theatre without paying or kissed a boy her parents wouldn't have approved of, in his car after school.

Fran shook her head. 'No, I mean . . .' she paused. 'Because of my brother. He died, you see. So now it's just me and . . .' She trailed off and looked down at her drawing.

'Goodness, that's terrible. How?'

Her face resembled a startled rabbit. Perhaps I wasn't meant to ask. 'Oh . . . of the flu,' she said. 'Back in fifty-one, during that awful epidemic in Liverpool. He was only twenty-one, just married with a baby on the way, but he was asthmatic, so . . .' She looked away. 'I was eleven at the time.'

'How awfully sad. You poor thing. My big brother is a total pain to live with but I'd be just beside myself if we lost him.' I threw my arms around her and squeezed. 'And now you've grown up with all your parents' hopes on your shoulders.' I released her from my hug. 'Whereas I don't think my parents hold out much hope for me at all. In fact, that's probably why I'm here. A last gasp attempt to make me into a *lady*.'

She smiled then but I saw her eyes were glistening. 'I've never met anyone like you, Lenny,' she said.

I laughed and stood up, did a little twirl in front of her. 'I hope you think that's a good thing, unlike Head Girl Sandra.'

She didn't answer right away; instead, she picked up her pencil and I watched as her eyes flicked between me and the sketchbook. Afterwards, I realized I'd been holding my breath in that moment, silently praying for a positive answer, for the same feeling of connection that I'd found with Jen when we'd first giggled together at the back of American history class in junior high.

'Yes,' she said finally, turning the sketchbook around so I could see. In just a few strokes she'd captured me so brilliantly – posing in hat, scarf and pearls, a wide smile on my face and a swagger in my stance. 'I rather think I do.'

3

A blackbird is pecking at a worm on the lawn, oblivious to Eric stalking silently towards it, ginger haunches low to the grass. Flo watches through the kitchen window but her mind is elsewhere, absorbing what she's just read in the book that sits in front of her on the table. She hardly recognizes herself in Lilli's words – in this *Frances*, this fictionalized version of her – because she is no longer that girl and hasn't been for such a long time. But she knows it is her, that she was once that poor little rich girl with her tailored dresses and meek acceptance of her impending marriage. If only she could leap back in time and scream at herself: *Get out now! Get away from there before you waste ten years of your life!* Instead she gets up from the chair, opens the door and startles the blackbird. It flies up into the sky as the cat slinks away.

He's quite nice. It makes her shudder.

Where would she be right now, if she *had* got out? *Who* would she be?

No. She shakes her head. She is old enough and wise enough to know that it gets you nowhere, wondering what might have been. Nowhere at all. Those years are part of her, as much as everything that came later, the good and the bad, the thrilling and the mundane, and she can't wish away one without the other. It has all shaped her indelibly, like gouge marks on linoleum.

But still. What might have happened if she hadn't let herself get trapped like that, when Lilli was offering an alternative, a way out? What kind of life might they have had together if she'd turned up that night?

Memories flit across her brain and a wave of nausea hits her. She sits down again, waiting for it to pass. She doesn't want to think about that, about what she did the very night the two of them parted.

It wasn't your fault.

She shakes her head.

You had no choice.

No, no, no. She screws her eyes up tight to shut out the memory. She can't think about it. Not after all these years. She packed it away a long time ago and that's where it needs to stay. She's put it behind her.

But Lilli, dearest Lilli, she does want to think about her. Lilli, with her wide smile and her laughter and her infectious confidence. A breath of fresh air.

She gets up from the armchair and walks up the stairs. She stands on the landing, hands on hips, and looks up at the square hatch in the ceiling. She hasn't been up there in years. The last time she needed something from the attic she waited until her niece, Ronnie, came to visit and sent her up. But right now she can't wait. She suddenly, urgently, needs to go up there.

She pokes the long stick into the ring pull on the hatch and it opens, releasing the folded ladder. She pulls it into place and tests a rung with one foot. Her knees may not be up to the climb, but it feels worth the risk. She takes it slowly, resting a little after each step, until she reaches the top. As she manoeuvres herself through the opening and into the attic, it occurs to her she may never get down again.

But she is here. One problem at a time.

The attic is full but fairly orderly, everything packed into labelled boxes that have hardly been disturbed since she moved in here fifteen years ago. The longer it's gone on, the more daunting a task it has seemed to clear it out. And now she may as well not bother; when she's dead, someone else will have to do it. She feels a twinge of guilt that this will likely fall to Ronnie – perhaps with her daughter Emily's help – but not enough to do anything about it beforehand. She doesn't want her death to be ordered, to cause so little dis-ruption that it's hardly noticed. She deserves to cause a little chaos, to make an impact in death as she's tried hard to in life.

There's a large trunk in the corner. That's probably where it will be – the trunk she's had since the fifties, when it went to boarding school with her. Over the years it's gradually become a depository for the detritus of her life, accumulating photo albums, folders of sketches and paintings, travel jour-nals, old greetings cards.

She sits on a wooden packing crate next to the trunk and starts to lift out its contents, piling things up on other boxes nearby. She takes out some photo albums from the nineties but resists opening them; if she starts looking at photos of her and James she'll be here forever, lost in reminiscence. Among them is Ronnie's wedding album from the latter part of the decade. *Here*, her niece had said, *a copy just for you, Flo, it'll be almost like you were there.* She remembers sitting with James on their bed, turning the pages, smiling at how beautiful Ronnie looked, how joyful teenage Emily was to see her mother happily remarried to someone decent this time; thinking how proud her late brother would have been to witness his daughter and granddaughter like this. James had covered her hand with his, squeezing it with what little strength the stroke hadn't taken from him. *I'm sorry you couldn't go.* But she'd shaken her head. *No, never be sorry.* She would have looked after him for ever if it meant he'd never leave her.

Next out of the trunk is a folder of nudes in oil paint – the fruits of an evening class sometime in the early seventies – then a box of slides going back even further. She takes one out of the box and holds it up to the naked bulb hanging from the ceiling. It is her and Alexander in Stow sometime in the mid-forties; she a beaming little girl with blonde curls and fat cheeks, her brother already a strapping teenager. His arm is around her and there's affection in his face. A sob escapes her throat. Alexander. How can it be possible that she is still here so long after time stopped for him in fifty-one? Such lonely, empty years they were, growing up without him in her life, an invisible shroud of unacknowledged grief hanging over the family home every time she was back from boarding school, always present but never spoken of. No wonder Lilli's direct questions were such a shock. Flo didn't know she was allowed to talk about it, until meeting her.

She puts the slide back in the case and the case on the floor and picks up the next item in the trunk, another album, a rectangular black book with a single photo on the front: her and Peter, on their wedding day in fifty-eight. She certainly doesn't want to look at that.

And then, underneath, there it is: the sketchbook she took to France with her in fifty-seven. She opens the cover, carefully turns the yellowed pages, and her mind skitters right back to those days. There's a pencil sketch of the chateau, with its ornate façade and kitsch turrets, and another of the big oak tree outside their window, the tree she'd gazed at so often, watching the seasons change and feeling a creeping sense of dread at what awaited her at the end of the year, a dread that only increased the more time she spent with the person who was awakening her to the impossible alternative. There are quick line drawings of shopfronts and bridges in Lyon — oh, how vivid everything seemed! — and a few caricatures of teachers at the school. Gosh, she was good, even then.

On a loose page tucked into the sketchbook is the drawing. A girl, wearing a scarf, hat and pearls, a smile on her face and self-confidence in her pose. Flo stares at the sketch for a long time. She takes in the girl's joyful expression, her exaggerated posing in Flo's accessories, and she wonders if this person still exists inside the woman she has become, the author in the South of France, the retired actress, teacher and small-business owner with a grown child and possibly grandchildren. Surely she must do, because however much Flo herself has changed, however much she matured and grew during the years that came afterwards, the cautious, reserved young woman who drew this sketch is still somewhere inside her.

A feeling pulses in her head. Panic and desperation, set against the sour tang of rubbish rotting in metal dustbins.

She drops the sketch in her lap. She is too hot. The attic is stuffy and airless and her eyes are swimming and there's a prickling sensation in her head.

And then . . .

Alice hears Ernie barking before she's even opened the door. He greets her with an urgency that's beyond his usual friendly enthusiasm and immediately bounds up the stairs, commanding her to follow. She takes them two at a time. When she reaches the landing, Ernie is sitting underneath an open hatch leading into the attic.

'Okay, boy, it's okay.' Alice strokes his head. She pictures a burglar rooting around for heirlooms; he's locked Flo in her workshop, or worse, bashed her over the head and she's lying somewhere, bleeding and in pain. *Oh God*. She rubs her scar, the flesh tender under her fingers.

'Who's there? Flo?'

No response. She doesn't want to go up there, but she has to; she wouldn't forgive herself if she did nothing. Her chest hammers as she looks around the landing for something she can use as a weapon. She takes some dried flowers out of a long-necked vase on the windowsill and brandishes the receptacle in one hand as she climbs the ladder, flinching at every creak of the metal. She peeks over the top, half bracing herself for a potential violent reaction from the intruder, but instead sees Flo at the far end of the attic, slumped on the floor.

'Flo!' She clambers off the ladder and ducks under the eaves to reach Flo's side. *She's dead.* Horror invades her head as she pictures Ella's pale, still face. But then Flo stirs, her eyes flicker open and relief washes away the images.

'Flo, are you all right? What happened?' She puts her hand on Flo's forehead; it is hot, clammy.

'Gosh.' Flo struggles to sit up. 'I think I must have fainted. Haven't done that in years.'

In her lap is a drawing. A girl in a scarf and hat, mischievous eyes and a wide smile. Alice puts it on a nearby packing crate and helps Flo sit up against an open trunk. Photo albums and sketchbooks are piled up around it.

'What were you doing? And how did you get up here?'

Flo snorts. 'I'm not completely useless just yet, dear. I can still get around my own house.'

'Sorry, sorry. But are you well enough to get down again? I'll call Mum, get her to come round and drive you to the hospital.' Alice doesn't drive. Doesn't trust herself to sit behind a wheel, to be in charge of something that could cause death and destruction – that *has* caused death and destruction, in front of her own eyes. She tried it, once, in a single lesson that terrified the life out of her, so she never booked a second, and her mum didn't push it, as she knew she wouldn't.

'Don't be ridiculous, I don't need to go to hospital. It's just hot up here, that's all it was. And your mum will be at work – don't bother her with this.'

They sit for a few minutes, colour seeping back into Flo's

face, and then Alice helps her down the ladder, worrying she will slip and fall, or faint again, and she won't be able to hold her. At the bottom, Ernie greets them with a whine – he looks as anxious as Alice feels – and follows them as Alice shepherds Flo into the nearest room, a guest bedroom with a large quilt covering the double bed.

'Here, sit down for a minute. I'll get you some water.' She opens the sash window before running down the stairs to fill a glass from the kitchen tap.

'It was a minor blip, nothing wrong with me,' Flo says when Alice returns with the water.

'But still, there's no harm in getting checked out. You never know.' Alice unlocks her phone to look up the number of the doctor's surgery in town. Why might someone faint? An undiagnosed disease, perhaps, the lead-up to a stroke or an aneurysm, or something else she can't even imagine.

'Alice, you're eighteen, not eighty, you're not supposed to be the hypochondriac in this situation,' Flo says, as though she's read her mind. 'Sit here.' Flo pats the bed, and Alice does as she's told. 'You worry a lot, don't you?'

Alice shrugs. *Maybe Flo doesn't have long left, maybe I'm going to come here one day and she really will be dead.* 'A bit.'

'A lot, is what I think.' Flo smiles. 'You know, things are hardly ever as bad as you fear.'

Alice looks down at the quilt. She would like to believe that. But the problem is it's not true. The problem is that the day Ella died, she realized all the bad things in her head could actually come true, because the worst thing she could have imagined up to that point was that someone she loved would cease to exist, and then it happened. So she can't believe Flo, she can't accept that things are never as bad as you fear, because she knows, with absolute certainty, that sometimes they are.

She manages, at least, to get Flo to take a nap. As she sleeps, Alice climbs back into the loft to clear up Flo's things and repack the trunk she'd clearly been looking through. She picks up the albums and sketchbooks from their various stacks on top of boxes around the attic and flicks through some of them. In doing so, she learns that Flo is a very good sketcher and painter (unsurprising, she supposes, given her talent for printmaking), and that she is widely travelled (journals and photo albums are labelled Egypt and Persia and Brazil and Greece). She picks up a wedding album and sees a black and white photo of a very young-looking Flo in a long white dress standing next to a tall, serious man in a suit, and she can hardly fathom it's the same woman in this house right now. The photo looks like something from a history lesson, a period drama. How did this young woman become the old one living here, now? How did she get from there to here? Alice suddenly wants to know everything about Flo, she wants to know the secret to living a life like hers, because right now she feels she's doing it all wrong and she worries – of course she does – that she'll never know how to do it right.

The loft sorted, she descends the ladder and folds it up into the hatch in the ceiling. The guest bedroom where she left Flo is empty; she finds her downstairs in the living room holding a cup of tea, Eric kneading her lap and Ernie curled at her feet.

'I brought you this.' Alice proffers the sketch of the

girl. 'It was in your lap when you fainted. I thought you might want it.'

Flo takes it. 'Thank you, Alice.' She looks down at the picture, and then up at her, and there's an odd expression on her face that Alice can't read, as though her thoughts have slid off into a different time and place, and a different person is standing in front of her.

Carla is trying to write a press release about the new edition of *Beach Walks Around Britain – A Colour Companion* when her phone vibrates on her desk.

Alice.

She immediately taps in her pin and opens it. Her daughter doesn't message her very often. Usually it's just a brief reply to something Carla has asked her. *Okay* (if Carla makes a suggestion for dinner) or *Probably* (if she asks if she'll be home straight after her shift at the café) or sometimes *Will sort myself out* (on the rare occasions Carla is out or has to work late and hasn't got any food in for dinner). But she hasn't messaged Alice today – something must be wrong. She holds her breath as she opens it.

> Flo fainted, do you think she should go
> to hospital?

Carla breathes out, a little guiltily. Alice is okay.

> It might be a good idea, she replies. What
> does Flo say? xx

The reply comes instantly.

> Don't be ridiculous

Carla smiles. She can just hear Flo saying that. She hasn't known her very long, nor does she know her well, but there's something about her – a certain self-confidence, a no-nonsense resilience – that Carla has admired ever since she met her in Harriet's shop last year. (*What a beautiful print, Harriet. Is the artist local?* she'd asked. *Speak of the devil,* Harriet replied, as the door tinkled and Flo stepped through it carrying a box of mounted prints, a black Labrador at her side.) Admired, yes – and felt a little intimidated by, if she's honest.

> Not sure you'll get Flo to do anything she
> doesn't want to xx, she messages back.

'Can I get you a cuppa, Carla?'

She looks up from her phone to find Andy smiling at her over the partition.

'Oh, yes please, that would be great.' She hands him her mug to add to the three already in his hands. Andy is one of the more frequent tea makers among the small team at Pulham Press and she likes that about him. It's usually the small things that say the most about a person. Alice is a good tea maker, too.

'That's nice.' He nods to her desk, where a mounted but unframed print depicting sunset over the local reservoir is propped up against the stem of her Anglepoise. She bought the picture just last week as a sort of thank you to Flo for employing Alice as a dog walker (*No need*, Flo had said, *I should be thanking you*), another beautiful piece to add to the modest collection of Flo's work she has now accumulated. It induces a sort of wistful envy in her every time she looks at it. To have the talent, time and means to be able to spend your days doing something so creative and fulfilling and . . . *independent* must be so satisfying.

'Yeah, it is,' she says to Andy. 'It's one of Flo's. Do you know Flo? Florence Carter?'

'The old woman with the dog? Yeah, I've seen her around. *She* did that?'

Carla bristles. 'Flo's a marvellous artist. Her stuff sells in Harriet's shop – the prints in the window are hers.'

'Huh,' Andy says. 'I had no idea. I thought she was just . . .'

An old woman with a dog? Indignation blooms in her chest. Flo doesn't *give a fig* what other people think of her (another thing Carla admires her for), but she is incensed on her behalf. Flo's not *just* anything. Older women aren't *just* old. Carla isn't *just* middle-aged, isn't *just* a mother – is she? *Are you* just *a receding, divorced, middle-aged father?* she wants to say, but she doesn't. Andy doesn't mean anything by it. He's a nice person, a good tea maker.

'Well,' Andy says. 'I'll have to take a closer look next time I pass the shop.' He nods to her mug. 'Yorkshire?'

Carla watches him walk away in the direction of the small kitchen, thinking back to that evening in the pub after work last year when the two of them spent the whole time together, sitting slightly away from their colleagues, dissecting their lives. It was refreshing, after so many years single, to have a man to talk to again, to feel that frisson of desire, of being desired. Carla was curious to hear his side of divorce: the agony of only seeing his boy every other weekend after his ex-wife moved away and they decided for their son's stability that he should stay with her. *I miss him like a physical pain,* he'd said, an emotional confession brought on by four pints and quickly modulated by: *he always was a pain in the butt.* She wondered, then, if Rich misses Alice. He tells her he does, but she's seen little evidence of it. The odd Facetime and the occasional WhatsApp message is all the relationship Alice now has with her father. He hasn't been here for her since the accident, leaving Carla to be both mum and dad, a double-strength parent in the absence of one.

Perhaps that's partly why she avoided Andy after that night in the pub, why she gave him the cold shoulder, stopped the invitation she saw forming on his lips. She shouldn't be doing something as self-centred as dating, not while Alice is as she is; she should be focusing all her time and attention on her daughter, on trying to figure out why she isn't healing, why her understandable grief has made her withdraw into herself and away from her mother.

She just wishes she knew *how* to figure that out, given asking Alice outright would likely only make things worse. Talk to one of her teachers, perhaps? But now she's left school, that doesn't seem right. One of her friends? She would . . . but the truth is she doesn't know who Alice's other friends are. It was always Ella – no one else ever came close. Wasn't there a Vicky, at one point? But Alice hasn't talked about her lately, hasn't socialized at all in the two years since Ella's death, come to think of it.

It is Lisa, not Andy, who brings her tea over to her. 'Here you go. Is now a good time, Carla?' she says, a bright smile on her face, the smile of a newcomer out to make a good impression.

'Oh, yes, now's fine,' Carla says, faintly irritated to have her thoughts of Alice interrupted. She'd forgotten all about Susan's request to show Lisa the release schedule. Doesn't even know why she has to, given Lisa has been employed as PA to Derek, Susan's husband and the CEO of Pulham Press, and not as part of the marketing and publicity team. 'How are you getting on so far?'

Lisa pulls up a vacant swivel chair and pushes one side of her long blonde hair behind her ear, the other falling thick and wavy down the right side of her face, partly covering one lens of her stylish black-rimmed glasses. 'Good, I think. I mean, first day and all. I just hate it when you're so new you don't even know where the toilets are, don't you?' Lisa laughs. Her skin is beautiful, Carla sees. The unlined, unblemished skin of a 26-year-old.

'I can barely remember,' Carla says. 'I haven't been the new girl for a while.'

'How long have you worked here?'

Carla hesitates. For some reason she doesn't want to say it. 'Fourteen years.'

'Wow, I can't imagine!'

Carla looks down, gives a half-laugh. 'No, well, neither could I.' She turns to her computer, puts her hand on the mouse to wake the screen. 'Shall I take you through our publicity priorities for the next few months then?'

For the next half an hour, Carla tells Lisa about the company's upcoming publications, the glossy coffee-table books, illustrated collections of *best bakes* and *beach walks,* and the occasional 'funny' (they all air-quote when they say the word, as if *humorous* is a generous description) that Carla does her best to publicize. It isn't her dream job, this. It isn't the sort of thing she thought she'd end up doing when, at more or less the same age as Lisa, she got her first job at a big fiction publisher in London, enthusiastic and excited about the career she envisioned for herself. But she remains grateful to have found this role at all. When she and Rich first moved to the town all those years ago – she, unexpectedly pregnant with Alice; he, headhunted by a big firm offering a juicy promotion and a fat salary – Carla thought she'd never get to work in publishing again. And though a town of 30,000 people didn't exactly offer an abundance of choice, and though it took four years before this position came up, at least it did, at least the town *had* a publishing company. And it has served her well over the years. Particularly recently, through the divorce and the accident. It's been reliable, certain, while everything around her has been so tumultuous; one less thing to worry about as she focuses all her attention on Alice, on keeping her safe, on making sure she's okay.

'And who else is in the publicity team?' Lisa asks.

'It's just me, reporting to Susan, Head of Marketing & Publicity.' The reason she hasn't progressed within this small company for fourteen years – there's nowhere to go.

'Oh, right. So I guess Susan thinks I could help you out a bit, if you need it?'

'Perhaps,' she says. 'I'll let you know.' She doesn't need help. She's good at her job. Not sensational, perhaps. Not emailing-on-Sunday, my-job-is-my-life brilliant, but reliable, competent, good enough, she thinks.

Lisa won't stay long anyway. In the time Carla has worked here she's seen young graduates come and go, spending a year or less as a PA or editorial assistant before moving on and up, heading to London or elsewhere, continuing on their intended trajectory, the trajectory you aim for – *expect*, even – when you're young and full of hope for the future ahead of you.

Careful, Lisa, the thought pops into her head unbidden, *you might end up having to quit a job you love and move away because your partner just can't turn down an incredibly well-paid opportunity. You might struggle to resurrect your career in a small town with a young child to look after. You and your husband might drift apart and end up resenting each other. You might get divorced after he's offered a new job abroad and doesn't bloody well want you to go with him.*

Lisa is saying something.

'Sorry, what was that?' Carla shakes her head to bring herself back to the conversation.

'I just said thank you, for showing me everything. I'm really looking forward to working with you.'

Carla smiles. 'You're welcome. It's great to have you here.'

As she watches Lisa return to her desk, long hair swinging, a bounce in her step, she is taken right back there: to being twenty-six, unsure what the future will hold but sure of what she wanted it to be. And it strikes her as vast, the gap between herself then and herself now, at forty-six, still unsure of the future but knowing it's futile to make a plan, because it never works out as you think it will.

She's all out of ideas anyway. No one tells you what comes next, after you've worked your way through the obligatory milestones of young adulthood and they haven't quite turned out as you hoped. Her daughter is her only real achievement of the last twenty years. Her marriage failed, her career isn't exactly the roaring success she'd hoped for, and now her wonderful daughter is mentally and physically damaged by an event Carla couldn't protect her from, and so she's failing at motherhood, too. And that's the worst failure of all, the one she simply has to overcome. All she wants is to figure out how to help Alice. It doesn't matter about herself, about her own missed opportunities and disappointments and sorrows. None of that matters at all, as long as she can make Alice happy again.

The Way We Were

LYON, FRANCE, OCTOBER 1957

The school was much more tolerable once Fran and I became firm friends. I could put up with sewing classes and pueri-culture lessons if I could laugh about it with her afterwards. I even started to enjoy flower arranging and cooking when I was paired up with Fran, though Madame Bouchard clearly considered me a bad influence on my new friend. *Please concentrate on the task in hand, Eleanor,* she'd chastise me when I'd make Fran laugh by, say, pinning a cloth diaper on a doll the wrong way, or doodling silly pictures in my notebook instead of writing down the correct way to manage household staff. *Please quieten your voice, Eleanor. Please sit up straighter, Eleanor.* But the more the headmistress reprimanded me, the more I wanted to disobey. I recalled what Ma had once said to me when I'd gaily related some fascinating titbit I'd learned in my high school science class. *Don't be too interested in things like that, Lenny, you'll only be disappointed later.* And yet I was meant to be interested in *this* instead?

Still, Fran's presence next to me always calmed my inner fire a little. I got the impression no one quite understood why we were now such firm friends, but somehow we complemented each other. Her gentle manner softened my brash ways just enough to bring me begrudging respect in the eyes of the other girls (even Sandra didn't dare look down her nose at me when Fran was around), and my already fulsome ego was indulged further when she laughed at my jokes, her face softening and brightening as she did. *I don't think she's had much to laugh about lately*, I wrote to Jen back home, *she's been too busy doing what she's told.* As for what Fran got from me, well, you'd have to ask her, but I like to think I encouraged her to be herself in a way she hadn't previously been allowed, to stick her head outside the pretty shell her family had put her in. Coaxed by me, she talked more about her brother, about the pain of being sent off to boarding school just months after he died, and the way her parents never asked her how she felt about his death. She told me how much she'd adored him, how he'd read her bedtime stories to help her settle when they moved in with her mother's cousin during the war, their own home having been requisitioned as a rehabilitation centre by the government. And how everything seemed just that little bit duller when he was away at university, as though he'd skimmed the cream off her life and taken it with him.

In turn I made her laugh with stories of growing up in Brooklyn, my mother's shopping obsession after years of having no money, and Pop's clumsy attempts to make our family something we would probably never truly be. 'I swear he'd try to marry me off to someone's son in exchange for membership of the country club,' I railed. I was joking (mostly). 'My engagement isn't exactly detrimental to my father's business interests,' Fran replied, and I knew she definitely wasn't.

In the evenings, tucked away in our attic bedroom, I'd encourage Fran to sketch as I posed in her tailored dresses and silk scarves, enjoying the attention as much as the dressing up. Sometimes I'd lie on my bed reading a novel as she drew me, or sit by the open window gazing out, a veritable Rapunzel in a tower.

Nevertheless, despite our friendship, I was restless. The view of the city from our bedroom became a siren call during those first few weeks at the school. We were technically allowed to venture out in the company of family members or friends on a list provided by parents to the school in advance, but since I didn't know anyone in Lyon, my list was blank and I, like most of the others. was held captive. Only Aurélia, whose brother lived in Lyon, was allowed to escape once a week. At least she brought back pralines and truffles from a chocolatier in the city, a sensible bribe to ease our envy.

In any case, what with lessons six days a week, followed by dinner and activities extending until 9.30pm, and curfew at 11pm, there wasn't time to go anywhere anyway. The most I could do was prowl around the grounds, light one of my precious few remaining Lucky Strikes and hang my hand out between the bars of the chateau's ornate wrought-iron gates (thus evading the ban on smoking on school grounds) as I imagined what might lie beyond them.

Relief arrived three weeks in, when that rumoured trip to

the opera came to fruition. I could hardly contain my excitement as Fran and I dressed for the evening in our room. I chose one of the gowns Ma and I had picked out on our trip to Saks a few weeks before Pop pressed that golden airplane ticket into my hands: a blue wild silk dress with a calf-length circle skirt, a structured bodice and a large bow around the waist. Ma had insisted this was what all the society girls wore, and though I'd rather have picked an outfit that *wasn't* exactly what everyone else wore, there was something about the rich colour and the feel of the silk on my skin that crumbled my resistance. That and the tears in Ma's eyes as I emerged from the fitting room. I couldn't bear to completely dash her hopes that her wayward daughter might finally see her way to fitting in with the society she and Pop so desperately wanted to feel at home in. So we bought it, along with long white cotton gloves, nylons, suspenders, brassieres and a girdle, and when I walked out of the store I felt like goddamn Grace Kelly.

When Fran – looking spectacular in a pink chiffon dress bought, she told me as though it was a dirty secret, *off the peg* in Marks & Spencer – and I joined the other girls in the chateau's reception room at 7pm on the dot, there was a frisson of excitement in the air. For all their obedience and politesse, it seemed the other girls were looking forward to getting out of there every bit as much as I was. Even Sandra grated on my nerves a little less than usual.

As we were transported into town in a private coach, my eyes followed the apartment blocks and boutiques and tree-lined boulevards I saw through the window. I only half listened as Monsieur Joussot lectured us about the opera house, the performance we would see – Puccini's *La bohème* – and the etiquette we were expected to follow as representatives of Château Mont d'Or. We were to stick together during the interval, go to the ladies' room in pairs, and under no circumstances were we to venture outside the opera house.

A group of sixteen pretty young women dressed to the nines was quite the sight, I quickly realized as we stepped off the coach and filed into the opera house, turning multiple heads as we went. I wanted to linger outside, take in the lights of the city, nip down the street to see the bridges over the Rhône, but instead I was ushered inside by Madame Bouchard and Monsieur Joussot like a heifer herded by over-enthusiastic Border Collies.

But my eagerness to see the city was partially mitigated by the glory of the opera house. It surely wasn't (as Sandra had once again reminded us) as grand as Paris, but that didn't matter to me. I gawped at the columned façade, which seemed like something out of ancient Rome (at least, the idea of ancient Rome I had in my head, which was probably quite far off the mark), while in the foyer I marvelled at the chandeliers and ceiling frescos reflected in the polished black stone floor. *Please close your mouth, Eleanor.* Further inside, framed photographs on the walls depicted the faces of singers who had previously performed there, and I was entranced by every single one, especially the women, each as impossibly glamorous as the next. It filled me with a rush of passion for the pursuit of my own desires – even if I was yet to discover exactly what they were. Shame I had no discernible singing talent whatsoever.

I was captivated, too, by the heavy red curtain, the low-lit auditorium and the hum of anticipation from the crowd as we all took our seats, the Château Mont d'Or girls and our teachers spread among two boxes at stage right. Having never been to the opera before (I think Pop was scared of that, too – *funny foreign singing*), I hadn't experienced anything like it.

Perhaps that's why I was so susceptible to *his* charms, too. Later on, after everything that happened as a result, I wondered if it was the opera house that had bewitched me, not him; if he was simply in the right place at the right time to slot into the picture forming in my head. I was seeking desires, passions, freedom – and there he was.

He was English, that's what first caught my attention. I was on my way to the ladies' room with Fran when I heard his voice cut through the general aural fog of French, a few words of clarity in an otherwise near-incomprehensible burr.

'Now they've lost Morocco and Tunisia, it won't be long until Algeria follows suit, no matter what the politicians say.'

His voice was rich and confident, and though I had no idea what he was talking about (my knowledge of current affairs and politics outside of North America was practically non-existent), it sounded fabulously grown up and exciting. I looked up to see who was speaking and to whom, just as someone in the crowd pushed past me, knocking me into the man's arm. 'Blast,' I heard him say, as liquid from the tumbler he was holding sloshed over its rim onto his hand and the cuff of his jacket sleeve.

'I sure am sorry,' I said. 'Someone knocked me into you.'

The man turned to see who had spoken and it was then, the very moment we clapped eyes on each other, that I was done for. He didn't respond straight away, and for what felt like minutes but was probably only a second or two, he only looked at me, an expression of surprise on his face – at my English words, my New York accent or something else, I didn't know. And for however long it lasted, I looked back, my eyes on his, as surprised by him as he was by me.

'Let the lady off the hook won't you, Hugo?'

The words of the man's companion broke whatever was floating between us, and he – Hugo – smiled broadly and shook his head.

'Forgive me,' he said. 'Where are my manners? Don't give this a second thought, it was clearly an accident and no harm's done.'

I looked between the two of them. 'I heard the English like to apologize, but I see no reason to do so when you're the wronged party. I'm the one who should say sorry. I hope it didn't mark your suit?'

'Not at all.' He smiled. 'You're American?'

'New York born and bred.' I smiled back, basking in his gaze. My feet felt fixed to the floor, as though I couldn't possibly move myself away from him, even if I wanted to. 'I'm at school over here for this academic year. Lenny Cranshaw.' I put my hand out and he shook it, never taking his eyes off my face.

'Hugo Bennett,' he said. 'And this here is my friend Fred du Toit.'

I transferred my hand, reluctantly, to Fred's, but my

eyes flitted only briefly away from Hugo's face. 'You're both English?'

'Indeed,' Hugo replied. 'We work in exports for Citroën. The French car company,' he added with a flutter of a smile, clearly assuming I'd never heard of it, which I hadn't.

'Of course.' My pulse was racing so hard I felt sure he could see it. 'How wonderful.'

'How do you like the city so far?'

'Oh, it's just swell. At least, what I've seen of it so far, which isn't a great deal, since the school likes to keep its students on a short leash, I'm sorry to say.'

Hugo laughed. 'I suppose that's quite correct. They wouldn't want you to come to any harm, after all.'

'Or have any fun, I shouldn't think.'

He leaned forward slightly and when he spoke his voice was low, conspiratorial, with something in his tone that sent a frisson through me. 'Well,' he said. 'That just won't do.'

I was about to reply *I know*, when Fran grabbed my arm. 'So sorry to interrupt,' she said, flashing a polite smile at the two men, and then, to me, quietly, 'Where have you been? You didn't come with me. You know we're not meant to wander off alone in the interval.'

'I met some nice people,' I said to her. 'Hugo Bennett, Fred du Toit, this is my good friend Frances Morrow.'

They shook hands and I watched Fran's reaction as she looked at the men, trying to see if Hugo had the same effect on her as he did on me, but she seemed more anxious about who else might be watching us to be in any way enveloped into our circle of four. Fran was often anxious about things,

I'd noticed, most unnecessarily in my view, and I wondered briefly if there was anything I might be able to do about that.

'How'd you do?' she said to the men, before adding to me: 'Have you seen the other girls? We should go and find them. It's nearly the end of the interval. Madame Bouchard will be looking for us.'

I smiled, faintly embarrassed to be reminded of my school-girl status in front of these grown men. 'I'm sure it's fine,' I trilled, and my cheeks flushed to see amusement on Hugo's face. For a brief, surprising moment, I wished Fran would go away again and take Fred with her, leaving me here with Hugo, because I had an overwhelming urge to find out what would happen if she did. But instead I caught the unwelcome sight of Sandra filtering her way through the crowd and suddenly I was being ushered off, shepherded back into the larger fold of my school friends.

'Which school do you attend?' Hugo called after me.

'Château Mont d'Or,' I mouthed back.

To this day I couldn't say what happens in the last two acts of *La bohème*.

4

Hugo. The name is not familiar. Flo doesn't remember a Hugo. It is a work of fiction, after all – only *semi*-autobiographical. The thought is something of a relief, but nevertheless her own recollections of that time float around the story, needling her. They *did* go to the opera. Lilli *did* meet someone there.

No. She shakes her head. *Shut it away, put it back in the box.*

She puts the book down and turns to the piece of lino on her workbench, the design she drew yesterday, ready to be carved. She picks up her favourite tool – a medium U-shaped Japanese gouge with a wooden handle. She bought it on holiday in Japan ten years ago, just after she'd started the craft, and it's turned out to be the best tool she's ever had. She sharpens it religiously and keeps it in an old jewellery box that James once gave her, many years ago. A special box for a special object.

As she carves, she thinks about what she said to Alice the other day, when the girl was worrying over her fainting episode. *Things are hardly ever as bad as you fear.* She meant it at the time, and it is true, actually, that over a whole lifespan, most things don't turn out as badly as you fear.

Mostly, the things she worried about when she arrived at the school in fifty-seven were laughably inconsequential. She worried about doing and saying the wrong thing, about offending someone, about using the wrong knife and fork at dinner, or forgetting to send a thank you note for a gift. She had larger worries, too, about not being a good wife to her future husband, about failing to effectively look after her future children, about whether she would enjoy the life set out for her and – with her brother's death in her head – how long she would survive it. But usually she suppressed those worries in favour of smaller ones, as though by fretting about her cutlery etiquette she would somehow forget about the more important concerns she had no way of addressing.

But what she knows now, what the long life she has led has taught her, is that worry is useless because the worst things are unforeseeable, they arrive by stealth, unexpectedly, when it is too late to worry because it is already done. She couldn't have foreseen the flu epidemic that took her asthmatic brother's life in fifty-one. Nor could she have anticipated the stroke that ruptured the idyllic life she had with James in the nineties. And never, in her most vivid imagination, could she have foreseen what happened as a result of Harry coming into her life in fifty-seven.

Harry. Hugo is *Harry*.

Her hand is shaking. She puts down the gouge and sits, waiting for the tremors to subside. She remembers his face, so handsome. She remembers his voice, rich and deep and well tended by an English private school education.

And the fear. She remembers the fear.

⌑

'Ease off on the cream, Alice, we're not the bloody Ritz.'

Alice looks up, the squirty cream can in her hand, as Merryn speaks over her shoulder. A rogue blob drops from the end of the nozzle onto the hot chocolate, which Alice is preparing for Harriet, one of their regulars, and she flinches at being caught red-handed.

Alice doesn't mind Merryn's bad moods (or not actually moods, but her usual demeanour, her personality, as Ella often said with a roll of her eyes). In fact, sometimes she feels grateful for them. The café is the one place in this town where she doesn't have to pretend to be cheery or be questioned as to why she isn't, since Merryn has already set the bar on that score. Happiness isn't part of the job description here. That may be why Alice has lasted longer than any other staff member. In the time she's had this Saturday job, she's seen staff arrive in a swell of anticipation and retreat in a riptide of animosity not long afterwards. But all the while Alice has stuck it out and felt grateful for it. Merryn has never told her to cheer up. She has never forced her to talk about things she doesn't want to talk about, has barely even shown interest in her life outside the café. And that's how Alice likes it.

Still, Merryn does seem to be in a worse mood than usual today. When she turns her back, Alice squirts a final flourish of cream on the hot chocolate, shakes over some cinnamon and takes the mug over to Harriet's table. It's late June, not really the season for hot chocolate, but Harriet comes here most Saturdays and always orders the same thing, without fail. People are creatures of habit, Alice has come to know. There are the two young mothers who always arrive for latte macchiatos around four, taking up half the café with their pushchairs. There's Mike, who turns up for a sandwich at one after his swim at the local pool, his little dachshund at his feet; and Carol, who always stops by for a takeaway cappuccino at eight-thirty before heading to her own job at the jeweller's where Ella used to work. This town is small enough that they all know what happened to Ella. At first, when Alice returned to the café just a few weeks afterwards, she could hardly bear to see the sympathy on their faces and batted away the condolences they offered; now, two years on, she struggles with the fact no one says or seems to feel anything at all. Gaps grow over quickly in a town like this.

'Thanks, Alice,' Harriet says. 'Though I really shouldn't.' She smiles and pats her stomach, another long-established routine. 'Flo tells me you're working for her now, too. Walking her dog?'

'Yes – Ernie.' Alice nods.

'So I bet you're getting a first look at all her beautiful prints! How's she getting on at the moment? I'm due some more in the shop – they're so popular, particularly with tourists. She could make a killing if she cared at all about money.'

'They're amazing,' Alice says, and she means it. Though she hasn't dared have another go herself, there's something about Flo's studio that leaves her in awe, and it has become a habit, now, staying for an hour or so after she's walked Ernie so she can watch Flo at work. The little shed looks so humble on the outside, yet inside it's a place of magic, where beauty is conjured from nothing but hands and imagination. It's like a secret world in there, with its smell of ink, its workbench strewn with the unfamiliar implements of a craft she doesn't yet know that much about, and the prints pegged across washing lines, a little more of the design emerging each time she visits. In there, away from everything, the constant worries in her head seem to ease a little, reducing to a faint hum instead of an invasive burr, and she is calm as she watches Flo choose a gouge, carve a piece of lino or − the magical bit, the bit she likes the most − bring the design to life on paper. She has never seen anything so wonderful.

Each day Flo asks if Alice wants to try it again. And each day Alice shakes her head. Sometimes she can picture herself saying yes, sometimes she yearns to say yes, but she knows it would only go wrong. So she sits and watches, much in the same way as she scrolls through Instagram and TikTok. She is good at watching other people's joys and triumphs.

'Well, tell her I said hello, and whenever she wants to bring some more prints over, I'll happily take them,' Harriet says.

'I will.'

Alice is weaving her way through the tables back to the counter when the door opens, and immediately that familiar twisted knot of emotions blooms inside her.

Her mother doesn't need to come into the café. She has perfectly good coffee at home. But she always comes in, without fail, every time Alice is working. And the café is usually so quiet that she can't even pretend she's too busy to chat.

I was just passing and wondered what you wanted for dinner?

*Just wanted to remind you it's your gran's birthday next week –
are you going to get a card?*

I just missed your lovely face.

Just, just . . .

'Hi Mum,' Alice says.

'Hi sweetie, how are you getting on?'

Her mum always looks so delighted to see her, as though
they haven't seen each other for weeks; her cheeks are flushed
and there's an actual sparkle in her eyes. For some reason this
only makes Alice act even more sullen than she feels, and then
guilt rises up in her, followed swiftly by anger and frustration.

'Fine,' she says. 'D'you want a coffee?'

'No thanks. Just popped into town to get something for
dinner so I thought I'd stop by. It's so hot, maybe we could
do a barbecue? What do you fancy, chicken drumsticks
or burgers?'

'Sausages.' Sometimes she thinks she says things just to see
if she can push that smile right off her mother's face, but it
never works.

'Okay, sausages it is!' She beams. 'See you at home after
your shift?'

Alice looks away and fiddles with the stack of takeaway
coffee lids. She has asked Merryn to find another solution,
told her she's killing the planet, helping to saturate the oceans
with tiny particles of plastic that get eaten by seals and birds
and whales, probably contributing to the extinction of multiple species in her lifetime. But Merryn only shrugs. *They're
cheap and I'm broke, so you'll just have to put up with them.*

'I'm going to Flo's first, to walk Ernie, then I might stay a while.'

'Oh, right,' her mother says, her smile flickering like a lightbulb on its last legs. 'Well, it's so hot today that it's bound to stay warm late into the evening, so how about I do the barbecue for around nine – that okay?'

Alice nods.

'Perfect.' Her mum's smile is back to maximum wattage. 'I'll see you later then. Be careful, won't you?'

'Yes, Mum,' Alice auto-replies to her mother's usual parting line. *Be careful of what?* she wants to say. *Don't be ridiculous,* she wants to say, Flo's voice in her head. But instead she thinks, *Yes, I'll be careful because I don't want to be attacked on the way home, I don't want to get run over by a joyrider when I cross the road, I don't want to slip down the steps outside the café and break my leg.*

She'll be careful. It's her default setting.

⸺

Carla blinks back tears as she leaves the café, choked after another failed interaction with her daughter. She puts so much effort into being bright and cheerful, in the vain hope of seeing similarly positive emotions reflected back in Alice's face, that when she leaves her the see-saw plummets the other way and plunges her into sadness.

She heads to the supermarket to pick up sausages. She knows Alice isn't bothered about a barbecue. Isn't bothered, really, about spending any time with her mother at all. But it seems important to Carla to do these things nonetheless, to sit outside in the warmth and attempt to re-create the kind of summer evening they used to have years ago, all four of them: her, Rich, Ella and Alice. Ella spent so many evenings with them that Carla always made sure there was enough food for four. Rich would baste chicken drumsticks as they sizzled on the grill, while Ella and Alice cried with laughter over some silly card game, and Carla watched them all, thinking how lucky she was to be there, wanting to hold on to that feeling, to capture it and put it in a locket around her neck.

It is as though she knew, even then, that it wouldn't last.

She's in the cake aisle, looking for something for pudding that Alice will probably ignore and she will eat too much of (maybe she should make something instead?) when she bumps into Flo, chocolate digestives in one hand, tiffin in the other.

'I'd just have both, if I were you,' she says.

'Carla! Gosh, you've found me out.' Flo puts both packets in her trolley and smiles. 'But you're quite right, life's too short to deny oneself treats.'

'I'm glad I caught you, actually. How are you?'

'Not too bad, thank you. Has Alice been telling you otherwise?'

'She said you fainted. She was worried about you.'

'She is a worrywart, isn't she?' Flo smiles. 'It was nothing to bother about. I'm fit as a fiddle.'

'Pleased to hear it.' She pauses. Maybe Flo could help her figure out what to do about Alice, get her to open up a bit. 'If you have time, could we go somewhere for a coffee, when you're done here?'

Flo nods. 'That would be lovely. I'm nearly finished.'

Carla takes her to Gigi's, which she knows wouldn't be Flo's first choice, but there are limited options in this town and they can't go to Merryn's Café, since Alice is there.

'I just wanted to have a quiet word about Alice,' Carla says when their coffees are delivered. Flo sits forward, perching on the edge of the low leather sofa, in order to reach her cappuccino on the table, and it crosses Carla's mind that she may not be able to get up again without help.

'It's been wonderful to have her helping me out with Ernie,' Flo says. 'She's a lovely girl.'

'She is, but . . .' Carla trails off.

'But?'

Carla looks down, fiddles with a sachet of sugar. 'But she's vulnerable right now,' she says finally. 'She's always been . . . *different*, not like other teenagers. Especially in the couple of years since . . .' She pauses. 'She's special, so special to me, Flo. And I'm worried about her, so I just wanted to ask you if you'd keep an eye on her and maybe try to find out what's going on in her head, let me know if you think . . . if anything seems . . . Because I can't lose her, I just can't.' She doesn't really know what she's trying to say. Lose her physically, like they lost Ella? Or lose their closeness for ever, their relationship so deteriorated that there's no way back. Both, really.

Flo's eyebrows knit together and a hint of a frown hovers on her lips. 'Why would you lose her?'

'It's just . . . we lost someone two years ago. Alice's best friend, Ella. They were so close, and she was practically a second daughter to me.'

Sisters from another mister. Later on, when the girls were teenagers, it seemed like something changed, though, like they were drifting apart a little, and Carla wonders if that's contributed to Alice's current malaise. Does she regret something that happened between them? Is she dwelling on a petty squabble? She wishes she could bring it up but she never dares, fearing Alice will only clam up even more.

'I'm sorry to hear that, Carla, I didn't know,' Flo says.

'No,' Carla says. 'We didn't know each other back then, did we?' The subject clearly hasn't come up during Alice's visits to Flo's house, and that worries her. It can't be good for Alice to hold everything in, to never talk about the thing she must be thinking about constantly.

Flo takes a sip of her coffee, destroying the wonky clover leaf stencilled in cinnamon on the foam. 'What happened?' she asks, and Carla takes a breath, bracing herself to relate the story that has haunted her for two years. 'You don't have to tell me. But maybe I ought to know, if I'm going to be spending time with Alice.'

'Ella was hit by a drunk driver when she was walking home from a night out,' she starts. 'He just drove right into her on the pavement, up there on the main road.' Her voice wavers. 'Alice was there too – they were together. She was injured but thankfully . . .' She can't say it, can't put into words the relief she felt to turn up to the hospital and find that Alice had survived, because it is permanently entwined with a sense of guilt that Ella didn't. Her death was devastating enough, but if it had been Alice instead . . .

'Oh, Carla, I'm so sorry,' Flo says.

'She was inconsolable at the time, extremely traumatized, which is completely understandable. But now, two years later, she doesn't seem to have got over her grief – if anything it seems worse. She's just in this . . . this funk, and I don't know what to do to help her get out of it. Every time I try to talk to her, I just seem to say or do the wrong thing. I even suggested therapy but you should have seen the look she gave me.' She shakes her head. 'She's completely shut me out.'

She can't stop her eyes filling up now and she blinks them back, draining her coffee cup to cover her face for a moment. But then Flo leans forward and puts her hand on hers and there's something about that gesture that breaks the dam and a tear slips down Carla's face. *Don't be nice,* she said to concerned well-wishers after the accident. *Don't be nice to me, I can't handle it.*

'I'm glad you told me,' Flo says. 'That must have been hard on you, too.'

Carla brushes her cheeks and looks up. 'Me? Well, yes, it was, it was . . . awful,' she takes a shaky breath, swallows down the self-blame that rises up like nausea, 'but it doesn't matter about me. I just want Alice to be okay. I want her to be happy again.'

Flo sits back and stares at her. 'Of course you do. But if you don't mind me saying so, Carla, you don't look all that happy yourself. So if I look out for Alice, will you do me a favour and try to look out for you?'

↻

When Alice arrives in the late afternoon after her shift at the café, Flo can almost see the cloud of misery sitting above her.

And now Flo understands why. When she heard what Carla told her at Gigi's, it was as though she'd found a crucial piece of a jigsaw puzzle down the back of the sofa. Alice's worry, her trepidation; that line between Carla's brows, just above the bridge of her nose. Grief will do that, Flo knows; grief and guilt can paint a person's face like foundation. She remembers those feelings well. Grief for James, for her brother, for the loss of her friendship with Lilli. Guilt for what she did, for the awful act that rears its ugly head in her mind when she reads Lilli's book and thinks of Lyon. The only thing that really helped her through all that was her art.

She remembers how Lilli would ask her about Alexander, encourage her to open up, to talk – something she'd never really done before – and how it helped, it really did. But it was in sketching that she found true solace, the way her quiet contemplation of a figure or a tree seemed to momentarily still her mind and in doing so, let it heal. And she will always be grateful that Lilli encouraged her to do that, too.

Alice grabs Ernie's lead and leaves immediately; Flo lets her go. She knows Ernie is a calming presence, that he will help Alice cast off her mood, or at least moderate it a little. Flo tinkers in her studio and waits. She has a plan – not necessarily the one Carla had in mind, but one that Flo considers just as effective: not to get Alice to talk, but to *create*.

'He did two poos and I only had one poobag,' Alice says when she returns. 'It was so disgusting.'

Ernie looks up at the girl, adoration on his face, and Flo laughs. 'And yet he looks as though butter wouldn't melt.'

Alice sits down on the armchair in the studio with a little

huff. Eric immediately jumps on her lap, as if to say *my turn for some fuss*, and Flo watches as Alice strokes the cat's head and tickles under his chin. His soft purr melts the tension in Alice's face and Flo spots a hint of a smile in her eyes. *Good job, Eric.*

'What are you doing?' Alice says finally.

'I started a new one today.' Flo holds up her sketchpad to show Alice the design for a three-colour reduction print. A cat curled in front of wallpaper featuring little red and orange fish. She forced herself to sit and do it, since it's becoming increasingly hard to concentrate with that book hanging over her, but she's glad she did.

'That'll look great. Did Eric pose for you?'

'He did. It's not his forte, but I caught him unawares.'

'Asleep?'

'Exactly.' She smiles.

'I saw Harriet in the café today,' Alice says. 'She says your prints sell really well so you should give her some more.'

'Good. I expect those will be ready to mount by Wednesday. I'll take them in to her.' Flo gestures to the washing lines strung behind her, where rows of prints are pegged and drying.

'I can do it, if you like.'

Flo tries not to react. She is surprised – and not surprised. She knows Alice wants to get involved in this. She knows she wants to carve and print her own designs, but she won't let herself – or fear won't let her. Flo aches for her to give in to that tiny, well-buried desire. She longs for Alice to throw caution to the wind, to cast off the heavy straitjacket she wears

102

and give herself a chance to breathe, to heal, to *live*. It took Flo far too long to do that herself, but she got there in the end. She hopes Alice can get there a little sooner.

'That would be great, Alice,' Flo says, then hesitates, her plan fluttering in her head. Fear isn't easily abandoned; it needs a push. 'It's good to have some help in these things as I get older,' she says. 'I can't do everything I used to. I suppose soon I won't be able to do any of it anymore.'

Alice's eyebrows shoot up and Flo feels a flush of guilt to be scaremongering towards someone so beholden to fear. But she knows, after her fainting episode in the attic, that the girl's anxiety is clearly overridden by her concern for others. And sometimes, as eighty years of life have taught her, you have to play dirty to get what you want; the end justifies the means.

'But you're okay, aren't you?' Alice says. 'You can still see and everything, right?'

Flo sighs. 'For now,' she says. 'And I'm going to carry on as long as this rusty old body can manage it, but my knees can be painful, as you know, and then there's the fainting.' She pauses for effect, even though she's positive she only fainted because the attic was too bloody hot. 'I'm sure there will come a time when I simply have to pack all this up.' She sighs again, casts a wistful look around the studio. 'And what a shame that will be. I'd truly love to pass it all on to someone, to inspire a younger person to pick up the craft. But my great-niece isn't interested, so . . .' She takes a sip of her tea. Alice isn't stupid, she probably understands exactly what Flo is doing, but that doesn't mean it won't work.

'I'd be rubbish,' Alice says.

'Probably,' Flo replies.

Alice looks at her. 'But I could give it another go, just to see.'

'You could.'

There is a silence, and Flo waits to hear the conclusion of her little game, to know if she has won. She very much enjoys winning.

'Okay then,' Alice says.

The Way We Were

'*How?*' I said to Fran, as I stared at the autumn leaves falling from the oak tree outside our window. 'How can I escape this place and find him?'

Since meeting Hugo at the opera house, I'd thought of little but him. I'd daydreamed about him while learning to knit baby bootees with Madame Grisaille, or pretending to listen while Madame Bouchard instructed us on public speaking. I relived the moment we met, the smile in his eyes and the turn up in his mouth when he looked at me, and my dreams at night were filled with his rich English voice when he said, *Well that just won't do.* I'd been sweet on a boy before – Walter Wilson back home in Brooklyn (we'd kissed once in his car after school, and a second time in the back row of the movie theatre) – but this was different. Hugo was a man. A man that I absolutely needed to see again.

Night after night I would ponder the conundrum of exactly how I was going to make that happen. Each evening after the day's activities had ended, Fran and I would go up to our room, kick off our shoes, lie together on one of our beds (usually mine since it was near the window, ideal for gazing at the distant city lights, the moon, or, I liked to imagine, the Soviets' newly launched Sputnik) and make our way through a packet of fudge or a tin of shortbread from Harrods (sent by Fran's mother in a fortnightly care package that usually included at least one new dress, blouse or scarf, which Fran freely let me try on), while I came up with increasingly harebrained schemes.

Poor Fran put up with me like a trouper – I did go *on* about it – but she never agreed that any of my proposals would actually work. She would only shrug and look at me with those big, anxious eyes. 'You'll just have to get over him. Nothing could possibly come of it, anyway.'

'I could climb out the window one day, shimmy down the drainpipe.'

'They'd catch you.'

'I could pretend he was a friend of my father's come to take me out to tea.'

'They'd never believe you.'

'I could sneak off next time we go into town.'

'And how would you find him exactly?'

Lovely as she was, Fran was a glass–half–empty kinda gal.

I wasn't, though, so I would dismiss my friend's pessimism and continue dreaming and scheming, because despite my limited knowledge of matters of the heart, I knew this sort of thing didn't happen every day. There had been something between Mr Hugo Bennett and me in that brief moment at the opera house, something some people went a whole lifetime without experiencing. I didn't know how I knew that; I just did. So I *would* find him, if it took me the entire school year, because the alternative was simply unacceptable.

Thankfully, it appeared Hugo felt the same.

'*Tu as une lettre*, Eleanor,' the dour school secretary, Madame Devillier, announced around a week after we'd visited the opera house. Letters weren't uncommon; most of the girls received something from their family every few days, including me, whose latest had been from Bobby – *Have you eaten frogs' legs yet? Dad's dragging me to the damned golf club tomorrow, wish me luck* – but I'd never had a letter with a Lyon postmark.

Dear Miss Cranshaw,

Please forgive the presumption, but I should like to inform you that I am regularly in the Maison Dorée in Place Bellecour on a Saturday afternoon from around 3 o' clock. Should you happen to be in the area and free to join me, I would be delighted to see you.

Hugo Bennett Esq. (opera aficionado)

'I knew it!' I said in an excited whisper, dragging Fran out into the school grounds, where I passed her the letter. 'I knew there was something between us – and he clearly felt it too.'

Fran read the note with her eyebrows raised so high, I thought they'd fly right off her head. 'You're not going to try and meet him, are you? I don't think Madame Bouchard would agree, nor your parents – at least not without a chaperone.'

I beamed and nudged her on the arm. 'I'm not planning on telling them, silly.'

But even I, with my unwavering optimism, knew it wasn't going to be as easy as all that. Though excursions and activities outside the school were more regular by then, they weren't always to Lyon city centre, and I had little opportunity to slip away in any case. The first Saturday after the note arrived, we went on a day trip to the Roman ruins in Vienne. Everyone was in high spirits as we explored the temple and the ancient amphitheatre, except for me, who felt torn from Lyon – and Hugo – like a button ripped from a beloved top-coat. The second Saturday we spent with Madame Grisaille learning to plan and prepare a picnic – baking ham pies and quiche Lorraine to serve cold, cutting the crusts off cucumber sandwiches, making lemonade and a vegetable juice cocktail – before taking the fruits of our labours to Lyon's Parc de la Tête d'Or, where the turning leaves glowed gold and umber and burgundy under the still-warm October sun.

It was fun, sitting on the grass eating our feast, laughing at the occasional shriek or honk floating over from the park's zoo. Even the teachers seemed relaxed, correcting our deportment a little less than usual. But my chest was tight with frustration. Hugo was likely in his regular café in town, thinking I didn't want to come – or perhaps, by now, having forgotten about me entirely – while I was forced to remain here, pining for him over cucumber sandwiches. Life was so goddamn unfair.

But on the third Saturday, things started to look up. There would be an excursion to the Musée des Beaux-Arts,

Madame Bouchard informed us the day before. We would have a guided tour of the collections, followed by – and here I perked up – additional time to look around the galleries by ourselves.

Her words were music to my ears. The fine art museum was in Place des Terreaux. It wouldn't take long to walk from there to Place Bellecour, according to my guidebook; both were on the Presqu'île, the sliver of land between the two rivers.

'After the tour, I'm going to slip out,' I told Fran the evening before the trip, when we were lying on my bed as usual. 'And you have to cover for me. If anyone asks, I'm in the ladies' powder room.'

Fran's brow fell into its now-familiar furrows. 'I don't know, Lenny, isn't it a bit risky? What if they find out? You'll never be let out again.'

'They won't. We'll have at least an hour to look around by ourselves. That should be enough time for me to get to Hugo and back before they notice.' I took her hand in mine. 'Don't worry so much. It'll be all right.' I jiggled my feet on the bed, unable to keep still. 'You've got to seize the day, Fran. You've got to take a risk or two, otherwise how dull would life be?'

Fran gave me a small smile. 'Life's never dull with you around, Lenny.' She squeezed my hand. 'Just be careful. I don't want anything bad to happen to you.'

'It won't,' I said. I was sure of it.

That Saturday was bright and sunny, a rich blue sky offsetting the white of Fourvière basilica and the red roofs of the

Croix-Rousse district snaking up the hill. A nervous energy bubbled in my chest.

'I'm glad to see you have such enthusiasm for fine art, Eleanor,' Madame Bouchard said, when I was among the first to line up for the coach.

'I simply adore the Impressionists, Madame. I hear the gallery has wonderful paintings by Manet and Renoir,' I said, aping my guidebook. I laughed inwardly at the flush of delight on the headmistress's face. I hadn't forgotten the way she'd looked at me at the welcome reception, the slight disapproval in her face which had lingered like a bad smell through most of her interactions with me ever since. So it pleased me no end to see that our esteemed headmistress now thought she was making me *shipshape*, moulding this brash *American* into a cultured, demure young lady. It also pleased me that tucked inside my handbag was my guidebook with its map of the city. I would need it.

It took every ounce of my patience to hold out through the guided tour and pretend to pay attention. (In hindsight, I wish I actually had, but on that day my genuine interest in art didn't stand much of a chance compared to my overwhelming interest in Hugo.) I nodded knowingly in front of Rodin's sculptures, feigned fascination with ancient Greek pots and Egyptian statues, and stood open-mouthed before paintings by Picasso, Gauguin and Monet, though I couldn't have told you much about them two minutes later. Perhaps, it occurred to me, I should be an actress.

But when the tour ended and we were told we had one hour to look around by ourselves, under the strict condition we did not leave the museum premises, my body jittered like a cat poised to pounce.

'Remember, if anyone asks . . .'

'You're in the powder room, yes I know,' Fran said. 'Let's just hope I'm not asked too often or people will start to think you've a problem.'

I laughed and grabbed her arm, announcing to anyone within earshot that we were off to revisit the antiquities room, and as soon as we left the hall, I blew a kiss to Fran and was gone.

Just being alone in the city and able to go where I pleased made my heart bloom. As much as I wanted to see Hugo, I also wanted to linger in the streets, to walk slowly, giving myself time to look up at the grand buildings, lean over the bridges of the Saône and the Rhône, mingle among the Frenchwomen strolling down Rue de la République, darling little dogs trotting at their feet. I wanted to ride the trolleybuses, find the chocolate shop where Aurélia bought those delectable pralines, sip a tisane at one of the big hotels overlooking the Rhône and browse the cosmetics in the department store Printemps. As it was, I only allowed myself a brief stop there to purchase a red lipstick at the Bourjois counter, telling the shop girl in my bad French that I was about to meet my fiancé for afternoon tea. I looked in the mirror, mussed my lips together and smiled at myself, admiring the sophisticated person I saw, somehow transformed from American schoolgirl to French ingenue by that simple slick of scarlet. Of course, when I think of that moment now I only cringe at how naïve I was, how silly and young. A lamb to the slaughter, you might say. But you really couldn't blame me for that.

After I left the shop I walked quickly, with purpose, until my heart just about stopped when, at the end of the shopping street, I came to the large dusty red expanse of Place Bellecour. I looked at my watch – a quarter after four. Place Bellecour was huge, and I didn't know which side of the square the café was on. I dithered, clenching my clammy palms. Perhaps he would have already left. Perhaps he didn't even come to the café today.

I walked a little way up the side of the square nearest to me, and then I saw it – not on any side of the square, in fact, but *in* it: the Maison Dorée.

I waited, feeling my heart pulse in my chest. A little voice in my head – Fran? Ma? – niggled at me. *Are you sure you know what you're doing?*

But there was no time to waste, so I ignored the voices and stepped inside the café.

I scoured the room and my eyes fell on a table in the corner. A man reading a newspaper, a cigarette dangling from his mouth. A waitress appeared at his side, placed a coffee in front of him, and as the man lowered his paper he looked up.

Hugo.

When he saw me, surprise lit up his face and my chest surged to see it. He stood up, and as he walked towards me, I knew this was the right decision, I knew the invisible thread that had connected us that night at the opera house was still intact, drawing us inevitably together.

'Miss Cranshaw. What a delightful surprise.'

I was momentarily mute, the words stopped in my throat by his handsome face, his adorable English accent, his wide smile.

'I was just passing and ... I remembered your note,' I said finally.

He smiled, and there was laughter in his eyes. 'You were just passing.'

'Yes, so I thought perhaps I'd stop by.' I beamed, enjoying his unspoken acknowledgement of my obvious pretence. Of course he knew finishing schoolgirls weren't allowed out without a chaperone, let alone to meet a complete stranger. I realized then that he also knew I was the sort of girl to bend the rules – in fact, I'd say that's exactly why he'd written to me.

'I am very pleased you did, Miss Cranshaw.'

'Do call me Lenny,' I said, as he directed me to his table. My body fizzed as his hand rested lightly on the small of my back.

'What can I offer you, Lenny? A café crème, perhaps?'

He signalled to the waitress and soon there was a coffee in front of me, though I barely noticed it arrive; I was as nervy as a debutante curtseying before the Queen of England.

'I come here every Saturday,' Hugo said, breaking the momentary silence. 'It's my relaxation time after a busy week at the office. A coffee or two, some time to read the news,' he tapped the paper, now folded on the table, 'and catch up on my correspondence, make good on my promise to my mother back in England. I do get chastised if I leave it too long to write to her.'

I seized upon these tiny details of his life and yearned for more. I wondered what his parents looked like, how his youth in England had been, and how he got from there to here. It all seemed so wonderfully enticing, the life of a man – especially an older, urbane, exotically foreign man.

'But I'm delighted to be distracted from all of that by your presence.' Hugo leaned forward. 'Tell me, Lenny, how is that school of yours treating you?'

'Oh, it's unbearably dull,' I said. 'Imagine spending hours learning the correct way to enter a room or compose dinner invitations. Last week we spent a whole morning taking instruction on how best to present oneself whilst doing household chores.'

'It does sound ghastly.' He laughed. 'What would you rather be doing?'

I hesitated a moment, rather taken aback by the question. I didn't think anyone had ever asked me that before. Perhaps he knew that, too.

'I should like to take a secretarial course and then apply for a position at one of the big firms in New York. Advertising, perhaps.' I didn't know that's what I wanted to do but I thought it sounded good. Any loftier ambitions had been knocked out of me by my high school science teacher and his pals.

He nodded. 'A girl who wants to make something of herself. I like that. But surely a modern young woman like yourself could aim higher. Executive, rather than typist, perhaps.'

I felt a rush of heat to my cheeks. 'Yes, perhaps,' I said. 'Or maybe I'll look into becoming an air hostess. I would very much like to see the world, and I so admired the girls working on my flight over here. Though I hear it's an extremely sought-after role and they only take women from society families.' I took a sip of coffee and looked at him over the rim of the cup, and I could have sworn his eyes were fixed on my scarlet lips. 'In fact, I would like to know how to become lots of things – and then I can decide which position would suit me best.'

'Quite right, too.'

'But I sure won't find out in that darn school.'

'Indeed, you will not.' Hugo proffered a packet of Gauloises and I took one, leaned forward as he lit it, so close I could smell his musky scent of aftershave and tobacco. My eyes met his and for a couple of long, intense seconds I felt he was looking right inside me, into every single cell. Then the lighter snapped shut and he sat back.

'You know, Lenny,' he said. 'Some people just don't have much imagination in life, wouldn't you say?'

A thrill rippled through my chest. 'I would,' I said.

'But you,' he pointed at me and I felt like he'd touched my heart itself, 'are different. I have the feeling you could do just about anything if you put your mind to it.'

He knew what he was doing, and it wasn't my fault I was so susceptible. I'd been waiting to hear words like these all my life, though I hadn't known it.

Don't be too interested in things, Lenny.

Don't waste your time on science, Lenny.

Go to college to get a diamond ring on your finger, Lenny.

I'd been absorbing this 'advice' for years. I'd seen the happy homemakers emblazoned across Ma's copies of *Good*

Housekeeping and *Ladies' Home Journal*. I'd watched Lucille Ball's funny but unsuccessful attempts to be anything other than a housewife in *I Love Lucy*; I'd noticed the way Ma and her friends always seemed to look down on Jen's mother, who worked on the front desk of our dental surgery. But none of it ever sat right in my stomach, somehow, though I didn't know why. I didn't know why Bill Haley and Little Richard and Elvis appealed to me more than Doris Day, or why I'd rather have gone with Bobby and Pop to nose around a housing development than stay home and help Ma with the housework, as I was usually ordered to do. I didn't know why I looked at Madame Grisaille and wondered what it would be like to earn your own money rather than thinking how sad she must be without a husband and child. I wasn't immune to the expectations placed on me, but the more I was shepherded into fulfilling them, the more I wanted, consciously or otherwise, to rebel. For some reason I was just made that way.

And the problem with Hugo, the reason he got under my skin so (apart from being an absolute dreamboat to look at) was that he knew it, and he told me what I wanted to hear.

'I'm extremely glad to have met you, Lenny Cranshaw,' he said as we parted half an hour later, pressing into my hand a folded piece of paper containing his address and telephone number.

I took a drag on my cigarette, looked into that beautiful face, and smiled. And then I rushed back up Rue de la République to the museum, grinning so hard I thought my face might break in two.

*

Fran was mad as hell that evening.

'You nearly got caught. They asked me three times where you were and I felt just horrid lying,' she said as soon as dinner was over and we'd retreated to our room.

I couldn't stop smiling. 'But I wasn't caught. And your fibs weren't discovered, so it's all fine. Stop worrying, Fran. It worked out. I saw him, I snuck back into the gallery, and no one was any the wiser.'

'All right, but I'm not helping you again. I don't think my nerves can stand it.' She gave a little huff and folded her arms, but there was a hint of a smile on her lips. Fran always did have trouble staying cross with me for long. And there was something else in that smile, too – admiration, I realized with a flash of satisfaction. I'd broken the school rules, dared to be brave, go my own way, and despite herself, she admired me for it. I *knew* there was something beneath Fran's good-girl exterior, and I was pleased to see my errant behaviour was coaxing it out. Perhaps that spark of rebellion was in all of us girls, deep down, whether we knew it or not (even Sandra occasionally smoked through the bars of the school gates).

I kicked off my shoes and flopped down on my bed, a stupid grin on my face. I kept revisiting moments from the café in my head; I saw his broad smile, felt his hand on my back, pictured him leaning forward and lighting my cigarette. Desire flooded my whole body and I revelled in the novelty of the sensation.

'Oh Fran, he's just dreamy! Handsome and cultured and sophisticated. He knows all about world affairs and politics and international trade, and he didn't treat me like some little girl who doesn't know anything. He asked my opinion, he wanted to know what I thought, and he didn't laugh at me when I said it.' I turned to her. 'I think I love him.'

Frances looked askance. 'You don't know him!'

'I do. I feel I've known him for years. He really *knows* me. We understand each other.'

I didn't expect her to comprehend. But I pitied my friend then. I wanted Fran to know what that felt like. I wanted her to meet someone like this, someone she could be truly passionate about, someone who would encourage her to fly instead of clipping her wings. But instead all she had ahead of her was marriage to a man for whom she could only muster the lukewarm and certainly damning praise *he's quite nice*. Fran deserved more than *nice*, and I hoped, through my budding romance with Hugo – which I knew, I just knew, would continue, whatever obstacles I had to overcome to make it so – I would show her that she didn't have to settle for anything less than simply wonderful.

5

Much to Flo's delight, a routine is quickly established. On weekdays, when Alice isn't at Merryn's Café, she arrives at the house around eleven. After walking Ernie, she returns to the studio, where Flo is already at work. She's cleared a corner of her workbench for the girl, removing stacks of discarded test prints, dirty rags and offcuts of lino (Flo is not, and never has been, a particularly neat artist) to uncover enough space for both of them. She has given Alice her own sketchbook, and started to teach her about the kind of designs that work well for a basic lino print – strong lines, silhouettes, simple shapes – and Alice has already carved and hand-printed her first design: a maple leaf, based on those on the tree in Flo's garden, its veins and fluted edges giving interesting detail to the monochrome print. Now she's working on another, a silhouette of Ernie by the tree.

Flo observes Alice as she carefully transfers the design onto the lino, or as she concentrates on carving, swearing occasionally when the tool slips, or when she peels the paper off the inked lino for the first time, her eyes lighting up to see her design become a print, and Flo knows this is what Alice needs.

As for herself, today Flo is carving the fourth layer of a complicated six-layer print of a landscape view. It shows the Westbury White Horse, the rolling hills and turning trees of the previous autumn, when she returned to the place she used to go with James, who always loved to walk near the White Horse. She's already printed three of the six layers – using her beautiful press, her pride and joy, which she will let Alice use when she's mastered the basics – and the picture is emerging in the prints hanging to dry on the line behind her. She loves seeing the image build up gradually, each new layer adding more depth and extra detail. It takes faith to do this, she thinks. The first layer usually looks like nothing, she had explained to Alice, when the girl questioned why she'd started this design by printing pale blue abstract shapes on twenty sheets of paper. Then she adds a second, and a third, and perhaps it starts to make sense. But it's only when she prints the last layer that the complete picture is revealed, and so all through that process – weeks, sometimes – Flo must maintain faith, must remember that by being patient and working on it step by step, she will eventually achieve what she wants.

'I don't know how you do such complicated designs,' Alice says, looking at her now. 'But I want to know because it looks amazing.'

Flo smiles. 'You have to start with something simple, as you're doing now. Master your skills in one-colour first, then I'll teach you a two-colour reduction print.'

Alice nods and goes back to carving.

'I saw a wonderful exhibition in Paris once,' Flo says. 'A contemporary lino printer doing just sensational work. I wish I could remember her name – I'd like you to look her up.'

'When were you in Paris?'

'Oh, many times. I went there frequently in the seventies for my job. We'd go for a few months at a time, myself and Guinevere, my boss.'

Alice looks up. 'Huh.' She puts down her gouge. 'I noticed some of your photo albums when I was in the loft,' she says. 'You've travelled a lot, haven't you?'

'I've tried. There's a lot out there to see.'

'And you lived in London as well as Paris.'

'Yes, and Lyon for a while, but that's another story.'

'Then how did you end up in this crappy town?'

Flo laughs. 'It's a lovely town. A little quiet, perhaps, but lovely in its own way.'

In truth, she mainly chose it because it was close to Ronnie and Emily, and after James died, she felt a need to be near family, her only family, now. But it has grown on her over the years; there is a sense of community in the café and Harriet's gallery and Gloria's art supplies shop and Moretti's ice-cream parlour. If London was a cocktail of flavours and experiences that invigorated her for so many years, this town is a single malt whisky – mellow and smooth, comforting and familiar; a little numbing, if she's honest.

Alice shakes her head. 'It's awful,' she says. 'It's in the sticks, there's nothing to do and everyone knows your business – or thinks they do. I hate it.'

'Well,' Flo says, 'I suppose you won't have to stay here much longer, since you're off to university. It's your turn to go and explore the world.' Alice doesn't answer, and Flo sees a veil come down over her face. 'What are you going to study?'

Alice doesn't meet her eye. Instead she picks up the gouge again and starts carving. 'Business,' she mumbles, and Flo almost laughs at how little enthusiasm is conveyed by her tone.

'Very sensible, I expect.'

Alice shrugs. 'Dad thinks it'll give me the best chance of getting a job afterwards and Mum thinks I should go to Birmingham because it means I can stay at home rather than live in halls.'

'But you just said you hated this town! Why give up the chance to go somewhere further away?'

Alice shrugs again and doesn't answer.

'Gosh, what I would have given to go to university. Not many women did, in late fifties Britain. I didn't even consider it, and no one suggested I should.'

Alice looks up and Flo sees a hint of relief in her face that the conversation is no longer about her. 'So you got a job instead?'

'No, dear. I got married.'

Alice's mouth drops open. 'At *eighteen*?'

Flo laughs. It must be so difficult for this young woman born in the twenty-first century to comprehend the social mores of a century long gone. But are things really that different now? Alice may face different pressures but the weight of them on her shoulders seems no less. Flo suddenly feels an overwhelming desire to help her cast them off, to stop her making the same mistake she did – the mistake of feeling you have to do as you're told.

You almost didn't make that mistake, though, did you? You were going to go with Lilli, you were going to tell your parents you didn't want to get married, until . . .

She's been having dreams lately. Vivid, terrifying dreams where she is back there, his face in front of her, panic rising inside her, and she is running, gulping at the air, near-blind with tears, bending double to be sick. She wakes bathed in sweat, a headache pulsing at her temples.

It is the book, of course. She can't stop reading it, but equally she can hardly bear to, and so she reads slowly, tentatively, scared of what the next page might reveal.

Does Lilli somehow know what she did? Is that why she wrote it? Is she punishing Flo for leaving her? Should she expect to end her days in jail?

'Listen,' she says to Alice, shutting off the thoughts in her head. It's been better since Alice has joined her in the studio; at times she's been able to push the past away, to find that meditative state and just revel in the pleasure of making art. But then sometimes, like now, something jolts her out of it and she is back there again, aged eighteen, traumatized and sleepwalking her way into marriage, and she can't sit there anymore, letting herself relive it. 'I've run out of a couple of inks,' she says. 'Want to come with me into town?'

Alice has walked past the art shop many times and been inside on the odd occasion, to get a new pen or pick up a birthday card for her grandmother, who likes arty photographs of flowers and animals. But today she is seeing it through new eyes. Today it seems as though she's stumbled across a treasure trove: there are shelves and shelves of inks and rollers and inking trays and barens. There are numerous different papers with exotic-sounding names (the best papers are handmade in Japan, Flo says), and stacks of lino in various sizes and colours (the grey, traditional lino with a hessian back is what Flo uses most).

'Hello, Gloria,' Flo greets the shop assistant, a middle-aged woman with a mass of unruly auburn hair, wearing an oversized top that slips down one shoulder and baggy, yoga-style trousers.

The woman smiles at Flo, who is clearly a regular. 'Lovely to see you, Flo. And who's this?'

'This is my friend Alice. She's just starting out in lino printing, and we're short of a few supplies. Do you have that lovely yellow ochre in today? And naphthol red in the biggest size?'

'Absolutely. Welcome, Alice,' Gloria says. 'Flo's one of my best customers. Keeps me in business, if I'm honest!'

'Nonsense,' Flo scoffs. 'You supply the local schools, don't you? That must be a good contract.'

'I do, but they're ordering less and less these days – government cuts,' she says, and Alice thinks back to her own school art classes, thirty kids mucking around as the teacher tried to get them to draw a bunch of fruit in a bowl. She never felt particularly passionate about art back then, dropped it at GCSE, but now . . .

Flo waggles her head and tuts. 'What a shame. So short-sighted.'

'Couldn't agree more,' Gloria says. Alice follows as she leads them to a vast wall of inks. 'Here you are, in the usual place. Anything else you need?'

'Thank you,' Flo says. 'We'll just have a little look around.'

'Absolutely. Take your time.'

When Gloria walks away, Alice runs her fingers over the tubes of ink. She wants to buy them all. The more she tries lino printing, the more she wants to do it again and again until she's as good as Flo. She is at once desperate to do it and frustrated that her efforts don't yet result in the kind of stunning prints that Flo produces. *Patience*, Flo says constantly, *you need to have patience. It will come, with practice.* And to Alice's surprise, she finds she's willing to put in the practice. She actively wants to do this, to spend her time in the studio with Flo, the radio on and the two of them carving side by side. And not just because she's avoiding her mother, who seems to have nothing to do but helicopter around her, causing a constant breeze that Alice can feel wherever she goes. *Get a life*, the phrase springs into her head, the childish insult thrown so often at school (but she'd never say it out loud, since she's hardly one to talk).

No, that's not why she's doing it. It's mostly because, as she feels the gouge slide through the lino, she is able to switch off from the thoughts in her head, from Ella, from her mother, from the constant catastrophizing. During those periods in Flo's studio, she finds she is no longer thinking about what might happen, about what could go wrong, about the worst-case scenarios that are usually present in her head. She thinks instead about which parts of the lino to cut out and which to leave, about which tool to use for which line, and which colour she might try this one in when it's ready to print. Or sometimes, when she's got quite a bit to carve, she thinks about hardly anything at all. She simply concentrates on the task in hand, as though there's nothing else in the world but the here and now, and in those glorious moments she feels free. Free of herself. Free to create something – some*one* – brand new.

They choose several more inks than they came in for, and various different papers for Alice to experiment with, and an apron for Alice to wear. She tries to pay, but Flo waves her away and gets out her purse, insisting it's the prerogative of an old lady to spend her money on whatever and whomever she wants.

'Thank you,' Alice says, as they leave the shop and walk up the street into the centre of town.

'You're very welcome. I'm delighted you're enjoying it, and it's nice to have company in my studio.'

They are walking down the high street back towards the car park where they left Flo's Mini when Alice sees her. She grabs Flo's arm and pulls her into the nearest shop, a newsagent.

'Alice, if you want to go anywhere just say so, but I'm too old and decrepit to be pulled about like that.'

'Sorry.' Alice hovers by the door, peeking out, relieved as Vicky continues up the street, oblivious to her presence.

'Oh, I see. Avoiding someone are we?'

She shakes her head and picks up a magazine, one of those ones about fashion and make-up that she's tried to read but gets bored with. Ella liked them. 'No, I just wanted this.' She takes it to the counter and pays. 'Sorry, we can go now.'

They are in the car driving back to the house when Flo asks Alice again. 'Look, you can tell me to mind my own business, but what was all that about?'

Alice looks out the window. It's around three, the time of day when normally, in term time, kids will spill out of school and walk into town, balling their ties in their pockets. They'll head to Moretti's for ice-cream or pick up cans of Coke from the newsagent before slowly wandering to their respective homes, or to the green to play football or sit around gossiping. It's what Alice did so many times, before. It's what she did with Ella, time and time again, when they were younger.

'A girl I know from school. I don't want to see her at the moment.'

Flo looks at her. 'You fell out?'

Alice shrugs. 'Not really. We were never good friends. It's no big deal. I just don't want to see her, that's all. I don't . . . fit in with that lot.'

She has tried to avoid Vicky for two years, though it's been difficult, as she would see her at school nearly every day during sixth form. It is indicative of how little Vicky thought of her that she barely acknowledged Alice's return to school several weeks after the accident. Instead it was all about Vicky. *Vicky* had lost her best friend, *Vicky* was completely devastated. So devastated that she's now going out with Nick – Ella's Nick.

With school over, Alice is relieved she never has to see the girl again, this symbol of what went wrong between Ella and herself, of how they grew apart. If she ignores Vicky enough, perhaps she will only remember the good memories, like that time in Year Six when Ella defended Alice against the bullies who mocked her for the braces she had just been fitted with; like the time they howled with laughter when they both turned up to a schoolfriend's thirteenth birthday party wearing the same colour trousers and top, as though they were twins; like the many times they lay side by side in the meadow, making up stories inspired by the shapes in the clouds.

Alice loved doing that. She thought Ella had, too.

'Listen,' Ella had said one day, turning on her side on the grass. 'Some of the others are going to the pub tonight. Vicky knows someone who can get us fake IDs. What do you think, shall we go?'

Alice turned her head to face Ella. It was the autumn they were both turning fifteen, school had started back a few weeks previously, but the sun was still warm.

'I don't know,' Alice said. She liked them hanging out together, just the two of them. And she wasn't sure about Vicky, who seemed to have changed over the summer holidays, both physically and mentally. She suddenly had a cleavage (*chicken fillets*, Ella had said), she wore thick black eye-liner flicked out at the sides of her eyes, and she was going out with Danny, who Alice had always found a little intimidating. 'I thought we were going to go to the cinema?'

Ella rolled on her back again. 'We can do that anytime. Don't you want to do something different?'

'We're under-age.'

'So? I told you, we can get fake IDs. Everyone does it.' Ella grinned. 'Go on, live a little.'

Live a little. The phrase hurt Alice, though she couldn't quite put her finger on why. She loved being with Ella, she loved being at home with her mother, she enjoyed school – apart from Physics – and she'd loved the long, hot summer holiday, the week she and her mum had spent camping in Cornwall, a second week in Stockholm with her dad, and the time she'd spent hanging out with Ella for the rest of the holiday. Perhaps she wasn't the most daring of people, perhaps change scared her more than it did others her age, but she liked her life, she was happy, on the whole.

Live a little. Though she didn't know it at the time, Ella's words marked the start of something, a tiny crack that would later widen into a crevasse she'd fall right into.

'Fitting in is overrated if you ask me,' Flo says now.

Alice looks at her and sees a smile on her face – such an open face, a confident, worry-free face.

Easy for her to say.

⟍⟋

'These are too good, Carla, what are you trying to do to me?' Andy smiles as he walks past with one of the brownies she made for Alice last night. But Alice didn't come home till late – *I'm doing something at Flo's,* she'd texted in response to Carla's *Where are you? Are you okay?* – and because she doesn't want to eat her way through the whole lot herself, she brought them into the office and put the Tupperware box in the kitchen.

'Glad you like them, Andy.' She smiles at him and goes back to sorting press releases into piles. The book fair is next week and she's preparing publicity materials for all their latest publications, printing off multiple copies of various press releases and inserting the completed press packs into plastic wallets. She's tried to tell Susan that they should put all this on USB sticks instead, but she wasn't having it, so here she is, mired in paper and plastic. Alice would be aghast.

When the phone rings she is glad to be interrupted from the mundanity of her task. It's Lisa, from the other side of the open plan. She can almost see her if she swivels her chair slightly to the left.

'Hey, Carla, Derek would like to see you in his office if you have a mo?'

'Oh, okay,' she says, failing to keep the surprise out of her voice. 'I'll go right in.'

She gets up from her desk, shrugging a response to Andy's questioning eyebrows, and takes the narrow stairs up to Derek's office. The company occupies the two upper floors of a creaky old townhouse, a delicatessen on the ground floor which Carla is sure only exists because the ten-strong staff of Pulham Press get their lunch there practically every day. But she rarely heads up here, having little to do with Derek on a day-to-day basis; it feels like she's been summoned to the headmaster's office.

She knocks and enters to find Derek sitting behind his desk and Susan beside him, their faces serious.

'Carla, do sit down.'

She does.

'I'm afraid we have some bad news.'

Her stomach plunges. *I'm afraid I have some bad news.* Those are the words she heard once, on the phone, two years ago, spoken by a nurse who summoned her to the hospital. Immediately she is back there, rushing through the corridors, unsure what she is rushing towards, petrified of Alice's injuries, horrified by what the nurse had said. *I'm so sorry to say there's been a fatal accident.*

'Oh God. Alice?' Carla says.

'No,' Susan says, confusion crossing her face. 'Nothing to do with your daughter. It's a work matter.'

Of course it is. Carla's heart rate slows again and her face flushes. *Thank God.*

'You've worked here a long time, Carla, and we're very appreciative of all you've done for us, but we've decided it's time for a . . . restructure.'

'Sorry, what?' She is still basking in the relief of knowing that Alice is all right.

'A restructure. As of next month, Lisa's role will be split between support for Derek and assistance in the marketing and publicity department, and I'm going to take on more hours myself, meaning your role will be' – Susan hesitates, as though about to say a dirty word – 'redundant.'

A clock on the office wall ticks through five long seconds before Carla speaks. *That's why I was told to brief Lisa on the publicity schedule.*

'You're making me redundant,' she says finally.

Derek nods. 'We're giving you a very generous severance package in recognition of your loyalty to this company, but yes, I'm afraid so.' He looks skywards and shakes his head. 'You know how it is, Carla, times are tricky, we've got to tighten our belts and you're just too ... experienced.'

Too expensive, he means. *Too old*. Carla grips the arm of the chair. How can they do this to her? She has a mortgage to pay, a daughter to support through university. She's given fourteen years to this place. *What else am I going to do?*

Susan cocks her head. 'I know this is a shock. We'll give you a good send-off when the dust settles, but for now, if you want to take the rest of the day off, we quite understand. We'll discuss the details of your severance in due course.'

She shakes her head, as if to dislodge the words. 'But what about the press packs?'

'Don't worry about that,' Susan says, her voice unusually soft, pacifying. 'I'll ask Lisa to finish them off.'

Carla leaves the room and walks back down the stairs to the open-plan first floor. She picks up her handbag and shuts off her computer, her colleagues' eyes following her as she does so. She is shaking a little in shock and she just wants to get out of there, to feel a cool breeze on her clammy skin, to calm herself down, to absorb this latest rejection.

'I'm so sorry, I didn't know that was going to happen.' Lisa has come over to her desk and the sympathy on her face sparks rage inside Carla, though it clearly isn't her fault. Rage seems to come easily to her these days, but it's justified today. Maybe it always is. Maybe she has every right to feel angry about lots of things in her life. About the professional sacrifices she made for the husband who thanked her by leaving her; about the drunk driver who broke her precious daughter and killed the next best thing; about her own inability to protect Alice from people like him, however hard she tries; about her treatment at the hands of a company she's done her best to work hard for, after shelving the dreams she once harboured. But she bites her tongue. Letting the rage out is not acceptable; she would only make a spectacle of herself.

'What the hell happened?' Andy says.

Carla shakes her head and doesn't answer. She will leave the tub of brownies in the kitchen. A parting gift, it turns out.

She walks out of the office and down past the deli, leaving her safety net, her comfort blanket. She's been *restructured* at forty-six years old. For some reason she thinks of that old film, the one where a boat leaves someone behind in the water at the end of a scuba diving trip, cut adrift, abandoned to the sharks.

It was a true story, wasn't it?

The Way We Were

They say love is blind, and I was certainly a touch myopic in the days that followed my meeting with Hugo in the café. I was near-dizzy with thoughts of him; I couldn't sleep at night, irritating Fran with my inability to lie quietly, while I bounced through the days on adrenaline. His beautiful face was a drug, his words the high I craved. *I have the feeling you could do just about anything if you put your mind to it.*

Oh, how young and silly I was.

While my giddy, lovelorn state meant I still wasn't exactly paying attention in class, there was clearly something about my permanently positive demeanour that worked in my favour.

'I'm delighted to see you responding so well to the school now, Eleanor,' Madame Bouchard said to me one afternoon after a class about laying the table for a formal luncheon. (*Servants should always remove plates from the left*, she'd told us, while I'd daydreamed about Hugo whisking me off for lunch

134

at one of those intimate little *bouchons* I'd read about in my guidebook.) 'Just remember to keep your mind on the task in hand, yes?'

'*Oui, madame.*' I beamed back. '*Absolument.*'

Playing the good girl was clearly the best way to enable me to be the bad girl when I got the chance. Because after escaping once, I was determined to do it again – if only I could figure out how.

It came to me the following Friday while I was attempting – and failing – to neatly topstitch an apron during sewing class. A letter had arrived from my brother that morning, half moaning about Pop's attempts to woo a local businessman with links to a prestigious social club, half ridiculing my stories about the school. But his words were instantly forgotten when the idea came to me. Of course! A letter with a New York stamp was all I needed. I could have kissed Bobby right then.

'Fran,' I hissed, and she looked over from her own sewing machine, where she was attempting to unravel a tangled bobbin of thread. 'I've had an idea.'

Fran rolled her eyes, a smile flickering on her lips. 'That's unfortunate.'

I laughed. 'My brother,' I said. 'I'll get him to write to me from New York, pretending to be my father – I know he can fake Pop's signature.'

'And?'

'Well, I have a cousin in town, don't I?'

'You do?'

Now it was my turn to roll my eyes. 'An English cousin.

Very dashing, opera fan, quite the respectable professional man.'

'Oh.'

I sat back in my chair with what was, I'm sure, an unbearably smug expression on my face. 'They can't stop me from going to tea with my own cousin, can they, if my parents put him on the approved list?'

'But, Lenny—'

'I suspect you two girls are doing more talking than sewing.' Madame Grisaille looked up from Sandra's workstation, where our *prefect extraordinaire*, already accomplished with a needle and thread, was sewing herself a dress to wear to one of the many debutantes' balls she would attend when she did *the season* in London next summer. *It's such a bore, but Mother won't hear of me skipping it,* she'd told us all several times when the subject had magically arisen without any of us bringing it up, but I knew better. A four-month whirl of fancy parties hosted by matchmaking mothers and frequented by eligible but insufferable bachelors? That was all girls like Sandra lived for. Thank goodness Pop had failed to buy my way into *that*.

Madame Grisaille walked over and peered at my apron, before stepping back as though what she'd seen had actually offended her eyes. 'More practising, less talking, Eleanor,' she said, before turning her gaze to Fran. 'Very nice, Frances – neat and precise.'

I pulled a face behind the teacher's back and enjoyed the tension in Fran's expression as she struggled not to laugh.

'You know, several students at this school have gone on to

become professional seamstresses,' Madame Grisaille added. 'Or accomplished cooks or nurses. The skills you gain here may well set you on an exciting new path – if you put your mind to it.'

Her words cut through my silly mood and my mouth damn near fell open. She was encouraging us to have a *career*?

'That's really good to hear, madame, I should like to have a career.' Had I misjudged this place? After all, Madame Grisaille had a career. By now the gossip about her sexuality had been usurped by an alternative rumour – that she had lost her fiancé during the Great War and never found anyone to replace him – and I believed that story. There was a certain wistfulness about her that I found rather affecting; she was far nicer to us than Bouchard, turning a blind eye when we snatched a finger of cookie dough from the bowl in her cooking class, and watering down any chastisement with a warm smile. *We're her surrogate children*, Barbara liked to say with a pitying tone that infuriated me.

'Well, perhaps it won't be dressmaking for you, Eleanor,' Madame Grisaille said now with just such a smile. 'But something else, perhaps. I've always felt it valuable for young women to enter the world of work before they marry. Not only does it enhance one's personal skills, but it gives one a better understanding of financial matters, working routines and professional relationships so that a woman may one day ably support her husband in his own career.' She paused and looked from me to Fran. 'But in taking steps into the professional arena, a woman should always remember her limits. A job will help her become cultivated and informed enough to be interesting and supportive to a man, but once she does marry, happiness cannot be found by putting her professional aspirations before the needs of her husband and children. A woman should always respect the natural order of things.'

I sat back in my chair and swallowed down my disappointment at this parroting of the party line. *Who says it's the natural order?* I wanted to say. *Are you unnatural, then? Am I?* But instead I pictured Hugo's face, thought of what he'd said to me, and bit my tongue.

It took two weeks, an achingly slow two weeks I thought I would never endure. And then came the day when a letter arrived in the morning post – I'd never been so glad to see a New York stamp and my brother's familiar handwriting. I accepted it from Madame Devillier with polite restraint and, linking my arm through Fran's, pulled her into the garden where I tore at the envelope.

I don't know what you're playing at, and I can't imagine it's good, but I'm pissed at Pop so you caught me in the right mood. Go have your fun, Sis, but look out for yourself, won't you? And if anyone says anything, it was nothing to do with me.

My darling brother had come good. I kissed the letter and silently thanked the image of him in my head.

'Has he done it?' Fran asked. She was chewing on a cuticle, frown lines cutting across her forehead, both of which she'd be royally chastised for if Bouchard caught her. *No amount of Pond's Cold Cream can prevent the formation of wrinkles if you insist on frowning.*

'He sure has!' I scanned the rest of Bobby's words. 'He says he's sent a second letter to the school, asking them to put Hugo on my approved list.' I clapped my hands together. All I had to do now was write to the address Hugo gave me when we were at the café and ask him to call for me. Then we'd be free to see each other as much as we liked. I beamed at Fran. 'I can't believe it worked!'

Though I'd been optimistic my older brother wouldn't let me down, or snitch on me to Pop, I hadn't been completely sure he'd do it for me. We had what I suppose was a typical sibling relationship – we bickered frequently and rarely expressed our affection for each other, but affection was there, nonetheless, despite the way our lives seemed to have diverged as we grew up, as distinct now as our physical differences. Bobby was at college studying engineering and would join Pop at Cranshaw Construction when he graduated. The only thing I'd been invited to join was Ma's Tupperware parties.

'I can't believe it either,' Fran said, her face like a wet fish.

I sighed. 'You could at least try to seem happy for me.'

Fran pursed her lips and hesitated before speaking. 'Lenny, you hardly know this man. And you're only seventeen. How old is he, do you know?'

'Mid-twenties I'd imagine, but what's that got to do with anything? I won't be the first girl to be courted by an older man.'

'Is that what he's doing? Courting you?'

'I certainly hope so.' I laughed.

139

Fran shook her head. 'Lenny, you don't know this man from Adam.'

'Honey, you worry too much.' I took her hands in mine. 'And I appreciate your concern, I really do, but I've had it with this place, with everyone telling me how I should be. I just want to be myself, but I've realized I don't even know what that is. Isn't that crazy? But I think Hugo might actually be able to help me figure it out. So I'm not going to do what the teachers say I should, or my parents, or even you, my dear friend. And if I were in your shoes, I'd do exactly the same.'

I scanned her face, trying to find that little hint of admiration for my rebelliousness that I'd seen before, but there was no sign of it behind her knotted eyebrows and downturned mouth. All I saw was an upper-class English girl used to keeping quiet even in grief, to being obedient even when facing a loveless marriage.

She shook her head. 'I couldn't.'

'I know you think that,' I said gently. 'But you could *try*. Only you can make things change. You won't be the first girl to stand up to your parents, however hard it may be.'

'I can't, I shouldn't,' she said, more harshness in her voice now, but I heard the quiver of fear in it, too. 'And maybe you shouldn't either.'

I sighed. 'I've had enough of *should* and *shouldn't*. I'm going to do what I *want*.'

'But, Lenny, maybe this man just wants to take advantage of you, have you thought of that?'

I had, as it happens, and the idea was rather thrilling. And then it occurred to me: was my friend a little jealous? Jealous of my ability to plunge, fearless, into this adventure? Jealous of my passion for a man, something she clearly didn't have for her own fiancé?

I squeezed her hands, leaned forward and said quietly but firmly, 'I'm willing to risk it.'

6

Fear skitters down her spine when he smiles at her. His body is so close to hers she can feel his breath on her face. Her legs are trembling and she puts a hand onto the wall behind her in case they buckle. Her nose fills with that familiar smell – tobacco mingled with rotting rubbish – and she heaves, momentarily suffocated as her lunch fills her throat, and then he is there again, face up on the ground, skin pale, hair matted with blood, eyes closed. *Are you jealous, Florence? Is that it? Are you jealous?*

She turns her head, feels something soft and moist against her face. She pushes it away and runs; she is running along a river, chest hammering, vision blurred, lungs screaming . . .

Flo's eyes open and the image is gone. She is drenched in sweat, heart racing. She turns her head on the damp pillow to see a shard of sunlight streaming through a gap in the curtains, dust suspended in its beam, drifting lazily, weightless and unhurried. She is awake and the dream has dissolved, but it has left her shaken.

She hears a meow and sees Eric push open the bedroom door and weave his way into the room through the smallest of gaps. Did he wake her? Is that what brought her back from the past? He jumps up on the bed and paws at the duvet, a low purr attesting to his satisfaction at this forbidden act. It has been a game between them for a good seven years now, since Flo got him from the rescue shelter. He is not allowed on the bed, never has been, and he knows it, just as she knows he will flout the rules every time she fails to properly close the bedroom door. But this morning she doesn't push him off. She is glad of his presence, glad of his easy contentment as he settles down on the duvet, paws resting on her right leg, and as she strokes him, she feels her pulse ease, her skin cool.

Memories flit across her mind like stills from a film, faces only half seen, events only partially clear. Even those she does think she remembers properly may be merged with later ones, or distorted by the filter of time, until it is near-impossible to know exactly what she felt, what she did, so long ago. Is it the same for Lilli? Is she, with the contamination of hindsight and the contrived packaging of a novel, relating things as they actually were or as she *thinks* they were? How much of her is embellished for the character she wished to put on the page? Did she really think Flo jealous of her romance with Harry – this *Hugo* she has created? Did she really feel that her worry was out of envy, not concern?

The only thing Flo knows for certain is that she loved that girl. Like the memory of a book read long ago, the plot forgotten, leaving only the emotions it provoked, she knows she loved Lilli like the sister she didn't have, like the sibling she lost. The feeling is distilled into an essence that has never left her.

She moves her legs and Eric looks up, annoyance on his whiskered face. She gets out of bed, walks to the window and draws back the curtain on another glorious day, but she is suddenly full of sorrow. She didn't intend to leave Lilli to go off alone. She only didn't turn up that night because she'd just killed a man.

She takes a deep breath and lets it out slowly. She hasn't wanted to admit that to herself for a very long time. She's pushed it away, buried it deep, but the book is forcing it back to the surface. She doesn't want it back in her thoughts once again, doesn't want to remember what she did.

She killed Harry.

Flo was in a strange mood when Alice turned up that morning — still in her pyjamas and dressing gown at 11am, that book she's been reading — *The Way We Were* — in her lap. But she wasn't actually reading it, just staring at the cover, eyebrows knitted together. And she said she didn't want to do any lino printing today, couldn't concentrate; she wanted to go on a day trip instead and would Alice come? Alice actually wanted to stay in the house, carve the next layer of her latest print, but she's never been very good at saying what she wants, so here she is, in the passenger seat of Flo's battered brown Mini, Ernie in the back.

'Is this car roadworthy?' Alice can't stop herself asking. A scene blooms in her head — the Mini a ball of flames on the motorway, the two of them trapped inside.

'Yes, dear. It may look like a rust bucket but it's very

reliable,' Flo says. 'Looks aren't everything, you know.' She laughs and Alice manages to smile back. At least Flo's mood seems to have brightened. She switches on the radio and starts singing along. 'Always loved Stevie Nicks,' she says. 'Such a colourful life.'

'Who's that?' Alice asks.

Flo laughs. 'I feel old.' She looks over at her. 'Who do you listen to then? Go on, educate me. Who do young people rate these days?'

Alice shrugs. 'Taylor Swift. Ariana Grande. Beyoncé. Dua Lipa.'

'I've heard of Beyoncé, at least,' Flo says. 'When I was your age, it was Cilla Black and Cliff Richard.'

'*Cliff Richard*?'

Flo laughs. 'Yes, dear. Back then he was a dreamboat. The British Elvis, they called him. Girls would throw themselves at him during concerts. I was desperate to go and see Cliff Richard and the Shadows play live but Peter didn't approve of rock 'n' roll. Thought it was a bit *common*.'

Alice looks sideways at Flo. 'Why did you split up?'

'Peter and me? Oh, we never should have married in the first place. It was arranged by our parents. I mean, they wouldn't have put it like that, but we grew up together in Stow and our families had always imagined we would marry, so they pushed us towards each other, encouraged us to go to dances and social occasions together, pressured him to propose and me to say yes. We were the right *sort* for each other, I suppose. My parents saw no need for me to look elsewhere.'

Alice looks at Flo. 'Did you love him? Did you want to be married to him?'

Flo shrugs. 'I don't think I knew what love was, back then. I was only eighteen when we married, remember. He was a couple of years older. I think we both thought marriage was simply what you did, and so I suppose we just accepted it as a fait accompli. I was born into a certain social class and my parents had very specific expectations of me. It wasn't in my upbringing to rebel.' She pauses and Alice wonders what she's remembering that she doesn't say. It surprises her to hear this, that confident, outspoken Flo didn't just tell her parents where they could shove their *right sort*. As if she's read her thoughts, Flo adds, 'It takes a strong person to swim against the tide, and I wasn't that person back then.'

Alice doesn't say anything. She isn't that person either, and she doesn't even want to be – at least, she doesn't think so. She hasn't ever *meant* to swim against the tide, but somehow it's happened anyway. She's never fit in, never been able to live up to anyone's expectations, however hard she's tried – and she really has tried. She tried to do what young people her age are supposed to do, to drink and smoke in the pub with Ella and Vicky, to go to parties and get pissed and dance, to get together with one of the popular boys like Liam, to *live a little*, but it only resulted in tragedy. And now she's trying to do what her parents want for her – the business degree, the stable career path, the good, safe office job with decent pay – but she knows she'll somehow mess that up, too; she won't fit in at university either and it will end in disaster, like everything she does. Instead she just wants to stand rigid and let life move around her. If she keeps still enough, maybe she won't cause any more tragedy.

'Anyway,' Flo is still talking, 'we expected children to come along, but when they didn't, things became fraught between us. I think both of us thought that, even if we didn't love each other, we would both love our children. That would be what made our union worthwhile. We struggled on for ten years, and then I discovered Peter had another woman on the side.'

'What an arsehole,' Alice says.

Flo laughs. 'Well, I suppose he was. But I can hardly blame him. In fact, I thank him for it daily. Though my pride was ripped to shreds, when I found out his mistress was pregnant and he intended to leave me for her, it was almost a relief. I could be free, you see.' She signals and pulls out to overtake the car in front. 'For me, life started at twenty-eight,' Flo says. 'But by God, I've made the most of it since.'

She laughs and turns the radio up. Ernie woofs his approval of the song. Alice looks out the window at the fields and the trees and wonders where she'll be when she's twenty-eight, *who* she'll be. Ten years feels like such a long time. She tries to picture a future version of herself but the scene is unclear. It feels out of reach, unattainable, like there's a gulf between the person she is now and the person she thinks she should be then. She has no idea how to get from here to there. Her life stretches in front of her like an endless blank page; she should find that exciting, but all she feels is fear. What if she does it all wrong? At what point on that blank page will she lose her mother? And how long will her own life last?

Will she reach Flo's age, or will she die next week, her life cut short like Ella's was? The sad thing is, she doesn't know which path she fears more.

⸎

'Where are we?'

'Oxford,' Flo says. 'Where I used to live when I was married. I just had the urge to see the house again.' She pulls the car into the gravel driveway and turns off the engine. 'This is the one.'

The large house is tucked back from the busy Woodstock Road behind carefully tended box hedges, a soft-top Audi parked in front of the garage. Honeysuckle creeps up its façade, trailing around the bay window and the front door. After last night's dream, Flo wanted to come here to remind herself that she was punished for what she did. That she gave herself a ten-year sentence after killing Harry in Lyon.

'I lived here with Peter, it was our first home together – our only home, as it turned out.' Flo peers out of the car window and up at the house. 'My father bought it for us as a wedding present – a sort of dowry for my husband, if you like – although Peter always had a chip on his shoulder about it, since his family weren't quite as rich as mine. It was rather nice inside. This street was quite well-to-do, back in the late fifties and sixties – still is, I suppose. Peter was an accountant for Oxford University; I stayed home and kept house because Peter would have viewed my getting a job as an affront to his pride.' She pauses. 'My God, I was bored!'

She pictures the inside as she remembers it – four bedrooms,

148

a sitting room, dining room, kitchen and pantry, family bathroom and downstairs toilet. So much room to be cleaned and dusted and tidied. So much space to sit empty, waiting for the children that never came. They had all the latest appliances, of course – Peter's idea of a gift was a vacuum cleaner or an electric kettle, rather than the books or the art supplies she wanted – but there was still the washing and the shopping and the cooking, tasks she performed with all the enthusiasm and passion of a prisoner under duress. After growing up at boarding school and in a house with domestic staff who not only ran the household but were company for a young bereaved girl, she was lonely as well as bored.

The house doesn't appear to have changed much, from the outside at least. The door is painted a rich burgundy, much cheerier than the black it had been in her day – Peter didn't want something *different,* he was all about fitting in – and there are flowers in boxes beneath the bay window. Something's missing, though. And then she sees it – a tree stump, thick and low to the ground in the front garden. Of course. The flowering cherry. Her chest jolts to see it and sadness washes over her.

She gets out of the car, walks up the drive.

'What are you doing?' Alice calls out the car window. Ernie hangs his head out and barks once.

'Just taking a look. Won't be a minute.'

She leans down, puts her hand on the tree stump, smooth and warm. Rings dilate out from the centre of the stump, some thicker than others. There should be sixty or so, if it was cut down only recently.

How often she sat on a chair by this tree, needing to escape the confines of the house, attempting to ignore the frustration, loneliness and despair of a loveless marriage. How often she would sit and talk to her dead brother, recounting the myriad reasons she was miserable. Were there *any* happy times? If so, they are dominated in her mind by the unhappy ones: Peter's annoyance if she failed to have dinner on the table when he got home from work at 6pm; hiding her sketchbook away under the bed (*a frivolous activity*, he called her art) and retuning the wireless from her favourite station, BBC Light Programme, to his, BBC Home Service; all the times he demanded his conjugal rights but never bothered to make it anything more than another chore for her.

To be fair, she can see on reflection that he was probably as miserable as she was. The only time they seemed to find some light relief was on the tennis court. Once a week they'd play doubles with Peter's work colleague and his wife, regularly trouncing them, and their mutual admiration for each other's skills (her difficult-to-read serve, his slice backhand) quelled the mutual disappointment just a little, until the wooden rackets were put back in the cupboard and the daily grind resumed.

But that isn't much to show for a marriage, Flo thinks. Not nearly enough.

All the things she could have done in those ten years sit in a parallel life, all the babies they never had in another.

Yes, she paid for her actions in Lyon. She paid for taking a life. She only got early release because of Peter's infidelity.

'Are you okay, Flo?'

She opens her eyes to see Alice has emerged from the car

and is walking tentatively towards her, a gazelle ready to flee at the slightest threat.

'I'm fine, dear. Just tripping down memory lane a little, and it's sometimes a bumpy ride.'

'I can't imagine you being pushed into marriage at eighteen, sitting around here doing housework,' Alice says. 'You're so ... forthright. Why didn't you just say no?'

'Like I said, I wasn't always so forthright. And it's scary, going against what others think you should do, isn't it?' Flo throws the girl a pointed look but she turns her head away, leaving the question unanswered. 'And, of course, first you have to figure out what you want for yourself.'

Perhaps Alice would have replied, but it's another, unfamiliar, voice that breaks the momentary silence between them.

'Can I help you?' A woman has come out of the front door and is staring at them, hands on hips.

Flo turns. 'Oh, I'm sorry to disturb you. I just wanted to see the tree.'

The woman gives her a look as if to say *mad old bat*.

'I used to live here, you see, a long time ago.' The woman's face barely softens at Flo's words. 'I planted this tree in fact, when we moved in. It was a memorial of sorts, to my late brother.'

She never told Peter that's what it was, since he wouldn't have understood. Grief was the sort of messy emotion they never talked about, and seeing as she didn't have Lilli to confide in anymore, a tree would have to do.

She looks at the stump again, sees the crude saw marks round the edges. 'When did you cut it down?'

The woman cocks her head. 'Last year. Got too big – was blocking the sun from the front window.'

'Oh,' Flo says. 'What a shame.'

The woman crosses her arms over her chest. 'Is there anything else I can help you with? If not, then . . .'

Flo nods. 'Of course. Yes. I mean, no, there's nothing else. Thank you for letting me look at the tree.'

I didn't, the woman's face says. Flo wonders if she is married, and if it's a happier marriage than hers was, if she is enjoying life in this house.

'Right-ho. Good day to you.' Flo smiles and walks back to the Mini, Alice behind her. They get into the car and Flo turns the key in the ignition.

'Miserable cow,' Alice says, a smile flicking at the corners of her mouth.

Flo laughs, and a moment passes between them that Flo can't quite identify. Understanding, perhaps. Kinship.

'Quite,' Flo says, and pulls away from the curb.

*

Carla is sitting outside on the deck under the sunshade, her laptop open on the table. She spent the morning cleaning the house, vacuuming, washing the kitchen floor, doing all the boring but necessary things she never really wants to do but can no longer avoid, now she doesn't have a job to fill her time. She's been to town and done the food shopping. She's marinated the meat for dinner and prepared a fancy salad, making sure to include cranberries, since Alice really likes them. There's a bottle of white in the fridge and she's even whipped up a cheesecake for dessert – Alice's favourite. One bonus of being jobless has been having more time to bake, and she likes doing that, at least; something for pleasure, not necessity. Today, as she prepared the biscuit base, mixed the lemon zest into the cream cheese, decorated the top with carefully arranged strawberry halves, it reminded her of when Alice was little and they'd sit side by side on stools at the kitchen counter, decorating cupcakes with Smarties. She hopes Alice likes the cheesecake, hopes it will make her smile, like she used to.

But Alice isn't here.

She doesn't know where she is, but presumes she's at Flo's again. She has resisted the temptation to message her, since it will only annoy her. *I know you like to know my whereabouts at all times*, Alice said once, her voice dripping with animosity.

So here she is, sitting outside in the early afternoon, scrolling through recruitment websites, her legs stiff from lack of movement. So far, she's applied for three jobs and found two more potentials. There are no other publishing jobs in the town – Pulham Press is the only such company for miles around – and she doesn't want to commute to the city every day, so the only PR jobs she's found to apply for are at a local wholesale retailer, an events company in the next town over and a *lifestyle start-up*, none of which are in her field of experience, nor are they filling her with joy. The start-up has invited her for an interview later today, though her continued scrolling tells her how little confidence she has in that.

It's clear that, in the fourteen years since she last applied for a job, she's become a relic of a bygone age. She scrolls past roles such as Social Media Manager and Head of Content as though they are written in a different language. Who wants to spend their days posting things on social media or writing for websites? It fills her with horror. And it worries her, too, because who's going to want a middle-aged, tech-inept books bore to work for them? Everyone wants young, clued-up, social-savvy people these days. Experience counts for little when technology moves so quickly.

'Could you retrain?' Flo asked when she popped round briefly the other day with a bunch of flowers, Alice clearly having mentioned her redundancy.

'In social media? I can't think of anything worse,' Carla had said, before adding, 'How's Alice getting on at yours?'

Flo had pursed her lips, just a little. 'You leave Alice to me,' she'd said, 'and focus on you. Maybe this is an opportunity for change, Carla, a chance to pursue a passion, perhaps.'

The problem is, she doesn't know what her passions are. She doesn't know what else she wants to do, what she even *could* do, and the more she thinks about it, the more useless she feels.

Redundant.

She shuts the lid of her laptop and stands, stretching her arms above her head. Her right elbow hurts, as it often does these days – a sort of RSI, she suspects, born of years sat at a desk in front of a computer; the twenty-first century equivalent of Flo's dodgy knees and another sign that she is getting old, that her youth is in the past. *Stop it*, she tells herself, *you're forty-six, not eighty-six.*

She goes into the house, opens the fridge and pours herself a glass of chilled apple juice. She sips it – sweet and cool down her throat – as she stands in the kitchen, the tick of the wall clock loud in the silence of the house. Two hours until her interview. Her eyes catch the print propped up on the mantelpiece in the sitting room, a picture of a dog in a garden surrounded by trees. Alice brought it home for her after she lost her job. *For you,* she said simply. *Sorry about the job.* It's quite simple, but there's loveliness in its simplicity, and to Carla it's the most beautiful thing in the world because making it put a smile on her daughter's face. When she gave it to her, pride and joy in that flicker of a smile, Carla had to work hard to stop herself bursting into tears, because in that small act was a glimmer of the old Alice, the pre-accident Alice, when she would share things with her mother, when they would talk and hug and laugh. When she was wanted.

'Thank you, sweetie, this is so lovely,' Carla had said, going in to hug her, but Alice had stood stiff, unable or unwilling to reciprocate, before turning away, eyes down, the shutters closed once more.

Carla drains her glass and puts it on the kitchen counter, walks through the sitting room and up the stairs, drawn, suddenly, to her daughter's bedroom. She pushes open the door and takes in the familiar sight: the pale yellow walls Alice painted herself several years ago, adorned with posters of bands Carla has never heard of; a dog-eared copy of *Hamlet* on top of a haphazard pile of school textbooks on her desk; photos and ticket stubs and postcards tacked to a corkboard next to the window. Carla is drawn to one photo in particular, of Ella and Alice in their early teens, standing in shorts and T-shirts in the foamy shallows of the sea, arms flung around each other's shoulders, smiling. Cornwall, she thinks – that summer when Ella came with them on a week's camping trip. Carla must have taken that photo herself – back then, back when she was wanted.

She used to be wanted so much it was exhausting. Years ago, she used to be wanted to read bedtime stories and play Guess Who? and tie shoelaces and mop up spills and prepare dinners. She used to be wanted at 5am when little Alice would come into her parents' room and snuggle under the duvet – promptly falling asleep and somehow taking up the entirety of their bed – an act that Carla loved, while Rich grumbled in annoyance.

She used to be wanted by Rich, too – at the beginning, back in London when her flatmates suggested he should start paying rent, so often was he at theirs; and later, when he asked her to marry him shortly after the shock of her accidental pregnancy had worn off, an old-fashioned gesture that seemed so right to both of them.

Pulham Press wanted her as well, when she first started. *Gosh, aren't we lucky to find someone with publishing experience in this small town?* Susan had said and Carla had beamed, eager to get stuck in after four years as a stay-at-home-mum, eager to use her brain again, to do more than just wipe up spills and prepare meals (though of course she still did that, as well).

Then Rich didn't want her anymore.

Now her job doesn't want her anymore.

And, she suspects, Alice doesn't want her much either.

So what's the point of her now? That's what she asks herself when she scrolls through job websites, when she reads descriptions of roles she has neither the skills nor the inclination to do, when she sips a cool glass of apple juice, waiting for her hot flush to subside. *What's the bloody point of me now?*

The thought depresses her and she sits down on Alice's bed with a *whump*, as though all the air has gone out of her. She smooths her hand over the bedspread they chose together on a shopping trip to Birmingham a few years ago.

Sometimes she wishes she could wind back ten years, to that chaotic, exhausting period of her life, when Alice was little and she and Rich were together. It wasn't perfect, that time, but it was certain, that's what differentiates it from now – back then, everything seemed *certain*. Now, it's anything but. Where will she be in five years' time, at fifty and beyond? She really doesn't have a clue – it's simply a blank page.

Alone. The thought pops into her head. She will be alone.

She shakes her head, exhales a short huff. Wallowing won't get her anywhere. She should get back to her laptop, back to the job search. She goes to stand, but as she does, her heels kick something under the bed. She reaches down and pulls out an old shoebox; it's quite heavy, and so full the lid doesn't fit properly. She pulls it onto her lap and opens it. Notebooks of different shapes and sizes are packed inside. No, not notebooks – diaries. Alice keeps a *diary*? She never knew that, has never seen her writing one. But judging by the number in this box, she's done it for years. Carla picks one up and flicks through it – her daughter's handwriting scrawled across pages and pages in various colours of ink. Her pulse revs up a notch. It's like finding the key to Alice's brain, a secret passageway into her head, which she usually keeps so tightly locked, so unavailable to her mother.

But no, she can't. She couldn't possibly read them. It would be a betrayal, an act of treachery. There's no question.

She puts the diary back with the others in the box and closes the lid, slides it back under the bed. Then she stands and leaves the room, retracing her steps down the stairs and back into the kitchen, where the clock ticks on in the empty house.

The Way We Were

LYON, FRANCE, NOVEMBER 1957

It was such a thrill to see Hugo walk through the gates and up the drive and announce himself to the school secretary as my cousin one Thursday early evening. The only downside was seeing Fran's anxious little face as I near-skipped my way down the corridor to meet him. I did so hate making her worry, but I also felt it would do her good to see that taking a little risk now and again wasn't going to do me any harm. I mean, Hugo was an upstanding member of the community and a sophisticated gentleman; and if he did have any wicked intentions towards me, well, I confess, that only enhanced his appeal. I was ready for wicked intentions; I positively craved them, and where was the harm in giving in to what I craved?

I just about melted at the sight of him, and it took all my acting abilities to hold back from throwing myself on him in front of Madame Devillier, lest our school secretary suspect we were anything other than cousins. But still, I was surprised she couldn't see the gravitational pull between us. To me it was a tangible thing, a visible thread that wound me towards him – to those arms, that face, those lips.

'Shall we?' Hugo said, putting his arm out for me to take, before turning to the secretary and saying in French, 'I'll have my little cousin back by curfew.'

Madame Devillier nodded and smiled, clearly won over by his charm – who wouldn't be? – and I linked my arm through his and we walked out through the door, down the path and through the gate to freedom. Oh, the relief! I could feel the weeks of frustration at being cooped up in that place drain out of me like pus from an infected wound.

As we turned the corner, hidden now from the school by the high box hedge, Hugo turned to me and said in a low voice that seemed to turn my whole being to Jell-O, 'Well, Lenny Cranshaw, you summoned me to fetch you, so tell me, what exactly should I do with you now?'

I took a deep breath to steady my voice. 'I think you should take me somewhere we can have obscene amounts of fun.'

He squeezed my arm and raised his eyebrows. 'I had a feeling you might say that. As it happens, I know just the place.'

Well, of course he did. The place was a little café in a suburb of the city. He drove me there in his 2CV, a modest car with an impossibly French allure which delighted me almost as much as Hugo himself. Everything delighted me that night – the way he lit my cigarette and laughed as I blew smoke out the open window, the way the trees lined up with such precision along the riverside, the way the city's many bridges were reflected in the water of the Rhône below. I can see now, looking back, that my view of everything that night was absurdly rose-tinted. Lyon was rather grubby in the fifties, its buildings grey with pollution from its many factories, its Old Town dilapidated and insalubrious. But I didn't see any of that, just like I didn't see anything but loveliness in Hugo. I was desperate for new experiences and easily impressed; as a result I viewed everything through a filter of delight and naivety.

The café was nothing special from the outside. We parked nearby and I took his arm as we walked down the side street, my face aching from smiling. I could hear music and laughter as we approached. The door was propped open and several people stood outside clutching drinks and cigarettes.

'Hugo, *chéri*, you made it!' A woman touched his arm as we reached the group and he leaned in to kiss her, once on each cheek.

'Celeste Pascale, may I introduce you to the delightful Lenny Cranshaw.' He smiled at me and I felt a rush of pride that I, the delightful Lenny Cranshaw indeed, was on the arm of this delicious Englishman.

'*Enchantée*,' Celeste replied, her eyes flicking almost imperceptibly up and down my body and I felt a thrill to realize this woman envied me Hugo's arm.

'Very pleased to meet you,' I said. 'This place looks just swell.'

'You're American,' she said, and I wondered whether anyone I met tonight wasn't going to state the obvious the first time I opened my mouth.

'Don't hold it against me,' I replied with a smile, and she only laughed.

'You've got a live one here, Hugo.' She leaned towards him, so close he could surely feel her breath on his face. 'Trust you,' she said in a low voice. Then she took my hand and I reluctantly relinquished my grasp of Hugo's arm. 'Come on, let me introduce you to everyone.'

Celeste was half English, half French, and she seemed to embody everything I wanted to be. She spoke perfect French, of course, and switched easily between the two languages depending on who she was introducing me to. She was tall and glamorous and sassy and smoked incessantly and wore chic clothes and worked with Hugo at the car company – and it was this last detail, more than any other, that had me in awe of her. She wasn't in a managerial role, like Hugo, but as an administrator in the European exports department, she was a crucial part of everything that went on there. She was the grease in the wheels, Hugo told me, the oil in the engine. *As necessary to us as air is to breathe.*

It was clear they had once been more than just co-workers. But I didn't mind. *I* was on Hugo's arm now, and despite that initial flash of envy in Celeste's face, she was warm and welcoming to me, and made it her mission to introduce me to everyone in that little café. For the life of me now, I can't remember any of their names and hardly any faces, but I know they were a mixed bunch: wiry young men smoking Gauloises; older, paunchier ones sitting at the bar gesticulating over their drinks; a smattering of wives and girlfriends setting the world to rights at a long table at the back; all of them clearly used to occupying this nondescript neighbourhood café on a regular basis.

What linked them all that night – perhaps all nights, but especially *that* night – was wine. It was a Beaujolais Nouveau party, Hugo had told me in the car on the way. Earlier that afternoon the year's vintage had been released, and that night, in that little café, it was our job to sample it and, hopefully, give it our seal of approval. In other words, I realized quite quickly after entering the café, we were here to get absolutely sloshed.

'Here,' Celeste said, passing me a glass. '*Santé.*'

I touched her glass with mine in a toast and took a sip, and I swear as soon as the plum-red liquid touched my lips, I felt giddy. I'd never tasted wine (Pop preferred beer and bourbon, Ma was partial to a martini), and now there I was in a place where it clearly flowed freely, with no rules or regulations as to how much of it I should drink or how I should behave while I did. I don't think I'd ever been more excited in my whole little life.

Celeste lit a cigarette for me, and then herself.

'You make a nice-looking couple.' She nodded at Hugo, who was standing at the bar talking to a man of a similar age. Hugo's shirt sleeves were rolled up and his tie was loose, which only enhanced his appeal, and when I caught his eye and he flashed his electric smile at me, I felt a little wobbly that I was here with him, that Celeste and probably most other people thought he was mine and I was his. I couldn't stop a very unsophisticated grin from invading my face.

'Oh dear,' she smiled. 'I see it's already too late to save you.'

My eyebrows shot up. 'Whatever do you mean?'

Celeste put her hand on mine and gave it a squeeze. 'I don't think it's even worth me giving you any advice, *chérie*, you're clearly too far gone for that. But just remember,' she leaned forward, 'Hugo's no schoolboy.'

'I know that.' I beamed. 'I don't want a schoolboy.'

Celeste sighed. *'Evidemment.'* She took a sip of her wine and I saw that her eyes were glazed – who knew how long she and the others had been there already? Then she laughed and shook her head. 'Come on, let's have some fun.'

The evening passed in a blur. What I remember of it now is simple food – thick slices of cooked ham and boiled potatoes in thin gravy – eaten at long tables, with copious amounts of wine and hunks of bread to mop up the bouillon. I remember the delight on Hugo's face as I made the table laugh with embellished anecdotes about Pop's attempts at social climbing and my exploits growing up in Brooklyn – tales that, in my memory, became ever more hilarious to everyone the more we all drank. I remember Celeste leaning in to me, planting a kiss on my cheek, telling Hugo he had to take care of me, and I recall how my innards turned to purée when he put his arm around me and said *nothing would please me more*. And I remember the dancing. I don't know what happened to the tables, or where the music was coming from, but I remember how we danced until we were breathless, how I smiled until my cheeks hurt, how we paraded around the room, hands on each other's hips in a snake formation, doing the cancan.

And then it was time to go.

'I can't bear it,' I said to Hugo as he led me out of the café, determined to drive his 2CV in an approximation of a straight line to get me back to the school before curfew.

'I want to see you again,' he said, his breath a heady mix of wine and tobacco, 'so I have to be a good boy and deliver you to matron in time for bed.'

He smiled wolfishly, but I took his mocking personally. That night I'd finally felt like I was being treated as an adult, as the person I wanted to be, but here he was reminding me that I was a 17-year-old schoolgirl stuck in a prison.

'I just can't go back there.' I grabbed his arm. 'Take me somewhere else, or back to the café – anywhere but there.'

He looked at me and turned the key in the ignition. 'If there's one thing I've learnt, darling Lenny, it's that playing the game can get you a very long way.'

He was right, of course.

Then, before I even knew what was happening, he leaned over and kissed me with such passion I thought I'd faint on the spot. I felt the roughness of his stubble on my face, his hand in my hair, the taste of Beaujolais and Gauloises in my mouth, and I just wanted it to keep going, on and on. After he pulled away, it was like I'd had a revelation: so that's how it was meant to be. Poor Walter, the boy whose wet kisses had introduced me to the activity back in Brooklyn, really hadn't had even the slightest clue.

'Stealth,' Hugo said. 'It's all about stealth.' He grinned, sat back in the driver's seat and pulled away from the curb to a screech of brakes behind us. If I hadn't just dissolved on the spot during that kiss, I might have wondered if I was going to make it back to the chateau in one piece.

7

Alice feels lighter, somehow, after her day out in Oxford with Flo and Ernie. They have wandered around the covered market, eaten pasties by the river in Christchurch Meadow, visited an art shop on the high street that Flo remembered from years ago, and now they have left the city limits and are on their way home, Ernie asleep on the back seat.

'What a lovely day!' Flo says. 'Shame my blasted knees are playing up after all that walking.' She turns to Alice. 'I don't suppose you feel like driving back?'

'*Me*?' Alice points to herself and then feels silly, since it could only be her – unless Ernie has become the world's first driving dog.

'You *can* drive, can't you?'

Alice shakes her head. 'I haven't got my licence.'

'Oh, I see. Still learning?'

'No,' she says. 'I had one lesson after I got my provisional licence, but I didn't like it.'

Her head spirals back to that day, a couple of months after her seventeenth birthday, when her mother stood at the doorway biting her nails as the instructor invited Alice to sit

166

in the driving seat. The feel of the wheel beneath her hands, the power of the accelerator under her foot, the danger and destruction they promised. She could crash the car. They could end up in a ditch somewhere or in a ball of fire on the motorway. She could kill someone just like Ella.

So she told her mum she didn't want any more lessons, she didn't need to learn to drive – she'd just use public transport, it was better for the environment anyway. The look of relief on her mother's face convinced her she'd made the right decision, even though a tiny part of her wished she'd at least tried to persuade her otherwise.

Flo nods, as though what she's heard is no surprise to her. 'Want to try again? I could teach you if you like?'

Alice shakes her head.

'Go on, just give it a go.'

She fiddles with her hands in her lap. Ella couldn't wait to learn to drive, to have the freedom to go anywhere she wanted, whenever she wanted. She'd been saving the majority of her Saturday job money in the vain hope that one day she'd have enough to buy a second-hand banger.

C'mon, Alice, live a little.

Alice doesn't trust herself to open her mouth because she knows a negative response will come out of it. So instead she forces herself to nod.

'Wonderful!'

The smile on Flo's face gives her a rush of confidence. Perhaps she can do it, perhaps she won't mess it up. Perhaps she won't harm anyone.

Flo drives them a short way along the road home before

turning right down a country lane. She puts on the handbrake and turns off the engine.

'Looks pretty deserted here – let's give it a go. Out you get.'

They swap seats and as Alice slides behind the wheel, her fleeting confidence drains away. *What am I doing?* She touches her scar, feels the rawness of it, the uneven skin, remembers the broken glass searing her flesh. She hears the screech of tyres on tarmac, the smell of rubber, the sickening crash as it ploughed into the wall. *I can't do this. I can't do this.* She looks at Flo, holds her gaze in a silent plea.

But Flo nods to the wheel. *You* can *do this.* She doesn't need to say it out loud; her face is set, determined, calmly confident. 'Now, put your hands at ten and two, push down very lightly on the accelerator and bring up your clutch foot until you feel the engine engage,' she says. 'Then take off the handbrake.'

Alice does as instructed and the car stalls.

'Again.'

Her hands feel sticky on the wheel. She does it again and the car bunny-hops once and then stalls. Ernie barks, awake now, and she catches his expression in the rear-view mirror: *what on earth are you doing?*

'I can't do it.' Panic bubbles up inside her. *Take a chill pill,* Ella would always say when Alice worried about something.

'It just takes practice. Just like your lino printing. You made mistakes with that at first, too, but now look what beauty you produce!' Flo smiles. 'Give the accelerator a little more power and try to be smoother with the clutch.'

Alice tries again and the car revs alarmingly, but then starts to move down the lane.

'That's it, you're doing it!' Flo claps her hands and Ernie gives an appreciative *woof.*

Alice looks at her and smiles, before the car stalls again.

'Better. Now try again.'

They spend half an hour in that lane, until the bunny-hops become less frequent and the distance covered before stalling becomes ever greater, and with each attempt Alice feels a little less incapable, a little more in control.

'What a great start,' Flo says eventually. 'But I think you're right, it's best if I drive home.' She laughs. 'We'll do this again, though, yes? Make it a regular thing?'

Alice hesitates. There's something about being with Flo that takes the edge off her fear, makes her feel that perhaps things aren't as scary as she thought. *She's* the chill pill.

'Yes,' she says, 'okay.'

Carla's job interview doesn't last long. The position appealed because it was close by, in the same town, and by the time the interview is over she realizes that location was, in fact, the job's only appeal.

She'd put on her best suit especially, the one she wore to big events at Pulham Press – sales conferences, press events, book fairs – but as soon as she arrived, she felt like a besuited dinosaur next to the bright young things wearing T-shirts and jeans who occupied the offices of BoxYourLife, *a new monthly subscription box carefully curated for the Millennial lifestyle,* as the job advert had said.

'We're looking for someone who's *hungry* for it,' the man

who'd interviewed her – Max, a bearded twenty-something wearing skinny jeans, a checked shirt and a flat cap – had said, 'who's willing to put their heart and soul into this company, to really be a key part of the team, y'know? We're not a nine to five sort of place, Carla, d'you know what I mean? It's a lifestyle thing, right?'

She knew then that she wouldn't get the job, that she wouldn't fit in with this group of dynamic young entrepreneurs who seemed as alien to her as she undoubtedly looked to them. She knew, too, that she didn't really want it, that she'd turned up to the interview out of fear of what she'll do when her redundancy money runs out, not out of passion for a business she doesn't really understand, run by a team half her age.

It is five o'clock when she walks into the empty house, kicks off her shoes, throws her suit jacket over the back of a chair, pours herself a glass of wine and collapses onto the sofa. What's wrong with her? The excitement and enthusiasm of her early career seem a long time ago. It's as though those years at Pulham Press have numbed her somehow, and she has no clue what would excite and enthuse her now, let alone how to pursue it.

She stares at Alice's lino print propped on the mantelpiece. At least her daughter has found a new passion, even if it's keeping her away from the house, from her. She *still* isn't home. *Where are you?* she longs to text, her fingers fiddling with her phone. *I miss you.* But she doesn't send the message, she picks up her wine glass instead, blinking back tears as she drinks. How did it get to the point that she won't tell her daughter she misses her for fear of driving her further away?

Her mind wanders back to the box of journals. If she read them, maybe she could figure out how to put a smile back on her daughter's face; perhaps she'd know how to regain the closeness they once shared. Carla *needs* that closeness. It's the only good thing in her life, her only passion. And surely Alice needs it, too; surely it can't be good for either of them to live with this ever-widening gulf between them?

But no. She couldn't possibly read them.

Could she?

She takes another sip of wine as her brain answers quietly, *perhaps*.

The back gate creaks and she jumps, spilling wine down her top.

'Alice?' Her heart leaps.

'Hi, Mum.' Her daughter appears through the patio doors. Her cheeks are flushed and there's a brightness in her eyes that Carla hasn't seen lately.

'You okay? Where have you been?'

'Oxford, not really sure why, think Flo's on a bit of a nostalgia trip or something.'

'But you had a good time?'

'Yeah.' Alice pauses. 'I drove.'

Carla's eyebrows shoot up. 'What?!'

'Well, I mean I didn't really *drive*, but on the way back Flo gave me a lesson. She says she'll teach me, if I want.'

Carla doesn't know what to say. Her daughter, behind a wheel. She might crash – all new drivers have a minor crash or two, don't they? Or worse, someone might crash into her. A useless driver. Someone texting on their bloody mobile phone when they should be paying attention. Or a drunk, veering over the centre line. It happens. Just like that car crashed into Ella. It really *happens,* it's not just her thinking the worst. It's proven to happen, time and time again. And she can't bear it, she can't bear to think that her beautiful daughter, her only passion, could end up . . .

Alice is looking at her and that brightness has gone from her eyes. Something has switched off in her face and a blind has come down. 'You don't want me to,' she says and Carla flinches at the coldness in her voice.

'No, it's not that. I just think . . . after everything . . . are you sure it's a good idea? I thought you'd decided it wasn't for you?'

Alice shrugs. 'I don't know.'

'I mean, if you want to you can, of course, sweetie.' Carla hesitates. 'But you don't *need* to drive, you can get the bus into Birmingham for uni. It's probably quicker anyway, with the bus lanes.' She steps forward towards her, but Alice moves back, out of reach. Carla thinks she's going to say something else, going to insist, but she doesn't, she only lets out a sigh – a huff, really – and turns away, stomping out of the room. Carla hears her daughter's footsteps heavy on the stairs as she stands there alone, an odd mix of feelings competing for space in her head. She didn't tell her no; she didn't say she couldn't, and it *is* quicker with the bus lanes – so why does she feel like she's done something wrong?

'Dinner won't be long!' she calls after her, her voice fading as she adds, almost to herself, 'I made cheesecake.'

'Not hungry,' is the muted reply.

The next morning, Alice walks quickly down the street to Flo's house. Tension fills her chest, rising up from her diaphragm to her neck, clutching at her heart and twisting around her windpipe.

Are you sure, Alice? Her mother had said. *I thought you'd decided it wasn't for you?* An innocent comment on the face of it. A true comment, in fact. But it's the anxiety on her mum's face, the quicksand of her worry, that frustrates Alice. As much as she tries to stop it, as much as she tries to picture Flo's contented, open, carefree face instead, she can't help her mother's expression erasing that and invading her head like a virus. If she does this, if she keeps learning to drive, it's only going to end in disaster or tragedy, so it's best not to risk it, it's best not to even try.

When she reaches Flo's house she knocks – three short, sharp raps – and then uses her key to let herself in. Ernie is at the door to greet her, tail wagging furiously, and she bends down to pat him, the delight on his face easing her frustration just a little. She walks down the hall, expecting the place to be empty, Flo ensconced in her studio, but instead she's in the kitchen, and it occurs to her that Flo hasn't done much printing lately.

'Hello, Alice, dear.' Flo looks up from the kitchen table, where various papers and a map are spread over the surface. 'Are you all right?' Alice feels sure she can see her bad mood like a dæmon on her shoulder.

'Fine.' She can't quite bring herself to smile. 'What are you doing?'

'Oh,' Flo says, looking back at the map. 'Just thinking, I suppose.'

'Are you going somewhere?' One of the items lying on the table is a holiday brochure, Alice sees. The Eiffel Tower, some lavender fields, a picture of a city at night, its bridges glowing golden in the dark. Alice hasn't been to France since that week in Biarritz with her parents years ago, before they divorced, before Ella died. She had the chance to go on a history trip to northern France with school last year but it wasn't long after Ella's death and she couldn't – too distressed, too fearful to leave her mum and go abroad. Now, going anywhere foreign feels out of reach, the idea languishing somewhere on the other side of the barrier that has solidified in the two years since she lost her friend. Anything could happen if she went abroad – the plane could be shot down, the coach could crash in a tunnel, she could get blown up by terrorists in Paris or mugged in Barcelona or pickpocketed in Berlin, or worse, something could happen to her mum while she's away. *I'll take you to France sometime instead,* her mum had said at the time, *we'll go together.* But they never have.

'I'm not sure – maybe,' Flo says, with a half-laugh. 'I suppose I'm thinking of visiting an old friend. We used to be very good friends, but that was a long time ago.'

Alice slides into a chair, looks at the places Flo has circled on the map. Paris. Lyon. Avignon. 'What happened?'

'Life conspired against us, I suppose.' Flo shakes her head. 'It's been sixty-two years, can you believe it?'

'Wow.' Alice's eyebrows shoot up. 'You're so old, Flo.'

Flo laughs. 'Ain't that the truth.' She looks at Alice. 'What do you think? Can a friendship be resurrected after sixty-two years?'

Alice shrugs. 'I don't know. I can't really imagine being friends with someone for that long.' She used to think she and Ella would be like that. They'd always be friends because she couldn't imagine her life without Ella in it. But it's only been fourteen years since they met on the first day of primary school and yet it's over already.

She fights it, blinking hard, but she's not strong enough and with an unintentional intake of breath, she feels the tears spill over.

'Oh, Alice, I'm so sorry,' Flo says. 'I didn't think. Your mum told me about your friend. I shouldn't have spoken about this, reminded you.'

Alice jabs at her cheeks, brushing off the tears. 'It's not like I ever forget.'

Flo smiles at her, but there's a sadness in it; of course she understands. She's eighty, she must have known loss – far more than Alice has. Her parents presumably, and a brother, she seems to remember, and didn't she mention she'd lost someone called James, the love of her life?

'I know you don't,' Flo says. 'I was eleven when my big brother died and I still think of him every day.'

Alice can't meet her eyes. Instead she stares at the brochure on the table. 'I think it could,' she says finally.

'Sorry, what?'

'I think a friendship could be resurrected after sixty-two years, if you were really good friends,' she says.

It suddenly feels very important that it is.

Flo can't work today. Can't throw herself into a new project. She's tried, but she can't concentrate, and she's come to the understanding that she won't be able to – not until she's got her past out of her system. Instead she sits at the kitchen table drinking tea, with the book, her laptop and the holiday brochure that came through her door at the beginning of the summer in front of her. Lyon. Lilli.

After Oxford, after reliving those years, she feels compelled to go back to France. It's been sixty-two years since she stepped foot in Lyon, the scene of her crime; sixty-two years since she abandoned Lilli, leaving her to go off alone. She thought she'd put it behind her long ago, thought her marriage was punishment enough, but it turns out it has only lain dormant, waiting to be woken by Lilli's book. Now, in her eighty-first year, it is time to face it again. She needs Lilli to understand, to forgive. She needs to see her old friend again.

After her third cup of tea, she makes another for Alice and carries it out the back door, down the garden path towards the studio, Ernie at her side. She hears the witter of the radio and when she opens the door, Alice greets her with the widest of smiles, an expression of pure happiness that is so unfamiliar yet so glorious on the girl's face – and that, like nothing else has managed throughout the day, lifts the tension from Flo's head in an instant.

'I brought you tea,' she says.

'Thanks, Flo.' Alice takes the mug from her. 'Are you okay?'

'Oh, I'm fi—' Her words are stopped in her mouth by the

sight in front of her. '*Alice.*' She stares at the prints hanging on the line, the prints she can't take her eyes off. She moves closer and inspects them up close. 'These are magnificent.' She looks at the girl and sees the flush of pleasure in her cheeks.

'They're not perfect, I made a few mistakes.'

Flo shakes her head. 'No print is perfect, but those little imperfections create character and make each one unique. They're perfectly imperfect.' She stands back, viewing them with a more critical eye, and though there are indeed some small errors, what she sees most of all is talent – and potential. 'You know,' she adds, 'if you keep this up, you'll have compiled a nice portfolio if you want to apply to art school.'

Alice's smile drops and Flo sees the old frown creep into her features.

'Oh, I couldn't,' she says. She puts the mug to her lips, blows on the hot liquid, eyes cast down.

'Why not?'

'I'm not good enough.'

'I think you are.'

Alice shrugs. 'Well, I'm going to Birmingham to study business, anyway.'

Flo nods. 'Business. Yes, you said.'

'Dad said it'll set me up well for jobs.'

'You said that, too. And it allows you to stay at home while you study.'

'No point spending money on halls, especially now Mum's lost her job.'

Flo looks at her. She can see the worries spinning around her head at the thought of leaving this small town and heading elsewhere to study. And she can picture Carla, telling herself that Birmingham University would help keep her troubled daughter safe. She can see both of them convincing themselves that this low-risk option is the best thing for Alice, but Flo knows it is the worst. She has been there, she once let herself be ushered into the low-risk option – her punishment – and it led to ten wasted years of her life. She can't let Alice do the same, she can't let fear and inhibition and low self-esteem and trauma undermine the talent and sheer joy she clearly has for art.

She just needs to come up with a plan.

The Way We Were

I felt like a changed woman after that night in the café – or two different women, depending on where I was. Hugo called for me once a week, sometimes on a Thursday evening, other times on a Sunday, and I lived for those days like an inmate on day release from Sing Sing.

Though Bouchard didn't appear to suspect a thing, I knew my two lives could never cross in public or I'd surely give myself away (I wasn't *that* good an actress), but they nearly did once, in mid-December, when Hugo had taken me out to see Lyon's famous illuminations (an annual affair that had something to do with the Virgin Mary, a statue and some flooding in 1852, according to my guidebook). We were meandering arm in arm through the crowd near Bellecour, sipping mulled wine and marvelling at the candles in the windows and the lights strung across the streets, when I saw them – a gaggle of girls corralled by two older women, Bouchard and Grisaille. I stopped dead and slid my arm from his, mentally winding back the last few moments in my head. When did he last kiss me? When had I laid my head on his shoulder? Might any of them have seen? But no one in the group appeared to have noticed us at all. Perhaps when I was with him, I looked as different as I felt.

I pulled Hugo a little further away and watched them. I'd known they were going to the festival, too, but I'd thought the city too big to bump into them. And now here they were. It was strange, standing on the outside looking in.

'Missing your friends?' Hugo said in a low voice, a smile on his lips.

'Gosh, no,' I replied, scouring the group for Fran. And then I saw her, standing slightly apart from the rest, looking up at the lights overhead.

Fran, I wanted to call out. *Come and meet Hugo*. The two most important people in my life in Lyon; I wanted them to get to know each other a little. But of course I didn't call out to her and she continued to stand there, among the others yet strangely alone. Perhaps it was the wine, but I had to blink a few times to clear my vision.

When we compared evenings later – The lights! The crowds! The smell of the *vin chaud*! – I didn't tell her I'd seen her and I don't exactly know why.

For the most part, Fran commented little on my escapades with Hugo, though she certainly heard plenty about them. Every week she would lie on my bed and listen to me wax lyrical when I returned from another illicit rendezvous. She humoured me with aplomb (a skill I imagine she'd been trained in since birth), almost appearing to accept this double life I was leading. Almost. But for that fine line on her forehead, which creased ever deeper the more I talked about him.

And then, eventually, she said what I think I'd been expecting her to say for weeks.

'Lenny.' It was early evening and we were standing by the school gates before dinner, mainly so I could sneak a cigarette. 'I know you're having tons of fun, but you're not going to do anything silly, are you?' Her words made soft clouds in the frigid December air.

I smiled. 'I don't know what you mean.'

'Yes, you do. I'm worried about you, Lenny. Worried about what Hugo might do.'

Frankly, I was a little worried, too – about what he hadn't yet done. I was desperate for him to take things further, but so far he'd remained a perfect gentleman. There had been plenty more of those delicious kisses, yet he'd never suggested we go to his place. *Curfew*, he'd say, looking at his watch and giving me a sly grin before driving me back to the school. If he was trying to make me beg for it (and in hindsight I'd say that's exactly what he was doing) then he was certainly succeeding. I didn't even really know what *it* was (I was as ignorant as I was bold, a dangerous combination) but I knew I definitely wanted to find out.

'We're just having fun,' I said to Fran. I took a drag of my cigarette and stuck my hand out between the bars, tapping ash onto the cold ground. The gates were unlocked, I noticed. Did Monsieur Chatagnier, our lacklustre caretaker, ever think to lock them? 'And, hell, I need some fun after being cooped up in this place all week. My time with him is the only thing that makes it all bearable.' I realized what I'd said as soon as I said it, but it was too late to stop Fran's face from falling. 'Apart from you, of course,' I said quickly, squeezing her hand. I meant it – but I didn't mean it quite as much as I used to. Being with Hugo was like living in a Technicolor movie, throwing my days at the school into contrasting black and white. Bouchard's dull lessons now seemed all the duller, Fran's worries all the more wearisome.

She pulled her hand from mine and wrapped her arms around her body. 'I know I'm not as fun as him, Lenny,' she said. 'But I'm only looking out for you. There's something about him that's . . .' she shook her head, 'I don't know.'

'You've only met him once! He might be the love of my life, for all you know. He might be my future husband.'

'I thought you didn't want to get married yet?'

I shrugged. Lately I'd started to see the appeal of marriage if it was to someone like Hugo. I imagined us travelling widely, going to parties, pursuing our professional interests in parallel. Hugo wouldn't hold me back. He was different from other men, just as I was different from other women. That's why we were so perfect together.

'No, not *yet*,' I said to Fran, 'but I wouldn't say no to some-one I love and who loves me back; I simply want to marry the person I choose, Fran, at the time of my choosing, not rush to marry someone selected for me by my parents because he looks the part and comes from the right family.' I saw the hurt on her face but I didn't stop. 'I'd rather take a risk and be happy than play it safe and be miserable. Do you want to be happy, Fran, or stuck in a miserable marriage with someone you don't love?'

In my head I was trying to do her a favour, but the tears in her eyes told me she clearly didn't take it that way.

'I've told you, I don't have any choice,' she said quietly.

I stubbed out my cigarette on the stone wall, threw the butt out between the bars of the gate, and put my hands on her arms. 'You *do*,' I said, looking her in the eyes. 'You absolutely do – you just have to take some risks and be a bit of a rebel.' I paused, remembering what Hugo had said after the Beaujolais Nouveau party. 'A stealthy rebel.'

She shook her head. 'I can't,' she said quietly.

I huffed. I was sick of *can't* and too obsessed with my own life to spend any more time trying to help Fran with hers, if she didn't want to help herself. 'Suit yourself,' I said. 'Come on, I'm ravenous.'

I walked up the driveway back to the chateau without looking back to see if Fran was following. I curse myself for that now, for that small act of dismissal towards my good friend, because it tells me that however much I loved that girl – and I did, I really did – I absolutely took our friendship for granted.

'You can't know how glad I am to see you again,' I said the day he picked me up from the chateau – the last day of 1957 and the start of what I thought would be such an exciting 1958 spent on his arm. Christmas had been agony, since he'd gone away to spend it with his family, as had many of the girls at the school (we crowded around the window when

Gina's movie star mother came to collect her, complete with entourage), but those of us from farther-flung countries or less attentive families had been stuck there over Christmas week, abandoned by our parents who clearly had the means but not the inclination to pay for a well-deserved break from the tedium of French lessons and formal letter writing. To be fair to Madame Bouchard and her pals, they tried their best to make the festive period enjoyable – in their own way, of course. We spent an entire afternoon decorating a giant Christmas tree in the main entrance hall, an activity overseen with dictatorial relish by Sandra, who seemed to be in a permanent huff that her parents had chosen to spend Christmas with friends in St Tropez but hadn't summoned their daughter to join them; we helped Madame Grisaille plan an extravagant Christmas lunch, timings recorded with military precision; and a good couple of hours were occupied writing formal place cards and menus in elegant calligraphy for every student and teacher (had they no one else to spend Christmas with?) who would attend on the day.

By the time Hugo came to collect me from the chateau on New Year's Eve, the anticipation was killing me. I'd been granted special dispensation – with the help of another letter from my darling brother, whom I knew I now owed for probably the rest of my days – to spend the celebration with my 'cousin,' including staying out past midnight, and I'd built it up in my head to be the best night of my whole damned life.

I'd put on my best dress, the one I wore to the opera the night I met him, and Fran, in a simple act of forgiveness (or, at least, acceptance) that seared my heart, had lent me one of her beautiful silk scarves to wear with my coat. 'Be careful,' she'd whispered as I walked out the door. 'I'll have it back in one piece,' I'd joked, purposely obtuse – I just couldn't help myself. The idea that I should be careful, that there was any-thing to be careful *about*, wasn't something I thought worthy of any consideration at all. Fran would understand, one day, when she came to know him properly. I'd hugged her hard and skipped out the door.

But Hugo mocked my enthusiasm. 'You've been locked up in that place all week and now your saviour's come along with the key to let you out. Let's face it, I could be anyone, so long as I had that key.'

My face fell. 'No.' I shook my head. 'Not in the slightest. I don't want it to be just anyone – I want it to be you.'

He laughed, and I saw he was joking. He didn't need me to tell him how much he was wanted, he knew he'd had me from the very instant I first saw him. When I think of myself back then, I cringe at my eagerness, at my inability to hide my feelings.

'Did you miss me even a little bit?' I said, because that was the sort of thing I couldn't stop coming out of my mouth.

He looked at me sideways as we drove along in his 2CV and grinned again. 'I should think a little bit.' He laughed at my expression and leaned over to kiss me. 'Don't worry, Lenny Cranshaw, you are damned difficult to forget about.'

I was beaming all the way to the hotel.

He'd booked us tickets for a masked ball at one of Lyon's most glamorous hotels. It had been built at the end of the nineteenth century, Hugo told me as we drove there, and was

quite the place to be in the pre-war years. I made appreciative noises as he spoke, only half listening as I stared out the
window. Honestly, the past was something that I, so in thrall
to the here and now, struggled to attribute any importance.
Granted freedom from the school on those dates with Hugo,
I simply treated Lyon like my playground, with no real concept of what it had been through in recent history – and of
course it had been through so much. War, to me, was something distant, remote. It had happened when I was too small
to remember on a continent I had no concept of at the time.
Pop never talked about his experiences as a GI, and I'd been
told little at school, where history lessons focused mostly on
the Founding Fathers and the War of Independence. So when
we drove along Avenue Berthelot and Hugo pointed out the
former military building where the Gestapo tortured and
interrogated during the occupation, all I could muster was
a simple *Gosh, how awful* before my mind flitted back to the
excitement of the evening ahead.

I walked into the ballroom on his arm, the black feathered
mask he'd bought me disguising me from forehead to cheeks.
His own was based on a Venetian bauta mask, which gave
him a slightly sinister air. At the bar he bought us both mar-
tinis, and when we toasted each other's health, a thrill went
through me as his eyes met mine.

There was something about Hugo that night – and it
wasn't just the mask. There was a darkness about him that
both delighted and scared me. He drained his martini quickly
and bought another. He kept me close, a hand on my back, a
whispered comment in my ear, as though I was his possession,

his party accessory; and when we danced, he flung me around so vigorously I felt my hair slip out of the pins I'd used to carefully construct the look I wanted. When I tried to pin it back up, he took my hand.

'Leave it,' he said. 'I like you a little dishevelled.' He tucked a strand of hair behind my ear and I near-flinched from the electric charge in his touch.

'The cat still has his cream, I see.'

I turned at the voice. Despite her mask, I should have recognized her from the colour of her hair and her statuesque height, but it had been a few weeks and the only face in my head had been Hugo's.

'Celeste, I should have known.' He kissed her on both cheeks, but I caught a little irritation in his tone.

'Where else would I be? It's the hottest ticket in town.'

'I just thought you were . . . unwell,' he said.

'All better,' she replied with a bright smile, but there was something in the way her eyes locked on his that made me think she was saying something else entirely.

'Hello there H, good to see you.' A man stepped around Celeste and put his hand out to Hugo before his gaze fell on me. 'I don't believe we've met. Although it's hard to tell with these ridiculous masks.'

'We're at a masked ball, Fred, that's entirely the point.' Celeste laughed. 'This is Lenny Cranshaw, the most delightful young thing you ever did meet.'

I flushed under my mask, not so much at the praise but at the fact her tone sounded slightly sarcastic. But hadn't we got on so well, last time?

'How do you do?' I said, taking Fred's hand. 'I think we did already meet – at the opera. That's right, isn't it, Hugo?'

'Oh, yes, I suppose it is,' he replied, though he was looking at Celeste, whose plump red lips seemed all the more pronounced for the mask covering the top half of her face. 'You've a good memory.'

I didn't really, but how could I forget anything about that night?

'Ah yes,' Fred said. '*La bohème*. Frightfully dull, I seem to recall. Pleasure to see you again, Lenny.'

'You should have saved her from his clutches, Fred.' Celeste took a drag on her cigarette. 'Poor little thing.'

Hugo slung his arm around my shoulders and pulled me into him. 'Lenny here can look after herself,' he said. 'Now, can I offer you two a drink?'

Whatever tension I'd detected between Hugo and Celeste I quickly forgot about the more I drank. With Hugo and Fred talking and smoking cigars at the bar, Celeste led me onto the dance floor where we flailed about through several numbers, my hair becoming ever wilder as we jived and bopped to the band, neither of us even slightly bothered to be the only pairing of two girls among a sea of couples. Celeste was infectious company. I was glad her mask didn't cover her mouth because her broad smile seemed to make everyone around her smile, too, and when she danced her happiness seemed genuine and free of the undercurrent I thought I'd noticed earlier. But I was curious about her and Hugo. So when the band began playing 'Que Sera, Sera' I claimed exhaustion and pulled her over to a table.

'Oh, Lenny, that was so much fun!' Celeste said as we sat down. She beckoned to a waiter to pour us two glasses of white wine and immediately put one to her lips, draining half the glass as though it was water. My head was spinning and I imagined I hadn't drunk half as much as her.

'It sure was,' I said. 'I wish we could see each other more. I so enjoy spending time with you.'

She leaned forward then and kissed my cheek. 'So do I, Lenny. You're such a darling. Far too good for . . .' Her face fell as she looked towards the bar.

'For Hugo? Why, Celeste? What do you mean?'

She took another large gulp of wine. 'Oh, he's perfectly charming, but don't be fooled, he's emotionally empty inside. It's like there's something missing. Of course, you can feel sorry for him in some ways, given what happened to his father, but hasn't every family had to endure that sort of thing? It's not an excuse for acting like a . . .' She stopped herself and waved her hand for the waiter.

'What do you mean, what happened to his father?'

She looked at me and laughed. 'You really don't know him at all, do you, Lenny? His father died at Normandy. His mother never got over it and is a nervous wreck, by all accounts. He purposely looked for a job abroad so he could get away from her.'

'He just spent Christmas with her!'

'Is that what he told you?' Her laugh was loaded with cynicism. 'Probably galivanting around London with some chums, I expect, when he should have been here, when I needed him to . . .'

She trailed off and I didn't press her on what she needed Hugo to do. I was too young and naïve to realize what she wasn't saying, what I later came to understand had happened between the two of them.

Instead I looked over at the bar, where Hugo and Fred were laughing at something. Hugo's mask was pushed up off his face and his black tie sat a little askew. When he saw me looking, he raised his glass and smiled in that way he had of utterly melting my insides. But this time it was shame that brought heat to my cheeks. I'd spent all these weeks so concerned by what Hugo thought of me, so determined to make him like me, want me, so excited about having this grown man to distract me from the tedium of the school, that I'd talked far more about me than I'd ever asked about him. In my head I'd wanted to know everything about him, but in fact what little had he told me? A mother in England, yes, though I'd assumed a father, too. A job in the French car industry. A love of wine and current affairs and opera. But nothing deeper, nothing about his background, his childhood, his feelings.

'He lost his father? That's terrible.'

Celeste took a packet of cigarettes out of her clutch purse and offered it to me. I took one and she lit it for me. 'Of course, but as I said, so did many people so that's really no excuse for acting like a . . . *connard*. It was more than thirteen years ago.' She lit another cigarette for herself and took a long drag. I thought about asking what a *connard* was but decided against it – whatever it was, it wasn't a compliment. 'You'll see, Lenny, I'm afraid to say,' she continued. 'You'll see what he can be like, if you stay with him – and if you want my advice, then don't.' She looked at me with an expression I couldn't interpret and then something seemed to occur to her. She fished around in her clutch bag and brought out a pen. 'Here,' she said, scribbling something on a paper napkin. 'This is the address and telephone number for my apartment.' She handed it to me. 'You never know when you might need it.'

'Thank you.' I folded the paper and put it in my purse. My chest swelled a little to know she cared about me, this slightly older, fun-loving, glamorous career girl, the sort of woman I was now determined to be, but nevertheless I pretty much dismissed her warnings about Hugo, as I'm sure she knew I would. Maybe he'd been a brute to *her* (though I could hardly believe it), but he was perfectly charming to me.

Clearly, I was simply the right girl for him.

We didn't make it to midnight. It was around eleven-thirty when he took my hand, pulled me to him and said, 'Let's get out of here.'

I nodded. Tight after all the booze, and with Celeste's words in my head, words that had only increased my fervour for this poor, fatherless man who simply needed someone to open up to (how predictable I was in my quest to be exactly the opposite!), I would have done whatever he wanted.

We left Fred, Celeste and his other friends in the ballroom and slipped out the door. It was cold as we walked down to the river in the direction of his apartment, which he told me wasn't far. The lights from the buildings along the riverside glittered in the water, and we stood for a minute on a bridge over the Rhône, looking down. I couldn't believe I was here, in this beautiful city with this beautiful man, while Fran and the others languished in their suburban prison.

'What a swell city this is,' I said, clutching his arm.

He stared into the water below. 'Damned Krauts blew up nearly all the city's bridges when they retreated.'

'Gosh,' I said. I didn't quite know how else to respond to that, but his mention of the war reminded me of what Celeste had said. 'Hugo, you do know you can talk to me about anything? I know I'm only seventeen, but I'm not a little girl.'

My words seemed to snap him out of whatever reverie he was in. He pulled me to him and kissed me deeply, the warmth of his body flooding into mine. 'Oh, I know,' he said.

'Really – anything,' I repeated. 'I mean, if you want to talk about your father . . .'

A shadow passed briefly across his face before he seemed to recover himself and his mouth broke into a smile. 'Right now, talking is the last thing on my mind.'

He took my hand and pulled me across the bridge, walking quickly, and I felt my skin bristle. His mouth was on mine again before he'd even got the key in his apartment door, and as it slammed shut behind us, his hands were undoing the buttons on my coat, pulling at my dress, sliding up my thighs. So this was it, I thought. This really was it. I was about to find out what all the damned fuss was about.

I really didn't know much about Hugo; Celeste had been right. But I think I learnt more about him from his actions that night than I'd discovered from his words over the time I'd known him. I learnt that he was a little selfish, a little angry; I learnt that something darker, rougher, lay beneath the charm, just as Celeste had said. But I admitted none of that to myself that night. It was only much later that I realized I could have seen it coming, if only I'd been more honest with myself. But I was infatuated and intoxicated, and whoever sees things clearly like that?

Fran woke when I entered our room in the early hours of the morning after Hugo drove me back.

'You're here.' She sat half up and eyed me dozily. 'How was the ball?'

I didn't look at her as I slid into my bed and closed my eyes, my head still full of him, my body still reverberating with the things we'd done. 'It was wonderful,' I said. 'Simply wonderful.'

8

Alice doesn't know where they're going. All Flo said that morning was that they weren't going to do any printing that day – they were going on another outing, a surprise.

'But Harriet's low on stock, she asks me every Saturday when you're going to bring her some more prints,' Alice had said.

'Maybe you should take her some of yours,' Flo replied, as she opened the front door of the house and Ernie bounded out into the driveway, eager at the prospect of a trip.

Alice gave Flo a withering look – *as if* – and followed Flo to the car. 'Just don't make me drive,' she muttered and received a loaded glance in return – Alice's decision to not continue with driving lessons has not gone down well with Flo.

Now, there's a devilish smile on her face that makes Alice think she's up to no good, and it annoys her slightly. She doesn't like surprises, doesn't like being left in the dark, where her imagination can run wild. Still, she likes being in Flo and Ernie's company, so she is content enough to sit there in the passenger seat and be driven to this mystery place, trying to contain her imagination to a low hum in the back of her brain.

'Are you going to try and find your friend, then?' Alice says, when they are on the M40 going south.

'Lilli?' Flo looks at her. 'D'you know, I think I am. In fact, I've already booked a ferry.'

'That's good.' Alice is looking out the window, the fields rushing by. As a child, on long car journeys, she'd pass the time imagining herself leaping and dancing along the telegraph poles like some circus trapeze artist. She could spend hours doing that. She told Ella this once, when they were older, but her friend only laughed and looked at her like she was crazy, so she's never told anyone else. 'I can look after Eric and Ernie when you're gone,' she adds.

'Thank you, dear,' Flo says. 'I could do with a holiday, and France is so lovely in the summer. But I can't imagine how it will feel to see her again, after so long – if I can find her, that is.'

'But you haven't forgotten what she was like.'

'Gosh no – Lilli wasn't the sort of person you forget.'

'Like Ella, then.'

Flo turns to her and smiles. 'Ella must have been a wonderful girl.'

'She was,' Alice says. 'But she could be really annoying sometimes.'

Flo laughs. 'Ah yes, Lilli certainly could be, too. But sometimes you need someone to challenge you a bit, drag you out of your comfort zone.'

'I'm happy in my comfort zone.'

Flo looks at her and a slight frown crosses her features. 'Are you?'

Alice shrugs.

'It's about finding a balance really, isn't it?' Flo continues. 'It's good to be pushed to try new things, to do things you're not sure about – if only so you can find out whether you like them or not.'

'S'pose.'

'Well, that's my theory and I'm sticking to it.' Flo laughs. 'Which is sort of why we're going out today.'

She says no more about it and Alice doesn't dare ask. She stares out the window as Flo hums along to the radio. An hour passes until they turn off the main road and, soon after, pull into a car park. Alice catches a flash of nervousness in Flo's expression, which makes her immediately suspicious. Where are they? What has Flo done?

They get out of the car, put Ernie on the lead and walk towards a building. When she reads the sign she stops dead and her left hand flies to her right arm, finds her scar. Winchester School of Art.

'Now just hear me out.' Flo puts her hands up in a defensive gesture. 'They've got a taster day thing going on today, mainly for the adult education classes they're holding next term, but I thought it wouldn't hurt to come down and take a look so you can see the place. That can't be a bad thing now, can it? No pressure.'

Alice looks around her. People are streaming into the building and there's an energy in the air that prickles the skin on the back of her neck. What would it be like to study here, to spend all day lino printing, to discover other creative activities she might like as much, or even more, if that were possible?

She looks at Flo and nods, and the expression of delight that spreads across Flo's face propels her to take a step towards the building.

Inside, the place is buzzing. Students sit at tables loaded with brochures and flyers, and a big piece of paper sellotaped to a table urges visitors to *Sign up here for taster classes.*

'The life drawing and watercolour sessions still have places available.' A girl in a strappy white top and short shorts smiles at them. 'Starting at 2pm.'

'Do you want to do either of those?' Flo turns to Alice, who only manages a shrug in response. Her head is crowded with thoughts she doesn't want to be there. She rubs at her scar, the skin tender under her fingers, but the thoughts keep coming. She shouldn't study art because it doesn't lead to a career so she'll end up with no job, skint and having to sign on, and then maybe she'll meet the wrong people and something bad will happen. She shouldn't move away from home for university because anything could happen to her in a strange city, with strange people, and her mum will be left behind, sad and lonely in an empty house, and she might get depression and it'll be Alice's fault – all her fault, once again.

'We're actually here to enquire about full-time study for my young friend here.' Flo is talking to the student, but Alice hears her words as though she's underwater. 'It's too late to apply for the coming academic year I know, but could we take a prospectus anyway?'

'Sure,' the girl says. 'But there are sometimes places in clearing, or you could do a year's foundation course first and apply here next year.' She is looking at Alice, talking to Alice, but she can only shake her head. Ernie whines by her side.

'I need to go.' She tugs on Flo's arm. 'I really need to leave.'

A wave of nausea hits her and she is far too hot. The noise in the room is amplified in her ears; people are screaming at her, laughing in her face, telling her *you can't do this, Alice, you shouldn't be here, Alice, it's all going to go wrong, Alice, someone's going to die, Alice*, until she is shaking and she gulps at the air, a fish flapping on the shore, gills fluttering.

'Alice?' Flo says, but she barely hears her; she is running from the room, out the front door and into the open air, pushing her way past people until she reaches a tree and bends over, one hand on the rough bark, taking greedy breaths.

Her pulse is slowing when Flo and Ernie reach her.

'Alice?' Flo says again. 'Are you all right? What happened?'

She shakes her head. 'I can't do it. I don't want to be here.'

Flo looks perplexed and Alice wants to scream at her *it's so easy for you, you've got life all figured out* but she only shakes her head again. 'I told you I didn't want to apply to art school.'

'It was only to look.' Flo puts her hand on Alice's back. 'I thought it would be fun.'

Alice stares at the ground. She thinks how she tried – she really tried – to do the things Ella told her to do, to mould herself into someone she isn't. She thinks of Vicky's party on that awful night, of the make-up Ella put on her and the clothes she gave her to wear, like a uniform to make her seem like everyone else even though underneath she was still herself, still boring, freaky, anxious Alice. She thinks of Ella snogging Nick, pushing her towards Liam, cocky, greasy Liam, and she remembers the panic she felt, the sudden need to be anywhere else but there. Yes, she tried. And look what happened.

'You're as bad as her,' she shouts now, her voice cracking on the last word. She shakes off Flo's hand. 'Stop pressuring me to do things I don't want to do!'

Flo's hand drops from her back and she takes a step away. Her eyebrows crinkle into an expression of what – hurt? puzzlement? – and she observes her as if trying to analyse the thoughts in her head. Alice's breathing slows and her anger dissolves in front of this kind, open face, its smile lines and wrinkles testifying to a long life well lived. She can't imagine having lived so long, having lived so well. *Perhaps*, a small voice says, *if you did go to art school you could be more like Flo.*

'Can we just go home?' she says, her voice soft now.

The old woman smiles but it's full of sadness. 'Okay, dear,' she says.

They walk slowly back to the car in silence, but when they reach it, Flo puts her hand on her arm and Alice sees she's been mulling something over, considering how best to phrase it. 'I'll just say one thing and then I'll be quiet about it,' Flo says. 'You need to figure out the difference between being pushed into things you genuinely don't want to do and being too fearful to do the things you *do* want to do.'

Alice doesn't answer. On the trip home she stares out of the window, half hearing Flo singing along to Fleetwood

Mac, 'Go Your Own Way,' as thoughts tumble over each other in her head.

⚊⚊

It is silent in the house, as it always seems to be when Alice isn't there (and sometimes when she is). Carla sits outside on the patio with the journal in her hands. She smooths her palm over the cover, the word *diary* printed in embossed gold letters. She was hoping to find Alice's current journal, but riffling through the box under her bed, she found there was nothing recent there. Her daughter hasn't written a diary since the day before Ella died two years ago. Perhaps that's reason enough not to do it. What could they possibly teach her, these thoughts from two years ago? But maybe the seeds of her current melancholy were planted back then. Perhaps, if she reads it, she will finally know what's going on in her daughter's head. Maybe she will understand why she heard Alice crying softly in her room last night, and why she felt unable to go and comfort her, for fear her daughter would reject her, wouldn't want her there, would turn that cold stare upon her and tell her to go away.

Standing there on the landing in the dark, barely able to breathe, tears had slipped down Carla's own cheeks at the awful sound of her daughter in distress, at her own inability to take that distress away. Who else did Alice have to turn to? Her best friend gone. Her father and grandparents living abroad. No other close friends to speak of. What if she felt so alone she did something silly? You heard about it – teen girls harming themselves and putting it on the internet. What if

Alice did something like that? What if . . . ? Carla squeezed her eyes shut, forcing the thoughts away. She couldn't even contemplate it, that Alice could hurt herself, or worse. And it would be her fault – again – for failing to protect her, for failing to do all she could to keep her from harm.

And so she will do all she can.

This morning, when Alice left to go to Flo's with barely a backwards glance in Carla's direction, she went up to her daughter's bedroom and brought out the box of journals and picked out this one – the last one.

Now, she flicks through it, sees her daughter's familiar scrawl in black and blue and red and green over pages and pages and pages. How would she have felt if her own mother had read her teenage diaries? Horrified. Embarrassed. Furious. But then her own mother was never interested enough in her to do something like that, always too preoccupied with herself to be overly concerned about her daughter.

For the umpteenth time she wishes there was someone else here to talk to about this. She doesn't wish Rich was back here with them, but she misses what he embodied: a partner in life, a partner in parenting, someone to use as a sounding board, someone to console and sympathize, to be positive when she was negative, to raise her up when she was down, someone to share both the joy and the burden of loving a child.

What would he say if he *was* here? That she shouldn't do this, of course. But something she's learnt over the past eighteen years of being a parent is that she is willing to do anything – even the things she knows are wrong – if she thinks it will help her daughter.

She smooths out a page, the last entry, the day before Ella died, and reads.

I just don't know whether to go to Vicky's party or not. No, actually, I know I don't want to go, but Ella really wants me to, and I just worry that if I don't, she'll be cross with me again. Lately I feel like I can never do anything right and I don't understand why. Doesn't she like me anymore? Aren't I good enough, fun enough, as I am? She just keeps banging on about how I have to put myself out there, how it would be good for me to be more sociable, how I should get together with Liam because he fancies me and then we could double date with her and Nick. But I don't like Liam! He's got greasy hair and intentionally fouls the Year Sevens on the football pitch. I do like Michael, but I'm not going to bring that up again after last time.

So I think I have to go to the party. I just feel really scared that if I'm not careful we might not be friends anymore. If I don't change, she's going to dump me and only hang around with Vicky and Nick. But I don't want to, I REALLY don't want to. WHY don't I want to? Why am I so rubbish and crap? Why don't I like doing the things that Ella does? I'm SO fed up with being me. Why can't I just be like the others? Why can't I be normal? I hate myself!!!

Carla's heart skips when the gate bangs and Alice emerges on to the patio. She stuffs the diary in the pocket of her cardigan, pulse racing.

Did she see?

'Hi, sweetie,' Carla says. 'Good day?' She has to force the

words out and they sound strangled, unnatural, because her head is still taking in what she's read.

Alice hates herself. Alice doesn't want to be herself. Is that how she's felt for the past two years or more? Is that why she cries in her room and rubs her scar until it's red raw?

It shatters her.

Her daughter looks at her, clearly debating what to say. 'Flo took me to an open day in Winchester,' she says finally. 'For the art school.'

Carla's chest sinks, but she smiles. 'Art school? How come?'

Alice comes over and sits next to her on the rattan sofa. She looks down at her feet, then takes a deep breath, as though about to launch into a speech she's been preparing. 'Flo wants me to apply, says I'm good enough.' Alice looks up then, and the hint of a smile on her face makes Carla's heart clench.

'But you're already going to Birmingham. You've got an offer and you're bound to get the grades.'

'I don't have to go.'

'I thought you wanted to?'

'*You* want me to. *Dad* wants me to. But I don't know.' She picks at a loose strand of rattan on the arm of the sofa. 'I've never really known.'

Carla hesitates, looks at the silvery-pink scar trailing down her daughter's forearm.

Perhaps it'll be all right, perhaps it'll make her happy.

If she goes, you won't be able to look after her. If she goes, you won't be able to stop her doing something silly.

'I know you're enjoying the lino printing but is it really a career?' she says finally. 'The job market is tough these days

and degrees are expensive now so it's important to do something that will lead to decent prospects.' Carla hears herself
and cringes. She sounds like her own father twenty-five years
ago. And was he right? She isn't so sure, now. She's had a
steady office job for years and look where it's got her.

'Flo says there are plenty of jobs you can do with an art
degree, it's not just about being an artist exactly.'

'Well, that could be true I suppose . . .' She pauses. *Keep
her here with you, she's safe here.* Perhaps she could do art at
Birmingham uni instead, don't they have a good art school?

'Flo says Winchester's one of the best places to do it,' Alice
says, as though reading her mind. 'And I so like doing it,
Mum. I really like it, it makes me feel good, better than anything else. So I'm thinking maybe Flo's right, maybe I should
apply. I mean, I probably wouldn't get it, it's too late for this
year in any case, although someone said I could try clearing
after I get my exam results, or I could do a foundation course
first, and Winchester's quite far away and I know the living
costs are expensive so maybe I can't do it anyway, although
Flo mentioned that she'd help financially, if I wanted to go,
and maybe I could get a part-time job while I'm there, and
of course I could get the loans and everything, so perhaps I
could do it?'

Carla feels winded. It's the most Alice has spoken in one go
for as long as she can remember. It's the most animated she's
been since before Ella died. *It makes me feel good, better than
anything else.* Isn't that what she wants for her daughter, after
what she's just read? She aches for Alice to feel good about
herself, for that smile to be permanent.

So let her go.

She opens her mouth to say *yes, yes, my darling girl, I just want you to do what makes you happy* but then she's back there, running down the hospital corridor, reaching Alice's bedside, seeing her arm bandaged, feeling the sheer relief, the flood of joy, that she will be all right.

They said she's dead, Mum, Alice had said on that dreadful day. *She's dead. How can she be dead?*

Ella would have gone far, everyone said so. She was vibrant, confident, cheeky, boundary-pushing. She would have done great things. But for that you have to live. You have to stay alive.

'I just don't know, Alice,' she says eventually, hating herself with every word. 'I don't know that it's such a good idea.'

⌁

When Alice arrives later that evening – unexpectedly, but she doesn't mind – Flo is abruptly taken out of Lyon in 1958 and back to the creaking knees and battered old armchair of her front room. She closes the book. Alice says hello but heads straight past her, and the expression on her face makes Flo get up from the chair, book in hand, and follow her down the hall and out the back door. When she gets to the studio, Alice is at the drying lines, inspecting the prints she did the other day, touching them gently to see if they're dry. Flo stands there for a few seconds, taking in the intense expression on the girl's face, the vulnerability in her thin frame, and affection floods her body.

'Alice?' she says softly. 'Are you all right?'

Alice nods but doesn't say anything, which in Flo's short but intense experience of this girl usually means she isn't.

'Looking good.' Flo gestures to the prints, and then she can't help herself. 'That would be a great one to put in a portfolio. Really shows your design talent, and the way you handle colour.'

Alice turns around and there's a shine in her eyes. 'I'm not doing a portfolio because I'm not applying to art school.'

'Alice—'

'Just leave it, Flo, okay?'

'Did you talk about it with your mum?'

Alice nods.

'And what did she say?'

The girl turns back to her prints, ostensibly inspecting them more closely, though Flo knows it's to stop her seeing her face.

'I can't,' Alice says finally. 'It's not a good idea.'

Flo sighs. She turns the book over in her hands. *The Way We Were*. She may have changed considerably since she attended that finishing school so long ago, but she now knows that you're never really *finished*. Everyone's a work in progress. Even now, she doesn't have all the answers. No one does. Even Lilli. But the difference between the two of them back then is that Lilli was always willing to ask the question. She always wanted to know *what would happen if?* Whereas Flo, when they first met, was too scared to ask. That changed, she knows, during the time they spent together. It wasn't easy, but she did it; with Lilli's encouragement (or doggedness), she changed from a girl who would say *I can't* to someone who would rather say *maybe I can try*. And she *was* going to try; by the end of that academic year in Lyon she was going to tell her parents she didn't want to marry Peter, she was going to try to figure out what she *did* want to do. She was going to follow her heart, her passions – her friend.

A sudden fury rises up in her. Harry took that away from her. He made her waste ten years of her life. She needs to explain this to Lilli. It's time now, it's been long enough. She needs to go to the place where it happened and stare it full in the face.

Flo puts the book on the workbench. 'Come on,' she says to Alice. 'Let's go.'

'Go where?'

'To your house, to see your mum.'

Alice shakes her head. 'No, Flo. I don't want to talk about it. It's between me and Mum. I told you not to pressure me.' Her voice rises and Flo hears the panic in it.

'I'm not going to,' she says. 'Just trust me.'

They get in the car and Flo backs out of the drive at top speed, barely missing Eric, who makes a run for it just in time. They skim the speed limit all the way to Alice's house, neither of them saying a word.

When they arrive, Flo parks at a wonky angle in front of the house. Alice lets them in and they walk down the corridor and into the living room, where Carla sits on the sofa in the semi-dark, the TV on.

'Carla, dear, may I have a word?'

Surprise alights on Carla's face but she nods, switches the telly off and gets up. 'Can I offer you a cup of tea or something, Flo?'

'No thank you, dear. I'm here with a proposal.'

'Flo—' Alice starts, warning in her voice.

'It's not what you think. Just listen.' Flo smiles, takes a breath. 'I've made a decision,' she announces. 'I'm going on a road trip. To France. And I want you both to come with me.'

Carla and Alice look at her, and then each other.

'When?' Carla says finally, at the same time as Alice says, 'In *your* car?'

Flo laughs. 'Ferry's booked for next week,' she answers Carla, before adding to Alice, 'Yes, dear, it's perfectly capable.'

Carla shakes her head. 'It's very kind of you to suggest it, Flo, but I couldn't possibly. I'm meant to be looking for jobs – and Alice has her shifts at the café.'

'You can still look for jobs, the internet isn't confined to the UK. And Alice tells me the café is on the verge of closing anyway, so I'm sure Merryn will be glad not to have to pay her Saturday girl for a couple of weeks.' There is an abruptness in her voice, Flo knows, but it's necessary. She won't take no for an answer.

'Well, I suppose so but ... I should really be saving my redundancy pay rather than spending it on an impromptu holiday.'

'The trip's on me,' Flo says, before pre-empting Carla's inevitable protestations. 'I'm a well-off old lady and I can spend my money however I damn well please. So there are absolutely no excuses. If you don't want to, well that's a different matter. But who doesn't want a free trip to the South of France? End destination Avignon, with stopovers in Paris and Lyon and anywhere else the wind should take us. I'd only ask that you share the driving – I get a little tired if I spend too long behind the wheel, these days. And Alice, we'll bring Ernie so I'll want you to continue walking him, wherever we are. I'll get a neighbour to come and fill up Eric's automatic feeding bowl occasionally.'

Flo watches as Carla looks at Alice and Alice looks at Carla. She knows what they're both thinking, can practically see all the fears and negativity rolling around their heads, barking out nonsensical reasons why they shouldn't say yes. Mother and daughter are as bad as each other – as bad as she used to be.

'But why?' Carla says eventually.

'That,' Flo replies, 'I will tell you on the way.'

PART TWO

The Way We Were

Oh, how I laugh at myself when I look back now! How grown up I thought myself, how sophisticated and worldly, how rebellious, simply because I'd been with a man. I clung to that feeling in the weeks that followed my first illuminating encounter with Hugo's naked body. It was all so novel, so wonderfully new, and I relished every moment, every sensation. He wasn't the most generous of lovers (as I learned, by comparison, later in my life), but he seemed to adore making love to me, and that was enough to make me feel glorious, since I didn't know any different in any case. I was fuelled by the fact that he wanted me, he couldn't keep his hands off me, he devoured me every time we saw each other, which was about once a week throughout January, as often as we could realistically pass off our meetings as cousinly catch-ups. He'd pick me up on a Sunday around midday, ostensibly to take me out for lunch, and drive me to his apartment on Rue Pasteur, where we'd spend the rest of the afternoon in his bed,

213

gradually making our way through a bottle of wine, a packet of cigarettes and each other.

My God, you're divine, he'd say, as his lips travelled over my body. And so I felt divine. He thought me a goddess, and thus I considered myself one. My ego was damn well full to bursting (so much so that I didn't give more than a passing thought to the potential consequences – surely Hugo, with all his experience, would do what was needed to avoid them).

However, as these afternoons continued apace into February, this divine being couldn't help but start to feel a little ... well, bored. Hugo no longer took me out to eat at a *bouchon*. We never went dancing. We hadn't seen Celeste or Fred or any of his other friends since New Year's Eve. All our time together was spent at his flat, in bed. Then one afternoon, as I stood at the window wrapped in a blanket, smoking a cigarette and looking out at the Vespas nipping down the street below (what freedom!), something unexpected happened: I found my thoughts drifting to the school, wondering what Fran and the others were doing. I'd heard talk of an ice-skating outing to the frozen lake in the Parc de la Tête d'Or today, and I imagined Fran and I tottering about together, arm in arm, shrieking at our ineptitude. I wondered who she was tottering and shrieking with instead of me.

'Darling, can we go out next time?' I said when he came back into the room carrying another bottle of wine. After several months of seeing him regularly, my tolerance for the local Beaujolais had increased significantly since that evening in November. I couldn't match him, but I wasn't far behind.

If Hugo gave me any enduring legacy, it's my ability to keep up with the men in my life nearly drink for drink. It's not much of a legacy, though, really, is it?

'Why?' he said. 'We're perfectly all right here, aren't we?' He came over and wrapped one arm around me, while the other took the bottle to his lips. Then he handed it to me, but I shook my head.

'I'd like to see a little more of the city,' I said. 'I want you to show me. You've been here for years, you must know all the best parts, but I feel I've hardly seen it. Maybe we could go to a Sunday market, or stroll along the quay. It's my birthday next week, after all.'

'Is it?' He took another swig of wine and I smelled it on his breath when he kissed my cheek. 'That's perfect – I have a bottle of Moët & Chandon in the fridge just waiting for the right occasion. We can drink it between the sheets.'

I looked out of the window, where the light was already fading in the mid-afternoon of a cold February day, and I wondered if my excitement about Hugo hadn't, in fact, been more about the possibility of escape that I'd thought he offered me, rather than the man himself. The lovemaking had been enlightening, yes, but I was rather tired of it now. And here I was looking out at the city with a certain wistfulness that reminded me of my early days at the school. Had I swapped one gilded cage for another?

I must admit, too, that while I seemed to have quite successfully maintained my status of divine goddess in Hugo's eyes, his status in mine had waned a little – just a little – since I'd seen him at such close quarters. It still thrilled me to peel off his clothes and encounter the smooth skin of a real man beneath. It still amazed me to touch him and feel him react, and to hear with some incredulity the sounds he would make when exploring my own body. However, in some ways I approached it with the same scientific curiosity I'd had for those bugs in jars during high school, because I found, after a few weeks of it, that the act itself didn't provoke a whole heap of physical feeling in me. The desire I'd felt when we met, and while he was courting me (toying with me, more like), had clearly been sparked at least in part by the anticipation of the thing, and now I'd actually *experienced* the thing – multiple times – I was sad to realize it had dissipated rather. Now I observed the animalistic shudders and groans of Hugo with a certain detachment, as though watching a sea lion copulating with his mate, which I'd once accidentally witnessed as a child at Central Park Zoo. *Oh! Don't look, honey, don't look!* Ma had screeched, though of course I had.

Sometimes I'd try to engage him in conversation before we got down to the act, hoping to glean a little more about the man beneath the flesh, to dig out the frisson of darkness I'd encountered on New Year's Eve, or prod at his feelings about his late father, his frail mother, in the hope of disproving Celeste's claim that he was *emotionally empty*. Other times I'd try to discern what his plans for the future might be, plans that I was still, strangely, hoping might include me. Once I asked him about Celeste's job at the car company, thinking he might suggest I could do something similar once I finished at the school. (I'd imagine us coming back to his apartment – *our* apartment – after a day at work, discussing

current affairs and office politics over a late dinner, him prais-
ing me for being so well informed, intelligent and funny.)
But he'd usually silence my attempts at conversation with a
kiss and that was that.

Once the sex was over, there was little to keep me occupied
while Hugo dozed beside me. I would light a cigarette and
explore his apartment. I'd browse his books, flick through the
newspapers and magazines he left lying on his desk, inves-
tigate the usually meagre contents of his fridge, and then sit
on the little balcony smoking, listening to his soft snore and
wondering if I should make an excuse for him to drive me
back to the chateau a little earlier tonight.

So you see, it wasn't quite the escape I'd had in mind.

But I forgot all that the minute I returned to the school.
When I related everything to Fran in our room when I
came back each Sunday afternoon, I gave it all a glossy
sheen: Hugo's post-coital snoring forgotten in favour of the
glamour of smoking out his apartment window wrapped in
a blanket; my lack of passion glossed over while I recounted
the extent of his own. Poor Fran received far more detail
than she could ever have possibly wanted to hear; it was an
education for her, that's for sure, and certainly not one the
school would have approved of. I had to go into detail about
the sex, of course, because there was very little else to say
about our encounters.

One day, however, someone else was waiting for me in the
school entrance hall when Hugo drove me back. Normally,
I'd sweep past any loitering staff member or student with a
breezy *bonsoir* and head straight for my room, lest the odour of

Gauloises and Beaujolais waft their way. But on that particular Sunday in mid-February (just before St Valentine's Day, I seem to recall, and even in my distress about what was about to unfold, I could appreciate the irony in that), there was an obstacle in my way.

'Madame Bouchard,' I said, my stomach plummeting to the cold stone floor.

'Eleanor.' She didn't smile. 'Come this way, please.'

She led me into her office, a room on the second floor of the chateau with a splendid view of the school grounds and the mountains in the far distance. She invited me to sit on the couch and took the armchair opposite. My heart galloped as I prepared myself for a dressing-down. She knew about Hugo, she was going to kick me out, I was headed back to New York never to see him again. But for a moment she didn't say anything, she just looked at me, an ambiguous smile on her perfectly made-up face.

'I've worked at this school for thirty years and run it for twenty, bar a break during the war,' she said finally, and I nodded, attempting to engage with whatever it was she was going to tell me despite the whirl of thoughts fighting for attention in my head. 'So you see, Eleanor, I know how girls are. I've seen every type: the obedient ones, eager to please and unable to take criticism; the Head Girls, born to lead the others; the quiet, intelligent ones, who tend to hide their light under a bushel; and the deceitful ones, the rebels, who enjoy being the exception to the rule.' She was looking at me the whole time, and though I met her gaze with all the defiance I could muster, I had to hand it to her, it made me a little uncomfortable. 'And one thing I've learnt in this job, Eleanor, is to trust my instincts. I knew from the beginning that you were one of the exceptions, one of those who like to be *different*.' She layered the word with so much disdain that it was clear she didn't mean it in the same way Hugo had. 'But in my folly I thought perhaps the education we were offering you would be enough to turn you into the fine young woman you had the potential to be, as it has for so many girls before you. For a time, I thought we were succeeding, until you started to come back from your *outings* smelling of cigarettes and alcohol and in a distinctly dishevelled state, expecting us all not to notice. However, it's my job to notice, Eleanor. I therefore wrote to your father to inform him that I was concerned your cousin wasn't being the positive influence on his daughter that I'm sure he hoped he'd be.' She leaned forward, hands clasped in front of her. 'And do you know what he said?'

I thought about replying, but it felt rather pointless. I breathed out, smiled, and held my head up as I waited for the inevitable answer to come.

'Of course you do,' she said, when she received no response from me. She stood up and walked over to the window, turning her back to me as I tried to digest this demasking of my 'cousin.' 'Your father is furious, of course, as am I. You have disrespected this school and let down your family.' She turned to face me then, but rather than anger I saw pity on her face – and that, more than anything she'd said so far, made me squirm in my seat.

She sighed, a short, sharp puff of breath which seemed to

contain all her frustration with me, before saying, 'I don't suppose he intends to marry you?'

The image of us discussing work and politics around the dinner table flickered and then faded in my head. The truth was, I had no idea of Hugo's intentions towards me. I shook my head and saw the rather desperate glimmer of hope for my salvation dissolve in her face.

'I thought not.' She paused. 'What makes it so much more tragic is that you don't even realize what you've done. You think this man respects you, after what you've no doubt let him do to you? You think he wouldn't have just cast you aside for the next arrogant and naïve young woman who crossed his path?' She shook her head. 'You've demeaned yourself, Eleanor; you've jeopardized your future and wasted all that potential.'

Potential for what? I wanted to say, but I didn't dare. *For keeping house?* Perhaps she was right, I was just a type. But if that type was independent and life-loving like Celeste, if it meant drinking and laughing and doing the cancan in cafés, or dancing to exhaustion in hotel ballrooms, if it meant the thrill of sneaking out of an art gallery and rushing down the street to meet a man, and the delight of seeing his clothes fall to the floor for the first time, then I wanted to be that type and no other. Because how could joy and delight and thrill be wrong?

'I have consulted with your father,' Madame Bouchard continued. 'You will not receive what you would no doubt see as the reward of being expelled from this school and sent home. You will stay here and see out the academic year – but you shall not join any excursions or extra-curricular activities. The walls of this school are all you will see for the next few months, Eleanor.' She paused. 'You may go.'

I stood up, smoothed my dress down and turned to the door.

Fuck.

9

Flo feels free as she drives down the motorway. The principal joy of living alone has been the ability to do as she pleases, when she pleases. There's a loneliness in that, too, but mostly she has enjoyed the freedom of being able to make decisions like this one, to act on a whim, purely because she wants to. Though this isn't really a whim; it's been brewing in her head ever since she started reading that book, a plan forming as she flicked through that travel brochure and started googling hotels. And now feels like the right time to do it – for her, and, she is sure, for her travelling companions, too.

She glances in the rear-view mirror – Alice is in the back seat, staring out the side window, mirroring Ernie looking out the other. She wonders what the girl is thinking, what awful thoughts are whirling around her head this time. She seemed sullen this morning, when Flo picked them up, Alice's unsmiling face a contrast to Carla's almost too-bright smile and forced enthusiasm. Tension floats around the pair of them like an invisible forcefield.

But Flo isn't going to let the tension distract her from her mission, because she wants – no, *needs* – to go on this journey, to make peace with the long-dormant demons in her head, and she has come to realize that these two also have demons to pacify, that they also need to go on this trip.

'What time's the ferry again?' Carla says from the passenger seat.

'One o'clock. Plenty of time. If the traffic's good we'll get there early and then we can have a quick lunch in Portsmouth. Fish and chips?'

Carla looks at her watch and nods, smiles. 'Sounds good.'

'Okay, Alice?' Flo glances in the mirror again.

'Sure,' the girl says without turning her head from the window.

Flo wonders if Alice recognizes the route. It is the third time in two weeks they've driven this road, after their day trip to Oxford, and then Winchester. As they pass the turn-off for the A40, signed to Oxford and London, Flo's thoughts slide back much further, half a century in fact, to another time she drove down that road – the trip that marked the start of a new phase of her life. A suitcase full of clothes, a few pieces of jewellery, an envelope of cash and an agreement for a regular stipend (it was the least Peter could do for her, after all), plus his car as a parting gift. She was also gifted her parents' disapproval and social embarrassment over the impending divorce. As she drove down the motorway towards London after leaving the marital home in the spring of 1968, the words of her father were still ringing in her ears: *what did you do to drive him away?* She wondered if her faithless soon-to-be-ex-husband had been asked the same thing.

Flo laughs to herself, and Carla and Alice both look up at the unexpected outburst. There's a quizzical look on the girl's face, as though she thinks Flo the mad old bat the schoolkids consider her. Mad as a fruitcake! She'd rather be considered that than someone who just plays by society's rules. She spent too much of her early life playing by those silly rules.

'What's so funny?' Carla says, a smile on her face.

'Oh, nothing dear. I'm just happy to be here with you two. I've always loved the beginning of a trip, the anticipation of all the fun to be had, the freedom of being on the open road. And I suppose it made me think of leaving my marriage because that felt like the beginning of a trip, too.'

'Divorce must have been quite a big deal back then,' Carla says. 'Were you scared to leave?'

'Petrified! But I had no choice. Our marriage was dead and he wanted to move on and marry the mother of his forth-coming child, so off I went. I drove down to London and started my life again.'

'I'm so sorry, Flo. What a way to be treated.'

'Don't be. Do you know what happened as I fled down the M40?'

Carla shakes her head. Flo glances in the rear-view mirror and sees Alice looking at her, listening. 'Beneath my fear and my sorrow and my shame and my sense of failure, I felt this little glimmer of something else.' She pauses for effect and then slams her left hand on the wheel. '*Excitement.* And it made me think of someone, of Lilli, this friend I'd had back in the fifties. You've heard me talk about Lilli, Alice.' Her eyes flick to the mirror again and Alice nods. 'Lilli was such a bon vivant, so courageous and forthright and sure of herself, and I knew she would have said to me *well it's about time, honey, just go for it, seize the day.* When I knew her, I was never very good at *seizing.* But on the day I left Peter, something changed. I suppose I felt I'd done my best to play by the rules, to do what everyone wanted me to, and it hadn't worked out very well for me, had it? And after it all went wrong, I felt I had nothing to lose. So that's what I decided to do – seize the day.'

'How did you do that?' Alice asks.

And so Flo slips back into 1968 and tells them about finding a bedsit to rent in London, about the austere landlady Mrs Butler, and the other women in the building, mostly younger than her, unsaddled by the burden of divorce but all making their way on their own for now: Linda, who worked as a secretary to someone important at the Ministry of Defence; Anne, a sales assistant in Selfridges; and Samantha, a teacher at a girls' school. She tells Alice and Carla about sitting on her pull-out bed and thinking *what now?* About wandering the streets aimlessly, both intimidated and enthralled by the buzz of the city. About scouring the job pages for some idea of what she might do with herself, the sheer novelty of even having to contemplate a paid job after ten years as a housewife (she didn't want to retreat back to her parents, nor did she want to live off her trust fund, which she might need one day), and the slight inferiority she felt at living with these younger women who seemed far more qualified and competent and 'now' than her. But all the while she heard Lilli's voice in her head. She remembered her friend's confidence, untrammelled by what had happened to her, her defiance against the odds, her refusal to feel shame, and when Flo felt fear and shame herself, she told herself to be like Lilli. That's what she whispered to herself as she went for a job interview for a library assistant post and was told she was too inexperienced. That's what she kept in her head when she went to a bar on the Strand with her new friends and felt her confidence waver and fear creep in. *Be like Lilli.*

And after a while, it began to work. So when Samantha said a friend of hers knew of a job opening as assistant to a fashion designer with the fantastically exotic name of Guinevere De Souza, she told herself to be like Lilli and applied.

Guinevere De Souza's office was in the attic space of an old building in Covent Garden near the Theatre Royal Drury Lane. Flo could just make out the crackly voice over the intercom telling her to make her way to the top floor, so when the door buzzed open, she picked her way up three narrow, rickety flights of stairs and knocked as confidently as she could on the wooden door at the top. Her heart pounded in her chest and she swallowed hard. *Be like Lilli.*

'Come in.'

Flo just about managed to prevent her jaw from dropping when she saw the woman sitting in the chair by the window. She had bright pink hair, for starters, cut in a short, thick bob; long eyelashes that couldn't be real and thick slicks of eyeliner flicking out from the corner of each eye. She was older than Flo – early forties, perhaps – but wearing a floral-patterned minidress so short Flo hardly knew where to look, with a diamond brooch in the shape of a lizard pinned to the oversized white collar. People hadn't looked like this in

226

Oxford – had they? *She* certainly didn't look like this. She could well imagine Peter's face if she'd gone out in public in a dress like that. But this was London, this was sixty-eight, not fifty-eight, and Flo was beginning to see that the world had changed in the ten years she'd stood still.

'Um ... I'm here about the job,' Flo said eventually, a tremor in her voice.

The woman didn't speak for a moment, only looked at Flo, an undefinable expression on her face. Eventually she stood up and walked towards her. 'Florence, you said?'

Flo nodded.

'Where did you buy that dress?'

Flo looked down at her blue cotton shift, so staid and conventional compared to this woman's outfit. 'Oh, a department store in Oxford I think. Elliston & Cavell, probably.' Peter's salary hadn't stretched to bespoke tailoring and fabric from Harrods, and he hadn't liked her to dip into her trust fund. *I'm your husband, I should keep you in dresses, not your family.*

Guinevere De Souza gave a little sigh, as though that were the wrong answer, and sat down again in the chair by the window. There were sketches on the table in front of her – women in miniskirts and belted shirt dresses and other, more obscure outfits that made Flo's eyes pop. Along the far wall was a rack of clothes in vibrant colours that Flo longed to riffle through. A tailor's dummy sat in the corner, an enormous feathered red hat on its head, as extravagant and expressive as the dummy's face was empty. She thought of the tweeds and twinsets her mother bought her as a teen, and the equally prim, sensible outfits Peter wanted his respectable wife to wear; God, how she wanted to put that feathered hat on her head!

'Why do you want this job, Florence?'

Flo's eyes flicked back to the designer. 'Well, I was told you wanted someone very organized and that's certainly me. I've experience of putting together events and throwing dinner parties, and I'm good with paperwork and managing a budget. I know I don't have any references to give you, but I'm eager to learn and I pick things up quickly.'

Guinevere pursed her red lips together. 'You didn't answer my question. I asked why you wanted this job, Florence.'

Flo took a breath and tried again, her words coming out rushed. 'I think it would be marvellous fun to work in the fashion industry. I've always loved clothes, and I can sew and sketch a bit.' She cringed at her own words, childish and ridiculous; felt herself wither under the woman's gaze. Hot tears brewed behind her eyes and she worked hard to beat them back.

'And?' Guinevere said. She was still looking at her, waiting for something else, something more satisfactory.

Flo sighed. She'd blown it anyway, so what the hell. *Take a risk*, Lilli would have said. So she held her head up and looked the woman right in the eyes. 'My husband of ten years left me for another woman whom he got pregnant, so I've moved to London on my own and I don't know what to do with myself now because I got married at eighteen and I've never worked so I don't really know what kind of job I'd be good at but I'd really like to find out.' She paused. 'And I'd like the money.'

Guinevere smiled. She lit a cigarette and blew smoke up to the ceiling. 'Can you start on Monday?'

Flo put a hand to her mouth and laughed. *Really?* As she clattered back down those wooden steps, she felt giddy. She was in London, the city of miniskirts and pink hair and opportunities, and for the first time in her life she was free to do exactly as she pleased.

'You worked as an assistant to Guinevere De Souza?' Carla says now. The astonishment on her face makes Flo laugh again. She grips the wheel as pride blooms inside her; once, she would have found that a fantastical statement, too.

'Who's that again?' Alice pipes up from the back seat.

'Only one of the most famous British fashion designers of the sixties and seventies,' Carla tells her.

'I did, for many years,' Flo says. 'Both in London and Paris. It was such great fun and we became good friends as well as colleagues. She was like an older sister leading me astray. And it really was a wonderful time and place to be led astray. London was just so exciting back then, and once I'd got over the shock of it, I allowed myself to fully embrace it.' She remembers the sense of release it gave her to don one of Guinevere's minidresses and dance to the Stones and the Kinks in Covent Garden clubs, to watch naked hippies on stage in *Hair*, to join anti-war protests in Trafalgar Square, to attend life-drawing and pattern-cutting evening classes at St Martin's (art school, finally — she'd wished she could tell Lilli) and to expand her idea of fashion beyond Harrods and John Lewis under Guinevere's encouragement and tuition.

'Incredible!' Carla shakes her head. 'You're full of surprises, Flo.'

'No more than anyone else, dear,' she says with a laugh,

but when she looks at Carla's face she catches a sadness in it that she wasn't expecting.

They are driving past the turn-off for Basingstoke now. Only another hour or so until Portsmouth, where their trip will really start. Anticipation expands to fill her chest. She feels full of life, literally full up from all the experiences she's already had and all the others she knows are still to come, if she gives herself the chance.

You didn't deserve it, after what you did.

She shakes the voice out of her head.

'But wait, what happened to this friend of yours, this Lilli?' Carla asks.

Flo smiles. 'That's what I'm hoping to find out on this trip.'

⚬

Alice pushes open the door and walks onto the deck to be hit by a blast of air that almost makes her cry out. The spray is refreshing, like she's wiped her face with toner, which instantly reminds her of Ella, since toner was one of the many products Ella once told her she should be using. Toner and micellar water and exfoliator and undereye lotion. Hair-removal cream for the fine down on her top lip, moisturizer to soothe her bikini line after waxing, BB cream to cover up her acne scars. Michael, the only boy at school she actually liked (but who she had to pretend she didn't, since Vicky and Ella thought he was a geek), once laughed when he bumped into her in Boots with a basketload of it, on Ella's instructions. *What do you need all that gubbins for?* he said, and she only shrugged, because she certainly didn't know. After two weeks her acne was worse than ever and she had a line of small red dots above her top lip that made her far more self-conscious than a few hairs ever had.

She puts her hands on the railing and looks out at the sea. It's pretty calm, though there's a gentle swell that has made her stagger like a drunk when walking around the boat. A trail of white foam is gradually dissolving into the water at the stern, while a trio of gulls catches a ride on the air wake like skateboarders hanging off the back of a bus. Maybe she could try and draw them, compose a design for a new lino print. She finds herself doing that a lot these days, looking at things in new ways, creating compositions in her head. Her thoughts flicker to the conversation she had with her mother about art school. *I don't know that it's such a good idea.*

She shakes her head; she doesn't want to think about that now, not when she's actually feeling content to be here on this ferry, on this trip. Though worries rise up when she thinks about Flo having to drive on the wrong side of the road (what if she forgets and crashes into an oncoming car?), about the big cities they will visit (what if they lose each other and someone gets mugged?) or about the prospect of finding Lilli (what if she doesn't want to reunite with Flo and Flo is overcome with grief?), there is something comforting about being taken under Flo's wing and chaperoned on this trip. The old woman's presence seems to lift a weight, as though her optimism and positivity are gradually eroding Alice's own fear and negativity, albeit one wafer-thin layer at a time. She wishes she could say the same about her mother. Part of her didn't want her mum to come with them, and then she felt instantly guilty, not least because another part of her wants her here, needs her here, like a safety blanket she knows she's too old for but still clings to.

Alice stares out at the grey-blue sea and screams into the spray, a long howl of she doesn't know what, but whatever it is, it makes her feel good. 'Ahhhhhh!' she screams until her lungs feel fit to burst. 'Ahhhhhhh!'

'You all right there?'

She jumps at the voice and stands back from the railing. *Shit.* She'd thought this side of the deck was empty. 'Oh,' she says. 'Yeah. Sorry.'

The boy laughs. 'Doesn't matter to me. Was just checking someone wasn't being thrown overboard or something.'

Alice smiles. 'I just . . . felt like yelling.'

The boy steps forward, puts his hands on the rail and yells, louder and longer than Alice did. 'Ahhhhhhhhh!' When he's finished he looks at her and nods. 'See what you mean. Feels bloody good.'

Alice laughs, despite herself. He's probably about her age, this guy, though he doesn't look like the popular boys in sixth form, in their branded hoodies, black trackies and Nike trainers; he's wearing a slightly grubby white T-shirt with a hole in the left shoulder seam and faded blue jeans all scuffed at the bottom, over flip flops.

'Again?' He gestures to the railing but she shakes her head, feeling her cheeks redden. It's not the same in public. 'Sorry,' he says. 'Ruined your moment. I was just bored. Finding out why someone was yelling over the railing of a ferry was more interesting than playing Snap with my little sister.'

'It doesn't matter,' she says. 'I don't know why I was yelling anyway.' All she knows is that she feels better for it.

'Fair enough. Well, see you then.' He turns to go and then looks back. 'Unless you want to get a beer or something?'

She hesitates. Flo is snoozing in a recliner on the front deck, her mum next to her reading a book, Ernie asleep in the shade under their chairs. She has nothing better to do for the next few hours, and there's something about this boy's easy manner and unselfconscious clothing that is reassuring.

'All right.' She shrugs.

'Cool. I'm Adam.'

They sit at the stern of the ferry with their French lager. It's in shade, this part of the deck, so there aren't many people sitting on the fixed plastic chairs; they're all at the bow, lapping up the sun like they've been starved of it all year, which perhaps they have. So the two of them sit nearly alone, trying to defend a shared packet of crisps from predatory seagulls as they talk – or, at least, Adam talks and Alice listens, which she is happy to do, since the more he talks, the less she has to and therefore the more comfortable she feels.

Adam is going on holiday with his parents and sister, Alice learns. A camping trip to Brittany, which they've done every year since he was ten. This will probably be his last one, he tells her, since he's off to university in the autumn and can't see himself wanting to hang out with his family next summer. He's only doing it now because his 12-year-old sister, Rosie, begged him to come. Alice asks what he's going to study and he surprises her by saying music. He doesn't look like a musician – though she doesn't really know what she thinks a musician should look like – but then he shows her the callouses on his fingers from playing guitar and starts talking about Django Reinhardt and John Abercrombie and other names Alice has never heard of and she can start to see why this scruffy guy's passion and knowledge might have convinced the Guildhall School of Music & Drama to let him on their jazz guitar course.

'Do you know who's studied there? Cleveland Watkiss, Phil Robson, Dave Holland, Jules Buckley …' He reels off the names on his fingers as though Alice should know them and be impressed by each one, but although they leave her blank, she knows how amazing they must be because Adam's enthusiasm leaves her in no doubt. It reminds her of Michael, of the way he talked about books, of the light in his face when he related the plot of a new sci-fi trilogy he'd come across, and the way he'd press a book into her hands, wanting her to read it so they could discuss it together. Ella had laughed when Alice finally admitted she liked him, which she only did because Ella had enquired if Alice's lack of interest in boys perhaps meant she was gay. *It doesn't matter to me, everyone's a bit fluid these days.* Her eyes had widened when Alice, as nonchalantly as she could, mentioned Michael's name. *Oh, Alice, but he's such a nerd! You could do so much better!* She wonders where he is now, how he got on at the new school he moved to for sixth form. She hasn't seen him since that party, since Ella died.

Adam is still talking. About moving to London from his home in Bedfordshire, about the prospect of meeting all the other student musicians and getting to play in public concerts and watch professionals in the Barbican Centre down the road, about the teachers he tells her are leaders in their fields and the one-on-one tutoring he can't wait to have. As she listens to him, to this *geek*, this *nerd*, Alice is struck by one singular thought: he feels no fear at all. He knows he wants to do this and there's nothing stopping him whatsoever.

'How about you?' Adam says finally. He pops a crisp in his mouth.

She hesitates. She doesn't want to tell him about going to Birmingham to study business because she can't express the same enthusiasm for it as Adam clearly has for his own future. She pictures the cheerful student in Winchester signing up visitors for taster classes. She feels the puckered skin of her scar. *What if I don't make any friends? What if the teachers think I'm talentless and deluded? What if I can't do it?* But today, looking out at the vast expanse of sea, with this untroubled, enthusiastic, easy-going soul beside her, she allows the alternative question to pop into her head: *what if I can?*

'I'm not sure yet,' she says. 'But I'm thinking of going to art school.'

***

Carla feels a childlike sense of glee as she drives off the ferry. It's 7.30pm, she's spent the past five hours or so relaxing in the sun on the deck of the boat, and now they're in France, somewhere she hasn't been for years, on holiday with her daughter and a fascinating 80-year-old who wants to pay for everything. She almost feels happy – and that's not a word she's used a lot lately.

Almost happy, but not quite, because her daughter has

barely spoken to her properly since they embarked on the trip. One-word answers, delivered without eye contact, are all Alice has given her, and her daughter's standoffishness hurts Carla to her very soul. It should feel normal by now, so long it's been going on, but it doesn't, it never will. Still, she will put up with it for the whole trip if it means she can be here with her daughter twenty-four seven, able to look after her, to make sure she's okay. *Why am I so rubbish and crap? Why can't I be normal? I hate myself!* The words Alice wrote in her diary have reverberated around Carla's head ever since, sending a chill down her spine as she lay in the sun on the ferry. Yes, she is glad she is here.

'Go around again,' Flo says, wrestling with the map as Carla circles the roundabout on the outskirts of Le Havre. 'I'd forgotten how terrible French signage is. We're looking for the D6015 to Honfleur – perhaps it's that one?'

Carla sees nothing resembling that, but so they don't spend ten minutes riding the same roundabout she takes the third exit. As she does, she sees the sign to Honfleur at an odd angle just after the turning.

'Well blow me, what's the point of a sign after you've made the turn?' Flo laughs. 'Reminds me of driving over here with James. The arguments we'd have when we couldn't find our way! He'd always blame it on me. I'm sure the lack of decent signage must fuel the divorce rate over here.'

'James?' Carla asks as she drives them away from the coast. They'll spend their first night in Honfleur, where Flo has booked a guesthouse for them, before continuing to Paris the next day.

'My late partner,' Flo replies. 'My soulmate.'

Carla's eyebrows rise, just a little. She doesn't know why, but she assumed Flo had been on her own since her divorce, but now she feels a little silly. All that time? Of course not. Of course Flo, who was clearly in the thick of things in the late sixties and seventies, who dressed famous names in Guinevere De Souza for goodness' sake, would have met someone else. Of course she hasn't been single all her life. *Just an old woman with a dog.* Andy's phrase comes back to her. *Don't do what everyone else does,* she chastises herself. *Don't assume.* They have only just begun getting to know each other properly and already Flo has blown any assumptions out the window. Her stories are joyous, fascinating, and Carla is happy to sit and listen, all the while suppressing the little voice that asks herself *but what have* you *done since* your *divorce?*

'You spent time out here together then?' she asks.

'Oh yes. In fact, we met in Paris when I was there with Guinevere for fashion week in 1975. We'd spend plenty of time in Paris each year, she and I, sometimes staying for several weeks at a time. I met him because I dropped my purse on the metro. He found it, and thankfully there was a business card from the hotel where we were staying tucked inside it. He came to the hotel later to return it to me and I thanked him with a drink.'

Carla smiles. 'And how did you go from that to a relationship?' She thinks of meeting Rich in a bar in Hoxton, their drunken snog and the subsequent taxi ride back to hers. Not quite as romantic.

'It's a good question, especially since he was married at the time.' Flo looks at her. 'Have you ever just felt that you were meant to meet someone? If I hadn't dropped my purse, if he hadn't picked it up, if neither of us had got on that particular train carriage at that particular time, we'd never have met, and yet I've always felt as though we could never have *not* met, that we were always meant to.'

Carla doesn't say anything. She's never really felt that; in fact, she spends most of her time obsessing over the opposite idea – if she'd paid more attention, she might have been able to salvage her marriage, if she'd been a better mother Alice might be happier, if she'd asked more questions about what the girls were doing that night, she might have been able to save Ella. Her 'if onlys' have never been positive.

'You had an affair with a married man?' Alice pipes up. Carla glances in the rear-view mirror and sees her daughter's eyes are wide. She's stroking Ernie, whose head lies in her lap on the back seat.

'In a manner of sorts,' Flo says. Carla looks over at her and sees a melancholic smile on her face. 'We knew – right there and then in that hotel lobby over G&Ts. We didn't even have to say it. It was as clear to both of us as the bird on that fence post over there. We swapped details that night, and afterwards we started writing to each other. I suppose there *was* a betrayal, an affair, emotionally, but nothing physical happened until he divorced his wife and that was more than two years later. I insisted on that because I didn't want to be the other woman – I knew how it felt to be the cheated wife.'

Carla's mouth drops open. 'He divorced his wife for a woman he'd met in person only once?'

Flo laughs, but Carla sees her eyes are watery. 'Yes, I suppose he did. Although he hadn't been happy in that marriage for quite some time so it wasn't just about me.' She pauses. 'We met for the first time in two years under the Eiffel Tower and I had exactly the same feeling I'd had the very first time I saw him.'

'I didn't think things like that actually happened in real life.' Carla's never heard anything more romantic.

'Well, don't go all glassy-eyed over it,' Flo says. 'He snored like a foghorn and hated losing arguments; he certainly wasn't perfect. But he was perfect for me, I know that. Perhaps I knew it because I'd experienced the opposite. Peter was so wrong for me in every way. For starters there was no passion between us. So when James and I went to bed together, I finally, at the grand old age of thirty-seven, understood what all the fuss was about.' She leans sideways and whispers, 'Mind-blowing.'

Carla laughs and blushes, despite herself. She glances in the rear-view mirror where Alice is clearly listening. She catches her eye and the smile on Alice's face fades away. She doesn't know if Alice has ever slept with anyone. She had the 'talk' with her daughter several years ago, but Alice only brushed her off and told her to stop being so embarrassing. There was a time when she thought Alice would have told her. She'd always thought the two of them would remain close throughout the awkward teenage years. It was always her and Alice against Rich in any argument. If anything, Ella was more like Rich – confident, jokey, upbeat – while Alice was always more sensitive and reserved, much like herself.

They understood each other, Carla used to think. But lately, when faced with the expressionless brick wall her daughter has become, she has wondered if their similarities are pushing them apart. Maybe that's why it feels so good to be here with Flo, because she balances them out. In doing so, perhaps she can bring them together again.

Honfleur is a delight. They get a little lost trying to find the guesthouse, but Carla welcomes their unexpected tour of the town for the chance to glimpse the tall, narrow, colourful houses lining the beautiful harbour. She can't wait to come back here in the morning and have a wander. She'll find a little bakery and pick up some fresh croissants and strong coffee and sit on the harbour wall over there, looking out at the boats.

When they find the place – carefully selected by Flo because it accepts dogs – they check in and are quickly ushered into the small dining room by the landlady, a cheerful white-haired woman with a face so lined it's as though every year of her long life has been etched into it. She gives them menus and rattles off something in French that Flo responds to easily.

'I'm impressed,' Carla says.

'Oh, don't be, I'm pretty rusty.'

Carla supposes she shouldn't be surprised that Flo speaks French, given what she said about spending so much time here, but somehow she is, anyway. She wonders what else is packed into that head of hers; what other talents and skills and knowledge and experiences are lined up in the storage cupboards of her mind waiting to be dusted off and used once again as the occasion arises. She imagines, after what Flo's told her so far, that her cerebral shelves are pretty full. And for the first time she feels a flicker of possibility for the second act of her own life. Could she improve on her schoolgirl French, if she tried? Could she live in Paris, or change career, or take up a craft, or learn another new skill that hasn't even crossed her mind yet? Could she meet someone spontaneously on the metro and embark on a passionate love affair? But then she looks at Alice's unsmiling face across the table and thinks, *No, I shouldn't be thinking about me, I should be thinking about how to help my daughter.*

They dine on pâté and confit duck and an exquisite lemon tart so sharp it makes her brain hurt, and then comes the coffee, rich and dark, accompanied by tiny petit fours. If they eat like this for the next two weeks they'll hardly fit in the car. She wonders if she could ask the landlady for the tart recipe.

'Alice, would you mind taking Ernie for a spin around the block before you go to bed?' Flo says when they've finished. 'He'll need to do his business. There's a bumper pack of poo bags in the car boot.'

'Okay.' Alice nods but Carla sees a flicker of anxiety cross her features at the same time as she feels it herself. Alice doesn't know this place. She might get lost, or wander into a dodgy part of town, or encounter someone with bad intentions.

'You don't have to go, sweetie. I could walk him instead if you want,' she says, before turning to Flo. 'It's getting late, and she doesn't know the area. Why don't I go?'

Flo cocks her head. 'It's not dark yet,' she says. 'You've got your phone on you, haven't you?' she asks Alice, who nods again. 'And anyway, Ernie will be with her. She'll be absolutely fine. Honfleur is so touristy, there'll be tons of people about. We're not talking dark alleyways here. Just go to the port area we passed in the car, it's not far.'

Still, Carla thinks. *You never know what could happen.* She resists the temptation to grab Alice's arm and say *be careful, be careful.* It'll be a piece of cake, a walk in the park. It may be *literally* a walk in the park, if there's a park in Honfleur. But she still wants to put herself in Alice's place, to take whatever small risk there may be on herself, so that it doesn't fall on her daughter.

'Well, perhaps I could join you, then? Walk off that delicious dinner.' She pats her stomach and laughs, trying to keep her tone light, trying not to say what she thinks constantly these days, the thought that infuses her every action and reaction when it comes to her daughter: *let me protect you, let me do the job I failed to do two years ago.*

But Alice gives her a look that cuts the smile off her face.

'Just stop doing this, okay?' she says. 'You're doing my head in.' Her expression is one of such anger that Carla shrinks a little in her seat.

Stop what? she nearly says, but she doesn't, because in that moment she knows, she knows, but she just can't stop it because Alice's safety is more important, because she realizes she is willing to endure her daughter's anger for ever, if she has to, as long as it means she is safe.

'I just thought it might be nice to go together,' she says in a small voice.

'Well, it won't,' Alice says. 'Just let me go by myself.'

She grabs Ernie's lead and he emerges from under the table and wags his tail, delight all over his black velvet face, and the contrast with her daughter's own expression brings tears to Carla's eyes. Alice throws a glance at Flo, who sits passive, observing them both, and walks out of the room.

The Way We Were

Who knows how it got out – I doubt Bouchard would have told them – but however it did, my little affair with my fake cousin was quite the scandal among my fellow students in the weeks that followed. Sandra revelled in my downfall to the extent that she was visibly torn to have to travel back to London to curtsey before Queen Elizabeth II with her fellow debutantes, since it denied her a week of ridiculing me. ('I hear they let any old tart take part these days,' I'd goaded her, aping my heroine Princess Margaret. 'You should know,' she replied, and I had to admit I'd set myself up for that one.) Some of the others, including Barbara, skittered past me in the hallway as though being a fallen woman was catching, while a few looked at me with a mixture of awe and admiration that I quite enjoyed. 'What was it like?' Catherine whispered to me one day in class, before being swiftly silenced by Bouchard. Madame Grisaille, at least, showed me an ounce of sympathy, stopping dead the in-class giggling and ill-concealed staring with a sharply delivered, 'That's enough, girls,' though she didn't return my smile of thanks and I was momentarily subdued after that. Of all the teachers, it was her opinion of me that mattered most.

And then there was Fran, who to my great relief and gratitude, treated me exactly as she had before. She never said *I told you so*. She never said I deserved it, that I had it coming, that I shouldn't have been so stupid. She was simply there for me, in her calm and steadfast way, as I fluttered about our bedroom like a caged bird, railing against my exclusion from school excursions, a punishment that pained me far more than losing my Sundays in bed with Hugo. I think she was just glad to have me back there with her all the time, and the only humility I ever felt about my situation came from realizing that. *I'm sorry*, I wanted to tell her, though for some reason I didn't.

'Do you regret it? Was it worth it?' she asked me once, when she'd returned from an outing to the puppet theatre in town and found me lying on my bed reading, as I often did when the others had disappeared, an attempt to fall into another world and thus forget my own. That day I'd picked up a book that one of the other girls had left lying around, a Barbara Cartland romance called *The Kiss of the Devil*, whose heroine, Skye, is a feisty young woman who shirks marriage and domesticity to seek adventure in South America, only to be kidnapped by a bandit and forced to marry him. Trying to guess which of my buttoned-up schoolmates this might have belonged to was almost as entertaining as the book itself.

'No,' I said to Fran, 'and yes, in that order.' And when

she asked me why, with genuine curiosity, I told her what I'd thought when I was sitting in front of Bouchard being reprimanded like a 4-year-old: 'Whatever the outcome, how could I regret something so thrilling, something that, at least initially, made me feel so alive?'

She'd nodded and given me a small smile. 'I think I can understand that,' she said.

However, my faith in my own actions was shaken more than a little when I realized, several weeks down the line, that the consequences of my dalliance with Hugo were far greater than mere exclusion from school activities.

While I knew that what the two of us had done together was what caused babies to arrive, I was clueless about the actual biology of it, and for that I can't possibly blame myself. How were girls expected to know how to protect themselves against such things when their only education on the subject had been a half-witnessed copulation between two sea lions at a zoo? Madame Bouchard would have said by abstention, of course, but a more realistic method would have been education. However, the closest my high school had ever gotten to sex education was explaining the reproductive habits of earthworms, while God forbid Château Mont d'Or's mission to mould us into the ultimate models of womanhood should involve teaching us about a woman's actual biology. It still astounds me to think that if Bouchard and her staff had dedicated a little time to talking about the facts of life instead of teaching us to monogram napkins, then the whole course of my life could have been entirely different.

'Hugo?' I called him one Saturday morning when the other

girls and most of the teachers had gone to explore Lyon's covered food market in Cordeliers, an outing that gave me more than a small pang of self-pity since my guidebook said it was one of the most fabulous markets in France.

'Oh, hullo there, Lenny.' His voice sounded gravelly, as though he'd just dragged himself out of bed after a late night, and I think I knew then that my absence had created no more than a barely detectable ruffle in his otherwise calm life. He'd called for me again in his car the Sunday after our liaison was exposed, only to be sent away in no uncertain terms by Madame Bouchard; looking out of my bedroom window I'd seen him get back in his 2CV, light a cigarette and drive away. I'd like to say he'd written to me to declare how much he missed me and tell me he'd wait for me to leave the school at the end of the summer term and whisk me back to his apartment, but if he did, I never received it (not that I necessarily would have, since Madame Devillier was now tasked with opening all my correspondence).

'Well, I'm in a bit of a bind,' I said, keeping my voice low. Since I had no legitimate reason to use the telephone, I'd waited until Devillier (whose other new task was to ensure I didn't leave the school) was snoozing in her chair and snuck into Bouchard's office to use it. I had to be quick, so it was best just to come out with it. 'I think I'm expecting.'

For a moment I heard nothing, then came a long hiss, as though he was letting out all his breath into the handset. 'That's unfortunate,' he said finally.

'It is,' I said. I didn't know what I thought he would say. I didn't even know what I wanted. I certainly wasn't desperate to marry him – not only because I'd feel a fool to be the first of all my friends to do the one thing I'd said I would do *last,* if at all, but because my ardour for him, which had waned in the latter stages of our affair, had declined further since I'd seen him light that cigarette, get in his car and drive away without a second glance. But neither was I so ignorant that I didn't know what this would mean for me, and so I suppose I did hope he would at least *offer* to do right by me. I mean, what else was I meant to do now? Go home, tail between my legs, and be banished to an 'aunt' or a home for unmarried mothers while my parents hushed up my situation? It would be worse than being locked up here in the school. Worse, I decided, than being married to Hugo. Perhaps he would grow on me again – just as the bandit grew on Barbara Cartland's feisty heroine (she fell madly in love with him, naturally).

In hindsight, however, I'm extremely glad that *doing right by me* was clearly furthest from his mind.

'It's really not ideal,' he said.

I half laughed at the obviousness of his words. 'It sure isn't. But it is what it is. I expect we can make a go of it.'

Silence again. 'Look, Lenny. We've had fun, you and I, but this was never going to be for the long term, was it? I know you understood that. We got what we wanted from each other, didn't we? And all this,' he paused and I pictured him waving his hand dismissively, 'just can't be. So what you should do is call Celeste. She'll tell you what to do.'

'Celeste? Why? What do you mean?'

'Just call her. Do you have a pen?' I reached for one on

Bouchard's desk and scribbled down the number he gave me, forgetting I already had it. 'She'll arrange everything.'

'Arrange what?'

'Take care, Lenny. It was fun while it lasted.'

And he hung up.

I stood there for a moment after the line went dead, a little taken aback by Hugo's reaction – though I think, deep down, unsurprised. I was more surprised by my subsequent call to Celeste. When she sighed down the line at my news, when she remonstrated against Hugo, when she gave me a name and address and a price and said she would come with me if I wanted her to, I realized with a significant dent to my hitherto fulsome ego that Bouchard was right: I wasn't the first. Celeste had been where I was, and probably many other women before her. I finally understood her snippy comments to Hugo on New Year's Eve. I understood her warnings to me, and the melancholy that lay under her party girl exterior. She had been with Hugo, she had been dropped by Hugo, and she'd been to the address she was giving me now.

'Do you have the money? I don't suppose he offered to pay,' she said, and I mumbled a no, my head struggling to process the situation I seemed to be in. Would the dwindling packet of spending money I'd brought with me be enough? 'Well, I can't help with that, I'm afraid. Call me when you've got it. And Lenny? You might be quite ill afterwards – I certainly was.'

And that was the end of that phone call.

I allowed myself a little cry as I sat on my bed, waiting for Fran to come back from the market. Did I want to do what

Celeste had suggested? I didn't think so – it was a criminal act, and even if it hadn't been, it felt quite unsavoury to me – but the enormity of the alternative made my stomach plunge. Why was this to be so life-changing for me, when Hugo could just walk away? Not for the first time, and certainly not for the last, I felt the gulf between myself and the menfolk in my life.

But standing there, twisting the phone cord in my hands, something else prickled my skin.

I knew from the beginning that you were one of the exceptions, one of those who like to be different.

You are different, Lenny. I have the feeling you could do just about anything if you put your mind to it.

Bouchard's words mingled with Hugo's in my head. They hadn't meant it in the same way. But they were both right. I'd always harboured a desire to forge my own path and now here I was, the prospect of unmarried motherhood ahead of me. *Well then,* I told myself, *here it is, the chance to be different.*

Sure, when I'd thought about forging my own path, I think I envisioned getting an incredible job to earn my own money and going to parties and having wild affairs with a succession of roguish men, not falling pregnant at just gone eighteen, but there I was, and to my credit, once I'd absorbed the shock of the situation and Hugo's reaction and Celeste's suggestion, I saw another kind of different life ahead of me. Perhaps it would be all right, I thought. Perhaps I could deal with this just fine.

Perhaps.

10

Flo closes the book after finishing the chapter. It is their first morning in Paris and she woke early, a good couple of hours before she was due to meet Carla and Alice at breakfast, so she propped herself up in the sumptuous bed of her hotel room, letting Ernie lie beside her, and started to read. It feels appropriate to read this book here, in France, on her way to hopefully meet the person who wrote it, more than sixty years after they last saw each other.

Lilli's pregnancy was so shocking to her, back then. To a well-to-do girl with a conventional upbringing, it was a bombshell of immense proportions. Lilli had ruined her life, surely. She would struggle to find a husband; she might be disowned by her family. What would happen to her, on her own with a baby and no one to support her? Flo remembers sitting on Lilli's bed in their room and crying as she hugged her, telling her how sorry she was, how she'd do anything she could to help. And she also remembers Lilli's reaction to this outburst of pity and sorrow and despair. *Well, what's done is done, honey, let's not cry over spilt milk.*

251

Lilli wasn't upbeat, exactly. She wasn't happy about the situation she found herself in, but she wasn't going to let it drag her down either. She would remain hopeful and optimistic as she considered what she would do next. She still thought she would actually have some say in that; she still believed herself in charge of her own destiny.

And for that, Flo envied her. She envied this girl who had most probably messed up her life for having the courage to do what she wanted – or, at least, try to. Whatever life threw at her, she would see the best in it; however her future was now shaped by the actions of others, she would still try to go her own way.

Was that the first time she considered that perhaps Lilli was right – she didn't have to marry Peter? Perhaps she, too, could go her own way. If Lilli could, with all that she was now dealing with, why couldn't she?

Flo puts the book down on the bed beside her, pushes Ernie away, flips back the duvet and swings her legs out of the bed. Her skin is pale, wrinkled and paper-thin, purple veins snaking down her calves. So much time has passed since that year in Lyon, but some of the feelings it provoked have lingered more than others. *I'll do anything I can to help you,* she'd said to Lilli. But in fact she abandoned her friend and sent herself into a loveless marriage. She failed Lilli. Failed both of them.

Because of what she did.

No, because of him, *because of what* he *did.*

She stands up and a wave of dizziness washes over her. She sits down again and Ernie whines. 'It's all right, boy.' She pats his soft head. 'I'm all right.'

The four of them spend the day pottering about Paris. They browse the boutiques on Ile Saint-Louis, stroll past the pop-up beach along the Seine, and stop for lunch at a little place in the Marais that Flo remembers from the old days; it's hardly changed since she would lunch there with Guinevere on steak frites and good red claret, the owner always coming by to greet his regular customers and offer them a digestif on the house.

They go to the Eiffel Tower because Alice has never been. Flo sits on a bench with an ice-cream while Carla and Alice take pictures of each other under the vast iron arches. She smiles to see their heads huddled together, shielding the sun from the screen as they look at the pictures, and the delight on Alice's face as she poses for a photo, pointing to the top of the tower. It will take more than a day in Paris to fix whatever is broken in their relationship, but it's hard to be cross with someone when you're standing under the Eiffel Tower for the very first time.

'Come on, Flo,' Alice calls to her. 'I want to take your photo.'

But she smiles and waves her away. 'No, I like watching you two.'

Instead she sits, resting her knees, and lets herself slip back to the day she met James right here, recalls the flutter in her chest when she saw him walking towards her, a single flower in his hand – a vibrant orange gerbera, she was glad to see, not a red rose – and the way he shifted from foot to foot in front of her, silently asking if she'd changed her mind about him since they last saw each other in the bar of the Hotel

Bristol two years previously. But how could she have? The letters they had exchanged had been almost more intimate than any physical contact. Despite not having seen him for so long, she *knew* him – and she knew he was the one for her, with the certainty that comes from being with the wrong one for so long.

She misses him constantly, but she has got used to his absence, has learned to live with it; now she wears it like an invisible overcoat. These days, twenty years after his death, it's the little things that catch her out. When she buys apples and remembers he knew exactly how to pick the crunchiest and most flavoursome, while she invariably picks those that are soft and fuzzy in the mouth, as though they've been sitting in the supermarket too long. When she catches a film from the eighties or early nineties on the television and recalls them watching it together at the cinema, scrapping over the last dregs of popcorn. When she cooks a roast and thinks how he always did it better than her, how he'd hum away to himself in the kitchen while he chopped and baked and steamed, as Flo sat reading in the living room, a glass of wine in her hand. Knowing he was there – the smell of the chicken in the oven, the clatter of dishes and pans, his tuneless singing to 'When the Saints Go Marching In' or 'King of the Road' – that's what she misses the most. Just knowing he is there.

But when they first moved in together, Flo was skittish. Was this too good to be true? It was to be expected, she supposed, given how badly her marriage had turned out – and his. She was right to be apprehensive, cautious, protective of her heart. But gradually, as the days turned to weeks and the weeks to months, she knew they would be all right, that this was how it was meant to be. It simply couldn't be any other way.

'I don't think I've ever felt more content than I do right now,' he said to her one Sunday morning in bed. His legs were tangled with hers under the covers, his arm resting on her stomach.

She kissed his cheek and buried her nose in the smell of him. By the end of her marriage to Peter, they had slept in separate beds, much to both of their relief, and Flo had thought that's simply what happened, that all couples were like that.

'Nor me,' she said into his hair, and he hugged her tight.

She remembers the laughter they shared, even in the bad times. The hugs he gave her after each month's crushing disappointment. *At least we have each other.* The way he'd always remember her late brother's birthday and insist on toasting him. *He'd be so proud of you.* The small moments of triumph as he made progress after the first stroke – the first time he managed to walk unaided down the corridor, the first time he could pick up a pen again and write his name. And she remembers finding him the second time, realizing that that was it now, their time together was in the past.

Despite the pain of losing him, she wouldn't have given up those years for anything. To think she probably wouldn't have met him if she'd gone with Lilli that night! The thought is almost unbearable.

If she hadn't killed Harry.

If she hadn't failed her friend.

She looks over at Alice and Carla, the legs of the tower arching over their heads. It was worth it then, to have borne everything that happened, to have endured the traumatic end to her time in Lyon and the misery of her marriage, in order to have found James.

Wasn't it?

⌇

Alice follows her mother into the next room of the museum, past sculptures by Rodin and Gauguin, paintings by Degas and Cézanne and Manet. Flo insisted Alice and her mother go to the Musée d'Orsay, even though she would have to wait outside with Ernie. 'It doesn't matter, I've been here many times before,' Flo said, 'and I want you to see it.' And Alice is so glad Flo pushed them into it because it's unlike anything she has ever seen before. The sheer number of artworks on show and the magnitude of their creators' names – names that even she, with no art history education, has heard of, mostly from watching *University Challenge* with her mum – makes her whisper and tiptoe, as though in a place of worship. It both humbles and inspires her; surely she could never achieve such beauty and craftsmanship herself? And yet her mind is opening up to accommodate the possibility. People can do great things, if only they try – the evidence is right here.

'Look, Alice, isn't that just stunning?' Her mother points to a Rodin sculpture of a female nude, an old woman, her muscles and veins and wrinkles telling a life story in marble, and Alice wonders how it's possible to make stone seem as soft and delicate as flesh.

'It's amazing,' she says, her eyes fixed on the sculpture. She feels, rather than sees, her mother's smile.

'I'm so glad we're here together,' Carla says, and though Alice doesn't articulate it out loud, in that moment she thinks exactly the same. Perhaps it's because she's far from home, but she feels different in Paris. Freed, somehow. And despite that near row in Honfleur, she senses her mother feels the same. They both have other things to focus on, here in the French capital, things that don't involve their own lives. By walking through the Jardin des Tuileries, taking a Bateau Mouche down the Seine, people-watching from a restaurant terrace, standing under the Eiffel Tower, looking at the most beautiful art, Alice's brain seems to have been tricked into looking outward for a change, instead of goading her internal anxieties like a devil on her shoulder. She is still worried that Flo's knees might give in, that they might lose each other in the complicated metro system, that a terrorist might blow himself up in the café they stop for coffee in, but those worries are dulled, faded, by the beauty of the sculptures, the impressiveness of the architecture, the sheer wonder of seeing the Eiffel Tower for the first time.

'You love it here, don't you?' Carla asks as they leave the museum and head back to find Flo and Ernie.

'It's brilliant.'

'It's so nice to see a smile on your face,' her mother says, which, for a reason Alice can't identify, makes her mouth fall into a frown.

Carla puts her hand on Alice's arm and they stop on the steps of the museum. 'I know I worry about you, probably too much, but I just want you to be happy, Alice, you know that, don't you?'

Alice nods. She does know it, she always has. She just isn't always *able* to be happy; sometimes she just needs to be sad.

'And I hate it when we fight, or when you're cross with me. You used to tell me everything, but now ... sometimes I feel you don't even like me anymore.'

Her mother looks tired; she has aged a lot in the past two years. Alice is suddenly aware she is looking at her properly in a way she hasn't really, since Honfleur or before, since the ferry, since home, since ... when? A long time.

'But I want you to know that you are the most precious thing in the world to me, Alice, and I would do anything for you. I'll be here for you even if you never speak to me again. Always, for ever, as long as I'm still breathing. Do you understand that?'

Alice nods again. It's one thing in her life she has never doubted. Not when her parents divorced and her dad moved to Sweden. Not when Ella died. Not during all the times she's ignored her mother, or spoken harshly to her, or failed to show her own love. She has always known that her mother loves her. She just wishes it wasn't such a heavy burden on her shoulders, because sometimes it's so weighty it's suffocating.

But something shifts in her standing there on those steps, seeing the pain in her mother's eyes. Didn't she love Ella, too, wasn't she also traumatized by what happened? Hasn't she always tried her hardest to do the best for Alice, even if she doesn't always succeed? Isn't it, ultimately, not really her mother's fault Alice is so anxious, so worried about everything? Or even if it sort of is – because it's in her genes, because they are two peas in a pod, as her dad always said – it isn't her mother's responsibility to change Alice, to fix her; it's her own.

'I know, Mum,' she says finally. 'I love you, too.' And the emotion in her mother's eyes makes her look down at the steps, her cheeks burning to realize how long it's been since she's said those words.

'Oh Alice, I'm so glad to hear you say that. Just try and talk to me a little more, won't you? Everything with Ella, I know how hard it's been for you, even before she died, losing her a little to Vicky, and her going out with that boy Nick, and things between you two changing a bit. You were very different people and friendships can be tough to negotiate sometimes, can't they? And she died before you had the chance to work things out, and I can imagine how hard that must be. Just know that I'm always here for you if you ever want to talk about that stuff.'

Alice turns the words over in her head. Something doesn't feel right. She never told her mum about how things changed between her and Ella, about how small and pathetic she felt after Ella started hanging around with Vicky. Nor has she ever said that Ella was seeing Nick, has she? Ella didn't want it to get back to her uptight parents, thought they'd have a go at her, say she was too young. So how could her mother have possibly known these things? The realization arrives in jerky snapshots, like viewing a moving picture through one of those zoetropes she once saw at the Science Museum. Her mother on the patio, holding a book. The familiarity of its colour and size. The way it disappeared into a cardigan pocket when Alice walked through the gate.

No.

Her stomach plunges. She wouldn't. She couldn't possibly do that to her.

But something must show on her face because when she looks at her mother, her expression changes, too, her features warping like storm clouds obliterating blue sky. When she puts a hand to her mouth, Alice knows.

She stands there a few seconds longer, the heat reflecting off the stone steps too much to bear, the glare from the sun an unacceptable burden. The paintings and sculptures are forgotten, the photos of the two of them beneath the Eiffel Tower deleted for ever. And then she runs – away from the museum, away from her mother – tears blurring her vision as she goes.

⌇

Carla doesn't know what to do. She has committed the worst crime. Her punishment may be that her daughter never speaks to her again.

Right now, Alice has literally shut her out – she is in the hotel room they are sharing and has locked the door, and no amount of apologizing and pleading forgiveness outside of it is going to get Carla in. So she has retreated to the dining room along with Ernie, both of their tails between their legs, where they join Flo at a table set for three.

'Wine?' Flo says.

'God, yes.'

Flo smiles and pours her a glass, but Carla can't look her in the eyes. After everything Flo has done for her daughter, she would ruin this trip with her awful behaviour.

As if Flo can read her thoughts, she says, 'Don't be too hard on yourself, dear.'

'It's unforgivable.'

'It's certainly not the best thing you could have done, but you're surely not the first. Who knows, maybe I would have done the same.'

Carla looks up and finally meets Flo's eyes. 'You mean that?'

Flo pats her hand. 'I wasn't blessed with children. But if I had been, I'm sure I would have worried about them as fiercely as you do.'

Heat prickles the backs of her eyes. 'Thank you, Flo. And I'm sorry – that you couldn't, I mean. Do you mind . . . I mean . . . can I ask why?'

Flo shrugs. 'I don't know, really. I'm glad, actually, that I couldn't have them with Peter – I shudder to think that I might have been bound to remain in that marriage if I had. And then later, after I met James, it was clearly too late.' She pauses, looks Carla in the eye. 'I used to think I'd missed out on the *full human experience* – I read that in a newspaper once and it chimed with me somehow. But as it turns out, I've had plenty of other experiences that I might not have had if I'd had children. Different ones, but no less valuable. Children aren't the only fulfilling thing in life.'

Not the only *fulfilling thing*, Carla thinks, *but the* most *ful-filling thing*. 'Well, nobody gets everything,' she says. 'And at least you missed out on all that worry, too.' She rolls her eyes – *lucky you* – but she doesn't mean it. She'd never known fear like this until she had a child, and although it has given her countless sleepless nights over the years and drawn lines on her face, no amount of fear or anxiety could ever make her wish she hadn't had Alice. The joy of her daughter is an infinite weight on the other side of the scales. Flo can't know this, though, and she would never say, would never make her feel like she has, indeed, missed out on the best human experience possible.

'Carla,' Flo says, then hesitates, 'you probably don't think I'm qualified to give advice where child-rearing is concerned, but I'm going to give you some anyway. You need to try and worry less – or at least, *pretend* to worry less.'

Carla feels her cheeks flush and she looks down, swirls the wine in her glass.

'Alice is debilitated by anxiety. I see it in her eyes, in her actions,' Flo continues when Carla says nothing. 'She practically had a panic attack when I took her to the art school open day and that's not healthy. And when I see you two together, I see all that worry mirrored in your own face.' She pauses. 'And if you'll permit me to say, I don't think it's doing her any good. Nor you, for that matter.'

Carla fiddles with her napkin, feeling Flo's eyes on her. How to make her understand? How to explain why the guilt she felt when Alice didn't pursue driving lessons was outweighed by the relief? Why she swallowed down her self-hatred when she advised her daughter against art school?

'All I'm doing is trying to protect her, keep her safe,' she says finally, her voice quiet.

'She's eighteen, you can't protect her from everything, and you shouldn't want to. She needs to learn to fight her own battles now, overcome her own fears, don't you think?'

Carla shakes her head, stops herself saying the thing she wants to. *You don't understand.* Instead she says, 'She's my child, my only child, I'll protect her until I'm no longer on this planet – whether she wants to be protected or not. Who knows what might happen otherwise? She might end up like her friend, Ella, crushed to death on the side of a road.'

'I understand it's been hard for the both of you,' Flo says, and Carla bristles at her tone, a parent pacifying a child. 'But what can you do, keep her home until she's your age? You have to let her go, physically and metaphorically. And in my humble opinion letting her apply to Winchester would be a great start.'

'She agreed business at Birmingham was the best choice,' Carla says, but she can't summon any conviction. A lump rises in her throat when she thinks of the light in Alice's eyes when she spoke of art school, when she stood in that museum today.

'That's because she's ruled by her fears – and yours. She needs to challenge herself, that's the only way she'll grow and learn, but she needs a push. You telling her it's a big scary world out there is not helping her.' She pauses.

'You're saying I'm holding her back?' She tries for indignation but her cheeks flame with the truth of it.

Flo puts her hand on hers. 'It's understandable, Carla, given what you've been through.'

Carla draws her hand away and looks down at the tablecloth, unable to meet Flo's eyes. 'You don't know what it's like to lose a child. And it *is* a big scary world out there,' she says quietly. What does Flo know anyway, this woman who has never had a child? How can she know what it feels like to hear your daughter's life has been threatened by a drunk driver, to know that if he'd steered a couple of inches to the left you'd have lost her for ever? 'I'm sorry, Flo,' she says, getting up from her chair. 'I don't feel hungry after all.'

Flo's hands feel sweaty on the wheel. The Mini's aircon is struggling in the August heat as they travel south, adding to the simmering tension between the three of them. Alice has barely said two words the whole journey, though her body language speaks volumes. She sits in the back seat with her arms folded across her chest, staring out the window, mute and unsmiling, ignoring Ernie, whose hope at laying his head on her lap was abruptly quashed as soon as they got in the car at the hotel. *It's too hot, Ernie.*

And then there's Carla, as morose as her daughter, no longer even trying to lift the mood or make conversation with Flo. She sits in the passenger seat, ostensibly staring at the beautiful landscape passing them by outside but actually – it is obvious to Flo – surreptitiously glancing at Alice in the wing mirror, as if waiting to spot even the slightest thawing in her mood. Flo fears she will be waiting a long time.

Neither of them has responded to Flo's occasional attempt to lighten the atmosphere – *Oh, isn't it a beautiful blue sky! Look, did you see that kestrel on the lamppost over there? Aren't we lucky to be here and not stuck at home* – with more than a grunt or a one-word answer.

Perhaps she should have jolly well come on this trip alone.

They are a couple of hours into the journey to Lyon, driving down the A6 somewhere past Dijon, when Flo sees a brown sign at the next exit.

'Oh, look!' Flo says. 'They do paragliding there.' The sign has a number of symbols under the name – a picnic table, a fishing rod, and the distinct outline of a paraglider. 'I did that many years ago,' she says, her thoughts flipping back several decades, to when she and James both took a tandem flight on a trip to the Dolomites. The adrenaline rush of running down a slope and into the air, the thrill of being up there with the birds, her laughter at the apprehension on James's face. He loved it, too, though, when he eventually plucked up the courage to do it. 'Gosh, it was the most wonderful feeling,' she says now. 'Free as a bird! And the view up there – oh the view! It was so marvellous. I don't think I've ever felt more alive in my life.'

'Good for you,' Carla manages, hostility in every word, while Alice says nothing.

Sod them. Bloody miserable pair. 'I think I want to do it again!' she says. 'I have the urge to fly!'

A snort of laughter comes from the back seat.

'Do we have time to stop?' Carla says.

Flo shrugs. 'Of course there's time. It's our trip, we can do whatever we want!'

'But what about your knees? It might not be so good for them.'

'Oh knees schmees! I've got to do these things while I still can.' She glances in the rear-view mirror and sees Alice smiling now. *Good.* 'And how about you girls come with me? We could fly together, all three of us, free as birds. What do you say? Carla?'

'Oh, I don't think so, Flo. The thought terrifies the life out of me.'

'Alice?'

The girl opens her mouth to respond and Flo knows exactly what's going on in her head. She might break a leg on landing. The instructor might fail to strap her in properly and she'll plunge to the ground and die. The wing might collapse if the wind changes direction. That's exactly what Flo would have thought, too, long ago, before Lilli taught her that caution wasn't all it was cracked up to be.

But Alice doesn't say no straight away.

Flo glances at Carla and catches her eye. *Pretend*, she wants to say. *Pretend you're not worried for her.* But when Carla turns around and looks at her daughter, Flo almost hears the words that she doesn't – to her credit – say aloud, but that are written all over her face anyway: *I don't think it's such a good idea.*

And then Alice reacts to her mother's expression with a swiftness that Flo knows will pierce Carla's heart. 'Okay,' she says. 'I'll do it.'

The Way We Were

Time ticked along at an alarming rate once I knew I was expecting. While once it had dragged when I was desperate for my incarceration on school grounds to skip by, now it seemed to have sped up, just as I wished it would slow down until I'd come up with a plan for what the hell I was going to do – because it was becoming difficult to hide my situation. Several times now I'd had to excuse myself in lessons to go to the bathroom and throw up. My appetite was insatiable yet I felt permanently queasy in Madame Grisaille's cooking classes, and I was so tired all the time; I could hardly summon the energy to play tennis or even, sometimes, lift my fingers to practise piano. Thankfully I could catch up on sleep on the weekends and some evenings when my exclusion from any extra-curricular activities became almost welcome – but not *too* much sleep, lest Bouchard become suspicious. I felt sure she was giving me funny looks.

But at least I had Fran, the only person I had confided in.

After her initial shock, she had been so kind, so concerned for my well-being and so angry at what she termed Hugo's despicable behaviour, that it made me want to weep. Her friendship was the rock I clung to, the lighthouse in a stormy sea. I wasn't sure I deserved her, especially after our run-in with Sandra on the tennis courts.

We were playing doubles with our ersatz Head Girl and her loyal sidekick Barbara, and though I didn't have the energy or the inclination for it, it was pleasant to be outside in the spring air instead of cooped up in the chateau, and Fran's superior skills went a long way to cover up my own depleted abilities. We were in the middle of the second set, which was going with serve so far, when a wave of nausea hit me. I bent over as a ball whizzed past me, then staggered to the edge of the court, where I threw up all over the red clay.

Fran rushed over to me. 'Are you all right?' she whispered.

I nodded, stood up, my stomach now settling, but it lurched again when I saw the expression on the other girls' faces.

'That's disgusting,' Sandra said, her disdain topped with glee. Barbara hovered behind her, a hand over her mouth.

'Too much exertion too soon after lunch,' Fran said brightly, but I didn't bother to join in the pretence. I could see in Sandra's face that she'd guessed.

There was a pause as I held Sandra's gaze; no one spoke. The truth floated around us on the breeze. And then: 'I suppose that's what you get for being a whore,' Sandra said.

Fran's mouth dropped open, but I wasn't surprised – I think I'd been expecting this to happen at some point.

'She's not a . . .' Fran faltered, unable to utter the word she had probably never said before.

'It doesn't matter, Fran.' I tugged her arm. 'I don't care what she thinks of me.'

'Well, *I* do,' she said.

'Perhaps you'll care more when I let Madame Bouchard know what state you're in,' Sandra said to me.

'You wouldn't!' Fran said.

Sandra crossed her arms, cocked her head to the side. 'I could.'

Fran looked at her in horror and I felt a rush of affection for my friend, this sweet girl who'd never done anything wrong in her life, who was defending me, someone who couldn't seem to even see the line, let alone toe it. But I couldn't picture a way out of this. I resigned myself to my fate there and then – Sandra would tell Bouchard I was expecting and I'd be shipped back to New York quick smart, before my growing belly could damage the school's reputation.

But I hadn't counted on Fran playing dirty.

'No, you wouldn't,' she said again, but with a steeliness in her tone this time. She stepped forward towards Sandra. 'You wouldn't do that, because if you did, I'd let it be known that you're not as pure as you make yourself out to be.'

Sandra laughed, but there was uncertainty in it. 'What are you talking about?'

'I'm saying that my mother is very respected in London society, and if she were to hear that a certain debutante wasn't the unspoiled creature she appears to be, I can't help but feel that the poor girl's prospects for a successful season might be somewhat damaged. My mother can be a terrible gossip, you see.'

The shock of her words hit all of us at the same time. Fran, spreading malicious rumours, attempting blackmail? Yes, she'd said she'd do anything to help me, but I hadn't expected *this*. I looked from her to Sandra, riveted to the spot, not daring to say anything that might spoil my friend's delicious bombshell.

'But it's not true,' Sandra said finally, her voice wavering. 'Unlike this.' She nodded to me.

'Maybe not, but you know how the society ladies like a rumour.'

Sandra didn't say anything to that, but I saw her eyes, usually so confident, fill up with tears.

'Are we clear?' Fran said, and Sandra nodded, threw me a glare and stalked off, Barbara trotting at her heels.

I held in my laughter until they'd disappeared into the chateau and then it burst out of me, shaking my whole body. 'Oh, Fran!' I said when I was able. 'Well played, my friend, well played.'

That evening back in our room, we laughed about it so hard we had tears streaming down our cheeks. We relived the expression on Sandra's face, and the uncharacteristic steeliness in Fran's voice. 'I can't believe I did that,' she said over and over, but *I* could believe it. It only confirmed to me what I knew all along – she had the ability to stand up for herself, and for others, if she really wanted to.

'Thank you, Fran,' I said when we'd calmed down a little

and the emotion of what she'd done for me caught in my throat. 'Thank you for sticking by me, for not thinking I'm ridiculous.' We were examining the latest parcel sent from England by her mother (who wasn't, she told me, a terrible gossip at all): a cashmere cardigan and pink silk blouse from Liberty, a pot of Yardley's lavender hand cream and some toffees bought from a sweet shop in Stow, which Fran told me were her absolute favourites. It made me think of the letter I'd received from my parents, saying how disappointed and furious they were with me for bringing the Cranshaw name into disrepute and embarrassing them in the eyes of the school by carrying on with Hugo. There were no toffees with that letter. And they didn't even know I was pregnant.

'Ridiculous?' Fran turned to me, eyebrows raised. 'Why would I ever think that?'

'To have done what I've done, to find myself in this very silly situation.'

Fran shook her head. 'No, Lenny. I'm sorry for you – I think you were playing with fire and you got burned, and it's not fair how that awful man has just left you to deal with everything on your own, but I could never think you ridiculous.' She paused and looked down. 'I admire you.'

Had I heard correctly? Could I, in my foolish predicament, be admired?

'What the hell for?' I said.

Fran was holding the silk blouse in her hands, running the slippery fabric between her fingers. 'Because you're always *you*,' she said. 'You always stay true to yourself, you always do what you want, never mind the consequences.'

'Pop would call that irresponsible.'

Fran shrugged. 'But you're brave, Lenny, you don't blame your situation on anyone else, you take responsibility for your actions and you deal with the result in your own way. Just like now. You could have done what that woman you know – Celeste? – suggested. It might have been the easier path, to just erase everything, even if it . . .' She trailed off but I understood. It seemed shocking to me, too, to put myself at the mercy of some backstreet surgeon. 'But you chose not to. You're going to see this through, somehow, and I admire you for that, Lenny.'

She was just so damned *kind*. How could I ever have taken her for granted? '*Somehow,* indeed.' I hesitated. Perhaps I shouldn't have said what I did next. I was being selfish; I needed her. But I also felt that she needed me, that I could offer her the one thing she wanted but wasn't confident enough to do alone – the chance to escape the life-by-numbers that lay ahead of her. With me, it would be a life without silk blouses and luxury toffees, that was for sure, but it would be full of fun and friendship and freedom. If we were together, we could make it so. Alone, I wasn't quite so optimistic for either of us.

'I have to leave, Fran.' She looked at me, eyes wide, as I spoke. 'Before someone else notices I'm expecting. My folks won't want me back to embarrass them further; they're better off an ocean apart from me, where they can safely lie and say I've married an eligible Frenchman from an appropriately grand family. And I don't want to just stay here, waiting for Bouchard to realize she's got a chance to humiliate me further. I want to go on my own terms, before I'm pushed.' I paused, and then took the plunge. 'And I'd love it if you'd come with me.'

Fran's eyebrows shot up. 'Go where?'

'I don't know. Maybe Paris? We could just lose ourselves for a bit. You've a little bit of money from your parents, haven't you? So do I, a small amount. That might keep us until we can find work and somewhere simple to live. Wouldn't it be fun, actually, just the two of us? And this baby of course, when she comes along; I feel sure it's a *she*.' I smiled, hoping to provoke the same in Fran. 'It could work, don't you think?'

I don't even know where the idea came from. It wasn't something I'd planned before that moment; it just came out of my mouth unbidden. But as I said those words, they felt right. Strange, too, and radical and a little crazy, but definitely right. 'Don't go home and marry this man your parents have picked for you,' I continued. 'Come away with me instead. Take a risk, Fran. You never know what could happen.'

She laughed then, a touch of hysteria in it. 'You can't be serious?'

'I am, I really am.'

Her face fell into its familiar expression of worry. 'We can't, I mean, it's just not *done*.'

'Doesn't mean it *can't* be done.'

'My family would never forgive me.'

'They'd surely come around, in time.'

'And what if we can't survive? What if I can't get a job, or we can't afford a place to live?'

'We will. There are always jobs if you're not choosy, my friend Jennifer's father always says.'

'What if people shun us for being two women with a child? What if they think we're . . . ?'

'Well, why give a damn? But if it really bothers you, we can say we're sisters and my husband died before my child was born.'

She considered this a moment and I held my breath. *Come on, Fran. You can do it. Be brave, like you said I was. Be bold, like you've just demonstrated you can be.* She hesitated, and then, 'But what if it all goes horribly, horribly wrong?'

I sighed. I've never really understood why I'm so different to other people, why I let negativity roll off me rather than soak into my skin. Naivety? That was certainly part of it, back then. But even now, so many years older and wiser, I pride myself on my sunny disposition and I see no reason to let others drag me behind the clouds.

'It's possible, Fran, of course.' I looked my friend in the eyes and I laughed then. It wasn't simply that there was no other way, it was that this was surely the best way. 'But consider this,' I said, 'what if it all goes right?'

11

Alice isn't really sure how she's got herself in this situation. In front of her, the landscape stretches out to the horizon, the trees and fields and houses tiny from up here on this hill. She's strapped into a harness, with long, flimsy strings trailing out behind her, attached to a huge piece of floaty fabric which doesn't look like it could hold up a cat, let alone two fully grown humans. What if there's a tiny hole in it? What if one of these straps isn't in the correct position or done up tightly enough? Why is the windsock being buffeted about, and what if the wind changes direction at the last minute? Her head is so jammed with questions that she isn't fully focused on what the instructor – a bearded man in his twenties called Cédric – is saying in his strong French accent. What if she's missed something or misunderstood? What if she doesn't run exactly as he says and the wing collapses or they topple down the hill before the wind can fill it?

'Okay, Alice dear?' Flo is standing a few metres away strapped into her own harness, currently being tightened by her instructor, Virginie, as tanned and fit and enthusiastic as Cédric. Unlike Alice, Flo is beaming.

Alice nods.

'Do you want to go first?'

'No! I want to see you do it.'

'Right-ho,' Flo says. 'I'll see you down there. And don't worry, you'll be just fine, I promise.' She waves. *'Bon voyage!'*

Alice watches as Virginie gathers up the ends of the strings, says a few last words to Flo – hopefully not her *actual* last words – and then the two of them are running awkwardly down the slope like a strange four-legged beetle, until the wing lifts up and they are walking on air, their legs dangling down as they float away into the sky.

'Woo-hoo!' Flo shouts. 'Woooo-hoooo!'

Alice takes a breath. She can do this. An 80-year-old just did it, and therefore so can she.

But then she looks over at her mother, standing with the dog a few metres away, chewing on a fingernail as Flo glides off into the distance, and as soon as she does, she wishes she hadn't. The worry line between her mother's eyes cracks Alice's fragile armour and then the fear rushes in, unstoppable, filling her to the brim. She only said yes to piss her mother off, to punish her for reading her diary, but she's not strong enough to resist those eyes, the eyes she inherited along with the anxiety they project. She's eighteen, for God's sake. An adult. It's pathetic. *She's* pathetic, she's a rubbish, stupid human being. Why can she only ever think the worst? Ella would have literally leapt at this chance. *Come on, Alice!* she would have said with a laugh, *live a little!*

She nods with a decisiveness she doesn't feel. As if in response, the breeze picks up and a chill slithers down the back of her neck.

'Okay, Alice. *On y va*,' Cédric says with a chivvying grin that fails to chivvy her. She's strapped to him now, practically sitting on his lap – or she will be when they're in the air. Her legs are shaking uncontrollably, and she doesn't know if she'll have the ability to move them when Cédric tells her to. She's going to mess it up. She'll cause them to crash and plummet to the ground and the only advantage of that would be that she wouldn't be around to hear her mother telling her she was right.

She pushes her sleeve up her arm and rubs at her scar so hard it's painful, but it doesn't stop her breathing from speeding up and her chest from tightening. She sees Ella's face, but this time she isn't laughing, telling her it'll be fun, encouraging her to *just try it*; she is lying across the bonnet of the car, crushed and broken, her face a hideous blank.

'Are you ready?'

Alice hears Cédric's voice but she can't move, can't respond in words, only shakes her head.

Things can go wrong so quickly and easily. One minute you're alive, drinking and dancing at a party with your friends, the next you're slumped across a car with the life gone out of you. This could go wrong, too. This is *going* to go wrong, she's convinced of it.

'I can't.' She grabs at the straps of the harness, trying to wrench them off. 'Let me out,' she says. 'I need to get out.' Her voice spirals higher and higher until she is shouting, 'Get it off me, let me out!' and Cédric is saying something in a calm voice and he's dropping the lines and undoing the harness and Alice is running over to her mother, who's pulling her into her arms, smoothing her hands over her hair and saying, 'It's okay, sweetie, it's okay' and Alice breathes in her mother's familiar scent and feels the comforting shape of her body against hers and she cries so hard she thinks she'll break apart right there and then.

It's quiet up here, but for the swoosh of the wing through the summer air and the occasional cry of a bird – an eagle, perhaps? Flo scours the sky, looking for the familiar shape, and her heart soars when she sees it in the distance. What a privilege to be able to share the air with such a creature.

'You want to take over?' Virginie says.

'Oh, can I?'

'Keep them level, no sudden movements.'

Flo takes the two handles from her instructor's hands, one by one, and then she is flying, really flying, as close to being that eagle as it's possible to be. The air is warm, even this high, and there's a slight breeze, soft on her face; perfect flying conditions, Virginie said. Flo breathes in the musky smell of sun-scorched grass – the smell of summer – and laughs.

'This is wonderful,' she says. '*C'est magnifique.*'

She can't see if Alice has joined her in the air, but she really hopes so. She wants the girl to feel this sensation, to feel free, at peace – not something Alice has likely felt recently. There's so much weight on that girl's shoulders it's a wonder she's still standing upright. If only she could release herself from those self-imposed chains and let herself do these things, then a life full of seized opportunities and unexpected experiences could await, a life where she may find her equivalent of spontaneously applying for a job as assistant to a fashion designer or taking a risk on a stranger at a Paris hotel. Flo's life hasn't turned out anything like she once expected, and though it has contained ups and downs, joys and sorrows, delights and regrets – yes, certainly regrets – it has taught her that it's best to dispense with expectation altogether. Have aims and desires, naturally, but not such strict ones that you won't let yourself be deviated from your path by unexpected events. Make sure you're well strapped onto the paraglider of life, but allow yourself to be buffeted by the wind, because who knows to what exciting places it might take you?

She looks out at the horizon, across hills and fields and villages that disappear into a fuzzy haze where land meets sky. They are still a good couple of hours drive from Lyon, but they will be there tonight, and then, after a day or two, they'll carry on to Avignon. She thought about writing an email to Lilli's publisher to pass on to her, but she didn't know what to say, and anyway, she feared Lilli might decline to meet, given how they parted all those years ago. She'd rather not give her the chance to do that. She wants to just appear in front of her and get her apology in before Lilli has time to turn her back. If they find her, that is.

There's so much she wants to say to Lilli. Sixty-two years! How do you cover that in one conversation? Where do you even start? She wants to tell her about her marriage to Peter, how she realized Lilli was right almost as soon as the wedding band was slipped on her finger just a few months after returning from Lyon in 1958. She wants to tell her about all those times she sat under the tree in the front garden in Oxford wishing she'd rejected this life and gone with Lilli instead. She wants to tell her about the children that never came and Peter's affair and the sense of freedom she felt driving down that motorway towards London, her scant possessions in the boot, and sitting on the mattress in her bedsit that first night, her new life stretching out ahead of her, unwritten. She wants to tell her about the pop stars and minor royals she dressed with Guinevere, the fashion shows they attended, the fancy dinners and trips to New York and Madrid and Berlin and, more than anything, the way Guinevere, with her pink hair and miniskirts, gently but firmly shepherded Flo into this second phase of her adult life, encouraging her to cast off expectation and convention and do as she pleased, just as Lilli had all those years before. And she wants to tell her about James, the man she never would have met if she hadn't seized that opportunity to work with Guinevere. James, the man who showed her kindness and passion and respect and made her feel truly and utterly herself, who demonstrated what love should be – not a set of rules to contain a person, but the desire to help them fly. She hopes Lilli has had someone in her life like that, someone who really understands the unique individual she is – or was, because Flo can't really assume to know her anymore, after more than six decades apart. But she *wants* to know her, so much, now. She yearns to see her old friend again – and to explain what severed their friendship.

She hands the reins back to Virginie and they drift higher. As they turn, she scours the air for Alice and Cédric, but she can't see them, and then she catches a flash of red on the hill they took off from – Cédric's wing, still on the ground. *Oh, Alice.*

Her joy at being in the air falls away. She is failing Alice. She so wanted to help her, but she is failing. She wanted this trip to be a turning point for her, and she'd thought, for a while in Paris, that it might be. And then today, when Alice agreed to go paragliding with hardly any persuasion, although Flo deduced it was mainly about getting back at her mother, she thought the girl had made a breakthrough, that this could be a symbolic moment for her, the start of her casting off fear and embracing new challenges, just as Flo once did herself. But she should have known that it wouldn't be that easy.

It took her ten years, after all.

As Carla drives down the hill to meet Flo in the car park near the paragliding centre, they are silent. Alice is in the passenger seat, staring out of the window, her face streaked with dried tears, her eyes red. Carla is shaking slightly; she grips the steering wheel as though her life depended on it.

What have I done to my child?

As she watched Flo drift off into the air with a joyful *woo-hoo!* and then witnessed the panic and distress in her daughter's face, the contrast hit her full in her chest. Alice shouldn't be this fearful. She should be eager to try new things, jumping at the chance to gather experiences so she can figure out which ones she likes and which she doesn't – just as Carla did at her age, when she went off to university full of excitement about leaving home, when she made new friends and fell in love and had her heart broken, when she bungee-jumped and swam with freshies in Australia and returned from her travels determined to work in publishing. But instead, her daughter is immobilized by pain and trepidation. And so when Alice disentangled herself from the wing and fled to her mother and Carla wrapped herself around her, she didn't feel relief that Alice had been unable to fly, she felt only guilt – overwhelming, unassuageable guilt. What's the point of keeping Alice safe only for her to live in fear and misery?

Flo was right – she *is* holding Alice back. She has always known what Alice is like, so she should be encouraging her timid, anxious daughter to live her life to the full, to embrace every challenge and accept every new experience when offered. She should be telling her that what happened to Ella was a terrible, unlikely accident, an anomaly, that it doesn't mean everything will always go wrong, it doesn't mean death and tragedy are around every corner. But she hasn't done that. Instead she has let her own fear exacerbate her daughter's to a debilitating extent.

What have you done to her? she asks herself, followed by a quieter, more unexpected question: *what have you done to yourself?*

'What happened, Alice?' she says finally. The animosity her daughter brandished like a shield during the car journey evaporated in that moment on the hill, but it has been replaced by something raw that rips into Carla's heart. Alice looks broken.

'I saw her face,' she says finally.

'Ella?'

She nods. 'I saw her lying there over the car bonnet.'

'Oh, Alice.'

Carla sees her, too, sometimes. She wasn't even there that night, and yet she sees Ella's face in her dreams, her broken body, crushed into the stone wall by the car, the light gone from her eyes. She doesn't need to have been there because her imagination is perfectly able to fill in the gaps, though she wishes it wouldn't. And sometimes, instead of Ella's face, she sees Alice's. She sees her daughter crumpled on the street, and she wakes from the nightmare with her heart racing and tears running down her face because it felt so real and she can't fathom what she would do if it was.

Pretend, she hears Flo say. *You need to pretend to worry less.*

'I just can't stop thinking how it was all my fault,' Alice says, her voice so small that at first Carla thinks she hasn't heard her properly.

She looks over at her. 'What? How could it possibly be your fault? It was that drunk driver's fault, no one else's.'

But Alice only shakes her head. 'It was my fault,' she says again. 'I caused it. She's dead because of me.'

The Way We Were

LYON, FRANCE, APRIL 1958

I snuck out of the school gates one Saturday afternoon when the rest of the school was in town and Madame Devillier was, as predicted, enjoying a little shut-eye at the front desk. I killed time at a café a few streets away, and then, after dark, loitered near the school at the agreed hour, waiting for Fran to join me. My side of the initial exit plan was complete. All Fran had to do was tell Bouchard I wasn't feeling well – thus explaining my absence at dinner – wait for curfew and then sneak out.

She'd said yes, you see. Despite all her fears, all her worry, after many evenings talking it over, she'd agreed to come with me – and I was so proud of her.

It's going to be wonderful, Fran, you'll see, I'd said. *I'm going to make it wonderful for you, I promise.* And I'd meant it, with all my heart. She was doing this for me, so I would make sure it worked out for her, too – somehow.

So here I was, yet Fran wasn't.

I looked at my watch again. It was nearly ten past eleven. *Come on, Fran.* There was only so long I could hang around before the lights would come on in the chateau, the alarm would be raised and Bouchard would send out a search party in an attempt to drag me back. And that simply could not happen.

I knew, then, that I was going to do this regardless. Yes, I needed Fran. Without her, how could I possibly manage? My stomach plunged at the thought. And more importantly than that, I *wanted* Fran, because I'd miss her so desperately if she wasn't with me. But she'd been right about something: I *was* brave (or perhaps foolhardy, as Ma would say) and I was going to deal with the consequences of my actions in my own way, whatever happened. *You're going to see this through, somehow, and I admire you for that, Lenny.*

I looked up at the clouds drifting over the moon. When the lunar glow shone down on me again, I'd go. I'd walk to the bus stop and head into Lyon city centre. I'd follow through with the plan – *our* plan – because I had to, because the alternative was unacceptable to me, and if she failed to show up, I'd leave her behind. That was her choice to make, just as this was mine. I nodded to myself – decision made, that's that – and swallowed down a lump in my throat.

A few moments later the cloud fell away and the road lit up, the moonlight so bright I could see my shadow on the pavement, the shadow of an 18-year-old woman, wearing a woollen dress, coat and hat, a small suitcase at her feet. I glanced up at the school building, this strange mock-castle which had been my home and my prison for the previous seven months, the place I'd entered as an excited young girl and was now exiting as the outcast – the *exception* – they'd all decided I was from the beginning. *And so I am, gladly.* I picked up my case and turned up the hill.

'Lenny!' It was almost hissed, a loud whisper that wasn't really a whisper at all. I turned to see Fran half running towards me, her brows knotted, her eyes a little wild, and relief washed through me. I'd never been so pleased to see that worried little face. I stopped and put down the suitcase, aware that the light of the moon was illuminating our clandestine reunion.

'You came.' My voice broke on the second word.

Fran stopped beside me, breathing heavily. 'Of course I did. I said I would, didn't I?' She paused. 'You weren't just going to leave, were you?'

'I thought . . .' I swallowed. 'I thought you might have changed your mind.'

'Sandra and Barbara were outside for ages, smoking through the gate. I had to wait until they'd gone.' She grabbed my hand then and looked at me. 'I wasn't going to leave you.'

I couldn't meet her eyes. I looked away and blinked back tears. 'Let's go,' I said.

And so it was that we ended our time at finishing school by stepping on the last bus to Lyon city centre. Just like that. After all that time cooped up inside the walls of the chateau, in the end it was quite simple to leave, thanks to Monsieur Chatagnier, the careless caretaker, and his unlocked gates. The hard part would be everything to come.

'Are you sure she'll take us in?' Fran said. She was jigging her leg up and down in her seat as the trolleybus trundled through the suburbs, and I leaned into her, linked my arm through hers. Did I realize how much she was giving up for me? In my own selfishness, I don't think so.

'I don't think she'll turn us away.' I hadn't spoken to Celeste since that revelatory phone call but I felt confident she'd help us, so I'd dug around in my handbag and fished out the scrap of paper where she'd scribbled her address at the New Year's ball.

She opened the door in a long cream satin dressing gown with a Japanese flower motif snaking down each arm. Her hair hung loose in messy waves and her face was devoid of make-up; her natural, casual beauty seemed so fabulously, exotically French.

She didn't seem particularly surprised to see us.

'Come in,' she said, stepping aside and opening the door a little wider. 'Who's this?' She nodded in Fran's direction.

'This is my good friend, Frances. I've left the school – for obvious reasons – and Fran has decided to come with me.'

Celeste sighed and brushed a strand of hair off her face. 'You didn't take my advice then.'

'I decided to do things my way,' I said, the determination in my voice as much to convince myself as her.

A smile tugged at her mouth as she welcomed us in.

We stood in her tiny, dishevelled living room as Celeste disappeared for a moment, returning with two glasses which she added to the single glass and bottle of red wine on the table in front of us. She ushered us onto the faded green sofa, curled up in a wicker armchair laden with cushions, and lit a cigarette.

'*Alors*,' she said, and the word lingered in the air like smoke. Fran and I exchanged a glance.

'We were wondering if we could stay here with you for the night. We had to leave after dark, but we'd rather not travel any further at night, two girls on our own, so if we could trouble you to put us up that would be terribly good of you, and then we'll head to the train station in the morning and get out of your hair.'

She took a long drag on her cigarette and blew smoke up to the ceiling, which was yellowed and peeling. For a glamorous girl, it wasn't exactly a glamorous place to live, but there was a certain rough charm in its tousled appearance and I wanted to look around – to browse the many books that lined the shelves, to feel the softness of the well-worn throw that lay in a heap on a chair, to touch my bare feet to the scratched wooden floorboards. The flat was endearing, interesting, slightly battered by life – much like its occupant.

'And then?'

'We'll take a train to Paris, lose ourselves in the city for a while. Hopefully find a small place to live and get jobs.'

She laughed. 'That city will eat you alive, *chérie*. Paris is the worst place to be. You'll end up waitressing in some dive, fending off advances from sleazy men – and that's the best-case scenario.' She leaned forward. 'You should just go home, back to your families.'

I shook my head. 'Never. I refuse to feel shame for this.' I touched my stomach. 'And that's all I'll be made to feel if I go back home. And she,' I nodded to Fran, 'will be married off to some man she describes as *quite nice*.' I rolled my eyes and Celeste glanced at Fran, one eyebrow arched. 'Instead, we're taking our lives in our own hands and we *will* make a success of it.' I drained my wine glass and poured myself another. Perhaps I was being ridiculous, perhaps it would all go wrong, but I had to at least try. I'd never forgive myself if I just went home under a cloud. 'I mean, *you* have,' I added.

Celeste laughed again, but this time it was slightly sardonic. 'Looks can be deceiving.' She put her cigarette to her mouth, and then smiled. 'All right. We'd better come up with a different plan for you then.'

We stayed up drinking, smoking and talking until four in the morning, when Fran fell asleep on the sofa and Celeste finally drifted off to bed, squeezing my shoulder as she did. Perhaps it was the lateness of the hour, or the amount of wine swilling around in our gullets, or the strangeness of the situation Fran and I were now facing, but the time the three of us spent together that night seemed almost dreamlike the next day, as though we'd been suspended in a surreal bubble of our own making, a safe space where we could say or do whatever we wanted, with no one there to judge us.

'Celeste,' I said at one point, wine-induced emotion in my voice, 'I didn't know when we first met that you and Hugo ...' I shook my head. 'I'm sorry, if I ... got in the way.'

Celeste gave a small smile and waved her cigarette hand in a gesture of dismissal. 'Oh no, *chérie*, he and I were over before that. It was no *grand amour*, simply a few encounters between the sheets.' She fixed her eyes on me. 'And anyway, who could blame him – just look at you.'

I smiled and struck a silly pose, a little embarrassed by her praise, but her steady gaze remained on me until Fran spoke, dissolving whatever hung there between us.

'You had . . . relations with him, too?'

Celeste turned to her, laughed. 'Sex, you mean? Yes, *chérie*, I did – though I can tell you it really wasn't worth it. That quack of a so-called doctor . . . I spent Christmas here, by myself, in agony. And Hugo couldn't have given two hoots.' She looked at me again as I remembered her hostility towards him at the New Year's ball, the way she'd warned me off him.

'You poor thing!' Fran put her glass on the table with a heavy clunk and leaned forward, her eyes wide and shiny. She was more than a little drunk – she hadn't had weeks of developing her tolerance like I had. 'I'm so angry that he just gets to walk away while you two suffer the consequences.'

Celeste stood up and walked unsteadily towards the window, her Japanese silk robe blooming out around her. 'Maybe,' she said in a loaded tone, 'he needs to be punished.'

'Yes!' Fran said. 'We could, I don't know . . . slash the tyres on his car?' She giggled and slapped her hand over her mouth, as though she couldn't believe what she'd just said.

'Oh no,' Celeste turned back to look at us. 'Think bigger!'

'Cut the brake cables?' I chipped in with a laugh.

'Bigger!' She flung her arms out and her head back.

'Pay someone to bump him off!' Fran squealed, and my mouth dropped open – not so much at what she'd said (clearly a joke), but at the unfamiliar confidence in her manner as she sat there, wine glass once more in hand, gaily playing along with Celeste's silly game. Maybe it wasn't the alcohol, maybe it was simply the heady realization that she was free.

There was a flush in Celeste's face when she flung herself back down in her chair, and a glimmer of excitement in her eyes when she looked at us and said: 'Or lure him to the river, bash him over the head and push him in.'

I laughed, but I wasn't entirely sure if she was joking.

12

Flo is a little discombobulated to be back in Lyon after all this time. In some ways it doesn't appear to have changed much at all – still all those bridges over the city's two rivers, still the magnificent Renaissance buildings along Rue Édouard-Herriot and the red roofs of the Croix-Rousse crawling up the hill, bright in the intense August sun. But the atmosphere is different – it's cleaner, much of Rue de la République has been pedestrianized, the alleyways of the once run-down Old Town are now jammed with tourists, and a driverless metro whisks passengers under the streets and rivers.

Why hasn't she been back since fifty-eight? There have been plenty of times when she's thought about it. All that time she spent in Paris with Guinevere; it wouldn't have taken much to pop down to Lyon on the train for the weekend. She remembers telling James about the school, how he laughed at the classes they had to do. By the seventies, it all felt so long ago, so outdated. She knew it closed in 1970 and she's always wondered what happened to the headmistress and the other teachers – long gone by now, certainly.

She has, on occasion, been tempted to come back here, to stand outside the school, to explore the places she'd first seen back then as an anxious and impressionable teenager. But she's never done it. She's always told herself it's because she's felt guilty about abandoning Lilli, about letting her friend down.

Now, finally, here she is, and yet her memories are confused and disorientating, because last night, in bed at the hotel, she read that she *did* turn up that night after all, that she and Lilli left the chateau together to embark on a life that Flo can't recall.

She shakes her head, as if to erase Lilli's fiction. It didn't happen. She didn't turn up. Lilli left on her own and Flo went home after the school year to marry Peter. So why hasn't she written it like that? *Semi*-autobiographical, the blurb said. Well, that was certainly turning out to be true.

'What's this building, Flo? A theatre?'

Carla and Alice are standing next to her, staring up at the grand building in front of them, Ernie by their side. Yesterday's tension in the car was blown to bits by the paragliding debacle, but the ash cloud it produced has subdued all of them – even Ernie is walking more slowly than usual, though that may be the heat. But Flo can't deal with that right now. She has tried and failed to help Alice – and she will try again, but for now, here in Lyon, she has to focus on herself, on her reason for being here, on the memories that swirl in her head.

'The opera house,' she says. 'It didn't look quite like this in my day. That fancy glass roof wasn't there. But I think the lower façade is the same. I went to an opera there, while I was at finishing school here. *La bohème*, I recall.'

She can picture the look of elation on Lilli's face as she pulled her away from Harry; she was smitten already. Everything spiralled from that moment – if she hadn't met him then, she never would have fallen pregnant, she wouldn't have left the school, and perhaps she would still be in Flo's life now. But then again, this was Lilli. If it hadn't been Harry, it would have been someone else. Lilli was never going to simply live out that school year quietly, doing as she was told.

They stroll down Rue de la République, Ernie trotting by Alice's side on the leash. Flo's knees are playing up today; running down a slope attached to a paraglider hasn't done them much good and now she is paying for it. But she wants to walk, never mind the pain; she wants to step in the shoes of her 18-year-old self, even if it makes her shiver despite the heat of the day.

That restaurant over there used to be a cinema, Flo remembers, while the boutique all the girls at school liked must have been where one of these modern shops is now. But she claps her hands when she sees the chocolate shop is still there. How excited they'd all get when Aurélia would come back from her trips into town with her brother and hand them around. The dark chocolate truffles were always Flo's favourites.

'Just hang on here,' she says to the others. 'I'll be back in a minute.'

Entering the shop is like stepping back six decades. Rows of truffles and pralines and chocolate-covered candied orange segments are neatly lined up in trays under the glass counter, while on the wall behind the till are display boxes in black and gold, tied with orange ribbons. But it's the smell that transports her back to the fifties – the rich smell of high-grade cocoa.

She chooses a selection, including some of those delicious truffles, and the sales assistant puts them into a clear plastic sachet, sealing it with a gold label and a ribbon. Flo pays and heads back to Carla and Alice outside. When the sun hits her, she stops for a minute, momentarily blinded and a little dizzy, and puts her hand to her head. As she does so, her brain plucks a memory out of its depths and presents it to her like a still from a movie. The image is only there for a second, and then it is gone, but while it lasts it's as clear as anything.

'Are you okay, Flo?' Carla comes towards her and steers her to a bench. 'Sit down a minute. Have some water.' She holds out a bottle.

'Thank you, dear.'

Alice flutters around her. 'You looked like you were going to faint again.'

Flo takes a gulp of water and shakes her head. 'I'm fine. I just felt a bit funny coming out of the air-conditioned shop and back into the heat, and it made me dizzy for a second. It's so hot out here, isn't it? I'd forgotten how roasting southern France can be.'

'It *is* hot,' Carla says. 'I'm feeling it, too.'

When Flo has been sitting on the bench for a few minutes and pronounces herself fine to carry on, they continue walking slowly down Rue de la République, past some fountains she doesn't remember, past the department store Printemps.

Perhaps they should head for the River Rhône and sit in the shade for a while. Perhaps she should send the two of them off to explore while she sits in a café, but she wants to revisit the *traboules* of Vieux Lyon, the beautiful trees and placid lake of the Parc de la Tête d'Or, the view from Fourvière basilica on the hill, the book market lining the Saône, the vast dusty rust-red surface of . . .

She stops walking. There it is.

'Wow, this is quite a square,' Carla says.

'Bellecour,' Flo says softly and then her eyes are filling up and her hand is shaking as she puts it to her mouth.

'Flo? Are you okay, Flo?' Alice puts her hand on her arm as Flo stumbles. 'Mum! Help me, Mum!'

Carla rushes to her side and puts her arm around Flo as her knees give way and she sinks to the ground. 'Flo! What's wrong? Flo, can you hear me?'

She knows now why she's never been back to Lyon before. Not only because this is where she let Lilli down. Not only because it's where she killed Harry. But because of what happened first.

⟋⟍

It's early evening when Alice, her mother and Ernie arrive back in the city centre after several hours spent at the hospital. After the shock of Flo's collapse in Bellecour, the horror of seeing her crumple into the red dust like that – *she's dying*, Alice thought immediately, *she's dead and I couldn't save her, just like Ella* – it was a relief to see the ambulance arrive, to watch the paramedics attend to Flo, to hear her disgruntled protestations when they arrived at the hospital. 'I'm fine, really, this is ridiculous.' But this time they had a doctor as back-up, and when he said it would be a good idea for Flo to stay in overnight for observation, she huffed a bit and gave in. 'Well, I suppose it's three against one,' she said. 'But there's no point you two hanging around here wasting your chance to explore Lyon. Get back out there and have fun, without an old lady slowing you down.'

They both protested fervently, but Flo held up her hand. 'No "buts," ' she said. 'If you're going to insist I stay here, then I certainly have the right to insist you do not. Now off you go and enjoy yourselves.' She smiled and added in a softer voice. 'Your faces! For goodness' sake, you'd think I was sending you into battle.'

'If you're sure,' Alice said.

'Well, we can't jolly well leave Ernie tied up outside the hospital now, can we? Someone's got to look after him.'

So Flo is there and they are here, the sun beating down on their backs as they walk along the banks of the Rhône in search of somewhere to sit. Ernie is panting hard. They come to what looks like an old barge moored up along the riverbank, its gangway strung across to a quayside full of people drinking and chatting at tables: a boat bar, perfectly positioned to capture the last rays of the sun as it descends over the city.

'Shall we stop? I don't know about you, but I could do with a drink,' her mother says, and Alice nods.

They find a free table, securing Ernie's leash under a leg, and her mum waves to a waiter and orders. As she sits down,

Alice feels a frisson that it's just the two of them now, for tonight at least. They have lost their guide, their French speaker, their leader – the person who pushes them to do things and makes it all seem possible, the person whose presence has allowed her to ignore her mother's clear but as yet unasked question following her panic attack at the paragliding site: *how was Ella's death your fault?*

'What do you think she meant?' Alice says after the waiter has brought them two Aperol Spritz and a dog bowl of water. *I had to kill him, I had to,* Flo was mumbling as she sank to the ground in Bellecour. At first Alice thought she'd misheard, but she hasn't been able to dislodge it from her mind ever since.

'What, about killing someone? I really don't know, but I don't see her as a killer, do you?' Her mum smiles. 'I think she's just a bit befuddled. Maybe it's the heat. It's so hot today, and we were on our feet quite a bit, and she clearly wasn't coping well with it.'

'I guess.' Alice shrugs. She doesn't buy that. Flo is the least *befuddled* person she knows. 'Or maybe she didn't mean it literally. Maybe she just meant she was responsible for someone's death, rather than actually killing them.' Her eyes prickle. Her mother leans forward and puts her hand on hers.

'Oh, Alice,' she says. 'Ella's death wasn't your fault. You aren't responsible. How can you possibly think that?'

'Because I was. Because she wouldn't have been there if it wasn't for me.'

Her voice wobbles with the truth of it, the truth that has festered inside her over the past two years until she's become so paralyzed with guilt and grief that she's been unable to do anything at all for fear of causing something else to happen, some other unfathomable tragedy.

'Talk to me,' her mother says.

And so this time, finally, she does.

She relates how out of place she's long felt amongst her peers, the feeling of being different, of being some indefinable 'other' and hating herself for it. She admits how agonizing it was to realize she and Ella were growing up differently, growing apart; how Ella was clearly so at ease with their schoolmates, with her changing body, so confident in herself and her actions, so able to throw herself into life, while Alice was only unsure and self-conscious. And she tells her about that night, when she tried, despite herself, to fit in, to be like the rest of them.

'I think we told you we were going to hang out at Vicky's.' She stares at her glass. 'But it wasn't just a few of us over there to watch Netflix, like we said. Vicky's parents were away and she'd decided to throw this huge end-of-GCSEs party, invite everyone from our year at school. And although I never feel comfortable at big parties, because Ella was going, because she wanted me to go and I wanted to fit in, I said yes.'

They spent hours at Ella's place getting ready – Ella plucking Alice's eyebrows, painting her nails a lurid colour she wasn't sure she liked, doing her hair, giving her one of her own outfits to wear. She was so happy to be with Ella in that bedroom before the party, the fun of getting ready together, the closeness they shared as Ella did everything she could to help her feel like a normal teenager. She was going to try her best to be like them, that night, if only to please Ella. She was going to drink whatever Ella gave her, she was going to try and flirt with boys (though she didn't really know how), she was going to force herself to be like everyone else.

But when she looked in the mirror, when she saw her carefully tweezed and pencilled eyebrows and the flick of eyeliner at the corner of each eye, the artfully mussed hair and the gypsy top that exposed her midriff, she hardly recognized herself and she had to work hard to stop herself crying. *This isn't me. But who am I, then?* What *am I?*

'But I went, Mum,' she says, and her mother nods her on, her eyes watery. 'I went to the party and I tried, I really tried. I drank some disgusting punch that made me want to retch, but however much I drank I was still self-conscious when I danced. I tried to talk to people other than Ella, but I just said the wrong thing all the time and I knew they were laughing at me, and so in the end I sat in a corner and stayed quiet. But then I saw Michael.'

She doesn't even know why he came; it wasn't his scene any more than it was hers. And it struck her then that perhaps she wasn't the only one who wanted to fit in, the only one who was trying and failing to be someone else. He squeezed in next to her on the beer-dowsed cushions of the sofa, ignoring the couple snogging next to them, and for the first time in the whole night Alice felt like she didn't have to pretend.

'I've finished the third book in the Anderson series. I can lend it to you if you like?' Michael pushed his glasses up his nose. They were lightly smeared with something; she was surprised he could see out of them.

'Oh, thanks, yes I'd love it.'

'It's brilliant. I just wish he wrote quicker. The fourth won't be out for ages, I hear he's still writing it. But there's going to be a Netflix series based on the books apparently.' He took a swig from a can of Heineken and made a face as he swallowed. 'God, I'm pissed.'

Alice grinned. 'Me too. The punch is disgusting.'

He laughed and his face was soft, kind, an oasis in a hostile desert.

'Hey, Alice, come and dance!' Ella yelled. She was holding out her hand and shooting Alice a look that said *don't worry, I'm here to rescue you*, but Alice shook her head.

'Oh, come on, Al,' she whined, 'don't be such a killjoy.'

'S'all right. Need the bog,' Michael said and got up, knocking a beer can over the carpet. Foam seeped into the pile.

Alice let herself be dragged up from the sofa and pulled into the mass of bodies writhing to 'Havana.'

'This is a right laugh!' Ella shouted in her ear. 'I knew you'd get into it!' And for a second or two, Alice thought perhaps it was, until she found herself pushed up against Liam. She smelt beer on his breath and something sweeter – whatever was in that punch, probably, mixed with that cheap aftershave all the boys wore. Her stomach turned and she put her hand on his chest to push him away, but he seemed to take that as an invitation, and before she could escape he'd put his arms around her neck and his mouth was on hers and she felt his tongue fill her mouth, warm and wet and unwelcome. For a few seconds she let him, the sensation so novel, so unexpected, that it almost paralysed her. She was vaguely aware of catcalls and cheering in the background, Ella's laugh over the music, and then she drew back and pushed him away. He smiled at her, but it wasn't like Michael's smile, warm and kind, it was a smile of triumph, of conquest.

'Tenner coming your way.' Nick slapped Liam on the arm and laughed, and Alice's stomach plunged. *Was that a bet? Did Ella set her up?*

The music stopped then, and in the brief lull between tracks she glanced to the doorway and saw Michael standing there, staring at her. When their eyes caught, he turned and left the room.

'I want to go home,' she said to Ella.

'No, Alice! Oh, come on, we're having fun!'

A wave of sickness washed over her. The punch. Liam's probing tongue, his aftershave. 'No, I'm going.'

'Just leave her.' Vicky had come up behind Ella and tugged at her arm. 'Just bugger off, Alice, if you don't like it here – no one's stopping you.'

'*Alice*,' Ella said again, her voice soft. 'Come on, have another drink.'

But she shook her head. 'You'll have more fun without me.'

Now, Alice picks up her Aperol Spritz and sucks down the cold, tangy liquid. Her mother hasn't spoken since she's been telling her this story; she just waits, clearly understanding that there's more to say. The worst bit. The bit Alice has rerun in her head over and over, a daily self-flagellation.

'I left the house and was walking down the road when Ella came after me,' she tells her mother. It pierces her heart that she did. Despite everything, Ella still cared about her, she wanted her to fit in because she cared. But she never understood how difficult she found it. Alice looks around the quayside and takes in the smiles and laughter, the easy camaraderie among the groups of friends sitting around tables in the late afternoon Lyonnais sun. Why has she always found it so hard? *Fitting in is overrated if you ask me.* She hears Flo's words in her head. Maybe, just maybe, she's tried too much. 'And then we just had this blazing row in the middle of the pavement. She told me I didn't try, I told her she made me feel like crap, and then I started walking again. I just wanted to get away from her as quickly as possible.'

'Alice!' Ella had run after her. 'Alice, for fuck's sake, it's only a party, it was only a snog.'

'Fuck off!' Alice had screamed at her then. 'Just fuck off back to it then! I don't know why you want me there anyway if you think I'm so pathetic.'

'I don't think you're pathetic,' she said. 'I just think you're . . .'

Alice stopped then. They were on the pavement along the main road leading back to town, the bus stop a few metres away, from where Alice could get back home, away from here, away from Ella and the party that had made her hate herself once again. 'What?' she said. 'You just think I'm *what?*'

Ella gave a little smile then. 'I just think you're a bit . . . *awks.*'

'*What?*' Alice said again. She could hardly see for the tears blurring her vision.

'A bit awkward, socially anxious or something,' Ella said softly. 'So all I'm trying to do is help you.'

Alice looked at her, unable to reply. *Socially anxious.* It wasn't a term she'd heard before, but it suddenly felt completely apt. She *did* feel anxious in social situations. She felt anxious most of the time, in fact. And as she realized this, as she considered that there was a label for it, a *condition*, humiliation prickled her skin. She was a freak, a weirdo, an oddball. She wasn't like everyone else and she didn't know how to be, she would *never* know how to be.

'I just felt so horrible about myself, even though she was right,' Alice says now. Her mother puts her hand on Alice's across the table and she feels the warmth of her skin. 'She felt sorry for me, I could see it in her face, and that just made it worse. And so I screamed at her to go away and I pushed her. I just wanted her to get away from me, so I pushed her. And it was then that the car came towards us.'

The horror of it is seared in her mind – seeing the car barrelling towards them on the pavement and realizing she'd just pushed Ella into its path. It happened in an instant, and almost as soon as she'd had that flash of realization, it was over – Ella was slumped over the bonnet, sandwiched between the bumper and the stone wall, and all Alice heard was a long, eerie wail. It took her a long time to understand it was coming from herself.

'See, it *was* my fault,' she says now, 'and I wish it had been me instead.' She looks up at her mother but she can barely see her because her eyes are swimming. 'The car should have hit me, not her. I should have died – weird, freaky me – not Ella, not someone so sorted and confident and brilliant. It wasn't fair.'

There is a pause in which neither of them speaks. Alice blinks and her eyes focus on another tear-stained face opposite, a near mirror-image of her own. Then her mother reaches both hands across the table and grabs hers. 'No,' she says, with a fierceness that makes the people on the next table look over. 'No, my darling, my wonderful daughter, it wasn't fair that Ella died but it wouldn't have been any fairer if you had. You are every bit as worthy of life as she was, you are every bit as precious. You don't have to be like everyone else to be worth something. You are *you,* and I love you for being you. And if that had happened to you instead, I just wouldn't be able to bear it. I just couldn't . . .' She looks down then and Alice suddenly thinks how silly it is that they've both suffered alone these past two years when they could have shared the burden with each other. Two peas in a pod.

She gets up and comes around the table to hug her mother so tight it's as though she'll never let go.

꧁

Carla feels freer, lighter somehow, when they leave the boat bar and cross the river, heading back towards the Old Town.

Social anxiety. Well, of course. She's always known this about her daughter, she just hadn't given it a name, like Ella did. And, of course, someone who is naturally so anxious, so worried, would only have those feelings magnified by the death of a close friend – a death she felt responsible for. Especially when her mother was compounding the problem.

All this time she's felt she failed Alice by not protecting her, by letting her get hurt that night, but in fact her failure has been to *over*protect, to not let her daughter face her fears and overcome them in her own way. So, as they walk over the bridge and through the streets, she makes a little vow to herself: from now on she will summon all the strength she has to lead by example. She will put her own fears in a locked box somewhere deep inside her and ignore their siren call; she will encourage her daughter instead of hobbling her with her own debilitating worries.

And if she can't, she will pretend to.

As they walk, Alice slips her arm through hers and a sense of peace comes over Carla that she hasn't felt once in the past two years.

Back in Vieux Lyon, not far from the hotel, they run the gauntlet of waiters touting for business outside the many restaurants lining Rue Saint-Jean. They finally choose one and take a table on the terrace, Ernie finding a cool spot on the cobbles under their feet, and the waiter brings the menus, a basket of bread and a small pot of wrinkled black olives. The still-warm air hums with chatter and the chink of cutlery against plates.

They have clearly already been identified as tourists because the menu is in English, to Carla's relief. She scours the suggestions. Among the familiar things – a salad with lardons and a poached egg, French onion soup – there are other, more unusual items: roasted pig's trotter, tripe sausage, chicken liver cake and fish dumplings called quenelles. She looks at Alice and her daughter's expression matches her own – thinly veiled alarm – and for once, it makes Carla laugh.

'What's so funny?' Alice says.

'Nothing.' Carla shakes her head, but for some reason the laughter continues to bubble up in her, like a dam has been breached. Tears are running down her face and a woman at a table nearby is staring and Carla tries to quell the hilarity that has consumed her. 'I'm sorry,' she says to her daughter. 'I saw all these strange things to eat, and then I looked at your face and I just thought, what scaredy cats we both are, and for some reason I found that so funny.'

Alice smiles. 'Ella would have tried them,' she says.

Carla nods, wiping her face. 'And Flo would tell us to order them.' She looks back down at the menu. Whatever she orders, it can't possibly be a disaster, even though her head is telling her that maybe tripe carries disease or it might make them ill because they aren't used to that sort of food and so they should really order the salad. But then she remembers her vow and tells herself no, this is an opportunity to be brave, to try something new, to put any worries in that box and take the plunge, all in aid of showing her daughter the best example. Maybe, by extension, it'll be good for herself, too.

'I'll have the chicken liver starter,' she says to the waiter when he comes, 'followed by the quenelles.'

Alice makes a face, but then she smiles. 'The *salade lyonnaise*,' she says, before adding with a decisiveness that makes Carla's insides light up, 'followed by the tripe sausage, *s'il vous plaît*.'

After the waiter leaves, they both burst out laughing and it feels so good, so unbelievably good.

When she can manage it, Carla takes a breath and picks

up the carafe of wine, pours two glasses. 'To Ella.' She raises her glass to her daughter's, and she isn't sure if the tears in Alice's eyes are from laughing or crying – or perhaps, right now, a little of both.

'To Ella,' she says.

The Way We Were

LYON, FRANCE, APRIL 1958

I didn't intend to do Hugo any harm, I really didn't. As much as I felt discarded like a piece of trash, there was a time not so long past when I'd thought I loved him. He'd enlivened my time at the school no end, and I had extremely fond memories of him exploring my body in his flat like I was a box of delectable luxury chocolates from that little place on Rue de le République. Though he'd sunk drastically in my estimation, I really didn't bear him any ill will.

But it was clear, for reasons I didn't quite understand, that Celeste did.

Still, I didn't believe she really wanted to physically hurt him. Humiliate him perhaps, drag his name through the mud, take him down a notch or two, but nothing more serious than that.

Fran and I didn't leave the next day, though countless times since, I've wished we had. Instead, the three of us took the bus to the Parc de la Tête D'Or to lounge in the spring sun, which we hoped would soothe our aching heads after our boozy night in Celeste's apartment. It was that time of year when everything seems new and fresh; a mother duck trailed a string of ducklings behind her on the lake, and new leaves were budding on the trees, nourished by a warm breeze that hinted at a hot summer to come. It made me a little antsy to be there, in public, in a place I'd previously been with the school, but I knew the other girls would be ensconced in the chateau playing croquet or practising piano that Sunday, after the excursion to town the day before. Still, our absence would surely have been noticed when we didn't arrive for breakfast; I wondered whether Bouchard had sent out a search party, alerted the law, telephoned the folks back home.

'I could invite him to come over,' Celeste said. She was lying on her back, gazing at the wispy clouds drifting across the pale blue sky. 'Pretend he's going to get what he always wants. I could put a sleeping draught in his wine, and then when he's out for the count we could undress him and con-fiscate his clothes. Between the three of us, do you think we could carry him out the door and down the stairs?'

'Naked?' Fran's eyes were wide.

'*Bien sûr, chérie.*'

'I should think so.' I peered at her over the top of my sun-glasses. 'And then what?'

Celeste didn't reply immediately. She took a long drag on her cigarette and then turned her head to me, mischief in her smile. 'We put him in his car, drive him out here and dump him on the grass. He'll wake up naked as a jaybird in a park in the middle of the night.' She laughed. 'It doesn't make up for everything he's done, of course, but it will give me considerable satisfaction.' She paused. 'Which is more than I can say *he* gave me.'

I laughed, though I didn't really know what she meant. Such was the novelty of my time with Hugo that it hadn't exactly taught me that satisfaction was something I should expect.

Later, I would wonder if she'd planned an alternative outcome all along, but right then we were just young girls letting off steam about a man who had trampled all over our feelings. We would have our fun, play our little trick on Hugo, enjoy his humiliation and move on.

I must say my pride took a blow when I heard Celeste on the telephone to Hugo that night and realized just how quickly he'd agreed to come over. She'd made it perfectly clear what was on offer, and he was there in a flash. He'd only stopped seeing me a few weeks ago – clearly, he wasn't exactly missing me.

We all had a couple of nerve-calming drinks as we waited. What on earth were we doing? But I urged myself on, told myself there was no harm in a silly prank, because it was obvious that Celeste was intent on doing this. As she went through the plan again, like a lady of the manor instructing her servants, Fran worried a loose thread on her dress and I picked at a cuticle. We were as skittish as horses at the stable door, ready to bolt. Celeste, however, was dead calm.

When the door buzzed, my heart leapt so hard I thought I was done for.

'*Bon, allez-y,*' Celeste said, and Fran and I scuttled into the kitchen to hide behind the door for the first part of our plan.

Fran wove her fingers through mine and I squeezed her hand. It would be over soon, and we'd leave the next morning. But Celeste's almost manic determination to do this was concerning me more than I would have ever admitted to Fran. I told myself to stop being so silly and concentrated on trying to listen to Celeste and Hugo. The sound of his voice still did something to me.

'*Chérie*, let me get the wine,' I heard Celeste say, and then she came into the kitchen, giving the two of us a wink as she grabbed two glasses she'd poured earlier, after squeezing droplets of a clear liquid into one. I prayed she wouldn't mix them up or we'd have a problem we really hadn't anticipated.

It took a while. We stood behind that door for a good half hour, listening to things I would have preferred not to have heard – Fran's eyes damn near popping out of her head – until everything went quiet and Celeste finally came back into the kitchen.

'He's out cold.'

The two of us poked our heads around the door and then crept from our hiding place. Hugo was sprawled across the sofa, stripped to his underpants and socks – 'I thought it would be easier to do it while he was awake,' Celeste said with a smirk – and the three of us stood there for a minute, surveying his pale, slim, muscular body. If I'd been asked to analyse our different expressions in that moment, I would have described them thus: Celeste, riding high on the thrill of carrying out her plan; Fran, scared and a little lost, as though she couldn't quite believe what she was part of; and me, aware of the new life in my belly and feeling a little sorry for the man who'd put it there, now so vulnerable, so exposed to Celeste's wrath. It wasn't fair, what he did, dropping me like that in my condition, but weren't we all human? Didn't we all have our bad points? I was willing to forgive and forget, not enact revenge.

It took all of our strength to carry him down the stairs, out the front door and into the little Citroën 2CV that I knew so well, its musky scent of tobacco and aftershave evoking all those times Hugo had picked me up from the school and whisked me away to more exciting environs. We did it as quickly and quietly as possible, but, as I learned that day – one of the many unexpected things my time in Lyon taught me that Ma and Pop certainly hadn't intended – it is near impossible to carry an unconscious grown man down a narrow flight of stairs without making a racket. Thankfully, the neighbours didn't appear, and given it was late evening on a Sunday in a backstreet, there was no one outside either. Fran got in the passenger seat and I took the rear, a semi-naked Hugo sprawled across my lap. As Celeste drove, I cupped my hand around his head to stop it lolling and looked into his face. I remembered how delicious it felt when he first kissed me, what fabulous fun we had dancing at the café, and how possessive he was of me at the ball. And I recalled what Celeste told me about his dead father and troubled mother, and how he'd been writing to her when I first met him in the café in Bellecour.

'Are you sure about this, Celeste? We could just turn around, leave him here in the car until he wakes up. He'll be mighty mad at us, but I'm sure he won't do anything.'

Celeste carried on driving. 'Look at what he did to you, *chérie!* He deserves this.'

I didn't exactly object to most of what he did to me, I thought, but I didn't say it. It would be fine. Celeste would get this rage out of her system, we'd stay in the park to witness his humiliation when he woke up, so we'd know he'd be all right. Then it would be over and done with, and we could leave Celeste to her demons.

Fran turned around and looked at me, before glancing down at Hugo, and it was clear she felt the same.

The park was so different at night. It was much colder, of course, and the wind was up. The unknown lurked behind every bush and tree, the lake shimmered silver in the moonlight, and the occasional growl or shriek coming from the park's zoo took on a menacing quality. I'd thought – hoped? – we wouldn't be able to get in, but it seemed Celeste had thought of that, too, since she produced a pair of bolt cutters from the trunk and quickly dispensed with the chain around the gates.

'I don't like this,' Fran said, as Celeste drove further into the park.

'Don't be a baby,' Celeste replied. She stopped the 2CV on the path near the lake. 'Help me get him out of the car.'

We carried him as best we could onto the grass. Celeste removed his underpants but not his socks ('he looks more stupid that way,' she said) and then we left him spread-eagled on his back in the open air. Celeste went to move the car out of sight while Fran and I found a shadowy spot for the three of us to hide ourselves in, about twenty metres from where he lay.

Then we waited.

'How long will it take, do you think?' I couldn't prise my eyes from the prone figure on the grass, his flesh unnaturally pale in the moonlight.

Celeste lit a cigarette and sat cross-legged on the ground, beckoning us to do the same. 'A while. I always sleep well when I've taken that draught.'

'But it's cold and he's naked, surely that will wake him up?' Fran was shaking and I wasn't sure if it was from the cool night air or the circumstances we found ourselves in. I squeezed her hand, a silent apology.

Celeste shrugged. 'Just be patient. It'll be worth it to see his face.'

We sat there an hour or more, but Hugo didn't wake. The grass was damp and it soaked into my stockings, sending a chill up my body. Celeste retrieved a tatty picnic blanket from the car and wrapped it around all three of us as we huddled together like penguins. I remember the rotten-apple smell of the damp wool, the constant tremor of Fran's body, and the feel of Celeste's hand on mine. I looked at her when she took it and she smiled at me, and there was a wistfulness in that smile that solidified a thought in my head, a thought I realized I may have had all along: it wasn't *me* she'd envied the night I turned up to the café on Hugo's arm, but him. I wondered then why she'd ever been with him at all.

A sudden growl pierced the quiet and I felt all three of us jump. Celeste dropped my hand and looked away.

'What was that?' Fran said, her voice high.

'Only a lion in the zoo, I should think.' I looked over at

Hugo, still and silent on the grass. He hadn't moved an inch. 'Shouldn't we go and see if he's all right?'

'No,' Celeste nearly shouted. 'Don't disturb him now, I don't want him to see us when he wakes.'

In hindsight I think she knew, then; she knew the situation had morphed from a silly trick into an awful act we couldn't take back.

'How much did you give him?' I said. 'Just a regular dose?'

She didn't look at me. 'A *soupçon* more, perhaps. I wanted to make sure he'd be out.'

I couldn't wait any longer.

My heart pummelled as I inched my way to where Hugo lay. Was he going to wake up now and grab me? But when I reached him I knew, right then, that he wouldn't. I crouched down beside him and looked at his face, but it seemed empty, devoid of himself.

As I picked up his limp arm and put two fingers on his wrist, it occurred to me how lucky it was that we'd had a class at the school about basic medical care. *When one has a young baby, it's always wise to be prepared to carry out basic first aid should the need unfortunately arise*, the teacher had said. It seemed I'd actually paid attention, though I never thought I'd use my knowledge in quite this way.

I moved my fingers, searching, hoping.

But there was nothing.

13

'There you are. Finally! What kept you?' Flo is sitting on the edge of her bed, fully dressed, her handbag and jacket by her side, when Alice and Carla arrive at the hospital. It is half past ten; she expected them half an hour ago, as soon as visiting hours began.

'Are you feeling better?' Carla asks.

'Much. So let's be off.'

'Are you sure?' Alice says. 'Does the doctor say you can go?' Worry streaks across the girl's face and for the first time since they met, Flo has to stop herself snapping at her. She doesn't want to be here any longer, she wants to be driving south, towards Lilli.

'He says I'm fine, tests are all normal, and I don't want to spend my whole holiday in hospital when I have far better things to do.' Flo stands up from the bed, wincing at the twinge in her right knee. 'We'll carry on as planned, head to Avignon.'

She sees Alice glance at her mother, silently seeking validation of her own concern, but Carla doesn't meet her daughter's eyes. Instead she looks at Flo and nods. 'Glad to hear it,' she says. 'Let's get going then.'

Flo smiles, her impatience neutralized, and takes Carla's proffered arm. 'Ernie okay?' she asks as the three of them walk out of the ward, away from the bed she couldn't get to sleep in last night.

She hardly slept all night, in fact, and it wasn't because of the snuffles of the other patients, the click of the nurse's shoes on the ward floor, or the dim bluish glow that remained when the main lights were switched off. It was because of the memories that rushed back to her, no longer only in her dreams but all the time, worming their way back into a brain that has tried so hard to forget. The bright green spring leaves budding on the trees in Place Bellecour; the pain of his hands grabbing her so hard his fingers left a bracelet of purple bruising around her upper arms; the smell of tobacco on his breath; her panic and desperation as she realized it was her against him, no one was going to rescue her from this situation. It had all come back to her that afternoon as she stood once again in Place Bellecour, six decades after it happened, and it felt as real to her as it had at the time.

And yet.

Now the memories swirling around her head are entangled with the scenes from Lilli's book until she isn't completely sure she can tell fact from fiction. Were the spring leaves in the Parc de la Tête d'Or instead of Place Bellecour? Was it the car that smelled of tobacco as Celeste (she doesn't remember a Celeste) drove them there? Did she feel panicked and desperate because she realized Harry – *Hugo* – wasn't going to wake up from where he lay, naked but for his socks, on the grass?

If only she could see Lilli again, talk to her, get things straight in her head.

Flo lay awake in the hospital bed for hours, hot and restless, until eventually, at three in the morning, she called to the nurse on duty and asked for a pen and paper. Then she propped herself up against her pillows, switched on the bedside light and started to write.

The Way We Were is Lilli's interpretation of their story, and now, on a single sheet of A4 in blue biro, folded and stowed in her handbag, Flo has written her own account of killing a man.

~

Alice looks out of the window as they drive down the motorway, her mother behind the wheel and the speedo displaying bang on 110 kilometres per hour. She is in the passenger seat this time, Flo having requested the back seat with Ernie so she can read the final pages of her book in peace. Alice keeps glancing behind her to look at her. She has never seen Flo like this and it bothers her. Her usual cheerful, untroubled expression has gone; instead, frown lines cross her forehead and she is agitated, grumpy. 'You can go at 130, Carla,' she said after half an hour on the motorway. 'We're being passed by practically every single car.'

Perhaps they should have cancelled the trip and gone home. Perhaps Flo isn't well enough. She expected her mother to echo these thoughts, to tell Flo they should return to England straight away. She expected her face to be engraved with worry. But instead she listened when Flo said she was perfectly fine to carry on, when the doctor confirmed that all the tests were normal. She didn't say *perhaps we shouldn't*, she said *okay, why not?* instead, and this change in her mum has altered something in herself, too. It isn't enough to prevent the little voice in Alice's head reminding her of the disaster or tragedy around every corner, but it is a lone voice now, not a chorus, and therefore has lost a little of its power. Just a little.

Alice glances behind her again and sees that Flo has finished her book and is looking out the window, absently stroking Ernie's head. Her eyes are watery and lined in red.

'Lilli's in Avignon, isn't she? That's why we're going,' Alice says.

Flo catches her eyes in the mirror. 'Yes, dear, I think so.'

'Lilli – your friend who inspired you to take that fashion job?' Carla says.

Flo smiles. 'My friend who has inspired me ever since I met her.'

'So why haven't you seen her since?'

'Because I let her down.' Flo sighs. 'And now it's time to explain why and say sorry.'

'Do you think she'll forgive you?' Alice says.

'I don't know, dear. But I think it's worth a shot. It's a friendship worth salvaging, I think.' She smiles, but there's sadness in it. 'Even after so long.' She sits forward then and grasps the headrest of Alice's seat, making Ernie whine in complaint as he's shoved off her lap. 'But the thing is, Alice, I don't know how to find her when we get to Avignon. Will you help me? Look online or something? She's an author. L. P. Henri.'

Alice turns around and looks at Flo. 'I know,' she says.

'Perhaps that's her married name, or a pseudonym, I don't know, but that's all I have. There's a website.'

'I looked it up already.' Alice smiles. 'She wrote that book, didn't she?' She nods to the novella lying on the seat beside Flo. 'I've seen it lying around your house for weeks.'

'Ah yes, she did indeed.' Flo puts her hand on the book next to her and an expression that Alice understands crosses her face. Regret. Sadness. Pain. Alice is well acquainted with all of those feelings, and so although sixty-two years separate her and Flo – just like they do, in a different way, for Flo and Lilli – she likes to think she knows something of how Flo feels. But what surprises her now is how the heavy weight of her own regret, sadness and pain has lifted slightly since her conversation with her mother last night. It is still there, but it's perceptibly lighter, less cumbersome, since they wandered arm in arm through the Old Town after dinner last night. They bought ice-creams from a street vendor, sat on a wall by the river and talked like they hadn't for years, her mother telling her how she, too, has felt anxious and insecure and out of place at times in her life, how she does still, when she thinks of her life now, when she compares herself – divorced, redundant, perimenopausal – to other people her age who appear so much happier, more confident, more successful than her. Alice had no idea her mother felt like that, none at all. And this shared unburdening seems to have lessened the weight on both of them, just a little. She owes that to this journey, to Flo.

'Will you do whatever it is you young people can do on your phone and try to find out Lilli's home address, or some other way to find her?' Flo is saying.

'Okay.' Alice picks her phone off her lap. 'I'll do it now.'

'Thank you, dear.' Flo sits back in her seat and looks out the window.

Alice types the name into the search engine. They must find Lilli, and Flo must be forgiven. For what, it doesn't matter to her in the slightest.

⚊

Carla is driving through the outskirts of Avignon when Alice looks up from her phone.

'Right,' she says, 'I read an interview with Lilli for some travel magazine where she talks about her favourite things about Avignon and she mentions this café where she goes to write. I thought we could try there? Even if she's not there now, they're bound to know her.'

'Good one, Alice.' Carla turns to her daughter in the passenger seat and sees a smile on Alice's face. She could bask in that smile for ever.

'No,' Flo says, and Carla's eyes flick to the rear-view mirror. Flo is frowning and there is a vulnerability in her expression that Carla hasn't seen before. She hasn't seemed herself today; barely talked when they stopped for lunch at an *aire* off the motorway, picked at her food while Alice tucked into her *steak haché* with gusto. 'Can we stop, Carla? Can we just stop here, please? Look, we're near the bridge.'

Carla doesn't reply but she nods and pulls into a car park

near the river. They have come here for Flo, and Flo has healed her relationship with her daughter along the way. She will do anything the woman wants.

'Why are we stopping?' Alice says. 'I thought you wanted to go and find her?'

Flo shakes her head. 'I can't, not yet. I'm not ready.'

They get out of the car and walk onto the Pont d'Avignon, the words from the song fluttering in Carla's head. *Sur le pont, d'Avignon, l'on y danse, l'on y danse* ... Funny how she remembers the words from her childhood. She looks over the bridge into the river and watches the water flowing by. So many years have passed since she learned that song in a primary school French class. Would she ever have thought, back then, that she would be standing here now, divorced, jobless and wobbly around the middle? *Redundant.* What would that young child have thought of what she has become?

'Maybe we should do this tomorrow,' Flo is saying. 'Sleep on it. I've booked a lovely hotel. I've waited sixty-two years – I don't suppose one more night will matter.'

'If that's what you want, Flo,' Carla says.

'No.' Alice's response is swift and decisive. 'It *does* matter,' she says. 'You need to do this now, Flo. You need to seize the day. That's what we've come here for.'

Seize the day. Carla sees a flicker of a smile animate Flo's face when Alice says the words she has, in effect, taught her. What strange role reversal is this? Flo cautious and fearful, Alice positive and encouraging – words Carla hasn't used about her daughter for a very long time. Words she hasn't used about herself either, for that matter.

Flo glances at Carla and when their eyes meet, Carla knows what the woman is thinking: Alice is ready to leave home and forge her own way in life, and Carla should let her. It's time. It's the right thing to do. And when she does, Carla knows she needs to forge her own way, too, to make a new start, just like Flo did. *Children aren't the only fulfilling thing in life.* Maybe it's time she figured out what else could be.

'You're right, Alice,' Flo says then, her usual decisiveness returning. 'Enough of this dilly-dallying. Lead the way to that café.'

They walk through the pedestrian area, following Alice's online map, until they find the Grand Café Barretta in a pretty square, its terrace shaded by a large tree. Carla sees Flo sweep her eyes over the few people sitting outside – a woman with a baby in a pram, two older men with coffees and newspapers, a young man with a laptop. No Lilli, then.

Flo pushes open the door and the three of them walk in. Alice and Carla hover with Ernie as Flo goes to the counter, where a young woman is drying coffee cups with a tea towel.

'*Excusez-moi*,' Flo begins, and then continues to speak in French, Carla catching only the name *Lillian Henri*.

The woman smiles and nods before replying in rapid French.

'She isn't here.' Flo turns to them, a mixture of disappointment and relief in her face.

'Ask her if she knows where Lilli might be now.'

Flo does so and the woman shrugs. '*Peut-être au magasin de sa fille. C'est un magasin de fleurs au centre-ville.*'

A daughter, a flower shop – Carla's school French identifies the simple words just as Alice steps forward and touches Flo on the arm.

'Flo? I was just looking on Google maps and I found something. There's a flower shop in town called *Fleurs de Florence*.'

Carla's hand goes to her mouth as she sees emotion flood Flo's face.

'*Fleurs de Florence*?' Flo asks the waitress, her voice little more than a whisper.

'*Oui, c'est ça,*' says the woman. Yes, that's it.

The Way We Were

LYON, FRANCE, APRIL 1958

Neither of us spoke for the first hour of the train journey south. We sat in second class and stared out the window. Our hands were interlinked on the seat between us and that was our only communication, but it said everything.

We'd killed a man. We didn't mean to, but we had, and I was sick to my stomach to think about it. We'd drugged the father of my unborn baby and left him for dead in a park in the middle of the night.

'It'll be all right,' I'd whispered to Fran as the three of us sped away from the park in Hugo's car, though my words were as much for my benefit as hers.

'We need to tell someone!' Fran's voice was a wail. 'Call an ambulance – maybe he's still alive!'

I shook my head. He wasn't alive. I knew it, Celeste knew it.

'No! Are you mad?' Celeste was driving erratically; if she kept going like that, she'd kill all of us, too. 'Do you want to send us to the guillotine?'

Fran started crying then. 'We can't just leave him there.'

'We can!' Celeste looked from Fran to me. Her mascara was smudged into shadows under her eyes, her pupils dark and wide. 'No one ever need know it was us. There's nothing to put us there.' Her voice broke on the last word. '*Please,*' she said. 'It was an accident, wasn't it.'

It was a statement, not a question, though I wasn't completely sure of the truth of it. But I was sure of one thing: I didn't want to spend my life in jail – or worse – because Celeste was too liberal with her sleeping draught.

'We won't tell anyone,' I said, with all the conviction I could muster. Fran and I would have to decide, later, if we would stick to that.

She dropped the two of us at Perrache station at 5am and we bought tickets for the next service out of Lyon – not to Paris, after all, but south, on the continuation of the line that had brought me here.

'What will you do?' I asked Celeste, when Fran had gone to the station washroom and the two of us were standing in the middle of the concourse. The electric lights were stark, yet everything seemed hazy to me. I didn't know how I'd got there, how my time in Lyon had finished in such a shocking manner.

She shook her head, her eyes full. 'I don't know.'

I hesitated. We'd had such fun together. I'd thought her so inspiring, such an example to me in my desire to cast off convention and life live to the full. But now I saw that she wasn't actually the emancipated, self-assured young woman I'd considered her to be, that she was as unsure of her place in the world as the rest of us – she was just muddling along, as we all were. 'Celeste,' I said gently, 'what happened?'

I meant *what happened tonight?* I meant *did you mean to kill him?* But what she told me was so much more.

'They didn't want me after they found me with her.' Her hand shook as she lit a cigarette. 'They don't speak to me now. My parents, I mean,' she offered on seeing my blank look. 'They thought I was disgusting, immoral. So I tried to be what they wanted me to be. I thought I would try to be with a man and perhaps I would like it. And he was there and willing.' She laughed but it was full of sadness. 'He was *always* willing. But afterwards I felt so . . . wrong. So used up. And he barely blinked when I told him I was expecting. "Just sort it out," he said. "Get rid of it."' She paused and I saw her eyes fill. 'I only wanted him to feel how I felt – discarded and humiliated and in pain. But I didn't mean to kill him, I really didn't. You believe me, don't you, Lenny?'

I took her hand and nodded, my mind racing back over what she'd told me. 'I'm so sorry,' I whispered, but there was no time to say more, to say how much I wished it hadn't been that way for her, how much I wished she could live the life she needed to, because Fran rushed up to us then, breathing hard, a wild look in her eyes.

'The train, Lenny.' She grabbed my arm, pulling my hand from Celeste's. 'We have to get on the train.'

I nodded and looked back at Celeste.

'Don't let anyone tell you how to *be*, Lenny. You're stronger than me – I think you can do it. *Bonne chance.*'

And then she turned and walked away, a lone figure

striding through the station concourse at 5am, and all I could do was stare at her retreating back.

I never saw her again. A day later we read the supposedly unrelated reports in the newspaper: a homicide inquiry opened after a man was found naked and dead in the Parc de la Tête D'Or; and a much smaller article, tucked away at the bottom of page four, reporting that a young woman had lost control of her Citroën and crashed into the River Saône. Her body was found behind the wheel when they winched the car out.

I thought about what she'd said as the train sped south, away from the city and towards we didn't know what. I thought about how life can turn on a dime so quickly, so easily, that you barely notice it's happened until it's too late.

'Lenny?' We were nearly at Avignon when Fran spoke for the first time. 'What on earth do we do now?'

I said at the beginning of this story that I had no regrets, that with hindsight, I wouldn't change a thing. That wasn't entirely true. I regret that Hugo died, that my actions contributed to his death and consequently Celeste's. But I'm not ashamed of my time with him or my pregnancy, which resulted in a daughter whose every hair, fingernail and eyelash is more precious to me than anything. I regret that in my self-centredness I once took Fran's friendship for granted, that the fleeting attentions of a man like Hugo were the glitter that distracted me from the solid gold she always was, but I don't regret convincing her to come with me on my journey into a new future. I think, if you asked her, she would say she's glad she came.

We've been lucky, in many ways. No one connected the dots between the man found dead in the Parc de la Tête D'Or and the two young women absconded from a finishing school – Madame Bouchard was clearly too fearful for the school's reputation to tell the law I'd had an affair with the deceased, and once they realized whose car Celeste had been driving when she plunged into the drink, it was case closed. They did track us down after Bouchard reported us missing, but it was more to make sure we were all right than anything else. My study visa was valid until July, by which time we'd moved on from Avignon and the police seemed to have forgotten about us. I've always wondered if it was our class, our supposed wealth (though we had little by then), that exempted us from further suspicion; we were too good, too well-to-do, too proper to end up hanged like that prostitute Ruth Ellis. For once, society's rules and assumptions worked in our favour.

We were lucky, too, to find something of a safe haven among the tourists and wealthy residents of the Côte d'Azur, where we eventually ended up. Fran found work as a seamstress and I waitressed, employing all the money-saving tips I'd witnessed Ma use when I was small to make our meagre earnings go as far as possible. When Élodie, our daughter – I have always thought of her as *ours* – was older, we set up our own business in our modest living room, Fran making clothes for local ladies while I managed the accounts and put on my best airs and graces to tout for clients among the wealthy denizens of the area. (Madame Grisaille had been right, then, we *had* embarked on an exciting new path using the skills we'd learnt at the school, albeit not quite the one she'd envisioned.) Fran's eye for elegance and skill with a sewing machine attracted repeat customers and soon our living standards improved no end. We were always considered an oddity in the town, I think, but Fran's *finished* ways, our soon-fluent French and a few stories about a deceased husband (which was sort of true, after all) meant our difference was accepted in the end.

Fran sits by my side now, as I write this, sipping a café crème in the place we regularly meet up in on the Promenade des Anglais in Nice – she to read, me to write. We talk when we want to but don't always feel the need; it is enough to know that the other is there. Her face is a reflection of all the experiences we've had together, her grey hair an echo of the hard times and the light in her eyes an expression of the joyous ones. Over the many years of our friendship, we've lived apart as well as together, we've had different jobs and interests, we've each married men and divorced them, we've each been blessed with children other than the daughter we raised together in those early years – the woman who considers herself lucky to have had two mothers, a counterweight to the sadness of never having a father. We've talked until midnight and sat in companionable silence just as easily, we've holidayed together, we've irritated and exasperated each other, we've helped each other through the worst times and laughed through the best.

'What on earth do we do now?' Fran had asked me back then, fleeing Lyon by train in the spring of 1958.

I didn't know. I'd looked at her and tried to smile in a

way that conveyed confidence. I had dragged Fran into this. I had persuaded her to come with me, to leave her conventional – but certainly more secure, safer, less accidentally murderous – future behind and embark on a new, unpredictable life with me, and now I'd made her a fugitive, too. It was up to me to make sure that what happened next would be worth it, that the life she was going to get – this third way between happy housewife and freakish spinster – would be better than the one I'd denied her.

I think – I hope – I've achieved that, but to find out for sure, you'll have to ask her.

As far as I was concerned, it didn't really matter what we did, as long as we were free to choose it.

I'd squeezed her hand and smiled as I answered her question. 'Whatever we want.'

14

Flo follows Alice as she leads the way to the flower shop using her phone as a guide. The girl is walking too fast and she asks her to slow down a little, which she does, but Flo can see the impatient excitement on her face and it warms her heart. Alice is determined for this to happen, for Flo and Lilli to reunite, for Flo to be forgiven – but she can't quite share Alice's optimism. It is easier to be optimistic about other people's lives, after all.

Reading the final chapter of *The Way We Were* in the car on the way to Avignon has left Flo more confused than ever. Lilli's vision of their life together, as two old women sitting in that café, having shared so much, having raised a child together and stayed friends through all their ups and downs, has floored her. Is that what Lilli wanted? Is that what she hoped for when she suggested Flo go with her? What kind of life has she lived since they parted, and will she blame Flo for not being there by her side?

'Look,' Alice says when Flo catches up to her. 'This is it.'

Flo stands in front of the shop and looks up. It's a small

place among a string of independent boutiques lining the terraced street. The window is full of flowers arranged in elaborate displays, and above it the shop name is written in ornate green script on a white background.

Fleurs de Florence.

The name gives her a little hope that Lilli doesn't blame her, hasn't hated her all this time.

'Are you going to go in?' Carla says.

Flo lets out a long breath. 'I suppose I should.' She looks at the pair of them, at their eager faces, like children at Christmas.

'No time like the present,' Alice says.

'Seize the day.' Carla smiles.

Flo pushes open the door.

It's the smell that hits her first. The heady scent of lilies and lavender and hyacinth and roses and orchids mingling as one. The shop interior is as overwhelming for the eyes as it is for the nose; buckets of pink roses and orange chrysanthemums and yellow gerberas line the floor around every wall, intricate wreaths hang on the walls and huge bouquets sit in front of the till. It is glorious. It is a place imbued with happiness and joy, a place that cannot fail to lift a person's spirits.

'*Bonjour. Est-ce que je peux vous aider?*' A woman speaks from behind the till, where she is wrapping a large bouquet with green paper and ribbon. Flo jumps at the voice; she hadn't noticed her at first, her auburn hair and bright pink top camouflaged among the colours of the flowers. She is probably in her early sixties, her face is warm, open, welcoming, and Flo can't bring herself to respond because she knows exactly who she is.

'Um . . .' Alice starts, when Flo doesn't say anything. 'We're looking for Lilli.'

'My mother?' the woman says in English, a hint of an American accent in the words.

Flo steps forward then. 'You're Lilli's daughter.' She can hardly believe it.

'You know my mother?'

'Yes, I . . .' She pauses and shakes her head, trying to dislodge the memories and bring herself back to the present. Her hands are shaking. 'I do apologize. Yes, I knew your mother a long time ago and I've come here – we've come here,' she looks at Alice and Carla, 'to find her. It's really important that we do. I knew her back when . . . well, before you were born, and I . . .' She shakes her head again. 'I can't believe it's you,' she says quietly.

Alice steps up to the till and puts her arm around Flo. 'We've come all the way from England and we'd be really grateful if you could tell us where we can find your mum. It's very important.'

The woman looks confused by these three strangers and a dog who have turned up in her shop, but after a few seconds she simply shrugs. '*D'accord,*' she says. 'I can give her a call. Who should I say is looking for her?'

'Florence,' Alice says. 'Tell her it's Florence – Flo.'

Élise – because that's what Lilli's daughter says her name is, not Élodie of the book – takes the phone into the back of the shop to make the call to her mother, leaving the three of them standing there, waiting. Ernie sits by Flo's side, panting.

'I can't believe that's her. Lilli's daughter,' Flo says, almost to herself.

'You didn't know she had one?' Carla says.

'Yes, I . . . I did.' *I killed her father. I killed him after he . . .*

Élise comes back then and smiles. Relief flutters in Flo's chest. Whatever doubts or confusion this woman may have felt about these three random strangers in her shop, Lilli has clearly put them to rest. 'She's coming here,' Élise says. 'Won't be long. Would you like a coffee while you wait?'

Carla busies herself helping Élise serve coffee, Alice pats Ernie, and Flo sits on the shop's single stool, staring at her hands. When the bell finally goes, Ernie barks and five pairs of eyes look to the door simultaneously. It opens, and a woman steps into the shop. She has a pixie crop of vivid white hair, her face is criss-crossed with laughter lines and her expression exudes contentedness and, right now, incredulity, because despite the six decades or so that have passed, she clearly recognizes Flo instantly.

Flo stands up from the stool.

And then: 'You came,' Lilli says. 'I wondered if you might.'

Flo opens her mouth to speak but nothing comes out. She is rendered mute while her brain processes the appearance of her old friend, standing right there, in front of her.

'Look at you,' Lilli says, and her face breaks into a wide smile. 'You really haven't changed one bit!'

Her words, spoken in that familiar voice – softer now, after years away from America, but still unmistakably hers – cut through Flo's reverie. She smiles, because it's such a simple statement but it couldn't be further from the truth.

'Well, maybe a little,' Lilli adds, and she laughs, comes forward and holds out her hands. Flo takes them and they stand there, eye to eye; she is right there, in front of her.

'Sixty-two years,' Flo says finally, her voice soft and tremulous. 'Sixty-two years I've been wanting to say sorry to you.' Her voice breaks and she sees surprise in Lilli's face.

'*Sorry?*' she says. 'What on earth for?'

Flo can't stop herself; she puts her hand to her mouth as tears run from her eyes.

'Oh, Flo.' Lilli steps forward and folds her into her arms, and Flo is taken back to all those times they sat together on Lilli's bed at the school in Lyon, gossiping about the other students and the teachers, munching through a tin of Harrods shortbread, and then later, planning their escape, their new life together.

'Has it been a good life, Lilli?' she asks over her shoulder.

They draw apart and Lilli smiles. 'It has. And I can't wait to tell you all about it. But first, who are your friends?'

Flo turns to see Alice and Carla hovering by the counter, Ernie at their feet. Alice is beaming and Carla's eyes are shining; they stand arm in arm watching the reunion they have helped make happen. They are here with her, for her, and she loves them for it.

'Lilli, this is Carla and her daughter, Alice. You two, this is my very old friend Lilli, from finishing school. We haven't seen each other since we were eighteen years old.'

'Less of the very old, please, Flo. Just old will do.' Lilli steps forward and the three of them exchange kisses and hellos and then Carla is ushering Alice and Ernie out, saying they'll leave the two of them to it.

'We'll check into the hotel, have a walk around. Just text one of us when you're ready, okay?' she says.

Flo nods. One afternoon won't be nearly enough to say all she needs to say to Lilli, but no amount of time would be enough, not really; they have a lifetime to catch up on.

When Carla and Alice have left and Lilli has properly introduced Flo to Élise, Lilli ushers Flo into the back room of the shop and there they sit, surrounded by flowers, while Élise makes them fresh coffee.

'She looks like you,' Flo says, when Élise has left them to it and returned to the shop.

Lilli smiles. 'And him, a little, though I like to pretend otherwise.'

Flo looks down at her hands. The hands that killed the father of her friend's child. How to say it? How to explain? Does the fact Lilli wrote a similar outcome in her novella make it any better? Then she remembers that one of the many things she so loved about Lilli back then was her ability to cut to the chase. *I do find small talk so terribly dull.*

So she takes a breath and starts. 'I read your book,' she says. 'I've read every word, slowly and carefully, and I thought I was reading about my life back then – *our* lives – but then I read that we killed a man, and that we went off together and had this long life by each other's sides, and the whole thing has disturbed memories that I'd long put away and frankly, it's rather knocked me for six.'

Lilli laughs. 'Oh honey, it's only a story. I mean, there's some of us in there of course, but I made much of it up, didn't I? Artistic licence, et cetera.'

'But Hugo, I mean Harry . . .'

'What about him?'

'You wrote that we killed him . . .' She pauses, memories mingling with the scenes in Lilli's story. She shakes her head, shakes the truth from the invented.

'You aren't imagining that we really did it, are you? I made it up, Flo! We didn't kill anyone. You wouldn't forget a thing like that, would you?'

'I tried very hard to, but I never could quite manage it,' Flo says.

Lilli's face is a question mark. 'Flo, listen to me.' She takes her hands and looks intently into her face, surely assuming her old friend has lost all her marbles over the many, many years they've been apart. 'I made it up. I just thought it would make a better story, a bit of drama. And maybe it was my own rather petty way of getting back at Harry for dropping me like that, the asshole. So I half-heartedly disguised him as Hugo and plotted a way to kill him off – fictionally, I mean.'

'But you don't understand,' Flo says. 'I *did* kill him. Not like that. Not with you and your other friend, but I did kill him. He's dead, Lilli, because of me. And that's why I didn't turn up that day, why I didn't come with you. I abandoned you, left my pregnant friend to go off on her own when I really meant to come with you, I really did, only everything with Harry happened that night and I was so traumatized and upset. And so that's why I need to say sorry, that's why I came here today, because my whole life I've felt so terrible about leaving you like that and I wanted to explain why.'

Lilli recoils. 'Flo,' she says, squeezing her hands, just as she used to do so many years before, when Flo needed comfort or reassurance or support. The gesture is so familiar it takes her breath away. 'I don't know what you're talking about. Of course you didn't kill him.'

Flo pulls her hands from Lilli's and reaches for her handbag. She roots around inside until she comes up with the folded sheet of A4 that the nurse gave her in the hospital, now covered with her own scrawl. It is a witness statement, a confession, a revisiting of an event long buried.

'This,' she says, handing it to Lilli. 'This is what I'm talking about. I need you to read it, and then you'll understand.'

Flo

I didn't intend to do him any harm, you wrote in your book, in *The Way We Were.* Well, neither did I. I didn't intend anything that happened that day. All I was trying to do was act normally, ahead of our getaway. We were going to leave together that night, Lilli, weren't we? You and I, we had it all planned out. I would go on that Saturday's excursion with the rest of the school while you, as per your indefinite punishment, would stay behind. You'd pack our most essential things into a single suitcase and then sneak out and lay low until I could join you.

But it didn't happen that way. You left without me, presuming, I suppose, that I'd abandoned you, chickened out, hadn't the guts. It would have been an understandable presumption, but the thing is, Lilli, I *was* going to come with you. You'd convinced me, won me over, and though I was apprehensive (I wasn't going to change overnight, after all), I trusted you, and I had faith that you would make everything all right. I want you to know that.

But instead, it happened like this.

We'd been at the school many months by then, and apart from you – my disgraced, fallen friend – we'd been given certain privileges by that time. We were allowed to explore the city in pairs without a chaperone on certain planned occasions, as long as we returned to the meeting point by the appointed time to catch the minibus back to the school.

I was a little bolder by then, too, which was entirely down to you. All your encouragement, your flouting of the rules had rubbed off on meek, fearful me more than you realized. So I didn't go with one of the other girls that day, but headed off on my own. I'm not sure I had any particular purpose in mind; perhaps I did, subconsciously, but I wasn't aware of it. My head was full of ideas and plans and apprehension and – yes, still – fear when I thought of what I was about to embark on with you. I was ready to do it, though. I didn't want to marry Peter, whom I thought of as an inoffensive but rather dull young man my parents liked far more than I did. I yearned to take a chance on the sort of life you'd promised we could have, a life full of adventure, unpredictability and freedom. It terrified me, but after all those months with you, I was ready to give it a try.

That day, I walked down Rue de la République and picked up a few toiletries from the cosmetics floor of Printemps, and before I knew it, I found myself at the end of the street, the dusty red expanse of Place Bellecour before me. I stopped. I remembered the first time you snuck off to meet Harry when I covered for you at the art gallery. He always spent Saturday afternoon in the Maison Dorée in Place Bellecour, that's what you'd said. Something rose up in me – that spark you'd ignited, that boldness I'd used so effectively against our Head Girl – and before I quite realized what I was doing I was walking towards the café and going inside.

He was there, of course, sitting at a corner table, a coffee cup and an empty glass in front of him, a newspaper spread across the table. His placid, untroubled expression told me exactly why I was there.

But once I was, I didn't know how to conduct my somewhat childish confrontation.

'Mr Beacham,' I began, when I approached his table, because that was his real name, the man I've been unable to forget, as hard as I've tried – Harry Beacham, not Hugo Bennett.

He looked up. 'I do apologize, have we met?'

His charming smile riled me and my body tensed, my hands curling into fists. 'You should have stood by her. You shouldn't be allowed to carry on as if nothing has happened.'

His face hardened then, his eyes narrowed. 'You're her friend, aren't you? I remember now, that night at the opera . . .'

'You just left her to deal with everything herself.'

'I told her how to deal with it,' he said, his voice low. 'If she didn't want to, that's her business.'

'And you think it's that easy, do you?' It came out louder than I intended. 'To leave a girl to go to some illegal doctor, to risk her life, to—'

The wooden chair scraped on the floor as he stood up. I was aware of his bulk, of how much taller he was than me.

'Not here,' he said. He looked around the café and I followed his gaze, saw faces looking up at us. 'Outside.'

He flung a few coins on the table, nodded to the waiter and ushered me out of the door. Once in the square, he grabbed me by the upper arm and marched me over the road and down a side street, where cooking smells mingled with rotting rubbish in the damp spring air.

'You're hurting me,' I said.

He pushed me against a wall and put his face close to mine. 'What's your name?'

'Florence,' I mumbled.

'How dare you come here and speak to me like that, Florence?' I felt his breath on my face. 'You don't get to tell me what I should or shouldn't do.'

I forced myself to meet his gaze. 'You just discarded her like she was all used up. You should be marrying her,' I said, but my voice lost its power on the final words. I didn't *want* him to marry you – he didn't deserve you – but while you can take the girl out of her society, it's not always easy to remove society from the girl, something I'm not sure you ever fully understood about me, Lilli. I didn't want him to marry you, but I thought he *should* have to marry you. My whole life to date had been dictated by the societal rules my family adhered to, by should and shouldn't, and I'd abided by them like the good girl I was. In that moment I was livid that the same rules didn't seem to apply to this man.

'*Marriage?*' He laughed. 'She's not the type you marry, she's the type you fuck on the side.'

I recoiled from the word like he'd slapped me in the face. He stepped back from me, lit a cigarette. 'Now run along back to school.'

My heart, jackhammering in my chest as we stood face to face, eased just a little when he released me. I should have left it there. I'd said my piece. It hadn't worked – I hadn't really expected it to – but I just couldn't.

'You're a hypocrite,' I said, more boldly than I felt inside. 'She's not a *type*. She's just a girl who wants to live life as she pleases, just as you do. Your affair was mutual, she was doing nothing that you weren't doing, too, and yet *she's* the one who suffers? You disgust me.'

He came towards me again, unsmiling this time. I caught the tobacco on his breath and something else – brandy, or whisky, maybe – something I recognized from all those nights you'd returned from seeing him.

'*Suffering?* You call that suffering, Florence? Suffering is having your legs blown off on a beach in Normandy. Suffering is watching your mother slowly kill herself with a diet of tranquilizers and sherry. But I suppose you wouldn't know anything about that, a pampered deb like you.'

He took a hipflask from his pocket and put it to his lips, never taking his eyes off me. They were a little bloodshot, I saw, and I shrank from them. I looked down at the dirty ground, thinking of my brother, of crying myself to sleep at boarding school after his death, of the wedding plans my mother discussed in her letters, plans that filled me with dread. Was he right? Did my suffering not count as much as his? Had I not suffered enough, or in the right way, for it to be as valid?

When I didn't reply, he seemed to take that as acquiescence. 'Girls like you don't know you're alive,' he said. 'You'll cajole some poor sod up the aisle, have the big house, the gaggle of children, spend the man's money on clothes and luncheons and then bore him half to death when he gets home from work.' He dropped his cigarette on the ground. 'At least your friend has some imagination.'

'And look where it's got her,' I said. 'Why is it that imagination has consequences for girls like us but not for men like you?'

He laughed. 'I see,' he said, taking a step closer to me. 'You want life to be *fair*, Florence, is that right? Well, it's not. It's damned cruel.'

He was standing right up against me then. I felt his spittle on my face as he spoke. My body was trembling and I tried to stop it, knowing he could see it, maybe feel it, too. I'd never been that close to a man before, not in that way. *Are you jealous, Florence? Is that it? Are you jealous?* I don't think he actually said that aloud, but I inferred it from the look in his eyes, the press of his body against mine. And then before I realized what was happening, his lips were on mine, his tongue in my mouth, roughly, forcefully, unexpectedly.

I thought about this a lot in the months and years that followed, Lilli, until I decided it was better not to think of it at all. It tormented me, afterwards. Because the thing is, when he first kissed me, I let him. I didn't push him away instantly; I even kissed him back, just a little. Why? I don't exactly know. The surprise of the unfamiliar, perhaps. Or that tiny spark of rebellion, a spark nurtured by you over so many months, which goaded me to do something illicit, to no longer be the good girl. Or maybe I wanted to prove I wasn't the boring, unimaginative person he'd painted me to be.

None of that passed consciously through my head in those few seconds, however. The overwhelming memory of it is confusion. But it happened mutually – until I told him to stop.

'No.' I turned my head and put my hand on his chest to push him away. 'Don't.'

He kissed my neck, pressed his body against mine.

'Please.'

He put a hand on my breast, squeezing so hard it hurt, while the other groped under my dress and the feel of his fingers against my flesh sent raw terror travelling up my body. A metal dustbin next to us clattered as I tried to manoeuvre myself out of his grasp.

'I don't want this, get off me!'

He didn't reply, didn't stop.

I don't know what he would have done next, honestly. I don't know how it would have turned out. Perhaps he would have stopped eventually. Perhaps he'd have stood back, shaken the brandy blur from his head, and apologized. Because he can't have been that sort of man, can he, the man you once said you loved?

Or maybe he was.

Right then I thought he was, I really did.

I pushed harder, I turned my face from his, but his weight was immovable, his body too close, and I panicked then. I reached down and my fingers closed around the handle of the dustbin lid and with every ounce of strength I could muster I smashed it onto the back of his head.

He took me with him when he fell, my ears ringing from the clang of the metal on his skull. I landed on top of him, my face touching his, and I scrambled to get off him, to get away from his warm skin, the brandy and tobacco smell of him. I stood up, breath ragged, body trembling. He didn't move.

'Mr Beacham?' I whispered, meek, polite, as though I hadn't just assaulted him – or him me. I wanted him to answer me – but I also didn't. I feared my legs were shaking too much to run if he opened his eyes.

And then my stomach plunged when I saw the liquid pooling behind his head, the same dark red as the mulled wine the teachers had let us try the night of the illuminations.

I bent down, touched him tentatively. Even now, after years of trying to forget, I still remember the shine of Brylcreem in his hair, the pores on his nose, the paleness of his eyelashes. I picked up his wrist, felt nothing. I watched the puddle of blood expand, two seconds, three, four.

No, no, no.

It turned out my legs were able to run after all.

So I ran, Lilli. I ran for as long as I could along the riverbank until I could no longer breathe and I had to stop to take greedy gulps of cold air which burned my throat raw. I threw up.

It felt like hours passed then – I don't know how long it actually was. But I know I was late back to the meeting point, receiving a severe reprimand from the headmistress both for my tardiness and the dishevelled state of me, for which I must have given her some excuse I can't recall. *I expected better from you, Florence.*

Back at the school I said I wasn't feeling well and went to our room. It was empty. Why weren't you there? It was only then, a momentary freeze-frame among the cacophony of thoughts in my brain, that I remembered. You'd gone, and I was meant to be joining you. And I so wanted to, Lilli. I so wanted to see you, *needed* to see you – to tell you what happened, to have you comfort me and tell me that it wasn't my fault, that I'd done the only thing I could. I desperately wanted to run away with you, to flee the horrific situation I found myself in. But I didn't. I couldn't.

Perhaps you would hate me, for killing the father of your unborn child, the man you had loved.

Perhaps you would blame me for those seconds I let him kiss me.

Perhaps I couldn't survive out there in the real world, away from the safe haven of the school – because look what just happened when I tried?

Cowardly, all those reasons, aren't they? But that's the truth, Lilli – I was a coward, and so I did the most cowardly thing of all: I abandoned you in your hour of need.

I lay on my bed, sheets pulled tight around me, body trembling, nausea churning my guts. I saw his smile when I closed my eyes, felt his lips on mine, his groping hands on those parts of me that had never been touched. I heard the vibration of the metal against his skull. I ran in my sleep.

I killed him. I killed him. I killed him.

15

Flo has been studying Lilli's face as she's read her words; she has followed every tiny change in her expression, every hint of what she might be thinking, but now, when Lilli puts the paper down and looks at her, all Flo can see, to her overwhelming relief, is compassion.

'I can't believe I never knew, all these years. He tried to force himself on you.'

Flo nods, and the tears come again and she has no inclination to brush them away. 'I'm so sorry,' she says. 'I have wanted to say that to you for so long. I'm so sorry for not turning up that night, for leaving you to go off alone. But now you know why.'

Lilli shakes her head and looks down again at the paper, blows out her cheeks. 'Having just gone through what you did? I'm not surprised you didn't come. You were in shock. No, I'm the one who should be apologizing – for bringing him into your life. And for not being there for you after he . . .' Her eyes are watery when she looks up. 'Oh, Flo, what you went through, all because you stood up for me. It breaks my heart.'

'I've always wondered what would have happened if I'd gone with you,' Flo says. 'But as it was, I think I sleepwalked through those last weeks at the school and then let myself be married off to Peter when I got home. I felt it was my punishment, I suppose, for killing him.'

'But you didn't, Flo,' Lilli blurts. 'You didn't kill him.'

Flo shakes her head. 'His face. You weren't there, Lilli. It's like you described in your story. Just empty, like all the life had leached out of him.'

'Well, there must have been a bit left. You didn't kill him because he's still alive now.'

Flo can't speak for a moment, and when she does, her voice comes out in a whisper. 'How do you know?'

'Élise tracked him down years ago. She must have been in her late twenties. I told her not to bother, but it was her right, I suppose. He left France in the early sixties and he's lived back in the UK ever since. He and Élise don't exactly have a relationship – he was never going to be decent daddy material – but they exchange Christmas cards, so I know he's still going. He'll probably outlive all of us.'

Flo breathes out, light-headed. She's never considered that he might not have actually died. And however much she told herself she was only defending herself, she couldn't bear the thought she'd taken someone's life. 'I really didn't kill him?'

'More's the pity.' Lilli rolls her eyes. 'Though you must have given him a nasty concussion, which he fully deserved. To think what might have happened if you hadn't! It boils my blood.' She shakes her head.

'I didn't go to a phone box, I didn't summon the police, an ambulance, *anyone*,' Flo says. 'I just left him for dead.'

Lilli takes her hand. 'No one would have acted rationally in that situation. You'd just been assaulted. You weren't thinking straight.' She sighs. 'Though I wish you *had* called someone, then you wouldn't have tormented yourself all these years thinking you'd killed him.' She shakes her head. 'I wish I'd known. I never would have left that night.'

Flo takes a breath before asking the question she's long wondered about. 'Did you think badly of me, for not being there?'

'Of course not!' Lilli near-shouts. 'I was disappointed, I suppose, and very sad you wouldn't be coming with me, but I respected your decision – it was yours to make. I've never resented you for it. I only wish, now I know what actually happened, that you'd had more faith in our friendship. I never would have thought you to blame, never would have hated you.'

Flo looks down at her friend's hand on hers. 'I'm so sorry.'

Lilli smiles. 'Will you stop saying that?'

Time passes without them noticing. Conversation flows easily, questions tumbling one over another as each seeks to understand what happened to the other after the day they parted. Flo learns that Lilli did take a train down to Avignon, that she got a job as a waitress in a café and that the owner, a widow in her sixties called Juliette Henri, took it upon herself to help the pregnant 18-year-old as much as she could, offering her a room in her home and, once the child was born, helping her cope with the demands of motherhood.

'I owe her everything,' Lilli says. 'I hate to think where I'd have ended up if she hadn't helped me. I was a silly, overconfident young upstart who thought she knew it all, but I really didn't have a clue what I was doing. She saved me – and Élise.'

Flo swallows down a pang of guilt. 'What about your own family? You didn't ever think about going home?'

Lilli shrugs. 'Perhaps I would have had to, without Juliette. I expect they'd have taken me back if I'd asked, paid for my passage home and squirrelled me away like a shameful secret until after Élise was born and then given her away. But I didn't want that. I wasn't ashamed of Élise and I wanted so much to keep her. So I stayed, and though it was hard in those early years, we survived. I went back to New York eventually, for visits, but I never wanted to return permanently. Ben helped me a little financially, and he still visits now – can't get enough of French wine.'

Flo smiles. Ben – or, as she called him in her story, Bobby – Lilli's letter-writing accomplice. Little could he have known how his actions would change his sister's life.

'You were always so brave, so willing to just go for it,' Flo says. 'You know the worst thing Harry did to me? He made me retreat back into myself after I'd been ready to go for it, too, with you. I took a risk going to confront him that day, and look what I got for it? It took me ten years to pluck up the courage to be brave again, and only then after my marriage ended – my punishment.'

'Flo, my dear, dear friend,' Lilli says, 'you need to stop calling it that. You didn't deserve what he did to you, and you didn't deserve the bad marriage you ended up in as a result.'

Flo looks up. She's always known that, deep down, but somehow she's blamed herself anyway. Not just for killing him — *thinking* she'd killed him — but for failing her best friend and her unborn child when they needed her most. She thinks of Lilli's story, of the vision she had of them raising her daughter together, of what might have happened had Juliette not taken them in. Her vision blurs as she looks at Lilli and sees the same emotion in her eyes.

'I never had anything to forgive you for, honey, but you certainly need to forgive yourself.' Lilli smiles. 'You're eighty — I think it's time.'

Flo nods, wipes her face. She is purged. Purged and exhausted. 'Perhaps you're right. You always were right, I think.'

'I sure liked to think I was.' Lilli laughs.

'To think if you hadn't written that book, I wouldn't have known where to find you,' Flo says. The thought is unimaginable now, to have never seen Lilli again.

'I think that's why I wrote it,' Lilli says. 'I hoped you would.'

Flo shakes her head. 'After all this time, you still thought of me?'

'Of course,' she says simply, as though it couldn't be any different.

'My friend.' Flo squeezes her hand. 'It's so good to see you again.' She smiles. 'But you know, perhaps you should have written what really happened to you, instead of expending any more energy on that man. You should have written about being a single mother in the late fifties and sixties, about Juliette, about everything your website says you've done – acting, and teaching, and opening this shop – all of which shows what a resilient and determined person you are. It would have made a better ending, I think.'

'Less dramatic.'

'More real.'

'But I wanted you in my ending.'

Flo feels her eyes fill again. 'I can be now.'

The house is a rambling old place with so much charm Alice simply stands still and stares up at it when they first arrive. She's never seen anything like it, let alone known anyone who lived in one. Green shutters and terracotta roof tiles accessorize the stone building, while a creeper covers the back façade like a fur coat, extending over a pagoda on the patio which provides leafy relief from the sun. The garden sprawls fifty metres or so down a gentle slope, and beyond it lie acres of countryside, a violet haze on the horizon that Lilli says comes from late-flowering lavender fields.

'Can you take this out, please, Alice?' They are standing in the kitchen, the large stone tiles welcomingly cool under her bare feet. Lilli hands her a big bowl of salad – feta and pomegranate seeds peppering the green leaves – while she picks up a huge platter of cheese. 'We eat well in this house,' she says, and a wide smile lights up her whole face.

Alice likes Lilli a lot. She doesn't seem like a regular 80-year-old, but she knows by now that there's no such thing. Flo isn't a regular 80-year-old either, any more than she is a regular 18-year-old. And for the first time, she's beginning to think that might not be a bad thing. Could her otherness, her difference, her inability to fit in, actually be something to cherish? Now the thought has come to her, she wonders why it hasn't before. When she's lino printing, it's not always the most perfect print, the most uniform, the most pristine that is the most appealing; sometimes it's the unintended flaws – a patchy area of ink, a discolouration or a mistake in the carving – that makes it interesting.

She puts the salad on the table and sits down opposite her mother. Élise is here, too, who seems just as fascinating as Lilli. A doctor of biology, she spent twenty-five years working in nature conservation before she and Lilli opened the flower shop together ten years ago. And then there's Flo, of course, a permanent smile etched across her face. After the wobble of the past few days, she is back to her old self again, thanks to Lilli. Alice spent much of the evening reading Lilli's book, then Flo explained everything to her and her mother when she finally returned to the hotel last night, hours after they'd left her and Lilli to talk. They read what Flo wrote in the hospital and understood what she'd been through; they heard how a friendship was severed by one man's actions, and what it had cost them both. And Alice understands that though neither Flo nor Lilli have lived the life they thought they would, both are richer for their resilience through good and bad, both are more themselves for having acknowledged what they are not. But how sad, Alice thinks with a familiar pang of grief, that they couldn't go through life's ups and downs by each other's side.

'Well,' Flo says when they're all sitting down, 'I don't think our esteemed headmistress would have approved of this haphazard table setting.'

Lilli laughs. 'No, dear, I don't suppose she would.'

'Why not?' Alice says.

'Because there are all sorts of rules for laying a table, don't you know,' Flo says, a smile in her eyes. 'For example, a place setting for a formal dinner party should include' – she takes a deep breath – 'a soup spoon, fish knife and dinner knife, and no more than three forks, laid from the outside in, one inch from the edge of the table. Glasses for water, sherry, red wine and dessert wine. And no butter knife or side plate, since bread should be left unbuttered.'

Lilli laughs. 'My goodness, Flo, you really were listening.'

'Well, *you* never did.'

'No, and I can't say I've suffered. There's never been anything formal about my life.'

'I like butter on my bread,' Alice says.

Lilli leans forward and pushes a ceramic butter dish towards her. 'So do I, honey, so do I.' She sits back and laughs. 'My God, how the world has changed.'

And hasn't, Alice thinks.

She thinks how out of place she felt at the parties Ella dragged her to. How socially unacceptable it was to like Michael, how embarrassing it was to admit she'd never kissed anyone. She thinks of the pressure to wear certain clothes and have the right haircut and buy the right make-up, of the Botoxed, gleaming-toothed women on the telly praised for looking ten years younger than they are, and the way those who don't are plastered all over the sidebar of shame.

The rules have changed a little – but there are still rules, and it's still hard to go against them, to be yourself when you don't fit in.

'You did remember a thing or two from the school, though, *Maman*,' Élise says, a glint in her eyes. 'For example, how to make a stunning floral bouquet.'

Flo laughs. 'Oh yes, Lilli, I meant to ask how that came about. All that time you spent mocking our flower arranging classes and you end up making a business out of it! Our esteemed headmistress would be laughing from her grave.'

'I spent twenty years teaching biology at the *lycée* first,' she says, a little archily, though there's a smile behind it. 'And you know, Flo, it was never that I hated flower arranging per se, it was about what it represented to me back then: a life of domesticity. Now, it represents something entirely different: an independent business, run by two women doing whatever the hell they want.'

'You've reclaimed it,' Alice says.

'Exactly, honey.' Lilli throws her a broad grin.

'I admire you, starting your own business,' Alice's mother says. 'It must be a little daunting.'

'I've never been one to be *daunted*, dear, I just throw myself in and see what sticks. I threw myself into acting when Élise was little, then I threw myself into a degree down here in Avignon when Élise went off to the Sorbonne, and then I threw myself into teaching young people to broaden their minds. So why not a business, too? And it's suited us well, these last few years, hasn't it, Élise? We've both preferred working for ourselves rather than following other people's rules.'

Flo snorts with laughter. 'I'm so surprised.'

'Speaking of rule-breakers,' Alice says. 'I have a question about your book, Lilli.'

'Yes, dear?'

'What happened to Celeste, or whoever she was? Did she really end up at the bottom of the river?'

Lilli smiles. 'Goodness, no. Celeste is loosely based on Cécile, a woman I met that year who became a good pal. We've stayed in touch ever since and I've visited her in Paris a few times. She's lived there for many years with her wife, very happily. In fact, she wasn't too pleased with her storyline in my book. As she told me in no uncertain terms, she's the very last person to drown herself in the drink because of a man.'

They eat and drink all afternoon, until Alice feels overfed and woozy. The sun is warm on her skin, the light dapples through the canopy of leaves above them and lizards sunbathe on the stone wall of the house. She sits back in her chair and the thought comes to her that she is content. The realization is instantly followed by a familiar gut-punch of guilt and her hand automatically goes to her arm, trails down her scar, but then she stops herself, places her hand carefully back in her lap. *Sorry? What on earth for?* That's what Lilli said to Flo when they were reunited in the shop. She hopes, if she were able, Ella would say the same. So she sits – yes, content – rolling the unfamiliar feeling around inside her, testing it, probing it, but it remains there like a ball of warmth in her chest, growing outwards, expanding. As though this feeling is visible, her mother catches her eye and smiles, and she smiles back.

✇

Later, when the sun is low on the horizon and its heat less of a burden, Carla sees Alice take Ernie down to the bottom of the garden and chuck an old tennis ball around for him. She watches the dog bounding about the lawn and smiles at his gleeful, guileless abandon. He started all this. He brought Flo into her daughter's life just when she needed her. He's the reason they are all here right now.

She and Élise clear the table, leaving Flo and Lilli to sit and natter over the end of the bottle – though there is plenty more, Élise tells her, stocked in the wine cellar. As Carla goes back and forth between table and kitchen, she hears snippets of the conversation between the two old friends. Lilli telling Flo about being cast as an extra in a short film shot in Avignon, something she did for a laugh but which turned into a modest career as a supporting actress in independent films and TV commercials. Flo regaling Lilli with stories of dressing Twiggy and Grace Jones and Jerry Hall in Guinevere De Souza's designs in the late sixties and seventies, and meeting a man holding an orange gerbera under the Eiffel Tower. Lilli describing Guillaume, whom she lived with for twenty-five years after they met teaching at the same school when she was forty-five, and recounting the trip around South-East Asia they took the year before he died – the boat trip down the Mekong, the markets of Hanoi, the street-food stalls in Singapore, experiences that inspired her to write her first novel.

Carla hears all this and for the first time the blank page

that lies ahead of her seems blank no longer. It is already filled with things, with chance encounters, with opportunities, with corners to be turned and days to be seized. She just doesn't know what they are yet.

She isn't redundant, she's just on pause. After this trip, she needs to press play again.

When she's finished stacking the dishwasher, she wanders down to the bottom of the garden.

'It's so lovely here, isn't it?' she says as she approaches Alice. 'I can see why Lilli stayed.'

The smile that greets her lights up Alice's face and Carla knows that seeing it has, in turn, illuminated her own. She feels different here, in this soft evening light, among these people whom she can now call friends. More relaxed, less tense; weightless, almost.

'It's amazing,' Alice says. 'I can't believe anyone would live in England when they could live here.'

'Nowhere's perfect,' Carla says. 'Everywhere has its problems.'

Alice nods. 'I know.'

'But it clearly suits Lilli. And that's the point, I suppose, isn't it? You have to find the place that best suits you,' Carla continues. 'And the people – your tribe, if you like. And those things are different for everyone.' She pauses and picks up the ball to throw for Ernie, who barks in delight and bounds after it. 'I'm so sorry, Alice.' She feels her eyes well.

'What for?'

'For holding you back and wanting you to stay home and not do your own thing. I was scared – I *am* scared – of losing

361

you, like we lost Ella. I thought if I wrapped you up and protected you from the world then I'd keep you safe, but all I was doing was stifling you and exacerbating your anxiety. I want you to live the life you want, the life that makes you happy, and you need the freedom to find out what and where that might be. And so, if you still want to, I think you should apply to art school.'

Alice steps back, and the expression of undisguised delight on her face socks Carla in the chest. 'Really?'

'Absolutely. Flo's right, you're talented. And I want to see how high you can fly. Much higher than me, that's for sure.'

'But what about you? Will you be okay?'

Carla smiles. 'I'll miss you like crazy, and I'll worry about you constantly, but I'll be all right.' And she thinks she means it now.

'You should do something new, too. Something that scares you.'

'I think you're right, but what?'

Alice shrugs. 'I don't know. Go on another trip, take up a new hobby, go back to university, or start a business like Lilli and Élise did.'

'A business?'

'Yeah, like . . . I don't know, your own book PR company. Or something totally different . . . like a cake business, maybe. You're such a good baker.'

Carla feels her cheeks flush. It's been a long time since Alice gave her a compliment. 'Thanks, sweetie, but I don't know – I have no idea how to start a business.'

'Ask Lilli,' Alice says, then pauses and Carla sees an idea

come to her. 'Remember that posh school in Paris, the one we walked by the day we went to the Eiffel Tower? You could do a pastry course there or something, spend some of your redundancy money on that. That would be a good start, a good selling point. *Trained in Paris . . .*'

'Le Cordon Bleu? I hardly think so,' Carla scoffs. Does she want to start a baking business? She doesn't know. Probably not, but perhaps she could start *something*. Lilli and Flo's experiences have seeded in her head, watered now by Alice's words – what might happen if she let something grow?

Alice shrugs. 'Why not? You don't know if you don't try.' She laughs, acknowledging Flo's attitude in her own words, before adding with a grin, 'Only if you want to, though, no pressure.'

Carla pulls her into an embrace again and as Alice hugs her back, the last of the tension between them seems to drain away and it reminds Carla of before, of that little girl coming into her bed in the early hours, of icing cupcakes side by side, of a time when their similarities brought them together instead of forcing them apart.

Two peas in a pod.

'I'm sorry, too, Mum,' Alice mumbles into her shoulder. 'I'm sorry for being such a cow.'

Carla squeezes her daughter hard in response; there is nothing more to say. They simply stand there together, the low sun warm on their skin, and Carla doesn't think she's ever felt as happy as right now. When she opens her eyes, she sees Flo looking at them from the patio, a smile on her face.

Epilogue

The sky is the kind of rich blue that Flo is beginning to see is typical of Provence. Everything seems brighter here, more colourful, bathed in a light that just can't be matched back in the UK. She can see why artists have been drawn here over the centuries, why Cézanne, Picasso and Van Gogh found inspiration in these fields, under this sky. It feels like the right place for an artist – and the right place for her, now. Which is why she is staying.

'Have fun, dear. We'll be waiting for you at the bottom.' She hugs Alice, hoping to imbue the girl with some of her own positivity and take away her nerves in return.

'I'll try,' Alice says, and Flo knows that she really will, that this is important to her, that she has worked out the difference between peer pressure and fear – and she no longer wants to give in to either.

'We both will,' Carla says, a nervous smile on her face. She is only doing this for Alice, Flo knows, to show her daughter that it's possible to overcome her fear, possible to do things without submitting to the catastrophizer living in her head.

Carla is learning to pretend not to worry, and perhaps it is doing her some good in the process.

Flo takes Lilli's arm and they walk back to the car and drive down into the valley. The limestone mountains of the Alpilles roll into the distance, and Flo knows that from on high Alice and Carla may see the wild expanse of the Camargue, the River Rhône, whose water has flowed through Lyon on its way here, and perhaps even the point where the land drops into the Mediterranean Sea.

Flo hasn't felt the need to fling herself off a high hill once again. She doesn't need to prove herself anymore, to challenge herself with things that scare her, to push herself beyond the anxious, contained, fearful young woman she once was. She has done all that already, and now, at the age of eighty, she knows she is fully herself and all she wants to do is just *be*. She will simply enjoy what she is and what she has.

Lilli pulls up at the landing site the paragliding company told them about and turns the engine off. They get out and fetch fold-up chairs from the boot, positioning them under the shade of a tree, looking out towards the hill that Carla and Alice will hopefully take off from. Ernie flops on the ground beside them.

'I might come out here to sketch,' Flo says, looking around her. 'There's so much inspiration in this countryside, it's just wonderful. I see a whole new series of lino prints coming on.' She is excited about getting back to her art. She has abandoned it for too long, but now, after finding Lilli again, she knows she won't struggle to concentrate, that she will find that beautiful meditative state again.

'I can't wait to see what you do,' Lilli says. 'You were always so artistic. I used to love those sketches you did of me.'

'I still have them,' Flo says. 'I found one in the attic when I was looking through old things from that year.'

It feels such a long time since Flo fainted in the attic and Alice came to find her. What a strange summer it's been, plunged back into the past, but today simmers with the promise of something new, the start of looking forward again. She will stay here with Lilli for the rest of the summer and perhaps beyond. They still have so much to catch up on. She wants to spend more time with Élise and meet Lilli's grandchildren. She wants to hear more about Guillaume, Lilli's late partner, and the life they had together here in Provence. She wants to look through photo albums and see pictures of Juliette, the woman who became Lilli's surrogate mother after Lilli left the school, the woman whose surname Lilli honours with her pen name. She wants to watch the films she was in, which Lilli says were terrible but well paid enough for her to support herself and Élise as she grew up. She wants to tell her more about James and Guinevere and Ronnie and Emily and even Peter, to relate how the ups and downs of her life have shaped the person she is now, and how Lilli was a guiding light throughout. They need time to get to know each other again, to figure out how they are the same and how they have changed.

In the meantime, until she goes home, Flo will lend her studio and everything in it to Alice – on the proviso she looks after the cat and waters the plants occasionally. Alice will need time and practice to develop her work and compile a portfolio if she's going to apply to art school next year. The light in the girl's eyes when Flo told her she could use her studio tells her that Alice will do everything she can to make it happen. In doing so, Flo hopes that light will become a permanent fixture. 'I'm going to message you a picture of every design I print,' Alice had said, 'and I want you to do the same. It's our thing, right?' Flo had simply nodded and squeezed her hand, unable to get words out for the lump in her throat.

She sits forward in her chair as she sees a speck in the sky, but it's just a bird, a buzzard, probably, circling on the thermals. Though she doesn't believe in it, she crosses her fingers – anything to help Alice launch herself into the sky.

'Do you think she'll do it?' Lilli says, catching her expression.

'Yes.' Flo nods. 'I really do.'

'You're so positive these days.' Lilli laughs. 'What happened to *perhaps we shouldn't*, or *what if something goes wrong*?'

'*You* happened,' Flo says, 'and I took notes.'

Lilli smiles. 'Well, let's hope Alice has taken notes from you.'

They sit in companionable silence then, like two old ladies who have been friends their whole lives, without the six-decade gap in the middle. They sit and they wait, until . . .

'Look!' Lilli points. 'Over there.'

Flo follows her finger and sees it, a tiny arc of orange in the air, its shape unmistakable. She laughs and claps her hands, giddy at the sight. She imagines Alice's eyes widening when she sees the craggy tops of mountains in the distance, fields and orchards and olive groves far below, church spires and rooftops like matchbox toys. She imagines the sun on her smiling face and the wind on her skin, and the purity of that glorious silence, but for the woosh of the air on the wing. And then there's a second arc, a blue wing. *Yes, Carla!* Flo punches the air. Lilli high-fives her and then they sit there in silence, two *sad old spinsters*, side by side, beaming at the glorious sight in front of them.

What if it all goes right? Lilli wrote in her book, in *The Way We Were*, the novel that has brought them all here.

Flo reaches across and squeezes her old friend's hand without taking her eyes off the sky, the sky where her new friends are flying like birds.

Given half a chance, she thinks, it usually does.

Acknowledgements

The idea for this book was sparked by my curiosity about the many former finishing schools in the area around Lausanne in Switzerland, where I live, so first I want to thank Anne Frei of Brillantmont International School, whose history encompasses a period as a finishing school, for taking the time to share some stories with me. However, the school, students and staff in this book are entirely fictional and not based on Brillantmont.

Finishing schools also existed in France, mainly in Paris, but I decided to set my school in Lyon because it's a city I know well, having lived there for a year as a student. I'm grateful to the unseen librarians of the Guichet du Savoir, an incredible online resource run by Lyon library, for answering my questions about the history of the city, and to Lyon-based author Diane Jeffrey for helping me with present-day detail when the pandemic prevented me from getting there for a refresher visit. My research into 1950s social mores was greatly informed by a fascinating and hilarious 1958 edition of *Amy Vanderbilt's Complete Book of Etiquette*, while Fodor's *Woman's Guide to Europe*, from 1956, also provided amusing background reading. Betty Friedan's seminal text *The Feminine Mystique* and Virginia Nicholson's *Perfect Wives in Ideal Homes* helped me get my head around the eye-opening attitudes of the era.

Given this is my second novel I'm now well aware of the number of people it takes to put a book out in the world, but sadly, due to the Covid-19 pandemic, I wasn't able to see most of them during the writing of it.

Firstly, thank you to my superstar agent, Hayley Steed, and everyone at Madeleine Milburn Literary Agency for being such champions of my writing. Huge thanks to my editors on this book, Clare Hey and Molly Crawford, for being so enthusiastic about the story and for the wise and thoughtful editorial advice that has made it so much better, and to Sarah St. Pierre and the team at S&S Canada for loving it enough to want to bring it to readers in Canada, a country very close to my heart. To the rest of the team at S&S UK – Alice, Sara-Jade, Harriett, Hayley, Dominic, Genevieve and every-one else who I'm sure do lots of things I'm not even aware of – thank you for doing so much for my debut, *The Other Daughter*, and for everything you have done and will no doubt do for *The Lost Chapter*. Thanks to Pip Watkins for the beau-tiful cover and to Clare Wallis for the careful copyediting. To my trusty beta readers – Emma, Mari, Steph, Dad, Matt, Heather, Sylvia and Sarah – thank you for wanting to read it and for all your brilliant feedback.

Since my first book was published I've been touched by the support I've had from so many people. Big thanks to Michaela Dignard, Rachel Bender, Sylvia Koller and Sarah Green for spreading the word so amazingly in Switzerland and beyond, to Rachel and Matthew in Books, Books, Books, Lausanne's English bookshop, for being so supportive (and for making me a shop bestseller!), and to Clare O'Dea for the joint publicity ventures and authorly support. To my friends in the UK and elsewhere who bought, read and shouted about my debut – thank you, you are all wonderful.

Massive thanks to the D20 authors for making me laugh and providing virtual support when we couldn't meet face to face, to Emma Christie for the title, and to all the other writers I've connected with over social media. Though publishing is clearly a very friendly industry in normal times, it's been particularly lovely to see how authors have clubbed together to boost each other during the Covid years.

Thanks to my colleagues at the Michelangelo Foundation for Creativity & Craftsmanship in Geneva for all the support. My time there inspired me to restart lino printing, a craft I first tried at school, and though I'm unlikely to ever attain the heady heights of the many extraordinary craftsmen and women the foundation supports, spending time with a gouge and a piece of lino kept me occupied and smiling during the pandemic, and motivated me to write about the power of craft to boost mental well-being.

The biggest of thanks to my wonderful family – Dad, Steph, Melina, the Radmores, the Canadian contingent, the New Zealand cohort and my US cheerleaders Kathy and Erin – you are the absolute best. And special thanks to Matt, the person I'd always choose to be locked down with during a pandemic.

I also want to acknowledge three women who are no longer here but who have partly inspired this story – my distant relative Mary, who never married or had children but who studied at Cambridge in the 1930s (when the university didn't actually award degrees to women), worked for the Auxiliary Territorial Service in World War Two and who I remember as a chain-smoking, Mini-driving, generous and quirky person; my grandmother Barbara (another Mini driver) who loved to travel whenever she could; and my wonderful mum, Joan, who moved country, spoke fluent French, was a popular teacher and Oxford tour guide, and an accomplished quiltmaker. I am inspired by them all to make the most of life.

Lastly, to all the booksellers, book bloggers, librarians and readers who have bought, sold, lent, read and reviewed my books – thank you, I'm chuffed to bits that you want to read what I write.

The Lost
Chapter

Caroline Bishop

A READING GROUP GUIDE

Topics & Questions for Discussion

1. The story starts out with 'Lenny' (the fictional stand-in for Lilli) letting us know that, regarding her own actions, 'I can tell you right now that I wouldn't have changed a damned thing' (1). What does this tell you about her character?

2. Flo and Lilli are very different young women when they meet, yet they become very close friends. What do they learn from each other in the course of their friendship? How do those lessons shape their lives?

3. Finishing school is a place that reflects expectations set for upper class young women of the time. How does 'Lenny' flaunt those expectations, and why are other young women like 'Sandra' determined to fit in with them? What freedoms or constraints seem particular to Lenny's social class and to Fran's?

4. Why does Flo decide to help Alice? Why does Alice begin to trust her?

5. Flo says that 'it takes faith' to create the complex lino prints she is working on—that it takes patience, working layer after layer, for the design to begin to make sense (120). How does this process relate to her journey throughout *The Lost Chapter*?

6. Both Flo and Alice lost someone close to them—a brother, a friend almost like a sister—at a young age. How did that change the expectations others had of them? How did they internalize those expectations?

7. When Flo visits the tree she planted as a memorial to her lost brother, she finds the new owners of her old home have cut it down. How do places and objects remind us of people from our pasts? How does it affect us when those touchstones change?

8. Why didn't Flo look for Lilli in the intervening sixty years? How did Lilli know *The Way We Were* would reach Flo and bring them together again?

9. How does giving a name—*social anxiety*—to Alice's struggles affect the way Carla understands her?

10. Why did Lilli fictionalize the end of the story in Lyon, after so much of it has reflected her reality? Why does she kill off 'Hugo' and escape with 'Fran'?

11. How does Flo's confession that she killed Harry change our perception of her? How does that perception change again when we find out her reason?

12. Lilli tells Flo that Harry survived her attack in self-defense. How does this knowledge affect how Flo looks back on her life?

13. Alice and Carla both carry a lot of guilt about Ella's death. How do they begin to overcome that guilt?

14. Alice thinks about how modern young women are shaped by expectations, too, although they may be different ones. What has changed between Flo's time and Alice's, and what remains the same?

Enhance Your Book Club

1. Flo sees a perfect opportunity to help Alice take a risk-free leap: by trying the art of lino printing. Is there an artistic hobby you've thought about trying? Arrange a night to paint, sketch, arrange flowers, sculpt, embroider, or anything that interests you, with friends—and share your pride in your results, however imperfect.

2. If you're curious to learn more about what it was like to be a young woman from an aristocratic family in the 1950s, consider reading *Last Curtsey* by Fiona MacCarthy. She writes about her own experience of being a debutante in 1958—the last time debs were presented to the Queen—and her time attending a finishing school in Paris.

Turn the page for a sneak peek at

The Other Daughter

AVAILABLE SUMMER 2023

OCTOBER 2014

London, UK

I became a different person only because I walked around a corner I hadn't intended to.

Until that moment, I hadn't ever considered doing what we did that day, and neither had Dad. It was a spontaneous decision, a spur-of-the-moment thing, simply because the van happened to be parked there, around the corner next to the card shop.

'I forgot – I told Patrick I'd pick up a birthday card for his nephew.' I tugged Dad's arm away from the entrance to the tube, just steps from the museum where we'd spent the afternoon. 'I think there's a place nearby. I'll only be a minute.'

He frowned. A fine drizzle was settling on his glasses. My feet burned from inching past Aztec artefacts, the cafe's cake selection hadn't been up to scratch; we were definitely done for the day, but the shop wasn't far. Two minutes, grab something colourful with a number five on it, then back to the tube. Dad would get the train to Chichester, I'd go home to Peckham, and we'd both get through another Saturday night, another twenty-four hours in this strange new life without Mum.

Dad rolled his eyes. 'Go on then, Jessie, be quick.'

Countless times I've wondered if I would have ever found out if not for turning the corner that day. If I'd bought a card somewhere else, the day before, like I'd said I would. If Patrick had been more organised and done it himself. If the van hadn't been on that particular street on that particular day.

It's perfectly likely I'd have gone my whole life never knowing.

Maybe Patrick and I would still be married. Maybe I'd be head of department at St Mary's Comprehensive. Maybe we'd have a baby on the way. There'd still be that hole in my life, yes. But it would be *my* life, at least. My life.

Instead we took a left turn and saw the van. And that's the moment, right there. That's the moment I became someone else.

PART ONE

You may agree with women's lib
But what would be your view
If you came home to your liberated wife
And she gave you the washing to do?
Would you change places with your wife
And do her daily chores?
She has to do them all her life
Cleaning windows, clothes and floors.
'A man works harder than his mate'
Oh surely that's not true!
Each works in their appointed way
With certain things to do.
So let us say each works as hard
As he or she is able
One earns the money to pay for the food
The other sets the table.

A Man's Nightmare, by J. L. Hale of Haydock,
Merseyside, printed in the *Liverpool Echo*, 1976

FEBRUARY 1976

London, UK

SYLVIA

'Feminism,' Roger said, each syllable thick with scepticism. 'Been done to death, hasn't it?'

Sylvia had been prepared for the snort of derision from Clive, the amused smiles from the other men around the room, Valerie's unfathomable gaze. But she'd also been prepared to stand her ground. She would not be cowed on this one; she would look her commissioning editor in the eye until he gave her a good enough reason to turn her story down. If only she didn't feel so damn nauseous. She really didn't have the stomach for a fight today.

'Hardly,' she said. 'And certainly very little about Switzerland. They're barely getting started with sexual equality. I mean, it's only five years since women got the vote at national level. They were the last democratic country in the Western world to get there.'

'Liechtenstein,' Clive said.

'Excuse me?'

'Liechtenstein still doesn't have women's suffrage. So Switzerland wasn't the last country in the Western world.'

'That's a tiny principality, it's hardly the same thing.'

She saw Clive mutter something to Ellis and they both laughed. She turned her gaze back to Roger. The less she looked at Clive's overstuffed face, the better.

Roger lit another cigarette and took a long drag. His shirt was crumpled, tie askew. Broken capillaries sprawled over his nose. In front of him on his desk, his usual mug — its British Press Awards logo fading and chipped after too many washes — was releasing pungent wafts of coffee mixed with whisky, only exacerbating Sylvia's queasiness.

'You've found someone to interview?' he asked.

Sylvia looked down at her notes. 'Yes, a woman named Evelyne Buchs. She's part of a campaign group out in Lausanne, in the French-speaking part. They're very active. She's already agreed to talk to me.' She'd come across the woman's name when she was scouring the paper's cuttings library for a spark of an idea, something to finally make Roger give her a damn break. Tucked away in the World News section of an edition from the previous summer had been a small article about an event in Geneva for International Women's Year 1975, and Sylvia's attention had been caught by the passionate words of one of the attendees, a young radical Swiss feminist called Evelyne Buchs.

Roger blew a long plume of smoke up to the ceiling where it joined the cloud that was a permanent fixture in this room. He shook his head. 'I don't know, Tallis. There could be a decent story in it, but I'm not sure the budget will stretch to sending you out there.'

She swallowed down a knee-jerk reaction. *Was he joking?* It was common knowledge that the paper wasn't short of a bob or two. Max had only recently come back from the Winter Olympics in Innsbruck. Marnie had spent a week in Italy last October following around Elio Fiorucci for a profile piece in the fashion pages, coming back with a new calf's skin hand-bag and a tan. And she knew the rumours about how much they'd offered veteran war reporter Ellis to poach him from Reuters last year. They could damn well afford a return flight to Switzerland and some meagre expenses.

'I think it's a good idea,' Max said. Her head flicked in his direction and he gave her an encouraging smile, though she caught a hint of mischief in his eyes as he continued. 'You know, comparing the situation of Swiss women with what's happened over here in recent years. Are British women really better off with this whole *liberation* thing?'

'That wasn't exactly the angle I was going for,' she said, careful to keep her voice even. 'I want to explore why Swiss women still haven't achieved the same legal rights as us on abortion, on maternity leave, on discrimination and equal pay, why their society is holding back and what they're doing to change it.' If she could only stop the waves of sickness washing over her, she'd be arguing this a lot better.

'But isn't this all a bit ... *political* for the women's pages?' Clive waved his hand in the air as if brushing it all away. Sylvia saw, with some satisfaction, that his jowls wobbled as he did so. 'I mean, sex tips and clothes and ... *menstruation*,' he almost whispered the word, 'that's what our female readers want to hear about, not all this vulgar bra-waving. We're not the bloody *Guardian*.'

'How do you know what women want, Clive, have you grown breasts?' Valerie said, and the room descended into titters. Sylvia threw her a grateful glance, but the columnist didn't return it. She knew better than to presume anything Valerie said came from a place of female solidarity – any support she offered was likely only a by-product of self-interest. 'However, much as I fail to agree with my esteemed colleague,' Valerie continued, her eyebrows firing disdain at Clive, 'I do think Sylvia's such a little whizz with her regulars and so marvellous at helping the whole team that I'm not sure we can spare her for a foreign trip.'

Little whizz? 'I can handle this on top, no problem.' She kept her eyes on Roger, willing him to listen to her. She could see him wavering. He knew it was a good idea. He *knew* it.

'I'll think about it,' he said.

'But—'

Roger held up his hand. 'I said I'll think about it. Now,

Max, did you get anything juicy out of that gay ice dancer in Innsbruck?'

The sickness dogged her all day. It made her head spin when she stood up from her desk. It sat in a dull ache in her stomach as she walked down Fleet Street, the air thick with the metallic tang of exhaust fumes. It made her legs shake as she negotiated the raised walkways of the Barbican, her heels echoing off the concrete walls. She wished she could go back to last night and refuse Jim's suggestion that they try that new restaurant in Clapham Junction. It occurred to her now that she was likely to see that prawn cocktail again.

'Tea, dear? You look like you need it,' Marjorie said.

Sylvia accepted and sunk into the dusty pink velvet of the armchair. The window from the fifth-floor flat looked out over the site where the Barbican Arts Centre was due to emerge, years late and over budget, if the construction workers, so keen on striking, ever finished the job. Ellis was writing a longform piece about that right now – the sort of meaty news feature she could only dream of. Of course, she had done much of the legwork – interviewing contractors, researching background material – but she wouldn't get a joint byline, not with the famous Ellis Barker, who wouldn't deign to share the glory with an underling like her.

'Marjorie makes the best cuppa.' Victor had crepe-paper skin and oversized ears, but the eyes he fixed on her were surely as bright as they had been half a century ago.

'Here you go, dear.' Marjorie handed her an elegant china

mug with a portrait of the Queen on it and sat down on the sofa next to her husband. Sylvia flipped open her notepad, fished a pen out of her bag and smiled at the two of them. Fifty years together and they looked like they were made that way. Like owners and their dogs, she thought, an unwelcome image of Jim's mother and her Jack Russell popping into her mind; after a while, they begin to resemble each other.

'So, how did you two meet?'

After so many months of writing the 'golden oldies' weekly feature, she had a good idea how the conversation would go. She knew what kept couples together for half a century – not blind devotion, not butterflies in the stomach, but compromise, patience, humour and a stoic tolerance of even the most unlovable of little habits – but something always cropped up that surprised her. There'd been the couple who'd recreated their first date on the same day every year for the past fifty; the man who said he once joked he'd only marry a left-handed woman – and then met his left-handed wife-to-be the very next day; and the 89-year-old who told her the key to not arguing was to stuff your mouth with marshmallows so you physically couldn't speak. Sylvia had already decided to present Jim with a bag of marshmallows on their wedding day, just to kick things off in the right direction.

However, although she didn't dislike writing the feature, it wasn't exactly why she became a journalist. It wasn't why she'd suffered through tutorials with Dirty Dan, Oxford's lecherous lecturer, or why she'd turned a blind eye to her student paper's 'prettiest undergraduate' competitions so that the editor, a belligerent third year from Eton, wouldn't refuse to publish her work.

Give it time, she'd told herself, when she started interviewing the wrinklies. *Give it more time*, Jim had said a few months down the line, when the political magazine he worked for gave him his first cover feature and she was still drinking tea with Marjories. *Fucking bad luck*, Max said when her feature ideas got rebuffed by Roger again and again.

After more than eighteen months in her role as junior features writer, Roger was yet to commission a story she'd pitched. It might have begun to make her think she wasn't good enough. But she had a first from Oxford and a portfolio of student writing that had won her a place on a graduate trainee scheme with a female acceptance rate of just 5 per cent. No, she knew she was good enough. The problem was something else – and she knew exactly what.

'You've been hired primarily to write *women's interest* stories, Tallis,' Roger had said after a few months, when she enquired, as politely as possible, why he always rejected her ideas. 'Any other junior would give their right arm to cover Ladies' Day at Ascot or the Chelsea ruddy Flower Show, but you're always pushing for something else. Don't be so bloody *serious*.'

Sylvia thought he'd missed the point on purpose. She didn't have a problem writing for the women's pages, but it was archaic to assume this meant covering only fashion, flowers and celebrities. She admired Valerie for having moved the conversation on in her decade-long tenure as the so-called 'Queen' of the paper, writing in her witty, biting way about once-taboo subjects including infidelity, sexual satisfaction and domestic sluttery. But Sylvia didn't want to write about any of that, either. She wanted to write about the big political and social issues that impacted women's lives. Issues she, as a woman, was interested in. With her Switzerland idea she'd thought she had a good chance – yes it was *serious*, but what could be more female-focused than a feature about women's rights? And yet still it didn't look like Roger was going to budge. Well, neither would she – she wasn't going to stop pitching features that actually mattered.

'When's your own big day, dear?' Marjorie asked when the interview came to an end, nodding to Sylvia's hand.

'Oh, next year some time.' Sylvia twisted her ring around her finger. 'We haven't fixed a date yet.' She'd be happy with a registry office and a Marks & Spencer dress, but Jim wouldn't hear of it. *You only get married once; it's got to be a big bash.* At least that meant he'd help organise the silly thing.

'Well, we wish you all the luck in the world,' Marjorie said. She patted Victor's knee. 'You're going to need it.'

'Thank you.' She smiled. 'Can I use your bathroom before I go?'

The toilet lid had an avocado-green shagpile cover; the loo roll was hidden under the voluminous skirt of a plastic doll. Sylvia peed, wiped, stood up. The smell of air freshener was cloying. She washed her hands and steadied herself against the sink as another wave of nausea hit her, sweat beading on her forehead. *Oh God, no.* She lifted the toilet lid again and promptly threw up.

It had to be last night's prawns. She hurried back to the office, stopping only in the chemist to get some paracetamol. It took her a few minutes to find the right section. Shampoos. Deodorants. Sanitary products. Her mind paused, discarding a thought as lightly as it landed in her head.

'Roger wants to see you,' Max said, when she got back to her desk. His eyes were bloodshot after what she imagined was the usual three-hour lunch break in the pub. *Just a few sharpeners*, he always said. The sort of social boozing that worked tongues loose, ensuring stories were told, career-enhancing friendships were made and gossip was shared.

She knocked on the door of Roger's glass-walled office and he beckoned her in.

'Tallis. You look peaky.'

'I'm fine.' His office was airless. With no windows and the heating ramped up to combat the February chill, the air felt stagnant and smelt stale, a bilious blend of body odour, fags and vegetable soup that made her want to run to the toilet again. The same thought she'd had in the chemist popped into her head again, more vocal this time, insisting its presence, like Max with a shorthand notebook and a sensational headline ready to go.

Roger gestured to the chair in front of his desk. It was just about the only surface not covered with paper. It spilled out of box files stacked in dense rows along the floor-to-ceiling shelves behind his desk, it lay in piles on the industrial-grey carpet, ostensibly propping up the glass walls, and it smothered his desk: rival papers, opened envelopes, an overflowing in-tray of letters and board-meeting minutes neatly typed by Janice. She wondered if he ever read them.

'I've thought about it,' he said.

'I'm sorry?' Her head was full of Marjorie and weddings and avocado-green toilet lid covers and how many days it had been since—

'Your pitch. Five years on from women's suffrage in Switzerland.'

Her head cleared and she focused fully on her commissioning editor.

'June, you said the first vote was?' he continued.

'Yes. They were granted suffrage in February 1971, and first voted in a referendum in June.' She picked her fingernails behind her back. Was he going to . . . ?

'I know you want this, Tallis. And I know you've paid your dues around here. So I'm commissioning you. Go off to Switzerland and bring me back a damn good piece, okay? We'll run it before June.'

Sylvia couldn't help her eyebrows from shooting up. '*Really*?' Her head felt woozy, but she wasn't sure if it was the shock or the nausea. 'Thank you, thank you so much,' she managed.

'When can you get out there?'

She mentally ran through her diary and discarded

anything she found. 'Next week? There's a rally in Bern I'd like to go to on 6th March.'

A smile twitched at his mouth. 'Good. Ask Janice to book you a flight to Geneva. Expense the hotel. And make sure you get all your regulars done before you go. Oh, and I'm not throwing in a photographer so borrow the office camera and get some shots yourself, okay?'

'Right, yes. Absolutely.'

'And Tallis?'

'Yes?'

'Take a decent coat. Bloody freezing country.'

About the Author

Caroline Bishop grew up in the UK where she took a degree in languages (which included a year studying in Lyon, France) followed by a postgraduate diploma in journalism. After a decade working in London, in 2013 she moved to Lausanne, Switzerland, where she works as a freelance copywriter and journalist. *The Lost Chapter* is her second novel.